Pathways to Love

PATHWAYS TO *Love*

a novel by
H. THOMAS PUTNEY

XULON PRESS

Xulon Press
2301 Lucien Way #415
Maitland, FL 32751
407.339.4217
www.xulonpress.com

© 2021 by H. Thomas Putney

All rights reserved solely by the author. The author guarantees all contents are original and do not infringe upon the legal rights of any other person or work. No part of this book may be reproduced in any form without the permission of the author. The views expressed in this book are not necessarily those of the publisher.

Due to the changing nature of the Internet, if there are any web addresses, links, or URLs included in this manuscript, these may have been altered and may no longer be accessible. The views and opinions shared in this book belong solely to the author and do not necessarily reflect those of the publisher. The publisher therefore disclaims responsibility for the views or opinions expressed within the work.

Paperback ISBN-13: 978-1-6628-3665-7
Hard Cover ISBN-13: 978-1-6628-3666-4
eBook ISBN-13: 978-1-6628-3667-1

Table of Contents

Table of Contents v
Introduction ~ Sarah & John Matthews ix
Prologue ~ George Edward Matthews xiii

Chapter 1 ~ A Bite of the Apple 1
Chapter 2 ~ 'the Crew' 6
Chapter 3 ~ Geena Elaine Michaels 10
Chapter 4 ~ Drive Back to the Hotel 17
Chapter 5 ~ The Flight 20
Chapter 6 ~ An Evening on the Town 25
Chapter 7 ~ Walk Back to the Hotel 30
Chapter 8 ~ In the Morning Light 35
Chapter 9 ~ SLC Festivities & Awards Dinner 41
Chapter 10 ~ Starfire Café & Lounge 55
Chapter 11 ~ Veronica Nicole Rodgers (Ronnie) 60
Chapter 12 ~ Matt and C J 68
Chapter 13 ~ Matt & Ronnie's Road Trip 71
Chapter 14 ~ Welcome Home Ronnie! 77

Chapter 15 ~ 'Brick'...................................83
Chapter 16 ~ Brenda Helena Davis 87
Chapter 17 ~ I Love Paris, Anytime 93
Chapter 18 ~ Time Spent Alone, Time Spent Well...99
Chapter 19 ~ R & R at Summit Meadows 103
Chapter 20 ~ Carolina Country Squall............ 106
Chapter 21 ~ Morning After the Storm............113
Chapter 22 ~ Ronnie's Surprise for Matt 116
Chapter 23 ~ Rob, Jason, and Brick............... 126
Chapter 24 ~ Summit for 'the Crew' 134
Chapter 25 ~ Hail, Hail, the Gang is All Here!...... 139
Chapter 26 ~ Ronnie and Geena 152
Chapter 27 ~ Girls, Time to Go Shopping!........ 159
Chapter 28 ~ The Gazebo 168
Chapter 29 ~ A Time of Reflection 174
Chapter 30 ~ Back to New York................... 181
Chapter 31 ~ Evening in New York................ 190
Chapter 32 ~ Crooked Pathways 197
Chapter 33 ~ Wrong Time, Wrong Place 202
Chapter 34 ~ Time to Finish Shopping 218
Chapter 35 ~ Back to Business....................224
Chapter 36 ~ Thanksgiving......................230
Chapter 37 ~ The New Starfire Café & Lounge 252
Chapter 38 ~ Just to Be Close to You 256
Chapter 39 ~ Coordinating the Surprise..........260

Chapter 40 ~ Ronnie's Affairs...................264
Chapter 41 ~ The Best Made Plans 279
Chapter 42 ~ Grand Rapid Falls, Texas 285
Chapter 43 ~ Preparation for the Holidays 297
Chapter 44 ~ Spill the Beans!...................316
Chapter 45 ~ Holiday Affair....................332
Chapter 46 ~ Preparations for the Starfire 380
Chapter 47 ~ The New Starfire Café &
    Lounge Grand Opening....................398
Chapter 48 ~ Culture for the Community.........410
Chapter 49 ~ Affair for a GEM 420
Chapter 50 ~ Up, Up and Away!.................440

Epilogue ~ Pathways to Love....................446
Pathways To Love – Poem 451
About the Author.............................453
Acknowledgements............................455

Introduction

Sarah & John Matthews

George Edward Matthews was born as the only child to John Edward and Sarah Monique Matthews who lived in the small Village of Congers, NY. Sarah was feeling a bit anxious and grew uneasy about when her child was going to enter the world. With all the bumping and kicking going on in her tummy, it seemed to her the baby was anxious to get started in this world sooner than anticipated. She told John, and they decided to call Doc Harrison, whose office was only a short distance away from them. He advised them to come on by, so he could check Sarah out to relieve her anxiety.

John wasted no time getting Sarah to the office. Doc was waiting for them when they arrived and took Sarah into the examining room right away. He told Sarah, "Relax, everything is going to be alright." Indeed, she was correct. Doc said to Sarah, "Our friend here is anxious to make their way into the world, I'm glad you called. No time to get you to the hospital, I'll have to deliver the baby here." Before she could even respond he continued. "We have everything here to make a safe and proper delivery for you and the baby. Do you think John wants to be present?" Sarah responding, "Yes, I believe so. He wants to be here by my side to hold my hand and witness the birth of our child." Doc smiling, "Well then, let's get everyone prepped and ready, this child is ready to get started. I'll go inform John and have the nurse prepare you for the procedure."

"Hey there big fella, how are doing?" Anxiously looking at Doc, "Hi Doc, are Sarah and the baby okay?" Doc smiled, "They sure are and I'm happy to let you know the baby is ready right now, are you?

Sarah informed me you wish to be present for the birth, is that correct?" Excited, "I sure am and yes, I want to be there with Sarah." Smiling, Doc said, "That's great John! The nurse here is going to help get you ready and escort you into the delivery room. I've checked Sarah over and there is nothing for you to worry about."

With the nurse's assistance John was ready and entered the room, coming to and standing by Sarah's side. Looking down smiling at her, he gently grasped her tiny hand placing it into his own. "I'm right here sweetie, with you all the way, I love you so much," tears of joy welling up in both of their eyes.

Just as Doc said, everything went smoothly. To their delight, Sarah and John witnessed their baby boy enter the world, kicking and screaming!

Doc advised Sarah he wanted her to stay until tomorrow morning. John wanted to stay, but Sarah told him she wanted him to go home, making sure everything is ready for the baby and to get a good night's rest, because he was going to need it. He did as he was requested, making sure from the list he and Sarah had prepared, the house was stocked with everything for the new arrival.

At first John could not get to sleep, excitedly thinking of all the plans he and Sarah had made for the baby. They were determined to be good parents and they vowed to each other they would protect and nurture their child in the best possible way. They were not rich, just your average everyday working couple, but their child would be richly filled with all their love. Still restless, John was remembering the first time he saw Sarah. He was in the military and had an assignment to prepare the Mess Hall for a special event for the men returning from overseas and their families. He and his team were given permission to enlist the services of an outside contractor. A member of his team had been to an affair he had really enjoyed, and he was quite certain he could find out who had overseen the event. With not a lot of time given to prepare, John decided to go with the suggestion given and contact was made. Turns out it was the best decision he had ever made. Having made the appointment with the event planner, John arrived early. To his surprise, she was already surveying the site and writing down questions and suggestions for the event.

There before him, dressed classily and stylishly was Sarah Monique Roberts, petite and a very pleasant sight to behold. Hearing his footsteps walking up behind her, she turned smiling with extended hand to greet him. Wow, he had thought, she has the most beautiful smile I ever saw and the prettiest brown eyes which were electric when they engaged you. He knew at that moment he would do everything in his power to win her heart, because she had grabbed and stolen his. He had found the woman he wanted to share and spend the rest of his life with!

He wanted to have a career in the military, but the more he saw Sarah, the more he knew he wanted to be by her side always.

The event went on without a hitch. She had done a fantastic job with the decorations and the entertainment which was enjoyed by all. Business now out of the way, John had a plan of execution, which could not have gone better. As he would learn later, she too was excited at their first meeting and thought to herself, she would always feel safe, loved, and protected with this man. A brief whirlwind romance, discussing plans with her about the future, getting released from the military, and the rest was history. Here they are now, happy and with their first child. John fell asleep smiling and dreaming of Sarah and his new son!

Prologue

George Edward Matthews

Before the baby was born, Sarah and John had decided to move to the city to raise their children. Even though where they lived was comfortable and worked for them, they wanted to be in a more eclectic environment to raise their children. They felt that in this manner, there would be greater opportunity for their children to learn about other cultures. To also have a greater understanding on how to get along with other people's ways of life. Coupled with their love, devotion to family, and Christian values, their children would be prepared to make a positive contribution in the world, to the things they were involved in and to establish a positive image to the people they met. With this in mind, they had saved their money and bought a three-family house in a quiet section of Brooklyn, NY. This would enable them to have additional income. John had left the military and was a good photographer, and he had decided to take a few courses to be better prepared. This enabled Sarah and John to work from home and be there for the baby. John was handy and with some of the men from the local church they had joined, converted the basement into a workspace and office in which they could work. This enabled them to have the baby nearby.

They had named the baby, George Edward Matthews. George was the first name of Sarah's father and Edward was John's middle name. George was a good baby, always smiling and gurgling, crying very seldom.

During his toddler years, George was always by his parents playing with his toys. It seemed time was flying by, and it was soon time to enroll George into school. He quickly and easily made friends with the other children at school and at church. He was well liked by all his teachers, who were always impressed by his work ethic. It was not too long before the kids at church started calling him Matt, which spilled over into school, as some of the children from church were in his class.

He did well with his schoolwork and was always helping his friends and the other children. His popularity grew and soon his teachers were giving him assignments to help around the school. He worked with the video and audio squad when there were presentations given and was on the monitor squad, always keeping peace in the hallways and in the schoolyard.

At church he established a close connection to a few children, and they became inseparable, always there for one another. His tight friends were Charles

Jackson, Samuel Johnson, and later, Geena Michaels. Charles became C J, Samuel became Brick, and Geena was G. Hence, 'the Crew' was born. They did everything together in church, school and at play, never letting one another down. Their friendship carried on through church, elementary school, junior high, and high school. Even though they all went to different colleges, they stayed in touch. It was easier for the boys because they attended college locally. However, Geena wanted to attend college elsewhere. They all made it work, setting up conference calls so they could all talk together and by individualized personal calls.

They used their talents, gifts, and things they learned at school and in college. Whatever they did, they had a passion to do the absolute best job they were assigned to. Matt briefly served with the military, Brick worked in a recording studio, C J became a police officer with the NYPD and after college, Geena returned home and began working in media. All of them did well at what they were doing, always keeping in touch with one another and making new friends and contacts along the way.

As time passed, they agreed to meet and decided to go into private enterprise in their communities. As always, they planned, organized, and assisted each other in attaining each of their goals, working beside each other, hand in hand. Picking up strengths from each other and utilizing their own talents. Never afraid to use assistance from contacts they had made along the way, thus enabling them to complete projects effectively and successfully. They established a company called Galaxy Quest, and over time planned to bring others with the same values as theirs into the fold. C J and Brick ran a security firm, a community center for youth and a recording studio. Geena did various things in media and both she and Matt were good at organizing events and pulling people together. All of them worked closely together, which was nothing new to them.

They were based out of New York, however, Geena and Matt had to do a lot of traveling across the country. Something Matt liked, as he enjoyed flying and meeting other people while traveling. In his travels, Matt came across a place he liked in North Carolina. It was quiet and peaceful and stirred his creativity. He purchased a home there, so he could recharge his batteries whenever he felt the need. He gathered, and meticulously placed everything he would need to let the creative juices flow, and to be comfortable. It soon became a haven for all of them.

Over time they had achieved their goals and made it. Now it was time to help Geena attain hers.

Chapter 1

A Bite of the Apple

It has been a few months since last being in the Big Apple and flying in now just at twilight brings to memory of just how much I have missed being here. As the pilot expertly and easily brought the jet around, he made his final approach for landing at JFK. Looking out of the window enjoying the sunset, Matt's mind was jolted back to the reality of just how beautiful the view of New York City is at this time.

Whenever coming home, I have always enjoyed the view of the city, remembering the first time I saw it from the air when I came home from overseas after serving there with the military. Since that time, I have been on many flights traveling here and there, meeting and becoming friends with a lot of people, something else I enjoy.

It was about the same time as it is now flying into JFK for the first time and just as beautiful for me to see. Upon entering the military, I found that I really enjoyed flying in all sorts of aircraft. I quickly decided someway, somehow, someday, I was going to learn to fly.

That dream came true. While serving in the military and getting my first assignment overseas I met Jonathan Eric Evans-Troissant (JET). He was a helicopter pilot and a friendship quickly developed between us.

JET was the pilot who flew me to my second assignment in country. It's where I began working for Captain George S. Yancy as his clerk.

Time passed and months later Captain Yancy advised me orders had been sent for me to report back to Battalion HQ and the General had given the order. Both of us were perplexed to the orders and I had wondered if I had done something wrong in my work, because to my knowledge I did not know the General. The next morning those concerns became quite clear. JET had a passenger on board who had all the answers. A jeep rolled up from the helipad with none other than Master Sergeant Kenneth Drake, who jumped out with that great big smile of his. It was a surprise to me, and it was great to see a friend so far away from home. He reported to Captain Yancy and explained the General had need for services, of which I had the qualifications.

General Bradford Wilford Smith had found out I was stationed at a location under his command. He sent JET, who was now assigned to him as his pilot, to pick me up and bring me back to headquarters from the field for a special assignment. I knew the General from basic training when I entered the service. At the time I met him, he had just been promoted from Lt. Colonel, becoming a full bird, Colonel. He had need for assistance administratively, of which I was qualified to do. The work to be done needed a special clearance for the person working on it, to fulfill the assignment. He had me vetted and got me the necessary clearance and credentials for me to complete my assignment. That began my very brief, but exciting military experience. Upon finishing up the work for him and moving on from basic training, I was given my orders for my first assignment to a group assigned to special duty. Colonel Smith liked my work and felt I would be beneficial to the group. I later found out he oversaw the group and was instrumental in getting me assigned. The group completed the special assignment, and it was time to travel back to their headquarters. Having met and worked for the colonel opened other areas of opportunities for me. Upon arrival to our home base, I was assigned to Battery HQ, where I met my First Sergeant and Captain. Top had a friend who worked in Battalion HQ for Colonel Smith. I got to meet him when he and Colonel Smith came to Battery HQ for a meeting with my Captain. First Sergeant introduced me to Master Sergeant Kenneth Drake. That meeting changed and enriched my life for the better. Not only was he in the military, but he was also a Deacon in his church. I joined that church while I was stationed there. Sarge and I became good friends. I met his wife and family and was often at their home for Sunday dinners. Everyone in town knew, liked, and respected him. He and Colonel Smith were instrumental in getting me other special clearances for other projects I was assigned to. I was stationed there for almost a year, until I got my orders for my first assignment out of country. I was given leave and was able to be with my family and friends back home, for Christmas and New Year's.

A soft voice was now bringing me back to the present, "Please make sure your seatbelt is fastened sir and your seat is in the upright position. The pilot is preparing to make his final approach for landing." She steadily moved on to complete her task with the other passengers. Over the years I have heard that statement many times before. Still some time left before landing and my thoughts drifted back to the present. I am here to help my business partners culminate a business project we have been working on for some time. It sure will be great to see them, especially C J and JET. After my time spent in the military and returning to the States, JET and I remained in contact with each other and upon his release from service, we rekindled our friendship. JET was now a part of 'the Crew.' He is based on the West Coast and will be joining the meeting as well. The only one missing from this meeting will be Geena. She was purposely left out of this meeting because the project we are working on concerns her. We have been working on this project for some time now and are extremely excited about it.

Her personal assistant and friend, Leslie Anne Howard is aware of the project. She has been instrumental in keeping Geena busy and on the go, thus allowing the rest of the team to work on the project, without her getting suspicious.

Geena is always there when we are working on major projects, and no doubt she would be wondering why she had not been included in the planning of this project. Thus far, everything is working out fine, as Lee Anne has been doing a great job running interference. It turned out JET had seen her name on a list of potential assistants for Geena and he remembered the name from the military.

Although it had been some time, JET recommended her highly, as she was a communications specialist in the service he had worked with on a mission. Since she has joined Geena's staff, she has been invaluable to Geena, and they quickly became friends as well. Geena has always been there for all of us, and we thought she would appreciate what we have planned. We are almost ready to spring the surprise on her.

Chapter 2

'the Crew'

Charles Franklin Johnson, Sr. (C J) and I grew up together and attended the same church as kids. In fact, other than my family, I have known him longer than anyone else on the planet. We have an amazing friendship and we have been through a lot of things together. We are more than just friends, we are brothers. I feel closer to him than some of my real family. A confident who has always been trustworthy, and we have always been there for one another. Both of us truly value our friendship and special connection.

    C J always wanted to be a police officer. As youngsters often do, we talked of becoming policemen, helping people in our community. He studied criminal law, took the exam for the NYPD, passed, and entered the police academy. Meanwhile, I went into the military, so we never did become police officers together. Upon entering the U. S. Army, I found I had other interests, which I started to pursue after I received my honorable discharge from the military.

He quickly advanced in the ranks, to the detective level where he gained notable attention for his work on a high-level crime investigation jointly conducted by the FBI and the NYPD. His efforts were noted, and the Bureau requested his assistance on other cases which they were conducting. Bringing to the forefront his experience, he was offered a permanent job with the FBI, where he quickly gained the respect of his peers and the attention of his superiors. Whether he was in the field or spear heading an investigation, C J excelled.

Still, something was gnawing at him to get back into the community. He missed helping and rehabilitating those who had gone astray and mentoring to the young people he encountered. He and Rob King organized and expanded their own private security firm, C2C (Coast to Coast) Security, assisting families and small business owners to secure their homes and businesses from unwanted threats, quickly becoming favorite leaders in their communities, especially amongst the young kids in the neighborhood. With the business still expanding, C J being an avid sports enthusiast and Rob, who had a love for jazz, decided to mentor the young people through sports and music. They called on what we all now call 'the Crew,' which consisted of close friends, who had similar interests to help in the community. 'The Crew' consisted of C J, Rob

King (his partner and friend from the NYPD), Geena, Samuel David 'Brick' Johnson, and me. Except for Rob, we all grew up in the same church.

C J and I met in Sunday School at church, and as time went by, we became friends with Brick and later, Geena. As the years went by, we met the rest of 'the Crew.'

Since the inception of the group, other close-knit friends we have encountered in our lives have joined us, such as JET. It is of great importance to us to be able to help those with needs in our community, rather than just talk about it. We spearheaded local events with our contacts, to raise money for a building for the kids to be able to go to, offering them an array of things which could benefit them. Sports, educational assistance, games, and the arts. A place they could hang out safely and be in an environment that would be able to offer mentorship to them, through various programs. The kids refer to C J, Rob, and Brick as coach, so we named the place, 'the Koach's Kids.' C J, Rob and Brick run it. Everyone has quickly learned, do not mess with the Koach's Kids, or else! They are the mentors and protectors of the kids. Everyone has great respect and love for them. They teach them to look out for one another, much the same way as the older guys in the church we grew up in, looked out for us. They would let no one bother us, as we were their little brothers and sisters. Something we all felt necessary to pass on to these kids. Business thrived and we were able to expand the business and extend into other areas. All our business dealings came together, bloomed, and became successful because of 'the Crew.' As the founders, we brought in others who had the same principles, beliefs, and aspirations as ours, extending our network across the country.

Through this method, we were all able to succeed, nurture and grow our businesses. Through our connections, we continue to find others who want to share in this experience. Some of the main things we do in our business is to assist and enrich the lives of single parents and their children, community youth, military veterans, those who have been wrongfully incarcerated and even those who are now just seeking another chance. Also, to those retirees who have been cast aside and still have something to share and offer through our mentorship programs.

As a group of individuals traveling along our own individual pathways, we continue to seek and reach out to others who want to share their passions. Being part of this continuing saga is quite rewarding, as we all love to engage other people, travel, and assist others through our own personal passions, enriching and assisting them to create their own legacies.

Chapter 3

Geena Elaine Michaels

What in the world is going on over there? Wow! Even though it has been quite some time, I would recognize that voice anywhere when I hear it and certainly the body that goes along with it. I wonder what has got her so excited, as she has a personality and temperament which usually stays calm.

"Hey C J wait a minute! Come and go with me to check what's going on over there. That's Geena over there." Looking in the direction of the commotion and C J nodding his head in acknowledgement, "Sure Matt, let's go." We had just finished a meeting over brunch. It felt good, the two of us rolling together just like old times. The two of us started to move towards what is taking place and getting closer, all the while we are noting Geena is quite upset. After approaching and closing the gap, "Hi Geena, what's going on over here? You seem to be upset. Is there anything we can do to assist you?" Hi Mr. Matthews, hi C J," reaching with outstretched arms to hug us. "What are you guys doing here?"

Crazy, after all these years she still calls me by my surname but calls everyone else by their first name or nickname. She started it on the first project we worked together on, shortly after she had graduated from college, even after I expressed to her it would be alright to call me Matt. Strange, as she used to call me Matt back when we were younger. It sure is good seeing her again. Brings back a ship load of old memories. "I'm here on business and decided to meet up and have lunch with C J and JET, who is also here on business. We were leaving and saw you across the way and came over to find out what is wrong."

About Geena. Educated and intelligent, having a deep and very discerning spirit, who is a spiritual person without being over the top. She has and possesses a kind, considerate personality. She is a supportive, helpful individual; knowledgeable, trustworthy, and extremely organized. Just the type of individual you would want to be on your team if you were working on any project. Over the years, she has been someone I have had the good fortune and pleasure to work with.

Physically attractive and confident about herself. Not just pretty, but beautiful inside and out. Boasting quite a figure, not glamorous, but extremely attractive and graceful, with great style and taste. Weighing in about 130 – 137 pounds and about 5'6" tall, with a pair of fantastic legs, especially when she is wearing high heels, as she has on right now, of which I am particularly partial to. A lady with a great gait when she walks, with your eyes paying close attention to her every move. Not forgetting those fabulous eyes of hers. One look into them and you become entranced and mesmerized with her, as they take you on a long journey deep within her soul and being. Once you have traveled there, you will never want to leave.

She also is armed with a beautiful pair of lips which broaden into a warm and engaging smile that lights up a room. The words which emanate from them when she parts them to speak, are like soft friendly caresses to the listener. That makes you want to listen to her every word. A successful attribute which has been a positive staple over her professional career. She is an adventuress person who is willing to try different things to learn about them firsthand. Geena is also a great hostess, and she knows how to prepare a great meal for you. Clearly a wonderful lady to be around and to enjoy. God, I have missed being around her and I am still madly enamored with her and will always be.

Anyone would be proud to be seen with her and call her a friend, or per chance if you were fortunate enough, to have an intimate relationship with her. Whether it would be friend, or having an intimate relationship, it really would not matter because with her, both would be great.

A voice from behind, "Yeah G, what's going on?" The deep sounding voice belonging to none other than that of Jonathan Eric Evans-Toussaint. Another old friend. C J. and I had just left him a few moments ago after having lunch and discussing business at a restaurant with him here at the airport. Continuing to say, "As per usual, you guys seem to be right smack dab in the middle of things," with that wonderful jolly laugh of his. "What the heck…" Geena turning surprised to see another old friend approaching, holding outstretched arms once again to give one of those great hugs of hers. Hi JET, what a mess this is turning into. I didn't mean for things to escalate like this."

Geena explaining, "There seems to be a problem with my reservation. I am trying to get to Salt Lake City, as I have interviews to conduct, and I am supposed to be hosting an award show tomorrow and attending a dinner afterwards. I booked in advance, but the agent is explaining that due to a glitch in their system, the flight is overbooked, and I am upset because I was not notified prior to getting here. Now it is too late for me to make other arrangements. Moreover, my escort had an unexpected family issue come up and cannot be there tomorrow. I do not know what I am going to do at this point. It seems I am not having a particularly good day."

JET continues, "Well if you are willing, I believe we can resolve this issue for you little lady, right Matt?" Oh, oh! I am afraid to respond. JET has come up with another one of his ideas, which always seem to have me mixed up in it in some form or fashion. Responding, "What is your plan?" JET starts to expound. "Seems like we can solve a few issues here. No doubt you of course remember our business luncheon earlier and the little problem I was having." A statement made, rather than a question. Here it comes ladies and gentlemen! He had requested that I ferry one of his aircraft out to Salt Lake City, but I had begged off to stay in NYC a couple of more days to help the team finish off a project we are working on. I felt guilty leaving C J alone to handle things by himself and JET was understanding and said he would probably have to fly it out himself, even though he was really needed here. Usually I would have complied, but circumstances seemed to dictate something else.

"It is relatively easy my friend, you take your girlfriend there and you can kill three birds with one stone." I gave him a quick sharp glare with my eyes, but to no avail as he continued. "One, you get my plane out there, two, you get her safely to Salt Lake City and three, you escort her to the awards dinner… easy as 1-2-3." Yikes, he's done it again! "You know that if you can help it, you would not let our girl here down." Beautifully executed, signed, sealed, and delivered, as C J looks on with amusement in his expression. My buddies, such great friends, wondering how I let them get me into this.

Geena pipes up, "I can't let you guys sacrifice what you have to do for me." Of course, your boy here cannot let that go by without responding. "G, now you know we've all been friends for a long time and have never let each other down when issues have cropped up. We have been there consistently for one another, and this is no different. Case closed!" Taking a deep sigh Geena replies, "I really care about you guys and yes, it is true, with life's complications, we have always been there for one another."

Quickly I began mentally going over some details in my head to make this all happen. "I've got some last-minute details to take care of and some packing to do so we can get out of here without any further complications or delay."

"JET, will you file a flight plan for me please and make sure the plane is fueled and ready to go when I come back. Take Geena with you and if you would G, book a reservation at the Hilton for me please. You know what I like." Geena shaking her head yes in reply and JET saying, "We're already on it," as they both waved their goodbyes. "C J help get me back to the hotel to get my things and get me back here in a timely fashion." C J was already moving towards the exit, "Let's get going," laughing all the while.

It's a good thing Brick was back at the center with Koach's Kids, otherwise he would have added in his two cents. My friends, always an adventure when I am with them. Who am I kidding? I wouldn't have it any other way. These guys are my best friends in the world, and we would never hesitate to help one another. That kind of friendship is rare and hard to find, not to be taken lightly. Nope, all the money and success in the world could never match up to this friendship of ours.

Chapter 4

Drive Back to the Hotel

C J knows me all too well. He had already leapt into action as we were listening to JET, and he solved the issues at hand. Apparently, he had already called or texted his driver to be ready to move out as soon as we got there, because he was already opening the doors to the limo as we approached. Chet Walters was his personal driver and was always ready for whatever occasion C J was thrust into. A young man dedicated to assist C J wherever possible. Some time ago, he had gotten himself in a tight spot and C J was instrumental in getting him out of the jam.

With C J's grooming, he has over time developed into quite a responsible finished product, who recently started his own family. A real nice kid. I introduced him to a friend's daughter at a wedding he had driven me to. They immediately took to each other. Over a period, they fell in love and the rest as they say is history.

My friend is really a terrific person. Along with his partner Rob King, they were doing well with their security business. I was introduced to Rob a few years back by C J, as they were partners who worked for the NYPD as detectives. They turned out to be good friends and C J would always refer to him in our conversations. When we met, we liked each other right away. In fact, it seems like we have been friends for years. He is a thoughtful individual who likes to assist young people to realize their aspirations.

Fastening our seatbelts and settling into our seats for the drive back to the hotel, he gave me that look I am all too familiar with. "Matt, when are you going to tell that girl how you really feel about her?"

Here we go again. "Don't start with me C J. You know this is a subject I do not want to speak about." He quickly fired back, "Start! Let me get this straight. I am just getting warmed up. Not only am I your longtime friend, but I am also your brother and I have a few choice words for you, and you are going to listen to them. By the way, I will not be finished with this until you do what needs to be done."

"It is a complicated issue…." Just like that, he jumps in before I can even finish the sentence. "George Edward Matthews, it is only complicated because you have made it that way with that crazy code of yours. You need to tell her you love her, because you are never going to be genuinely happy until you do. You cannot run forever Matt, bite the bullet and tell her already!" He has himself pretty worked up about this and truthfully, he is right about the matter, but I will never tell him that.

"Are you finished yet?" Glaring back at me, "No, and I will not be done until you man up and do the right thing," turning to look out of his window. Chet looking at me in the rearview mirror, nodding in agreement to what C J just said. "What are you nodding your head about, it is none of your business?" "Yes, it is!" he fired back. "You have become my friend too, and you know he is right about this. All of your real friends know too." Wow, does everyone know? I too now turn in my seat to look out of my window. The rest of the drive was silent.

Chapter 5

The Flight

Upon arrival to the hotel, I jumped out of the limo before Chet could get out to open the door, gladly leaving him and C J to watch my retreat. Once in my room, I contacted the front desk and advised I would be leaving sooner than expected and to please settle my account. The receptionist advised me she would make certain I received a detailed receipt sent to my email and wished me safe travels. I thanked her and scurried around, making sure I packed everything and was not leaving anything behind.

I was back downstairs heading for the limo. Chet had already popped the trunk and grabbed my bags, gingerly placing them inside of and closing the limo's trunk. I had already slid inside to my seat and was fastening my seatbelt. Chet slid under the wheel, and we were on our way again. I went over some last-minute details with C J and suggested he contact Sam 'Brick' Johnson to assist him. Brick was like a little brother to us, and we all knew each other for a long time. Lately, Brick seemed to be distancing himself. Not wanting to crowd him, we decided to give him space to see if he could work things out. Whatever the issue is, he was not spilling any information about it, so we decided to give him more responsibility and get him more involved in the project. Perhaps in this manner, it might distract whatever issue was bothering him. C J agreed and we both settled back for the ride to the airport. I guess he is really upset with me. With no further business to discuss, there was nothing but silence on the ride back, leaving me alone to my thoughts about Geena and the flight to Salt Lake City.

Arriving at the airport, Geena and JET were already striding towards the limo to greet us. JET exclaiming everything was in order, and we were set for take-off whenever we were ready. Relieved, I was glad to see Geena had changed into something more casual, as what she had on previously was a definite distraction to me. She had the flight plan and was advising the weather ahead of us would be ideal all the way into Salt Lake City.

Geena enjoys flying as much as I do, and she too has been certified and licensed to pilot this craft. I remember taking her up for her first flight with me. She sure was excited and up to the challenge to pilot the craft when I offered her a chance to do so. She leapt at the opportunity. JET started to train and teach her, just as he did for me all those years ago. He was extremely instrumental in getting us both certified and licensed as pilots.

We said our goodbyes to everyone. C J embraced me in a bro hug and whispered in my ear he loved me and was praying I get it together regarding Geena. I hugged him back and said "okay." One thing about us, we do not carry grudges. We say what must be said and we are done. Life is too short and it is far too hard to remember what you are upset about and keep track of it. Get it out in the open and be done with it.

Chet and JET made certain everything was stowed properly. Geena looked over at me smiling and saying, "Let's kick the tires, and light the fires," a line from a movie we had watched together. Once onboard, Geena and I went over the checklist in preparation for take-off and contacted the control tower for take-off instructions. We worked well and efficiently together. Plus, it kept my mind focused and off her, as there would be plenty of time to think about her once we reached our destination safely. I felt a lot more confident and at ease than I was when heading back to the airport.

With everything in order, we contacted the control tower for taxi instructions and runway assignment. Geena expressed the desire to get us up into the air and I agreed. Headsets in place and seatbelts fastened, we received instructions from the control tower, and she started to move the plane into position for take-off. I watched as she effortlessly moved the craft into position, remembering the time I spent with her when she was learning to park her tiny vehicle, of which she was so proud of. Now look at her handling this aircraft.

Take-off granted from the tower, Geena pushed the aircraft down the runway, now gathering speed for lift off and finally lifting off the ground for flight. Once airborne, she made the necessary adjustments, gears up, heading, altitude and air speed. After all was achieved, and everything in order on the instrument panel, autopilot was engaged and she looked over with a smile and asked, "How was that captain?" I chuckled and responded, "perfect" to her, and said to myself, just like you.

Both of us flew in silence for some time, enjoying the view, as it was an extremely clear day, perfect for flying. We had a slight tail wind behind us and were making good time. We had calculated we would arrive in SLC around sunset, which on a day like this would look magnificent. As always, I had my trusty camera next to me, ready to take some in-flight photos from the air and if she would let me, some pictures of the lady herself. From time to time, she would send me snapshots of her from the various places and events she had attended. I had wondered why I had not received any lately. It seemed she might be upset for some unknown reason to me. I decided to leave it alone, as I figured if there was something wrong, she would tell me. Right now, everything was perfect sitting beside her, and I was going to try to enjoy every moment I was going to spend with her. I was really feeling confident now. She brought me up to speed regarding her agenda for tomorrow and we agreed to have dinner with one another this evening. So far, so good. Maybe C J was right. Perhaps I should speak with her and let her know how I really feel about her. Suddenly Geena grabbed the camera and took a few shots, snapping me back to attention. She was a rather good photographer herself.

Time to get back to reality and the business at hand, as we were now entering air space for Salt Lake City. We were handed off to the control tower. We began preparation for landing. I disengaged the autopilot and prepared for descent and final approach instructions from the tower. After a smooth and non-eventful landing, we taxied to the hangar. JET had a limo waiting to whisk us to the hotel. Geena had arranged for us to be in the same hotel, which would be more strategic for the events of tomorrow.

This was going to be a fabulous event. Geena was certain to be a hit. She has worked hard at her craft, and she is extremely adept at doing her job. She has done well and is well liked by everyone. I'm so proud of her and the accomplishments she's made.

Chapter 6

An Evening on the Town

The driver grabbed our luggage and placed them into the trunk. I opened the door for her, and she scooted in and slid over so I would not have to walk around the limo. Once settled inside, she leaned over and placed her head upon my shoulder to rest. It felt nice and I realized it had excited me, as my heart began to race a little faster. I hoped she would not notice, as I was getting that exhilarating feeling I get whenever she is near. I was not prepared for her to do that, and I felt a little on edge about it.

Finally arriving at the hotel, I found out she had arranged for a connecting suite for us. The concierge arranged for our luggage to be taken to our suite. Here we go again. I feel like a kid again and I am a bundle of nerves. I am so nervous, there is no way I am telling her how I feel now. I have got to pull it together before dinner. We decided to dress up and go out, instead of dining in the hotel restaurant.

I am glad I had my tux with me, as Geena informed me tomorrow evenings dinner attire was formal. I had arranged for all my attire for tomorrow be pressed. There would be no half stepping with this lady. I wondered what her gown would look like. I am certain whatever it will be, she will look fabulous and amazing in it. I needed to be prepared to be cool, calm, and collected. Tonight, would be good practice at just that.

I had just finished knotting my tie and putting my jacket on when I heard her knocking at the connecting door to our suite. I yelled out "Come on in," and in walked this vision of delight, attired in a peacock blue dress, my favorite color. It was just the right length, just over her knees, showing off those beautiful gams of hers standing in matching blue heels. It also accented her lovely shape as well. She used make-up very sparingly and knew how and where to apply it to get the effect she wanted.

Cool, calm, and collected!!?? I need to stop worrying about tomorrow, I am already knee deep into trouble for tonight. Simply stated, she is one beautiful and delightful looking woman. For me, perfection!

Pulling myself together, "You look beautiful." She smiled back at me, "Why thank you kind sir, you look quite dashing yourself." Grabbing her hand into mine, "Are you ready for dinner my lady?" Giggling, "But of course kind sir." We laughed and headed for the door.

I had called down to the desk earlier requesting the concierge to suggest a nice restaurant, preferably one that had live music, smooth jazz. He knew of such a place and highly recommended it. It was near the hotel, and we decided to walk there, as the night was beautiful for just that. We walked hand in hand, slowly and in silence.

Upon our arrival I opened the door for her to enter and followed her in. The look and smile upon her face were one of pure delight. We were greeted at the entrance by the hostess, and I gave her my name. "But of course, Mr. Matthews, we were expecting you and your guest. Please follow me," as she escorted us to our table. "Your waitress will be with you shortly." Just before she strolled away to greet another guest, I told her thank you. I pulled Geena's chair out for her to sit, before sitting across from her. "This is beautiful," she stated in amazement. She was correct. The concierge had suggested a wonderful place to dine. Intimate setting, soft music, perfect lighting, and a seemingly attentive staff. We had a great table for viewing the live show which was scheduled to start soon.

Also, we had perfect access to the dance floor, should we decide we wanted to kick up our heels. Geena is a delightful dancer, me, not so much.

The waitress came over and we placed our order. We ordered baked salmon, veggies and mac and cheese. I ordered a light white wine to go with our dinner. We chatted with one another about the day's events. So far, the evening was working out perfectly.

"Good evening ladies and gentlemen. We are all in for a treat tonight, as we are excited to present for your listening pleasure smooth jazz group, Pacific Sunset." Applause. Indeed, we were in for a treat, as I had the pleasure of hearing them last year while on a business trip to San Jose, CA.

Our dinner was served to us just as the group was taking the stage, so there would be no further distractions while we were enjoying their performance. I looked over at Geena, whose eyes were glistening in the soft light as she looked back at me with that wonderful smile of hers.

Dinner was delicious and the entertainment was superb, leaving both of us in a great mood. Looking at me, "This has been a beautiful evening Mr. Matthews, you have planned it very well. I really needed this, as things have been hectic for me over the last year. I have not even had any time to send you any pictures of me as I usually do." There it was, she was not upset with me, just super busy. "I am glad you're enjoying yourself." Reaching out to touch my hand, "You make it sound as if the evening is over. I do not have to get started until midafternoon tomorrow and we can stay out as late as we want, because we do not have to get up early in the morning. Don't tell me you're not going to ask me to dance with you to the wonderful music playing."

"Now you know I'm not a great dancer Geena." Getting up from her chair, "What's the matter, afraid to hold me close in your arms?" I cannot believe I just said that to him. I must have had too much wine at dinner. I hope he is not upset with me for saying that to him. I am not able to discern the look he has on his face right now.

There it was, she had issued me a challenge. Step up and accept it my man, you've got this. She is relaxed and you have nothing to be afraid of, rising to meet the challenge and taking her by the hand, "Let's go," as I started leading her to the dance floor.

As she moved ever so gently into my arms, the music began playing a recognizable tune of Roberta Flack's, "The First Time Ever I Saw Your Face."

I gently pulled her as close to me as I could, as she looked into my eyes, gazing into them as if she were looking for answers. She smells great and this is quite delightful, something I would like to get used to on a regular basis. Holding her close like this is amazing. What am I afraid of? I've always known she is the one. I wish I knew what she was thinking of and what she feels about me. When it comes down to it, I have a hard time discerning what is on her mind regarding us.

Completely relaxed, Geena was thinking, I rather like this, and I wish we had more intimate times like this together. I sure wish I knew what he is thinking about. Sigh, I don't want this to end.

Chapter 7

Walk Back to the Hotel

What an unexpected romantic evening this had turned out to be. I am not certain what has gotten into Geena, but I like it. I could enjoy this all the time with her. She is fantastic. Maybe I should tell her how I feel. It would be amazing if we could retain this feeling, we are sharing this evening. She sure makes me feel happy.

I need to get her back to the hotel, as I am cognizant, she has a long busy day planned out for her tomorrow.

Geena was musing to herself. I have had a wonderful evening and I do not want it to end. Him holding me in his arms is a great highlight of a day which looked as if it would become disastrous for me. Out of nowhere he shows up and saves the day, just like he has always done for me. I have wanted to be with him in this way for so long, but I have been extremely cautious, as I know he has been hurt deeply several times. It seems like the right time never presents the opportunity for me to tell him how I really feel about him. Several times I thought the opportunity was there, but nothing would happen. He is a hard one to read and figure out.

Physically Matt is about 6'5" inches tall, about 220-225 pounds, brown eyes; trim and fit. He has a well-groomed style, and he always is dressed nicely for the occasion, whether for work, social activity, like now, or casually. He is charming, polite, thoughtful, gentle, sweet, and kind. Even though he is reserved, quiet and for the most part stays to himself, one should not let his passiveness suggest he cannot take care of business. Should anything negative come up, he is quite formidable and knows how to handle himself quite adeptly. He is not the one to cross. I know he would never let any harm come to me. He has always been protective of me and has never failed to come to my rescue when I need him to do so. I cannot figure out how to let him know how I feel about him, and Lord knows there have been opportunities, but the timing seems to always be wrong. Being in his arms tonight felt right. I trust him and I am sure he would not take advantage of me, as he has always been a perfect gentleman to me. However, tonight I could use some closer intimacy. Smiling inwardly, down girl! Do not let your emotions get the best of you and ruin a perfect day and evening with him. Tomorrow is another day, just wait and see what it brings.

Matt pondering, hmm, I wonder what she is thinking. I hope she does not think I was not enjoying myself with her. We have been dancing for some time now, and I must admit, it's better than I could ever have imagined. Besides, it looks as if they want to close. Don't want to wear out our welcome. Time to snap back to reality and get her back to the hotel so she can get some rest. It has been a long day for both of us.

The walk back to the hotel was fantastic, with us holding each other around the waist and Geena leaning her head close to my body, as we walked slowly. I was thinking the whole time, I do not want the evening to end. Well, we are back safely. Now walk her to the door, kiss her on the forehead and say good night.

Gosh, I don't want the evening to be over yet. Shall I kiss him good night? This is insane. It is the end to a perfect day and he sure deserves one, in fact, I do too. I so want to be back in his arms, with the soft gentle way he holds me in them, sigh.

What the….!? After this beautiful evening, he just kissed me on my forehead after walking me to my door and is now saying goodnight!? I'm not having it! Geena, girl you need to act on this right now.

What are you thinking about lady… you may never get this chance again? What should I do?

Okay, I gave him time to get back to his room, now just do if before you chicken out. Walking across the floor to the door which connects their suites, Geena knocked gently on the door.

Matt, what in thunder is wrong with you? You walk her to her door, kiss her on the forehead, turn around and walk away. You wimp! C J is right, you need to handle this. You are never going to be happy until you do. If she really is your friend, you will not lose her. Man take charge and do something about this for crying out loud! Snap out of it, she is knocking on the door. I wonder what she wants. Well, I am never going to find out unless I open it.

Opening the door, "What's the matter, miss me alr....?" Geena came into Matt's arms, pressing her body against his and kissed him smack dab on the lips. Oh my God, the look on his face. Am I out of line, I do not want to lose him? He has been a constant connection in my life forever and I am not certain what I would do without him in it. Maybe I acted to rashly.

"Geena, what are you doing? I mean, ahh... I mean, what the heck. Did you have too much to drink, or is this some sort of test?" Replying, "Matt, stop trying to analyze everything all the time. Didn't you like it? Just hold me and kiss me back before I lose my nerve with all of this."

"You don't have to ask me twice." Matt gently pulled Geena to him and enveloped her into his arms, looking down into her staring eyes, like that of a doe caught in the headlights of an oncoming car. Bringing his hand up to run his fingers lightly through her hair, brushing it back from her face, he leaned in and kissed her on her cheek, then moving to kiss her behind her ear and gently on her neck. Now looking into her eyes again and smiling down at her, he moved in to kiss her on the lips. She parted her lips to accept him and melted into his arms. His tongue gently probing and flicking hers softly and she in return. Matt suddenly scooped her up and walked across the room, gently setting her down on the edge of the bed and sat down beside her.

Geena put her arms around Matt and gently drew him back towards her to kiss again. He angled her back on the bed slowly and lovingly caressed her, as the two of them enjoyed the soft kisses being given, feeling their hearts pounding and racing uncontrollably. Matt's mind was exploding like fireworks on the Fourth of July, which were spiraling back down to earth in a beautiful array of colors. Finally, Matt ended the kiss. "I've wanted and tried to imagine this for so long Geena, and now that it's finally happening, there are no words to describe how happy I'm feeling. I love you so much and I cannot begin to imagine how my life would be without you in it. Please tell me you're feeling the same way too."

"Oh, Matt yes, yes I do. I have been so afraid I would lose you and you would never know how I feel and how much I love you. I buried myself in work and my career, desperately trying not to think about this. You have always been there for me, and I could not stand losing what we have. Please, please, we can talk later. Right now, all I want is for you to hold me and never let go, I love you so much," as she began kissing Matt softly and tenderly once again.

Chapter 8

In the Morning Light

Geena was still in shock and disbelief since Matt had said he loved her also, words she was beginning to think she would never hear come from his lips. She had kicked off her heels and was snuggled safe and warm in his arms. He was holding her ever so gently and she could feel his heart pounding, or was it hers? Whatever, it felt wonderful. After all this time, finding out he felt the same way too. It seems he had the same reservations I did. We have wasted so much time. The way he holds, kisses, and caresses me is so wonderful. Geena fell asleep in Matt's arms feeling safe and protected, with a smile on her face. She felt safe, and knew Matt would not take advantage of her.

What an amazing day and evening! Matt could hardly keep his mind focused. Geena felt so wonderful in his arms and her kisses were delicious and exciting. How he had longed to have her in arms in this manner. To think, he really was making a mess of things. That crazy kiss he had given to her on the forehead fired her up and she made it perfectly clear she was not having it! I am sure glad she did too, because I am not sure if I would have followed up. Just like her to always come through. She had snuggled up and fallen asleep in his arms. It had been a long and emotional day for them both. It felt good holding her. Finally, Matt closed his eyes and drifted off to sleep to dream of Geena, with a smile on his face.

Matt awoke early, just as he usually does every day. He had this wonderful dream of being with Geena and spending a wonderful evening with her. Thank God to his delight when he opened his eyes, there she was still snuggled in his arms, a dream come true.

He had a feeling this was going to be the first of many more wonderful and shared experiences with her. He gently separated himself from her, so not as to disturb her, she looked so peaceful. He placed a pillow under her head and covered her with a sheet. He then went into the next room and called down to order breakfast to be sent up for two. That being done, he quickly gathered up some casual attire for the morning and headed for the bathroom to get cleaned up. Job complete, Matt headed back to where Geena was still asleep. She lay so peacefully he thought, and she certainly was beautiful, like the bright rays of a glorious morning sunrise. The reality hit him like a load of bricks dropped on his head, no longer was this a dream, it was real. His dreams had come true. Amazingly he was here with her and so in love with Geena!

Across the room Matt watched Geena as she stirred. Maybe he was looking at her too hard, smiling to himself. She seemed to be reaching out for him, still half asleep, softly calling his name, "Matt." Geena remembered being in his arms and that she felt safe and loved in his arms. Oh, the soft kisses they had shared. She must have fallen asleep. It had been such an amazing day! Finally, she was with the man of her dreams, and he loved her, Geena Elaine Michaels. How I love him so!

A voice nearby jerked her back into the present, "Good morning G, did you sleep well?" "Good morning Matt. Yes, I did and you? I was dreaming of you and there you are, right here with me." Matt crossed the room to sit down on the bed next to Geena, leaning over and gently kissing her on the cheek, "Yes, I slept dreaming of you in my arms and when I opened my eyes, there you were. Good morning sweetie. I did not want to disturb you, as you looked so peaceful, so I let you sleep because I know you have got a long day ahead. I took the liberty of calling room service and ordering us breakfast. It should be here shortly. I hope that's alright with you."

"Just like you, always looking out for me the way you have always done. I so appreciate and adore you. What am I saying? That is an understatement. I am head over heels in love with you Matt and I'm so incredibly happy right now. I could just burst wide open."

"Yes, this is all so wonderful and amazing. I too am overwhelmed with joy. You are an amazing woman, and I should not have been afraid to tell you how much I care and love you, and I am terribly sorry for not telling you just that."

"Matt, it's okay. Please do not beat yourself up. I too have felt this way for so long, and I was also afraid to share my feelings with you just in case you did not feel the same way. So, I held it in and did not share how I really felt about you. I did not want to take the chance on losing you. I just let being near and working close by your side suffice. Some pair we are, lol."

"Yeah, I guess we were both feeling the same way. I will make you a deal. No more keeping secrets from one another. We need to communicate better on a personal level, much the same way we do in business. Deal?"

"Deal," enveloping him in her arms and giving him a great big hug. "I'm going to head over and get cleaned up. By the time I'm done breakfast should be here." Matt letting her go, "Okay, missing you already." Geena smiled, "Aww, you're so sweet, I love you."

"I love you too, Ms. Michaels…role reversal." They threw their heads back and laughed out loud.

Geena now showered and dressed, laid clothes out for the rest of the day's festivities, she collected her thoughts, and went over in her mind what she had to do for the rest of the day. A day she was now really looking forward to having. She wondered what would be ahead now for Matt and herself. It did not matter she thought, they would be together.

It had been just a few minutes since Geena had left to change, leaving Matt to his thoughts. He had wondered what laid ahead for the two of them. The prospects were bountiful, as well as exciting. There was a knock at the door, "Room service." Matt went over and opened the door. "Good morning sir, breakfast for two. Where would you like me to set it up?" "Good morning to you as well. Please set it up by the balcony doors and place the flowers in the center. I'll move them when we are ready to eat, thank you." "Yes sir, not a problem. Will there be anything else?" "No thank you. Here, this is for you and have a great day!" "Thank you, you do the same sir." Matt closed the door behind him after he left.

Heading back over to make sure everything was just so; Matt heard the door open to Geena's suite. She entered wearing a casual pair of white slacks, a light blue blouse, and a pair of matching-colored blue socks on her feet. "I see you have been quite the busy beaver. Matt, the flowers are lovely, you shouldn't have. You're so thoughtful and kind." "It was all worth it, just to see the smile on your face. I promise from here on out, I will make you smile, or laugh every day." Geena came into his arms and kissed him, "And I promise whenever I can, to give you a proper kiss every morning and a good night kiss every evening too."

"Sounds wonderful, let's eat, I'm starving!" Geena laughing, "So much for the romance." They both laughed and sat down to eat, looking into each other's eyes, wondering what lies ahead.

Chapter 9

SLC Festivities & Awards Dinner

After they finished eating, Geena and Matt lounged around in the room, just talking to one another, and enjoying each other's company. Matt was elated to have Geena close, snuggled in his arms. They both kept looking at one another and enjoying soft kisses between them. Geena loved the way Matt's eyes looked at her, softly and tenderly. She had been waiting for this so long, and now that it was happening, she was overjoyed with happiness.

Soon it was time for Geena to get dressed for her interviews at the red-carpet event. She reluctantly let go of Matt, so she could go and get dressed. Matt gently pulled her back close to him and gave her a long ardent kiss, to which she responded. Finally, softly saying, "You are taking advantage of me baby, please let me go Matt, or I am never going to leave. You know I love being in your arms, but it is time for me to get ready to go. Before long I will be back to get ready for the awards dinner this evening. I promise you can hold and kiss me all you want this evening." Reluctantly Matt let her go, "Okay honey. I am looking forward to this evening." Geena went to her suite and changed. Soon after, she returned and gave Matt a preview of what she was wearing to the red-carpet interviews. His heart was racing.

Geena was wearing a red and gold raw silk scoop neck sleeveless A-line knee length dress, with a matching red and gold three quarter length sleeve Bolero jacket, designed by Alberta Ferretti. Red and gold open toe three-inch pumps, by BCB Girls, accentuated with a brush gold necklace and matching hoop earrings.

She looked at Matt smiling, "What do you think?" The look on his face was all the compliment Geena needed. Laughing, "Judging by the look on your face, I guess you like." Still speechless, Matt was nodding his head in agreement. Geena continued, "Wait until you see what I am wearing this evening." She sidled up to him and gave a quick kiss on his cheek, turned and waved goodbye as she headed out of the door, still laughing at Matt standing there with that look on his face.

She looked fantastic. Matt knew the interviews would go well for her. He knew all eyes would be on her. He was going to tune in later to watch her. He did not want to miss a thing. The attire he was going to wear this evening was brought up soon after Geena left. Matt made a few business calls. Soon it would be time to tune in and then get ready for tonight's affair. He could not wait to see what she was going to wear this evening.

Geena was sure great at the red-carpet event, speaking with the various personalities who were arriving and offering in-sight to the many viewers watching the telecast. He was so proud of her many, many accomplishments and was sure they would lead to bigger and better things for her in the future. He looked at the time and realized it was time to prepare himself, so he would be ready when Geena returned.

Geena returned to her suite after the interviews, to change into her attire for the evening. The interviews had gone well, and she was glad that everything had moved smoothly. As she dressed, she wondered if Matt had watched the live telecast.

Geena was going to wear a gown designed by Adrianna Papell. It was a black fitted satin gown, trimmed with silver piping around a scooped neckline and V-back extending to the waist. Silver satin sling back three-inch pumps, by Michael Kors and matching clutch purse, by Gucci. Accentuated with drop white-gold earrings, with a matching bracelet. Her hair was fashioned in an upsweep. She looked forward to Matt undoing it and his hands softly running through it later this evening, ready to be in his embrace one more time, enjoying his kisses. Make-up all done; Geena took one last look at herself in the full-length mirror. Smiling to herself, she was ready to go knock on Matt's door, and she hoped she would knock him off his feet.

Matt had finished dressing a few minutes before Geena knocked at the door.

He was wearing a black tuxedo by Canali, black bow tie, a white handkerchief square neatly tucked into his jacket pocket, a white French cuffed dress shirt, with gold and diamond cufflinks. He had on a pair of black patent Oxford plain toe; ribbon vamp overlay slip-on shoes by Calvin Klein. He had just finished checking his gig-line before Geena knocked at the door.

He strolled across the room and opened the door to a vision of pure beauty and delight. "You look stunning and beautiful Geena." This time he had managed to put together a few words. She was smiling as he looked up and down with the same look, she had seen on his face earlier today. "Thank you, Matt. It looks as if you are ready and I must say, you clean up very nicely. You look very dashing." Offering his arm for Geena to take, "Thanks G." She took his arm and they headed out. The limo should be waiting. On the elevator ride down, Matt could not keep his eyes off Geena. The gown she was wearing really accented her beautiful shape.

When they reached the main lobby and stepped off the elevator, starting to stroll across the lobby floor, all eyes were watching them, as their look complimented each other. Matt entered the revolving doors first, pushing slowly so Geena could move through easily.

Taking her hand, they moved to the limo, where the driver already had the door open. Geena entered and Matt followed, sitting close and holding her hand. They rode in silence enjoying the ride and view, still lovingly holding hands. It did not take them long to reach their destination. The driver came around to open the door. Matt stepped out, turned, and extended his hand to assist Geena out of the limo. Once out, Geena put her arm through Matt's, and they slowly started to make their way through the crowd of fans. Video cameras were rolling, and lightbulbs were flashing as they made their way inside, Geena smiling and graciously nodding her head, Matt proud to be by her side.

This was a star-studded major event. It seemed as if everyone was there. As they made their way to their table, people were coming over to congratulate Geena, expressing a job well done on the red-carpet.

"Hi there Geena," said playwright and movie producer, Theodore Porter. "Great job out there today. You always have a way of making everyone feel comfortable when you interview them." Geena smiled and said thank you. "Hi Matt, good to see you again." Geena looking over in amazement. "Hi Theo, it's great seeing you as well. How are things going?" Winking, "Things are moving well my friend. You guys enjoy yourselves. I see a couple of people I need to speak with before things get started." Matt and Geena said thanks, as he moved away in the direction he had looked.

Still looking at Matt impressed, Geena said, "I did not know you knew Theo. I was nervous you would be bothered by all the hoopla and fanfare. You are handling yourself well and seem to be enjoying yourself." Smiling, Matt said, "Well Ms. Mitchell, if you kept in touch, you would be updated, and you would know such things. Also, how could I not be comfortable and enjoying myself when I have the most beautiful woman by my side?" Laughing, "Touché, you've got me there," both now laughing.

The evening was progressing well, everyone seemingly enjoying themselves and the entertainment was fantastic. Matt looked at G, who was having a great time. They were holding hands throughout the evening, only letting go to applaud.

Geena knew Matt was having a 'grand ole' time as she looked into his eyes filled with excitement, occasionally looking at her with that soft, tender look of his she adored. She was enjoying herself, but she could not wait until they would be alone again. She so wanted to be in his arms again, receiving his warm, soft, gentle kisses.

Matt was enjoying himself more than he thought he would, but he was ready to head back. He had arranged for a surprise for G when they returned to their suite. He was sure she would like it.

The evening's events were ending. Seth Howard and aspiring comedienne Brenda Davis had served as the hosts for the evening, and they had bid good night to all and wished everyone a safe journey home. They had done well, working seamlessly together on stage. They were hilarious together and Brenda was great, just as funny as Seth. She won the award for Best New Comedienne. She was going to have a great career. They ran into the group Pacific Sunset, who received the award for Best Smooth Jazz Group. Someone from the group said hi to Matt and they all waved at him. Waving back Matt said, "Congrats guys." Smiling Geena said, "You are just full of surprises tonight." Matt laughed.

    They made their way back to the limo. Geena now starting to relax from the day's events, snuggled closely to Matt, laying her head upon his shoulder. Matt kissed her gently on her forehead and held her hand. They arrived safely back to the hotel and took the elevator to their suites. Reaching the door, Matt turned and gently gathered Geena into his arms and began kissing her, which she gladly returned. When they entered the room, it was dimly lit, and Matt escorted her over to the table sitting in front of the balcony doors and pulled out a chair for her to sit. The flowers from earlier were arranged and centered on the table. Geena's eyes were now adjusting to the dimly lit room and saw there were two other roses laying on plates on both sides of the table. There was also cheese and crackers to the side and a bottle of white wine, with two wine glasses. Matt lit two candles which had been set up and pressing a button on a remote, soft music began to play.

He leaned over and kissed her softly on her lips. "It was lovely spending time out with you this evening. I enjoyed myself immensely. But as you see, I am not ready for this evening to end yet," kissing her again. The music started playing Roberta Flack's, "The First Time Ever I Saw Your Face." Matt extending his hand to Geena said, "Dance with me."

"My word, who would have ever guessed? You are an old softie, a real romanticist. I love it!" Moving into his arms, they began to dance, Matt carefully undoing her hair, letting it softly drift down to her shoulders. Gently brushing it from her neck, he kissed her softly behind her ear and along her beautifully sculpted neck. "Oh Matt, I love you so much, don't stop. It feels so good." Matt placed his hand under her chin, and gently tilting her head back, started kissing her on her lips. She parted her lips and their tongues meeting, slowly moved together softly in concert. Geena's knees were feeling weak under her, but Matt with a soft firm grip around her waist kept her steady on her feet.

They danced towards the bed, and each kicked off their shoes. Matt still kissing Geena, gently maneuvered her onto the bed, their kisses becoming more exciting and their passions swelling.

He continued, as Geena was trembling uncontrollably, full of desire and love for this wonderful man in her life.

Matt was caressing her along her body in the way she liked him to do, her heart beating wildly and her breathing now out of control. Both were enjoying the fierce passion which was becoming torrid between them. Matt sensing and feeling things peaking, gently moved away from Geena's lips, slowed things down, kissing her gently along the sides of her neck. Moving onto his back, he pulled her close to him and she placed her head on his chest. She had taken off his bow tie while they were dancing and undid the buttons to his shirt. Now she was gently caressing his chest with her hand, as he gently ran his fingers through her hair.

Matt said, "G, I am so in love with you. I cannot remember ever being this happy before. It has been a long time coming. Things were becoming a bit heated, so I tapped the brakes. I hope you are not upset I slowed things down. I do want you, but you need to know just how much I adore and respect you. I am aware it is not the first dance for either of us, so to speak, and I know you've been hurt before. I want to make certain you understand I care about and appreciate you. It is important to me you know you can trust me, and I will always protect you. Phew, that was a mouthful. I felt it necessary for you to know what is transpiring between us is serious business to me, and I want this to be everlasting."

Wiping tears away from her eyes, "Oh Matt, that was beautiful. You expressed yourself, much the same way I am feeling. No, I am not upset you slowed things down to a slower pace. I want you as well, and I want it to last forever. The way you look at and touch me is delightful to me and I will never get tired of the way you connect with me. Even while working with you on our various projects, I always felt this very connection we have right now, and I am glad it is out in the open. I love and appreciate you as well. You have always been there for me, and I appreciate you. You have always been protective of me and treated me as a lady. Being the gentleman you are, you have never taken advantage of me, and I trust you implicitly. How I want you so badly right now is indescribable, but I know we will manage. Again, I do not want to go back to my room alone, and if it is alright with you, I want to spend the night in your arms again."

"Music to my ears G, I don't want you to go either. I want you right here close beside me. Taking a page from your book, let's stop talking and kiss me. Kiss me the way you do that makes me almost lose my mind. I hope this lasts all night." Geena laughing said, "Very funny, you are such a comedian. Get over here and kiss me crazy man."

Once again, they had fallen asleep in one another's arms, both smiling and dreaming pleasant dreams of each other.

They awoke much the same way as they did the day before, Geena going back to her room and Matt ordering room service.

She had taken her shower, just gotten her things on and was about to go back to Matt's room when her phone rang. Her assistant had called, all excited with good news and wanting to know how soon Geena could get back to NYC. It seemed she had made a good impression yesterday conducting the interviews on the red-carpet. A group wanted to meet with her regarding an assignment in Paris. She said she would be free in maybe two, maybe three days at the most. Her assistant said it was not a problem and she would set it up. The interview would take place in New York.

Geena was excited, and hurriedly went back to Matt's room to share the good news. Matt was excited for her as well asking, "When do you have to be there?" She told him two, or three days. She was hoping he might want to spend some down time with her. "That is great G. It all fits in great. I just got off the phone with JET. He asked if we could bring one of his aircraft to NYC when we came back. We can spend another day here and maybe go to the club we were at the other evening and do some dancing. Up for it?" Geena jumping in his arms, "Yes, yes. I was hoping you wanted to spend some more time together before we jumped back into our busy schedules." Matt kissing her, "Great, then it's settled. I will get JET back on the phone and give him the news." Matt thought, life was starting to have favor for Geena and himself and he could not be happier.

They spent a couple of wonderful days together, enjoying each other. They had also set up a meeting with the owners of the club they had attended. They felt it would be advantageous to bring them into the fold. They had some ideas on how to bring some similar clubs into the group as well. It turned out the concierge, and the staff at the club were all siblings. He had some connections with other concierges, who had similar holdings. Geena and Matt asked if he could contact them and set up a meeting to see if they would also be a good fit. The trip to SLC was a success on many fronts.

Having enjoyed themselves, they departed Salt Lake City and went home to NYC. The flight back was smooth and uneventful. They spent the evening together and went back to Geena's place. Matt knew he would be leaving tomorrow. He thought, rather than deal with the traffic, it was best to get a room at a hotel near the airport. Geena made a reservation at the airport hotel. Matt left and returned the auto rental once he got back to the airport. He called Geena and wished her happy dreams.

The following day, Geena met with the group interested in engaging her services. Everything went well and arrangements were made for her to go to Paris. It was just about every girl's dream to go to Paris. She would be there working on the project for about two months.

She phoned Matt to let him know when she was leaving and would let him know when she landed at Orly. Matt updated her regarding the newly formed relationship made with the concierge in Salt Lake City.

The concierge had worked expeditiously in contacting the others and it was decided they would meet in Chicago, which was central for them all, to work out the details of the business venture. Geena wished him a successful and safe trip. Of course, she told him she loved him. He told her the same and said goodbye, missing her already.

Matt left for the airport to catch his flight to Chicago. He had figured it would take him no more than two, or three days to work out the details with them and to set things in motion. He would then give them time to complete the various tasks ahead of them and then they could set up a new meeting to finalize everything.

He had decided after he met with 'the Crew,' he would then take some time for some much-needed R & R in North Carolina, knowing he needed to be well rested, and his thoughts clear for the events that lie ahead.

It only took a day and half, so he decided to catch a flight back to JFK a day earlier before he was to meet with 'the Crew.'

Things had worked out well, and he looked forward to some rest and relaxation. His thoughts were of Geena, hoping her new venture would go just as well for her. Surely it would keep her schedule busy, making it easier for 'the Crew' to plan their surprise. He felt amazingly comfortable with their new relationship and looked forward to a future with her. The trip to SLC and the awards were great. As far as he was concerned, he got the best award… Geena! Things were working out favorably for them, and he felt blessed to have her in his life.

Chapter 10

Starfire Café & Lounge

Matt and the rest of 'the Crew' had been meeting at the Starfire Café & Lounge for quite some time. Before then, they would meet at the airport restaurant, not wanting to run into Geena. Matt had come across it when meeting with a client a while back and he had liked the atmosphere. It was in a quiet section of Queens, easily accessible to both JFK and LAG. They also had valet parking, a plus so as not to have to drive around looking for a parking space. The cuisine, service and entertainment were enticing as well. It was perfect for quickie meetings regarding the project they were working on. When in town, he often would come here by himself just to relax, get a bite to eat and listen to the live music. There was a lady who played piano and sang for the live entertainment, usually smooth jazz, which Matt liked to hear, as it was relaxing to him. He had seen her first working on the day shift as a valet. Whenever he was there in the day, she would personally come over and take care of him. She was always kind and saw to his needs. He remembered he was quite surprised to see her in the evening, playing and singing at the piano. He really enjoyed her performances, as she was excellent.

As per usual, everything was great. Whenever he was there for the show, she would always make eye contact with him, which made him feel as if she were singing to him. She had this amazing phrasing in her vocals and Lord knows, she certainly knew how to tickle those keys.

Matt had decided to meet with 'the Crew' and flew in a day earlier before the meeting, for some much-needed downtime. He had been going pretty much non-stop for some time now and needed to unwind. He had decided on the plane flight back from O'Hare, he would check into the hotel, get settled, rest and then go to the club for dinner and the show.

As per usual, the evening was exactly what Matt needed and hoped for. However, this evening was going to be a little different though. The performance now being over, he was preparing to settle his tab when the owner picked up the microphone and asked for everyone's attention. He thanked everyone for their patronage and support of his establishment but apologized and announced this would be the club's final night open. Some family matters had come up and he had to leave to address them. Last minute plans were made so he could leave immediately. He sold his establishment to a buyer who had other ideas for this space. Again, he apologized and asked everyone for their prayers. The staff was visibly shaken and upset at this development. Everyone seemed to be upset and in shock and the club was buzzing with the news just given.

Matt was not close to the owner, but he had always seemed pleasant and cordial. He decided to go over, introducing himself to see if there was anything he could do. Jacob Meyers, who was the owner said, "It's unfortunate, but nothing can be done. I needed the funds to help my family and the club has already been sold." The staff came over to ask questions and understandably so, as they all had bills and needed their jobs to support themselves and their families.

The pianist exclaimed aloud, "What are we going to do, I'm already behind in my bills and my rent is past due?" She seemed to be quite upset, as it appeared none of their services were going to be needed any longer. Jacob responded, "I am so sorry Ronnie, everyone. My hands are tied. This is the last thing I wanted to do, but I have to look out for my family."

Matt spoke up, "Listen, listen everyone. Please let me have your attention. Maybe I can be of assistance here. I have frequented this establishment many times and have always received the utmost courtesy and respect. Considering that, my partners and I have some establishments that are always looking for good staff. If you will all please provide me your contact information, I will see if we have a position available for you. If not, my partners and I have considerable contacts, with whom I am sure would also be glad to assist you."

Everyone settled down and started giving Matt their information and likewise, he gave them his information so they could stay in contact, and he could help get them situated.

Jacob came over, "Oh thank you so much Matt. These are wonderful workers and I just hated doing this." Matt said, "I wish you would have told me about your troubles, so I could have tried to help." Jacob replied, "I'm sorry, but this happened so fast, and I had no way of contacting you. The offer was on the table, and I had to take it. I leave tomorrow morning."

"I understand. Look, take my card and if there is anything I can do to assist you, please feel free to contact me."

"Thank you so much Matt, I will remember this. This is kind of you. These are really great people." Matt responding, "No problem. Where and when we can, we all need to help one another. Say, what happened to the lady you called Ronnie?"

"Hmm, I don't know, I don't see her now. I am worried for her as she has no family I know of who can assist her. Her parents passed a few years back and I've tried to give her as much work as I could."

"Well, if she contacts you, have her get in touch with me and I will try to help her as well." Shaking Matt's hand, Jacob said he would.

Chapter 11

Veronica Nicole Rodgers (Ronnie)

Matt was walking to get his car and thought to himself, this has certainly been a twist to the evening. It would have been a shame if I had not decided to come in a day earlier. I am certain I will be able to help them. I just wish I knew what happened to Ronnie.

As Matt reached the parking lot, he heard crying. It was Ronnie. She was pleading, "Please don't take it. It was given to me by my father and it's all I have left from him, please sir."

"Hi Ronnie," said Matt. "Do you remember me from the club?" She looked at me shaking her head yes. Handing her my car keys, "Here, take my keys. Why don't you go over and sit in my car and let me talk to this gentleman to see if I can help you."

Matt talked with the man, who explained he had to take the car in, but he gave Matt the information needed to contact his boss in the morning so he could pursue the matter. He told him he would take care of the car and would let nothing happen to it. Matt thanked him and offered him a tip, but he refused because he really felt sorry for the lady. He left with her vehicle in tow.

Matt turned to walk to his car. Upon seeing what happened, Ronnie jumped out of the car sobbing and crying. She said, "I thought you said you were going to help me." Matt grabbed her and held her close, as she was shaking uncontrollably. "Shh, please stop crying and let me explain." He told her of the conversation that transpired between the tow-truck driver and himself. Matt told Ronnie he had the necessary information to follow up with the matter in the morning. He promised her he would handle it, and for her not to worry.

She looked up at him into his eyes and asked, "Why are you doing this, what's in it for you?" Matt responded by saying, "Simply put, you need help, and I can provide it. You have always been nice to me and now I am able to offer you some assistance. Where do you live, I will take you home? I don't want you to be alone by yourself, especially while you are upset like this?" Ronnie said, "You don't have to do that." Matt saying, "Absurd, I am not leaving you stranded out here by yourself. If something were to happen to you, I would never forgive myself, so get in the car and buckle up!" She told Matt where she lived and gave him directions on how to get there. By the way, my name is Matt. Nice to officially meet you, even though the circumstances are trying for you. It will be better tomorrow, you will see, I promise. "Thank you, Matt, nice meeting, you too," Ronnie began crying again. They drove in silence; Matt observed she was still upset.

Finally reaching their destination, Matt was parking the car to walk her to the door, when she suddenly unbuckled her seatbelt and bolted out of the car. Matt finished parking and chased behind her. She was audibly crying aloud again, "Where are you taking my things? Please, please, my keyboards, be careful with them."

"Take it easy Ronnie, let me handle this for you also." Matt spoke to the men, who advised she was being evicted and her belongings were being repossessed. He made much the same arrangement as he did with her car. Matt came back to tell her what was going on. If she was not before, she was really upset now, once again crying and sobbing uncontrollably. Matt took her in his arms to comfort her. Let's go back to the car and get you calmed down, so I can speak with you.

"What am I going to do, I've lost everything and now I have nowhere to stay on top of it all?"

"Look at me Ronnie. I have come this far with you, and I am not going to turn and leave you now. I may have a solution, that is if you are willing to listen to it and you are willing to trust me to help you. Do you want to hear me out?"

"What do you have in mind?" Matt continued, "You can stay at the hotel I am staying at tonight and…" Ronnie excited and interrupting said, "I knew it. I am not spending the night alone with you in some hotel, just what type of girl do you think I am? You're all alike."

"Wait Ronnie, please let me finish. I am not trying to take advantage of you. I promise, you can trust me. What I was trying to say is, I will get you your own room. You do not have to worry about the expenses. I will take care of everything. I have a meeting with my partners tomorrow, which is why I am here. Before I go, in the morning I will take care of your car and your personal things and have them placed in storage until you get back on your feet. While I am doing all of this, you stay at the hotel and get some rest. When I am done, I will come back for you. I know you are afraid I will take advantage of you, but I promise you I will not. You can meet me downstairs and we can talk further. I have a home in North Carolina, where my friends and I sometimes go to clear our heads. There is plenty of space and if you desire to and trust me, you are welcome to stay there for as long as you would like to. I usually pay someone from town to watch over it for me when I am not there, as I do a lot of traveling and I am seldom there. You could stay there and watch over it for me while I am away. No one will bother you and you can take the time to collect your thoughts, as to what you are going to do. I know this is a lot to absorb but sleep on it tonight and we will talk tomorrow when I get back. Deal?"

"Well, I don't know. I'm not sure…" Interrupting Matt says, "Come on, take a chance. All of us are not alike. I promise I will take care of you." Ronnie looked deeply into his eyes said, "Ok, I will sleep on it. I don't have anywhere to go, and I could use some rest and take the time to calm down."

Matt said, "Great, then tonight is settled, and we can discuss your plans further tomorrow. Let's get going so we can get some rest. Tomorrow is going to be a long day."

As he promised, Matt got her a room at the hotel. He walked her to her room, said goodnight, and gave her his cell number in case she needed to contact him. Ronnie thought he really seems like a nice guy and genuinely wants to help me. Honestly, I don't know what I would have done without his assistance. I can't believe he's doing this for me. I don't know how I will ever be able to repay him. I guess this is what it means not to look a gift horse in the mouth.

Ronnie was really exhausted and was beginning to drop off to sleep when her phone rang. "Hello." It was her former boss, Mr. Meyers. "Hi Ronnie. I was calling to check if you were alright. You left so suddenly, and we could not find you. After you left, George Matthews jumped in to save the day for everyone, by promising to hire them, or to find them jobs elsewhere. He even offered to help me with my situation should I need his assistance. He was worried about you and gave me his card so I could share his contact information with you. This gentleman is on the level, so grab a pencil and paper and copy his info down. Better yet, I will text you the information. Please stay in touch with me Ronnie, as I want to make sure you are doing well. You have been wonderful, and I will miss you. I hated I had to do this but thank God for Matt stepping up to the plate." Ronnie saying, "Okay Mr. Meyers, I will and thank you." "You are very welcome Ronnie, and good night." Ronnie wished him a good night and disconnected the call. Wow, Matt truly is a good guy, as she finally drifted off to sleep.

Back in his room, Matt was reflecting on the events which had unfolded. I am glad I can be there for Ronnie. I hope she will think it over and accept my help tomorrow. Getting away and being able to think clearly will really help her to get it together. I have been there, and I know what I am thinking will be right for her too. She seems like a nice person but has been subject to a lot or personal disappointment. Over time maybe I will be able to help her. I certainly hope so, as he drifted off to sleep, he began thinking of and then dreaming of Geena.

When Matt awoke the next morning, he set things in motion should Ronnie take him up on his offer. He hoped she would. Something in the back of his mind told him this lady was special and she just needed a chance to prove herself. He was usually right about these things and would do everything in his power to make it happen for her.

Having put everything in motion for Ronnie, he was now set to meet with C J and Brick, so they could discuss the project and the surprise they were planning and working on for Geena. JET was still in California and could not make this meeting, but they would bring him up to speed later. He gave C J a call to explain they would have to choose another location, because of the circumstances which had transpired the previous night. He also asked C J to update Brick on the change of plans. They decided to meet at a restaurant in the airport, which would work out simply fine for him. In this manner, he and Ronnie could do some last-minute shopping, and then be well on their way before rush hour this evening.

Ronnie awoke somewhere around nine and decided to give Matt a call to let him know she had thought about his proposal and was willing to give it a try. Matt was just getting ready to sit down to the meeting and told her he would call her when he finished and would be there soon afterwards. "Please be ready so we can go shopping to pick up some things for you." By now she was realizing when Matt was hatching a plan, nothing would deter him from it, so she agreed with no further resistance. She thought he was interesting, and she now was eager to learn more about him. Ronnie realized she had been alone and fending for herself for so long, that she had developed trust issues. She had been taken advantage of far too many times and had her share of grief and disappointments.

Having met Matt, she was wondering if things were finally going to turn around into a more positive mode for her. Maybe she could now concentrate on her dreams of becoming successful with her music, fashion designing and artwork. She remembered discussing her dreams with her mom and dad so many times. She certainly missed them. They were killed by a hit and run driver, who has yet to be found by the police. She was devasted upon receiving the news. She had no sisters, brothers, aunts, uncles, or any other family members. She was alone with no friends, other than her boss Jacob, or a few of the other staff members at Starfire.

Her parents would always urge her to keep on pressing, because if she did, eventually she would attain her goals and realize her dreams. They also made sure to let her know they were proud of her and loved her very much. She now was determined to do just that. Matt seems to have rekindled a fire and desire within her. Perhaps he was correct about her taking time to clear her thoughts of all the things that have recently transpired in her life. Matt certainly was affording her a wonderful opportunity, for which she should be grateful. This was something she should really take advantage of.

She got up, took a relaxing hot shower, put her clothes on, and waited for Matt to come pick her up, thinking of the possibilities awaiting her.

Chapter 12

Matt and C J

Matt entered the restaurant and quickly saw C J waving at him from across the room. Matt ended his call with Ronnie and moved towards the table C J had gotten for them. They embraced each other, glad to see one another again. "Hi C J, good to see you again my friend. How are Mel and the baby?" "Hey Matt, they are doing just fine thanks and how are you doing?" As they began to take their seats, "I am doing great. I decided to come in a day earlier, so I could catch up on some rest and catch the show at the Starfire last evening. I'm glad I did too. It turns out it was their last night to be open." Surprised, C J said, "What do you mean their last night open?" Matt explained what transpired at the club last evening and, telling him about Ronnie.

"So then, you guys are planning to leave later today for Summit Meadows?" Matt nodding, "Yep, that's the plan. As soon as we finish here, I will pick her up, we will shop for a few things for her and get on the road before rush hour. She can pick up any other things she may need once we get to North Carolina. Say, where the heck is Brick?" Shrugging his shoulders, "He called me just before we were to meet and apologized saying he would not be able to come to the meeting day. He has been missing in action a lot lately and mostly keeps to himself when he is around. He has not been his regular jovial self. I'm worried about what is going on with him. I'm trying to give him the space he seems to want and hoping that he will come around to talk about what is bothering him. It has been pretty strange." The waitress came over and they placed their orders. Matt agreed, "Yeah, that is strange and unlike him. You have no idea of what could be bothering him?"

C J, shaking his head, "Nope. I guess he will figure it out sooner or later. If not, we can cross that bridge when we get to it." Matt agreeing, "I suppose so. Please keep me updated on how things turn out and keep a watchful eye on our little brother." Nodding, "I sure will Matt. Rob and I will look out for him."

C J changed the subject, "By the way Matt, what about our girl… have you heard from G?" Shaking his head, "No I have not heard from her since Salt Lake City. She did so well in SLC, she was afforded the opportunity for an assignment in Paris, France. She has an interview here in New York about it and is excited about the interview for the position. I hope she will be selected.

I have been busy as well and have not heard from her yet. I'm sure I will hear from her soon."

"Well, you know Matt, you can always call her," C J chuckling. "Don't start with me C J, in fact, let's get down to business. This event is not going to plan itself." Usually, Geena would be handling things like this.

The meeting with C J now over and goodbyes said, Matt took out his phone to call Ronnie, and headed for the car to go and pick her up. He calculated they could do what they had to do and be on the road no later than three o'clock this afternoon. He had already arranged for check out for both himself and Ronnie. Having already packed his bags and placed them in the trunk, all that remained for him to do was pick up Ronnie.

A man of his word thought Ronnie, as he called like he said he would. She picked up her belongings and headed for downstairs, so as not to create any delays. Matt had indicated he would be there shortly.

Chapter 13

Matt & Ronnie's Road Trip

Matt pulled up to the hotel curb just as Ronnie was walking through the revolving doors. I knew I would like this girl; she is punctual. I believe we are going to become good friends. Matt hopped out of the car and went around to open the door for Ronnie. Seeing him do that, Ronnie waited for him to come around while thinking, hmm, he conducted himself well last evening and now this; at last, a gentleman.

Upon reaching her, "Hi Ronnie, did you rest well last night?" He opened the door for her and assisted her into the front seat. "Hi Matt. Yes, I did get a good night's rest. It did not take me long to fall asleep. Thank you for asking." Matt returned to the other side of the car and slid into the driver's seat. "Great, I'm glad you slept well. Buckle up and let's get started."

Matt found a little boutique off Queens Blvd. Fortunately for them, there was a parking spot in front of the shop. Matt got out and opened the door and extended his hand to help Ronnie out of the car. He liked that she waited, she was very lady like. Matt fed the parking meter, and they went inside.

It did not take Ronnie long. She picked up a few pairs of slacks, a couple of blouses, some pullovers, tennis shoes, loafers, undergarments, PJs, and slippers. Matt had given her the space to do what she needed to do and was watching the television. He had already advised her she could go on a full shopping spree at her leisure, once she got settled in at the house in North Carolina. She was grateful for his help and wondered how and when she would be able to pay him back. As if he was reading her mind, he told her not to worry and he had her covered.

Matt seemed to be generous, thoughtful, and kind. Everything was paid for, packed and ready to go. Matt scooped up most of the bags and they headed for the car, where he placed them in the trunk. He opened the door to let her in, walked around and slid into his seat. They buckled up and were off to the races. The whole process had taken less than thirty minutes.

"Thank you, Matt, you have been so kind, understanding, and generous through all this and I am so appreciative of what you are doing for me. I am truly blessed to know you." Matt looked over at her briefly and then back at the road ahead. He saw she had tears welling up in her eyes. "Please don't cry Veronica. I don't like to see you cry. It's all good and everything is going to turn out alright, you'll see." Her dad would always call her Veronica when she cried and would tell her everything would be fine. Funny he would call me Veronica; this must be an omen. She reached out to his free hand on the center console squeezing it, he in turn taking her hand in his and gently holding it. She was beginning to feel comfortable and safe with him. He had quickly won her over.

Matt had turned on some smooth jazz, which was playing softly. The music was soothing, and Ronnie felt even further relaxed. She must have dozed off; she suddenly awoke startled. Matt was still holding her hand, squeezing it gently he said, "It's okay, I'm here with you and you're safe. Don't worry. There is a rest station up ahead."

Smiling, Matt continued, "We can get fuel for the car and food for ourselves." Ronnie smiled back, "That would be great, I am getting a little hungry. I have not eaten anything since this morning at the hotel. Trying to watch the old figure." Matt chuckling, "I assure you; you don't have to worry about anything in that department." Smiling back at Matt, "Why thank you sir." Car fueled up, they went inside to eat, both laughing.

Having finished eating and using the restrooms, they headed for the car. Matt let out a brief yawn, which Ronnie caught. "Looks and sounds like someone is tired. Would you like me to drive for a while?" He was hesitant in responding. Ronnie giggled, "Don't worry Matt, I am a good driver, I'm not going to wreck your car," now laughing aloud. "Come on, give me the keys!" Smiling, he gave her the keys and opened the door for her, went around and slid into the passenger seat. Ronnie adjusted the seat, rearview and side mirrors, and programmed in her settings. She familiarized herself with the dashboard controls, placed the car into gear, giving it a little gas and tested the brakes. All the while Matt was paying attention to what she was doing. Satisfied with everything she eased the car into motion, gathering speed and smoothly entered the highway. They were on the road again.

Ronnie winked at Matt, "How was that captain, smooth enough for you?" They both had a good laugh. Matt reclined his seat and settled in. Now it was his turn to enjoy the soothing music. Yep, I like this girl. We are really hitting it off. He closed his eyes and drifted away.

Now in Virginia, Ronnie's thoughts drifted back to Matt. It seemed as if they were hitting it off quite well and she now believed they were becoming what looked like to be good friends. She was happy with the prospect. He was still resting, but she knew she would have to awaken him soon. They would be approaching the 95/85 South split and she needed to know which way to go, as she had no idea of where they were headed for in North Carolina.

Fortunately, traffic was moving well all the way from the time they left New York and was still moving satisfactory. She woke Matt up about five miles from the split, asking him which way she should go. He told her to take 85 South. He reached over and programmed in the directions in the GPS, asking if she needed for him to take over again.

"No, that's okay Matt, I'm used to driving on the roads down here at night. I traveled them many times with my dad. I'm originally from Louisiana, so I feel quite comfortable driving down here." Matt smiling, "Wow, I've got a real Southern Belle on my hands. I knew there was something special about you. Coming down here is exactly what you need to clear your mind."

"You know Matt, I am beginning to think you are right about that. You have already made me feel special and this road trip has made me feel good again. Thank you so much!"

"No need to thank me anymore. This benefits me too, and I seem to have found what is going to be a real good friendship, so thank you ma'am." They both laughed at his attempt to have a southern drawl.

Matt was enjoying Ronnie's company. It was just what he needed because he had a terribly busy and hectic schedule coming up. Ronnie was humming to the music. He certainly did enjoy her voice. He relaxed and dozed off again.

Ronnie kept her focus on the road, but her thoughts always drifted back to Matt. The more she was around him, the more comfortable she was beginning to feel, and wondering to what extent and level this friendship would evolve. The GPS alerted her the trip was nearing its end. Not being familiar with the location, she decided to awaken him. Softly she called out, "Matt, wake up. We are nearing our destination." He moved his seat back to the upright position and glanced at the clock. "You made good time lead-foot and we are here safely in one piece too," he said jokingly. Laughing, "Very funny wise guy." They looked at each other and laughed.

Chapter 14

Welcome Home Ronnie!

Matt pressed a code into his cellphone and told her to make a turn into the gate now opening ahead. A path of lights lit the sides of the road up to the house. Again, pressing another code into his phone, lights turned on inside of the house and the outside entranceway. She pulled the car up to the entranceway and parked. On the drive up, she could make out the dwelling had multiple levels, as well as garages and a small parking area. The garages were connected to the main house and there seemed to be a dwelling over the garages.

"Let's go inside, I will give you a brief tour and you can select the room you want to stay in." Getting out, he came around to her side of the car, opened the door and gently pulled her out. He pressed another command into the phone, which unlocked the door. Still holding her hand, he helped guide her up the few steps and opened the door to go inside of the house.

Letting go of her hand, he raised both of his hands, "Welcome home Ronnie! In retrospect, let's get you settled first, and I can show you around tomorrow. If you are hungry, I am sure I can find something to rustle up for us."

He picked up a remote and soft music began playing. "Come on, let's go find you a room." He reached for her hand, and they began to ascend the stairs. I know it seems large, but it is perfect for when 'the Crew' comes in. We are all able to be together, whether working or simply relaxing. Usually, everyone has their room already picked out on this side. On the other side you have your choice of rooms to pick from. This one is across from the master bedroom, which is mine." Matt opened the door and turned on the light so she could see. "If you would rather something at the other end, it will be okay. Whatever you want. They all have king sized beds, and you will be comfortable with whichever one you pick."

Ronnie noted that the room was beautiful, and she wondered who had decorated it. "No, Matt, this will be fine." Looking around again, "It is beautiful, I love it. By now, I think I can trust you. It's me that you should be worried about," winking an eye. They both laughed.

"Great, it's settled! I will go downstairs, park the car in the garage and bring our bags in." She followed him down, "I'll give you a hand." Matt looked at her, "Relax, it will only take me a few minutes. There will be plenty for you to do tomorrow."

While Matt was taking care of their things, Ronnie decided to go into the kitchen to see if she could put something together for them to eat. She did not want Matt thinking she was lazy and would not share in the work to be done while she was here. She found some salmon in the freezer and decided to make some eggs with salmon bits. She also found some veggies in the freezer. She would mix them in with the salmon and eggs, make some toast and brew some hot tea for them. Ronnie had noticed he liked to order salmon when he came to the Starfire. It was a simple meal and would not take her long to fix.

Upon completion of his tasks, Matt came back downstairs to join Ronnie. "Umm, something sure smells good." Smiling Ronnie said, "Take a load off of your feet and sit down over there," pointing to a place she had already set at the table. She had been able to find everything she needed with no trouble at all, as the kitchen was well organized. She had wondered if he had someone do it for him, or if he had done it by himself.

Matt did as he was told, and sat down where she had indicated, admiring how she took charge and how fast she had gotten everything set up. "You keep on surprising me Miss Veronica. If you keep this up, you are going to spoil me." Laughing, "After all you have done for me, you deserve to be spoiled and more."

"Now, now. Don't start that again. You will start crying again and you know I cannot stand to see you cry and be unhappy. Besides, I will be out of here in a few days, running and ripping again. Nothing for you to worry about though. It is relatively safe here and I will input the necessary program into your phone for the security system and show you how to use it. It is simple to use and should make you feel safer. The local sheriff is a friend, and I will let him know you are staying here and to keep an eye out for you. Also, I will leave you the car, so you have transportation. Besides giving you a tour of the house, I will take you to town, show you everything and introduce you to a few of the locals."

Ronnie had finished preparing the meal and set it on the table for them to eat. She sat down, took his hands into hers and said a blessing for their meal and their safe arrival from NYC. They talked a bit more, each sharing more information about themselves. Upon finishing their meal, they cleared the table. Matt washed the dishes, she dried, both cleaning up the kitchen.

Matt showed her how to engage the alarm system and gave her the password. They started upstairs, Matt turning off the light's downstairs. "Goodnight Ronnie, happy dreams." Ronnie embraced him, stood on her tippy toes, and kissed him on his cheek. "Goodnight Matt. You sleep well also." She undressed, jumped into a hot shower, and got into bed in a few minutes, her head hitting the pillow, it was lights out. She fell asleep dreaming of Matt.

Matt jumped into the shower and got himself ready for bed. It had been a long, but very pleasant day. He was glad he and Ronnie were becoming fast friends and he was sure the rest of 'the Crew' would like her as well. Mentally making a note, he had to make sure to govern himself accordingly when he was around her. He found her to be quite attractive and realized she was his kind of lady, so he had better tread carefully. She reminded him in many ways of Geena and could see why he had hit it off with her so quickly. He was stuck on Geena and wanted to make sure there were no complications or misunderstandings between himself and Ronnie.

It was late and tomorrow was another day. He and Ronnie had much to do, so she would feel comfortable here and he could be sure she would be alright. He wanted to make certain she would have no complications and would have a peaceful and serene atmosphere to get herself together. He would see to it her dads car was delivered here, along with her vintage keyboards. He would let her meld them into his studio, which she would be free to use as well.

It had been easy speaking to her about himself, 'the Crew' and the various projects they were interested in doing for their businesses, so they could continue to help other people establish and reach their goals. They were continuing to bond as friends.

Soon it would be time to be on the move again and he needed to get some rest. Exhausted from the long day, Matt began to drift off to sleep, thinking of the great day he had spent with Ronnie, but eventually falling asleep and dreaming of the woman he loved and cared for, Geena.

Chapter 15

'Brick'

Samuel David Johnson, Jr., was like a little brother to C J and Matt. He was a few years younger than them, but a close attachment had developed between them in church. He and Matt were always working together, setting up mikes or providing music for the various activities held at the church in the evenings, or for Sunday afternoon programs. He loved to be the DJ for some of the events of which required music to be utilized when there was not going to be any live entertainment. Sometimes the church would allow him to put on various skits. He usually developed humorous skits about some of the members or officials of the church, of which everyone thought were hilarious. He loved to make people laugh and over a period of time he got better at it.

He always kept Matt and C J laughing and they always let him hang out with them. Matt and C J were close to one another, and they soon started calling him their little brother, which he liked, having no brothers or sisters of his own. Eventually, Geena came into the picture, and they developed a tight relationship with one another. When he was younger, he was a bit chunky, but solid. They dubbed him Brick and the name stuck.

Never thinking it would be profitable for him to perform comedy, he had made the decision to learn about his other interest, audio engineering. One of the deacons in the church was involved with it and would always encourage him to pursue it. He used to do the sound for the church services and started letting Brick help him in the sound room.

Brick got good at it and soon became head of the audio team. The deacon had recommended him as his replacement because he had become the Church Administrative Assistant to the Pastor and no longer had time to lead the team. Brick was grateful for the opportunity. He had gone to school and studied audio engineering and its applications.

Over the years he developed a good reputation regarding his skills in audio engineering, working on projects with comedians, coming up with ideas for sound effects which could help them on their recordings. Soon he was helping on many different projects and meeting some top-notch acts. On one of his many trips, he developed a bond with comedian Seth Howard. Recently on a trip, he ran into Seth, who invited him and a group of his friends to come hear him perform at his live comedy act. Excited, Brick was more than happy to accept the invitation.

He was glad he did, because it was the first time, he laid eyes on Brenda Helena Davis. She was the opening act for Seth, and boy she was funny. A petite ball of fire that lit up the theater with laughter. She was hilarious. Not only that, but she was also super cute and really appealed to him. Seth had gotten him a backstage pass and while standing nearby, Seth saw the interest Brick had in her.

Walking over, "Hey young blood, do you want to meet her?" Brick was excited, "I sure would, she is super funny and cute too." Seth laughing, "No problem. We are having a get together at my place later and she will be there. Invite your friends to come with you and I will introduce you to her then, is that okay?" Smiling, "It sure is. Thanks, so much Seth, I'll handle it from there." Cracking up, "Handle your business young man. In all seriousness, she is a lovely young lady. I have known her family from back in the day, so when she said Uncle Seth, I want to do stand-up, I went to bat for her getting some gigs. She did the rest herself. As you see, she really is gifted. You guys would make a great couple. Go for it young blood!" Smiling, "Watch out now, she is family, ya hear? Don't make me sorry about setting this up Brick." Winking an eye, "Don't worry Uncle Seth, I got this!" They both cracked up regarding the reference, letting Seth know he was serious about her.

Brick told his friends they were all invited to the after-party Seth was throwing. They all agreed it would be fun. He told them they would be on their own, as he hoped he would have plans afterwards. That seemed to be cool with them, as they all had their own plans.

Brick stood about 6' 2" and Seth spotted him as soon as he walked in and excused himself from the group he was with. Coming over, "Welcome, welcome." Brick made the introductions and Seth told everyone to have a good time. They all thanked him and spread out to do just that, have fun. Seth put his arm around Brick, and they began walking together. "She is not here yet, but I know she will be here very soon, as I am sure she went to change, so just stay loose and hang out with me, alright?" Brick responded, "Sure Uncle Seth." He laughed and asked Brick, "Are you looking for a gig too." Brick replying, "Nah, I already have a gig and I am happy with it. Just warming up my private act for the young lady." Seth slapped him on the back and laughed.

Chapter 16

Brenda Helena Davis

They were standing with a small group, Seth being the perfect host and making everyone around him laugh, when Brick saw her enter the room. She was a vision of pure delight. Seth was correct. She did change her attire.

She was now wearing a fitted ivory dress, with a V-neck. The dress was sleeveless, showing a pair of smooth shoulders. She was wearing red sling-back heels, with stockings and she had a small red bag with a gold chain hanging from her shoulder, gold chain necklace, gold earrings and a gold wristwatch. The dress really accentuated her fine figure.

Seth saw her too and waved her over to where they were standing. The others upon seeing Seth wave her over, moved to other groups, leaving Brick standing there alone with Seth.

Everyone else saw her also, all nodding or saying something to her as she made her way towards them, occasionally reaching out to shake someone's hand, as they congratulated her on her performance earlier in the evening. She glided across the floor to where they were standing. She was beautiful and had a warm smile on her face, which made her even more appealing. Brick was smitten.

Having reached them, she smiled, "Good evening gentlemen'" as she hugged Seth and gave him a kiss on his cheek. Smiling, "Hi sweetie, you did great tonight." Smiling back, "Thanks Uncle Seth."

"Where are my manners? Brenda Helena Davis, this is Brick Johnson. I'm sorry, I meant to say this is Samuel Johnson, Jr." Responding, "That's okay Uncle Seth, all my close friends call me Brick."

Continuing, "Good evening Ms. Davis." Laughing and smiling back, "Why hello there Brick, it is a pleasure to make your acquaintance," smiling and extending her hand towards him. Brenda asked, "Were you at the performance this evening and did you enjoy yourself?" Taking her hand in his, "Why yes Ms. Davis, your show was wonderful, and Uncle Seth did okay as well." Laughing, "Why thank you sir. Oh, I like him already Uncle Seth, he has a great sense of humor and a great delivery." Chuckling, "Yep, yep, that's my cue, umm hmm, my job is done, three is a crowd, time to boogie. You kids enjoy yourselves," waving and turning to leave. They were all laughing.

Smiling, Brenda continued, "May I have my hand back now Brick?" He responded, "If you don't mind,

I think I would like to hold on to it a little longer, in fact, a lot longer please." Wow, Brenda thought he was wasting no time. She liked his confidence, and he was funny too. "Well alright then Mr. Brick, what do you have in mind?" Brick thought, so far, so good. "Why don't we find a cozy corner and chat for a while, better yet, why don't we get out of here and find a nice quiet place to eat and get better acquainted. Are you hungry?" Brenda liked the idea. "Yes, I would like that." Smiling, he said, "Let's find your Uncle Seth and let him know we are leaving, so he won't be worried about you, and it will give me a chance to thank him for showing me a wonderful evening." She liked him now even more, as he was showing he was thoughtful and courteous, all the while being a perfect gentleman.

She knew of a place close by and they decided to walk there. Brick was still holding her hand, and she was loving it, thinking this man is sweet. They arrived at the restaurant, got a table, settled in, and ordered an Italian meal with the waiter.

They were at ease with one another and chatted away, relaxing, and learning about each other as they enjoyed their meal.

Taking a deep breath, Brick being serious now, "I know this is sudden, but when it is right, it's right. I really like you and I do not want to let you get away. You are someone special, I enjoy being with you, and I do not want this to end."

Brenda leaned across the table and gave him a kiss. "I am glad to hear you say that. Even though this is unexpected, I feel the same way, as this feels right to me also." Brick continued, "I know this will be difficult, given our busy schedules and living in different places. No long-distance relationship is easy. However, I promise you I will come to you as often as I can and further, I promise to call you every night. This way, we will make every moment count and it will be special. I believe it will be worthwhile for both of us. I know it is crazy, but I have developed feelings for you already. May I call you Lena?"

Brenda sighed and leaned in to give him another kiss, this time longer and more passionate. "This is wonderful. Not only can you keep holding my hand, but you can also have my heart. I believe you are correct. We can make this work, and yes, you may call me Lena."

It was getting late now, and Brick had an early flight back to NY. He paid the check and took Brenda back to her hotel. He walked her to her room, took her in his arms and kissed her goodnight. She responded warmly, wrapped her arms around him and held him tight. Fortunately, they found out they were staying in the same hotel. When he got to his room, he packed, laid out his clothes for tomorrow, took a quick shower, came back into the room, jumped into the bed, and called Lena.

They talked briefly and then said goodnight. They fell asleep thinking of each other. Although she did not have to leave until later in the day, Lena got up early, went to Brick's room and knocked on the door. She kissed him good morning and kissed him goodbye, promising to call him when she arrived at her next destination.

Lena returned to her room to begin packing for her departure. Thinking to herself, how surprised and amazed she was regarding her meeting with Brick and how fast he had won her heart. She was not really in the market for a relationship, but agreed with his analogy, "when it's right, it's right."

Lena did not want to miss out on having a relationship with Brick, because she had a feeling this was the start of a terrific romance. Plus, she was pretty confident with him because of his relationship with Uncle Seth, who's judgement in people was always spot on.

Brick was excited. He knew everything would be okay, and he had found a great lady. The way she came to his room, let him know he had made a good decision about her, and he was going to do everything in his power to make their relationship work.

It was going to be difficult, but he learned a long time ago, things always work out for the better when you must put in a little overtime to make things work. He must persevere and overcome any obstacles if this was going to work. He was certain things would turn out simply fine for Lena and himself, and discerned he made the right choice.

From the time he first saw her, he knew and had a great feeling about Ms. Brenda Helena Davis.

He would let 'the Crew' know soon enough, but for now, he just wanted to enjoy his relationship with Lena without any pressure. He knew they would be happy for him, and they would love Lena too.

When it's right, it's right!

Chapter 17

I Love Paris, Anytime

Geena's plane landed safely at Orly. The flight took just approximately eight hours. She had asked if she would be allowed to bring her assistant along and was told it would not present a problem. Her assistant was Leslie Anne Howard, who was not only her assistant, but a good friend. Geena was thinking, Lee Anne was very capable, effective, and trustworthy. Always keeping my very hectic schedule manageable, keeping tabs on the various projects I was working on, and most importantly, she made herself available to me around the clock. She never has complained about the workload and how time consuming her job was. Some time ago, I added on members to my staff, and she quickly developed a comradery with them, which made my decision easy as who should oversee the team.

She was extremely excited about the Paris project, and elated I had been chosen to participate in the event. After I received the good news, I went back to the office after meeting with the project managers to let her know personally. "Lee Anne, you have been an integral part of this operation for a long time, and I really appreciate all of your hard work, which I know is very time consuming and tedious. You always have a handle on things, making my job and life easier. On top of that, we have become good friends, so having said all of that, how about you pack your bags and accompany me to gay Paris!"

Screaming, "Oh my God Geena, are you serious? Don't play with me girl, do you really mean it?" Stepping forward and hugging her, "Yes, I really mean it. I would not kid you about this. We will have a great time together. You need not worry about any expenses; everything has been taken care of. We will have the time of our lives, sightseeing, and shopping, which will of course all be on me, you deserve it lady." Hugging Geena back, "Yes, I would love to go with you. Everything will be fine here, as we have assembled a great staff." Geena laughing, "See what I mean? You are always looking out for my interests. I have so many things to tell you. So much has transpired since we last saw each other."

"Fantastic Geena, I am excited to hear all about it. You seem different and happier than I have seen you in a long time. This radiant look you have, has any of this to do with…" Geena held her hand up, "Not now! We will have plenty of time to talk while we are in Paris. Most every girl wants to go to Paris at some time, right?"

Giggling, "I don't know about you Geena, but I love Paris, anytime!" They threw their heads back laughing. There was going to be plenty of work to do, but the two of them were going to have a great time Geena thought.

They worked diligently to make certain their part of the event would go on without so much as a hiccup. They worked well in concert with one another, making the necessary arrangements to ensure the project's success. They also made sure an effective contingency plan was in place. They knew this was the opportunity of a lifetime, and if all went according to plan, its success would open other doors for Geena.

In their down time, they toured the city, dined, talked, and of course shopped. Swearing her to secrecy, Geena told Lee Anne about the trip to the awards in SLC, and what transpired between her and Matt.

Giving her a hug, Lee Anne was overjoyed to hear the good news. "I'm so happy for you both. Lord knows it's about time. I was beginning to wonder if the two of you would ever get it together." Geena surprised by the remark asked, "What do you mean by that?"

Laughing, "Gosh Geena, everybody knows. We all see how the two of you act when you are around each other and we have been rooting you two would get together."

"Wow, I thought I was masking my emotions pretty well regarding how I feel about him." Smiling, "Geena, you love him and have been for a long time, and further, he loves you too! It is so obvious."

Geena replying, "Well, let's just keep this between us Lee Anne. Matt and I want to just enjoy each other right now, without any outside scrutiny."

Laughing, "Good luck with that girl. The whole office noticed this new aura about you and have been speculating if it had something to do with Matt. Don't worry yourself about it. Everyone loves you and they have been cheering for both of you. You both complement each other well and I know you will be happy together."

Hugging her, "Thanks so very much Lee Anne. I am happy I shared this with you. Indeed, you have proven yourself to be a good friend and I hope I stay worthy of your friendship."

Laughing, "Only if I am invited to the wedding. In fact, I am certain the whole staff will want to be there also."

"Easy Lee Anne let's not rush things. Matt and I just want to enjoy each other right now and we have not even begun to discuss any wedding plans."

"Don't worry Geena. Trust me, that man is going to be talking to you about it sooner than you think. Besides, don't you think the two of you have waited long enough?"

Geena replied, "I am not worried. Everything will come together when it is time."

Working on the project, time passed by quickly. The event turned out to be quite the success and it was now time to plan for the return to New York. She had told Matt the interview went well, and she got the assignment. As promised, Geena and Matt had talked to each other daily.

Previously, whenever she was away, Geena would always be thinking of, and secretly wishing he would be by her side. Now that they've become closer, Geena realized this was harder, and she missed him even more than before. She could hardly wait until she would see him again.

Geena knew she had a few more events to attend, but thought maybe Lee Anne could clear up her schedule for a week or two so she could spend some quality time with Matt. She was worried about him, as she knew he and the guys were working on something which seemed to be pretty much of a big deal. She was feeling guilty not being with 'the Crew' because they had always worked together on big projects. She had been so busy with things, she could not fit time into her schedule. When finishing up one thing, Lee Anne always seemed to come up with something else. She let Geena know the guys understood, and they would be okay. Geena had let Lee Anne know if they needed any assistance from her office, to make it happen and to be there for them. Lee Anne had promised she would.

Before arriving back to the Apple, Lee Anne promised Geena she would try to clear her schedule, so she could spend time with Matt. Geena thanked her and said she would be grateful if she could.

Chapter 18

Time Spent Alone, Time Spent Well

Since coming to North Carolina, Ronnie had made good use of the time she was spending there. Matt had been right. The location was just as he said it would be.

At first, she acclimated herself with the house, then she would sit in the back on the patio, listening to the birds sing, and enjoying the view. She had missed the peace and quiet the country offered. Becoming more relaxed, she started taking walks around the grounds, and soon she would drive into town and was becoming more familiar with it. The town of Summit Hill was quaint, and the people were friendly. She started to know the locals, who were friendly towards her.

The house, Summit Meadows, was special too. It was large enough to be able to host events and there was plenty of space for guests to stay over. Matt had made certain everything needed was there. The grounds were spacious and beautiful. There was a patio, with a place to barbecue and grill. Just beyond that was the pool and jacuzzi. There was also a beautiful garden, lined with benches, so one could just sit and enjoy its beauty. Above the garage, there was space for separate living quarters. Set in a serene location, it offered those utilizing the space, the peace of mind to be able to create, or just to relax. It also had its own airstrip and helipad.

Summit Meadows certainly had it all. It was secluded, but still relatively near enough to town, when she wanted to visit. She had also found a gazebo, set in a beautiful field of flowers, just on the other side of town. She liked spending time there also, as it was peaceful and picturesque.

Ronnie decided to go into town to pick up a few more things and found a few sundresses she liked, for those relaxing days on the patio. She also went to the local market to keep the house stocked. They told her they could deliver, but she preferred coming to town, as she enjoyed visiting with the people. She was accomplishing a lot, but being alone all the time, she wanted to go into town just so she could talk with someone.

Matt would occasionally call to check on her. She really missed him and could not wait for his return so she could show him what she had accomplished. Ronnie had found the studio Matt had at the house and took advantage of it. She was composing and had put together quite a bit of material, just needing to get it recorded. She had found the audio booth and the recording equipment, but she had no experience at recording and did not want to bother with any of it.

She had many interests and soon found the urge to do some sketches. She began designing some things under the name of Powder Puff Design & Fashions. She dreamed of one day having a business doing fashions, along with becoming an artist.

She also loved art. Her mom had been an artist and she would spend time with her in the studio. She began first with sketching and finally started painting scenery. Her mother told her she had a natural talent and encouraged her to paint. Maybe one day she could sell some of her work.

Ronnie had found an empty space in one of the rooms at the house and did not think Matt would be upset if she converted it into a small studio for herself. She had found an arts and crafts store in town and picked up some supplies, excitedly taking them home and setting up the studio. She had also found a camera in the house and did not think he would be upset if she used it. She loved photography as well, and soon blended some of Matt's shots into the studio alongside of her work. She loved the little studio she had created and hoped Matt would like it too.

Funny, she was beginning to feel as if this place were home and could not imagine being any place other than here. She had come a long way since that night in the parking lot and was feeling good about herself.

She had felt helpless, vulnerable, and terribly alone since she lost her parents. Having no other relatives, or close friends, she had no one she could turn to. Having the job at the Starfire kept her somewhat grounded. Seth Meyers had become a friend she could rely on, but his devasting news of him selling the club sent her reeling, and out of control. He gave her as much work as he could, but without the job at the Starfire and his support, she didn't know what she was going to do.

Thank God Matt was there to step in. Having been hurt and let down before, she did not trust him right away. Something in the way he conducted himself throughout the evening, coupled with the phone call she received from Seth, made her decide to take a chance. It helped her to believe and trust again.

Matt proved himself to be someone special, and she was glad she had taken the opportunity he presented to her. She felt her life had direction and purpose once again. She knew her parents would be proud of her, and she knew she wanted Matt to be proud of her also.

Most of all, she was proud of herself. Matt was right about taking time for herself to get it together. The time she was spending here, was turning out to be time spent alone, but time spent well.

Chapter 19

R & R at Summit Meadows

Time was passing quickly for Matt, as many different things had transpired, both personally and in business. He managed to talk with Ronnie a few times but sensed she was enjoying her newfound solitude and was finding a peace and calmness for herself.

Geena had stayed in contact with him, although the calls were brief because of the time difference between Paris and Chicago. When they spoke, she excitedly briefed him on the events of her day. Being short calls, their attention now turned to them personally, on how they missed each other.

Matt wanted to tell Geena about what had taken place at the Starfire but decided it could wait until she returned to the States.

At this point, all that mattered to him now was to have the surprise events 'the Crew' was planning take place without a hitch, and of course Geena, who was constantly in his thoughts and prayers.

Matt was planning for Ronnie's car to be shipped to Summit Hill. He would have it taken to a garage in town first, so he could surprise her. He would arrive at the house and stay a few days and then make up some errand for her to run, then have the car brought to the house and placed in the garage, tucked away for her surprise. He knew she would flip out. Meanwhile, he had picked up her keyboards and had carefully placed them in the car rental he was driving to Summit Meadows. Yes indeed, she is going to be an incredibly pleased lady!

Arriving safely, Matt pulled the car into the garage and unloaded the keyboards, safely putting them away so Ronnie would not find them.

When Matt entered the house, he heard Ronnie playing the piano in the studio. He was not familiar with the music and stood listening. When she finished, he applauded and said, "Surprise, I'm home!" Ronnie jumped from the piano bench and ran to greet him, giving him a big hug. Excited, "Welcome home, I've missed you. I have so much to show and share with you." Laughing Matt said, "Ms. Veronica, slow down there and letta man ketch his breath," attempting that southern drawl again. Ronnie giggling, "Why I'm so sorry sah," copying him, both now laughing aloud.

Letting Matt go, "How was your trip…was it successful? Tell me all about it! Are you hungry? I could rustle you up something to eat." Not letting him answer, she guided him back to the sofa, "Sit down and relax. I'll go fix you something to eat." Not wanting to disappoint her, Matt sat down, as she rushed off to the kitchen to get started.

"Wow! You are certainly a bundle of high energy. You seem to be more relaxed and happier since the last time I saw you."

"Yes, I am, thank you. We have so much to catch up on. I want to hear all about your trip, and I want to tell you what I have been up to. But first, I need to get you fed and you certainly must be tired too."

"Thanks. If you don't mind, after I eat, I would like to go upstairs, get undressed and take a nice long hot shower and then jump into the bed because I am exhausted." Ronnie said she did not mind. She prepared his food and they chit-chatted while he ate. When Matt finished eating, he headed upstairs and Ronnie cleaned up the kitchen, before heading up to bed herself. She was excited Matt had returned home, realizing she missed him more than she thought. Excited, she was wondering what was ahead for them.

Chapter 20

Carolina Country Squall

After eating, Matt headed upstairs for the long hot shower he told Ronnie he was going to take. Finishing, he got dressed and jumped into bed. Just as he did, the phone rang. It was Geena checking in. She sensed how tired he was and kept the call brief, telling him she loved him. Matt grateful, hung up and immediately fell asleep.

After Ronnie finished cleaning the kitchen, she set the alarm. She was tired as well because she had started her day early. She was satisfied and realized she had accomplished a lot, but then got a brief spark of energy when Matt had arrived earlier. She certainly was glad to see him. Ronnie showered and jumped into the bed.

Sometime in the middle of the night a severe storm had arisen, with thunder and lightning, accompanied by heavy winds. The loud crashing of thunder awoke Ronnie, and she was terrified. She had always been afraid of storms since a young girl and would run to the safety of her dad's bedroom, where she felt safe in his arms. With the noise in the city, she would always manage and would eventually go back to sleep. Another loud crash of thunder and the room lit up with the flash of lightning. Without thinking, Ronnie jumped out of her bed and headed across to Matt's room, pushing the door and jumping into bed with him.

Matt awoke startled, and could feel Ronnie's arms reaching out for him, feeling her shake with fright. Still half asleep, he let her into his arms and told her, "G, it will be alright, don't be afraid." Soon, Ronnie began to relax and soon after, the storm began to subside.

Feeling comforted by his arms wrapped around her, Ronnie began to relax. Now calmer, she realized she had invaded Matt's space. Ashamed, but also realizing she had longed of being in his arms. She liked how he held her and how safe she felt, reminiscent of how he held her in New York, calming her down then also.

Feeling stirred by his gentleness, Ronnie began kissing Matt. First on his neck and then moving around to kiss him on his lips. He parted his lips and their tongues met, the desire welling up inside of her, a fire growing hotter and more intense with every passing second.

Matt was responding but sensed there was an unfamiliarity with the kisses. He suddenly realized he was holding Ronnie and he liked it, responding to the curves and softness of her body, and the gentle kisses she was giving to him. He knew he had to stop now before it was too late.

Matt reached out and turned on the light, and Ronnie could see the upset look and frown now upon his face.

He began, "Ronnie, what are you doing?" Responding, "Matt, you seem upset. I'm so sorry, I was not even thinking, just reacting to the storm. I am terribly afraid of electrical storms, and it just transported me back in time, to when I would run into my dad's room and into his arms. Please don't be upset with me, I was not thinking or acting clearly."

"So, then you want me to believe you would run to your father and start kissing him?"

"No, no! Please don't be angry with me, let me try to explain." Matt sensing Ronnie was upset, started calming down, "Go ahead, this I have got to hear."

"I realized it was you I was kissing. I have been wanting to be in your arms ever since the night you came to my rescue. I feel so safe when I am with you, and I wanted so to be in them again, and I also wanted to know what it would be like kissing you. So, feeling safe and comforted in your arms just now, I realized I was aroused and started kissing you and when you responded, I kept on going and I allowed myself to become even more passionate and let myself feel more desire towards you."

Matt stared at Ronnie for what seemed to her an eternity, looking deeply into her eyes, which were now starting to fill with tears. "Matt please say something. I know this is all sudden to you, but I have developed strong feelings for you. I mean, I could feel you responding. Didn't you like what was happening between us? Please, you must believe me. I would never just offer myself to a man like this, without caring for him. I have been hurt so many times before looking for love and wanting to be treated like a lady, just the way you have been treating me. We have and are building a relationship that is evolving, and I went for it. But judging by your demeanor and your reaction, you don't seem to be so happy with me right now."

Matt now realized he needed to respond carefully and certainly he needed to be gentle and kind when doing so.

"Ronnie, I need you to please listen to me very carefully. I know you trust me, and you are grateful to me for being there in your time of need, but you need time to think this through with a level head. I have not lied to you in the past, and I will not start now. Having said that, let me respond to the concerns and questions you've raised."

Continuing, "Yes, I was into what just happened and if I am being honest, I desired you also. I know it would have been easy for me to let our emotions play out and let things just happen. Trust me when I say it was hard for me to stop just now, you are such a beautiful and desirable woman. But I would have been taking advantage of you and even though it would have been easy,

I am not that kind of person. Given the fact I know you've been hurt in the past, it would make me a low life." Matt paused and Ronnie not wanting to interrupt waited. It seemed as if he wanted to explain something further to her. "Ronnie, I was just now debating if I should tell you this and I have decided to tell you something, and you will be one of the first to hear this and I believe it would be better coming from me firsthand, rather than you finding out from another source."

Matt took a deep breath, because this was possibly going to be something difficult for her to fathom at this moment and he did not want to hurt her feelings, as she was in an extremely sensitive state right now.

"I have had feelings for and have been in love with someone I have known for an awfully long time now and we have recently gotten together and professed our love and feelings towards one another. It is to her my heart now belongs. Again, I know this is not much, but if not for her and how we feel about one another, I can truthfully tell you I would allow myself to become in a romantic way with you to find out where it would lead us. I can really understand why I am so attracted to you, because you remind me so much of Geena. The both of you are ladies and that is what I want in my life."

There it was. Ronnie knew he just was not making up a story to get rid of her because he was not attracted to her, because his eyes and expression became soft when he said her name.

Tears in her eyes, "Matt, I am so ashamed and sorry. I have been wanting someone like you in my life for so long, and I could not help myself for loving you the way I do and know I do love you."

Responding to her, "Ronnie, I know and can feel the love you have for me. However, you love me, as I do you, but you are not in love with me. Maybe in time it would develop, but there is a distinct difference between the two."

Ronnie saying, "I know this is going to sound super weird and crazy, but may I please stay here with you holding me in your arms tonight? I promise, just give me a few days please, so I can find a place and when I do, I will get out of your way." Starting to cry, "I apologize, and I am so sorry my behavior. Believe me, I would never hurt you Matt."

He pushed her back onto the bed and turned the light out. Gently gathering her in his arms, he told her to stop crying, wiped her tears away softly with the back of his hand and kissed her on her cheek.

"Ronnie, you are not going anywhere. You have not done anything wrong. You have been brave and shared your true feelings, something Geena and I have realized we should have done long ago. Close your eyes, hold me, give me one of those sweet kisses of yours and go to sleep. We will talk tomorrow. You are family and this is your home too."

Ronnie softly kissed him, and then curled up into his arms thinking, this is an incredibly special man and

Geena is a fortunate woman to have his love. She was now determined more than ever to do something special for him. Once again feeling safe and protected she fell asleep in his arms.

Chapter 21

Morning After the Storm

The next morning, as per usual, Matt woke up early. Ronnie was still cuddled in his arms sleeping peacefully. The sunlight was now filtering through the window and filling the room with bright sunshine. Matt thought to himself, this beautiful woman lying in his arms was an exceptionally charming lady and how she would make some man incredibly happy as his companion. Easy to talk with, sweet, kind, supportive, extremely sensitive, and so much more. Yes, what he told her last night was true, if it were not for him being in love with Geena, he would be extremely interested in pursuing a relationship with her.

Last evening had been emotional for them in many ways. But her honesty and strength enabled him to find just the right words to respond to her. In their chats, she had expressed to him how deeply hurt she had been and how much she missed her parents. She was alone and felt she no longer had a foundation beneath her. He knew not showing empathy towards her could prove disastrous and send her spiraling back into a deep sense of doubt and fear.

Ronnie stirred and opened her eyes. She looked like a child caught with their hand in the cookie jar. She softly spoke, "Good morning Matt," and started to move away, looking as if she had been guilty of doing something wrong.

Matt gently pulled her back into his arms. "I don't want to let go of you yet. I have some things to share with you and I would like for you to listen and feel what I am about to say to you. You look as if you are ashamed of what transpired between us last night, like you did something very wrong. I want to keep on holding you, so you can hear and feel the truth of what I am saying to you."

"Last night with you sharing your feelings for me was deeply emotional for me and it was a richly rewarding experience, one I will always cherish and fondly remember. One day you are going to make a man a fine mate, giving him an experience of loving he will never want to walk away from. Your sensitivity and love will fill him with warm desire for you and he will always enjoy being with you. You are a beautiful and desirable lady, and I am proud to call you my friend. You are family and maybe this is selfish, but I do not want you to go anywhere because I love you, so please stay and never think about leaving again. I would not want that, because I know many wonderful and beautiful things lie ahead of us and I don't want us to miss what we will share together."

Softly crying in his arms, "Oh my God, Matt. Your words and the way you are holding me does make me feel every word you said is true. I feel so blessed and I am overwhelmed with the generosity you have shown me. I understand now about the love you and I are experiencing and sharing with another. I am so glad you took the time to listen to me and you understand my feelings, even better than I understand them. Geena has a warm, generous, and kind man, who will endeavor to make her extremely glad you are in her life."

Ronnie smiling and continuing, "I too will fondly cherish our night together and I will never forget the warmth we feel for each other, and it will never die. This is something special and we will always have it, no matter what." Ronnie took Matt into her arms and shared their final kiss, getting up and starting back to her room thinking to herself, Geena better be good to him, or else she is going to have to deal with me.

Chapter 22

Ronnie's Surprise for Matt

Matt showered and dressed, glad he and Ronnie had been able to talk to one another and clear the air. He was whistling and feeling in a wonderful mood as he bounded down the stairs. Ronnie was already down in the kitchen preparing breakfast, something that would become a ritual always shared in this home.

He heard her happily humming away on another tune he was unfamiliar with, coming into the kitchen to be with her. "This is the second time I have heard you humming happily to a melody I am not familiar with, and I have been meaning to ask you what they are. They seem to be incredibly beautiful. Are there any lyrics to go along with the melodies?"

Turning towards him, "Yes there are lyrics. If you remember what I told you last night, I have so much to share with you. I have been quite busy, and I believe I have utilized my time well. You will be the first to experience the fruits of my labor and I hope you like it."

After they had finished eating and cleaned up the kitchen together, Ronnie excitedly took Matt's hand into hers, pulling him towards the music room. She placed a chair next to the piano where he would be near and facing her, so she could see his reactions firsthand. She was nervous, as she was about to give Matt a private concert, one of which she hoped he would enjoy immensely.

Ronnie played for at least two hours, transforming into something Matt had not witnessed in her when she played at the Starfire. It was a richly fulfilling, and personal experience, of which he was extremely enjoying. All the music she was performing was composed by her and she had intermixed them with favorites which he recognized, arranged, and performed in her own special way.

She continued to play, always engaging him by looking and smiling at him, making it an extremely erotic and personal performance for him.

Her timing, phrasing, and her care of how she played the chords on the piano was a mesmerizing experience, something Matt had noticed and enjoyed when she played at the club. Her own arrangements seemingly to be a mixture of Nina Simone, Roberta Flack, Nancy Wilson, and others, but performed in her own unique way. She ended by singing Flack's, "The First Time Ever I Saw Your Face," which had now become Geena and his love song. She locked her eyes upon him, smiling and singing each note for him, and for him only, noting the look upon his face, like the song was special to him. Finishing, "Well, how did you like them? Be honest with me because I need to know the truth."

Matt had risen from his seat clapping his hands with excitement, saying to her, "Ronnie, they were superb, and beautiful. Your performance of them was simply captivating and mesmerizing. You made the experience warm and personal for me, thank you so much. I am enormously proud of you. When I first heard you at the club, I knew you had this in you and your talent was exceptionally special."

Excited, "Really Matt?" Smiling and shaking his head up and down for emphasis, "Yes, really Ronnie. Your ability to engage people with your eyes and smile will do well for you when performing live, something I know you are going to be doing a lot of."

Coming over to hug him, "Thank you Matt, from your lips to God's ears I pray."

Matt asking, "You are planning on recording them, right? You certainly have more than enough material to do so." She said, "Yes, I saw the recording booth, but I am not knowledgeable enough to do my own recordings. Plus, on one of the arrangements, I am not completely happy with it. It's as if there is something missing in it." Matt saying, "Play it for me please and let me see what you mean."

Ronnie's Surprise for Matt

Ronnie sat back down to play and upon finishing, "See what I mean, something is missing, right?" Nodding, "It's beautiful, but I understand what you are saying. Listen, I've got you Ronnie, I believe in you. I have some ideas that may help you I learned from back in my choir days. Let me make some calls and see if we can set them in motion."

Surprised, I did not know you were into music that way. Do you play also… is that why you have this studio here? It is certainly large enough to hold a choir and a band too." Matt replied shaking his head and telling Ronnie there was nothing special about it. "Nah, you're the real deal here, I just dabble." Changing the subject, "Let me make those calls." Ronnie had a feeling there was more to it than he was sharing.

Matt reached out to Rob and Brick. "Hey guys, I have stumbled onto something which may be beneficial to you Brick and for your young protégé Rob. If you can clear your schedules, would you do me a favor and come on down this weekend?" They both agreed they could, Rob saying, "Sure Matt, Jason and I were talking about doing a little fishing this weekend. I'm sure he will be excited to come down and enjoy some country living."

"Great, I will be expecting you all, and ask Jason to pack his fishing rod along with his Sax too! I will arrange for you to use the chopper, so you can get down here Friday evening. Call from the chopper and I will pick you up in the SUV." Acknowledging, "We sure will Matt, see you then."

Matt hung up and then called the garage in town asking them to put Ronnie's car on a trailer for towing and he would pick it up tomorrow. He decided to have the guys use the local airport, instead of the helipad here. This way he could kill two birds with one stone, with Ronnie being none the wiser. This was better than the original plan.

Having finished, he went back to rejoin Ronnie. "Sorry I took so long. I had to make a business call also, but I am free again now. Oh, and while I am still thinking about it, I have three business clients coming in this weekend, Friday evening to be exact. Would you please do me a huge favor, be the hostess, and prepare some meals for us for the weekend?"

"Sure Matt, anything for you. Anything special?" Matt replying, "No, I will leave the menu up to you. We can use the large dining area, as I want to leave a favorable impression on them."

"I will get on it and show you what I come up with this evening, okay?"

Matt replying, "That will be great Ronnie, thank you." Thinking, she sure is going to be surprised this weekend.

Ronnie excited again, "Come on Matt, I've got more to show you. I told you I was really busy while you were gone."

Laughing, "Why ya'll got more for me ta see Ms. Veronica?" Ronnie laughing as well, "I sure duz sah," both cracking up now.

Ronnie eagerly took Matt by the hand again, leading him to the makeshift studio she had prepared. The room was dark, and she told him, "Cover your eyes please and do not open them until I tell you it's okay, promise me." Matt promised and covered his eyes as he was told, all the while wondering what else Ronnie had cooked up.

Ronnie held him by the waist and guided him into the center of the room. She went over and turned the lights on and came back to stand in front of him, so she could see his reaction. "Okay, you can open them now."

Matt opened his eyes to a very delightful sight. She had created a studio, which featured some paintings, photography, and sketches, all clustered around the room, hanging symmetrically on the walls, which gave the room a good balance. She had an easel in one corner of the room and had brought in a table and chair, where it seemed she worked from, as he saw the unfinished sketches she was working on and an unfinished painting on the easel. Also, he recognized one of his cameras on the table, along with a laptop and printer. This was her little studio where she could create her pieces. Obviously, she was very gifted at it and showed a remarkable eye for detail in her work, which he found to be exquisite and riveting.

On one of the walls, he noticed some photos he had taken he never framed. He had bought a lot of frames and promised himself one day he would frame his work and hang them around the house, which of course he never did get around to doing.

"What do you think? I found this room while exploring the house and continuing, I found the camera, frames, and the unframed photos of which I assumed you took. I took it upon myself to frame them for you and I used the spare frames you had to frame my pieces of work. I know it was rather presumptuous of me, but I wanted to surprise you. I hope you are not upset with me, because I just wanted to do something nice for you. You have been so wonderful towards me, so I prepared this little exhibit for you. I hope it's not over the top."

Matt rushed over to her and began hugging her, "Ronnie, I love it. You went to great lengths to put this together and I appreciate all of your efforts. I had been meaning to do something with the photos I took, but you have managed to select the best of them, and you have showcased them well. In fact, this whole room's set-up has been done tastefully and your work is beautifully exquisite. You are extremely gifted and talented. I am beginning to wonder what else you can do, because thus far, all you have shown me is simply fantastic. I am so glad you have shared this with me. Other people need to see your work, it's amazing!"

Hugging Matt back, "Thank you Matt." Sensing her emotions on the rise, she let him go and stepped back, not wanting to send any wrong messages to him. She realized she was still physically attracted to him and knew it was not going to go all away in one day. To be honest, she wondered if it would ever disappear. "I just got on this fantastic roll of creativity and kept on going, well, until what you see here before you," whirling and waving her hands around the room for emphasis.

Matt had sensed her heightened emotions and was glad she stepped away, as he had felt it too. After all, she was a beautiful, alluring woman to him, and he realized they had to be careful of the attraction they felt for one another. She was a good person, and he knew in time this would dissipate and be just a memory in the past.

He walked around the exhibit she had put together, paying closer attention to the detail of her work, noting her work was excellent. She also drew some sketches of fashion designs, which were beautiful.

It had been a full day and Ronnie and Matt decided to go for a walk and watch the sunset, Ronnie grabbed the camera, slinging it across her shoulder, just in case any good shots popped up. They walked quietly hand-in-hand, except occasionally she would let it go when she felt she could take a nice shot with the camera. Afterwards, she would put her hand back in his and they would continue walking.

Starting to get dark, they headed back to the house. They had decided to heat up some frozen pizza and to just sit around chatting and listening to music, before retiring for the evening.

It finally was Friday and Matt was up early and all excited about what the day would bring. He could not wait to see the look upon Ronnie's face when he springs the surprises on her. As she had promised, she had prepared and shown him the list of meals she would be serving to his invited guests. She was in for a big surprise.

He had received the call from the chopper, and it was now time to put the plan into motion. Ronnie was busy scurrying around the kitchen, preparing snacks and dinner. Matt heard her humming and called out to her, letting her know he was leaving to run some errands and was on his way to pick up his guests. She acknowledged and Matt heard her continue to hum, as he closed the door behind him.

When Ronnie finished, she went upstairs to change and get ready for Matt's guests. He said they were important clients, and she wanted to make a good impression on them, so Matt would be proud of her. She knew over time, she was going to pay Matt back for the kindness he showed her, and with interest. It was the least she could do for this wonderful man. He's done so much for me, and I will never forget it.

She had been meticulous in choosing what she was going to wear. She wanted to be ready when Matt returned with his guests. She hoped the preparations made for his guests would please him.

Ronnie was pleased at her choice of attire, and the way she looked.

Chapter 23

Rob, Jason, and Brick

Matt drove to the garage, where the trailer was ready to be hooked up to the SUV, with Ronnie's car. From there, he headed to pick up Rob, Jason, and Brick. They were happy to see one another again and after exchanging greetings, they threw their luggage into the back of the SUV, Jason gingerly placing his saxophones where they would not be damaged, along with Rob and his fishing poles. Everything loaded, they jumped aboard, and they set off for the house. Rob started, "What's with the car on the trailer in the back?" Matt began sharing what had transpired regarding the club and Ronnie. Explaining to them how he felt about Ronnie and bringing them up to speed about the reason he had invited them to come.

Brick responding to what had been said, "From what you are saying, it sounds as if we have a wonderful addition to our family," Rob and Jason chiming in to agree.

They arrived back at the house just at sunset. Matt backed the trailer up to the garage door and with the help of the guys, they placed the car into neutral and guided it off the trailer into the garage. Matt placed the trailer into one of the empty spaces in the garage and then backed the SUV into its spot. They unloaded everything and headed inside.

Matt called out to Ronnie, alerting her he was back, which would also serve notice to her the guests were with him.

Hearing him, she took one last look at herself in the mirror. She had put on a sleeveless white dress, which accentuated her fine figure, stockings and four-inch white sling back heals she had picked up earlier in the week. The dress was one of her own designs. She accented the whole look with gold drop earrings, a gold necklace, and with a matching bracelet. Now moving gracefully down the stairs, "Good evening gentlemen." Matt immediately went over to extend his hand, as she was about to reach the bottom of the staircase. She reached out to accept it and Matt escorted her over to where the group was standing, mesmerized with her beauty. Jason dropped his sax case with a loud thud. Matt thought good thing it was a hard case and it fell on the welcome mat. "Gentlemen, allow me to present to you, Ms. Veronica Nicole Rodgers." They all said good evening, except for Jason, who was still standing there agog. Rob nudged him whispering, "Did you forget your manners and training son?" Snapping out of it, "Good evening Ms. Rodgers," stepping out with outstretched hand to greet her.

"Gentlemen, gentlemen, please… we can do without all the formalities. Please it would give me great pleasure if you would just address me as Ronnie. Would you care to freshen up?" I hope you have brought your appetites with you, as I have prepared a delightful meal for you, of which I do hope you will enjoy. Brick now standing next to Matt, whispered in his ear, "Wow, she is treating us in much the same manner as Geena does when she is hosting our little get togethers. You're right, she is special." Matt was standing there, looking like he was a proud papa.

They went upstairs to settle in and to freshen up, before coming back down.

Matt hugging Ronnie, "Great entrance Ms. Veronica, you made quite the impression." Smiling back at him, "Well, you said you wanted to leave a memorable impression, just doing my part. Who was the younger gentlemen who dropped his case, he is sweet?"

"Alright now Ms. Veronica, I guess you are over me," laughing. "He is the young protégé of Rob's and he is quite talented himself."

The guys were now coming back down the stairs, of which Matt was grateful, because it was not yet time to explain who they were. Leaning over and whispering in her ear, he asked Ronnie to tell them she had prepared some snacks for them and for them to help themselves and then for her to accompany him outside, because he had something to show her.

"Gentlemen, please help yourself to the snacks I prepared for you in the dining room and make yourselves comfortable. You will find salad, shrimp cocktail, cheese, and crackers. Dinner will be served shortly. Please excuse us, Matt and I will be back with you shortly." They started into the dining room, Matt now taking her hand and starting for the door to go outside. Ronnie was trying to figure out what he wanted to show her outside and why they would leave his important guests by themselves.

She did not have to wait long to ascertain what this was all about. They had been walking towards the garage and Matt reached into his pocket pulling out his phone and entered the code for the garage door to open and turn the lights on. There standing in the garage was the car her father had given to her, detailed, polished, and gleaming red.

She shrieked with excitement, jumping into Matt's arms, "My car, my dad's car. You brought it home to me. Thank you, thank you!!"

Pleasure was all over Matt's face as he watched her run over to get a closer look at her baby. Letting her take it all in, Matt softly took her hand in his hand, starting to head back towards the house, "Maybe you will invite me for a ride tomorrow and we can put the top down." Both turning to look at it one more time before they entered the house, Matt now putting the code in for the garage door to close and the lights to turn off. "You betcha, and if you are a good boy, maybe I will let you drive it, that is if you promise not to wreck it." They laughed and went inside.

"Hope you guys are enjoying yourself and you are hungry." She had prepared baked salmon, baked chicken, macaroni and cheese, vegetables, and corn. They had already found the various drinks she had gotten for them. They joined hands, and she asked Matt to say the blessing. They ate, chatted, and laughed, enjoying themselves.

Ronnie started to rise to clear the table and to start cleaning up. Matt recognizing the look on her face, asked her to please sit back down for a minute. "It is now time for part two and the final part of this little surprise I've cooked up for you. The gentlemen you have been entertaining this evening, are my business partners and close personal friends. They are not some clients here for a meeting with me but are here to work with you. Here is the plan. You go with Brick and Jason into the studio. Brick is an audio and video engineer, and he is going to help you record your music, and if he likes it all, he is prepared to offer you a contract with Brickhouse Productions. As for Jason, he is here because I thought you two might be able to collaborate on the piece you were not satisfied with. Rob and I will stay behind and clean up the dining room and the kitchen, so you have nothing to worry yourself about."

Rob, Jason, and Brick

"You got me really good Matt," coming over to hug him again. Smiling, "One good turn, deserves another. Thank you." Matt replied, "Sure sweetie. There is an additional surprise awaiting you in the studio."

Brick rising, "Come on let's get started and see what you have got." The three of them starting for the studio, where upon reaching, Brick and Jason set everything up for Ronnie's first recording session. They took the covers off the equipment Matt had them bring in. To her surprise and delight, it was Ronnie's vintage keyboards. Turning to go back to say thank you to Matt, Ronnie bumped into him. He had followed, wanting to be there when she saw her keyboards. "Oh, thank you Matt, you are so wonderful. You did not forget my keyboards," hugging him.

Responding, "Just make us all proud," as Matt headed back to help Rob. They cleared the dining room, wrapping up, and putting the food away. After which, they cleaned up the kitchen and settled on the sofa in the living room to talk.

Rob saying, "I see what you were saying about Ronnie. She is a special lady, and it seems as if Jason is quite taken with her. I have never seen him react to a woman like that. The only thing he is ever focused on is his music and fishing."

"Really? It seems Ronnie is also interested, as she told me she thinks he is sweet. If they hit it off and it works out, they will both be getting quality individuals."

The recordings were going well and moving along effortlessly, many of which were recorded on first takes. Brick was hugely impressed with her performances and style. Jason was assisting Brick with the video recordings, of which she was taking to so naturally. Brick noting how she looked into the camera smiling in a very personal way, making the viewer not want to take their eyes from her. It looked as if Jason was really into her, making sure he was capturing her from an array of different angles. This lady was going to be extraordinarily successful, and Brick knew he had to sign her up immediately.

Not wanting to have everyone fatigued, Brick suggested they end for the evening, to be continued on tomorrow and Sunday. They went and joined Matt and Rob in the living room and chatted for a while longer. Finally, the guys decided to go up and retire. Rob and Jason planned on rising early to go fishing before going back into the studio. Ronnie and Matt said good night as the guys went upstairs to their rooms.

"Golly Matt, this has been a surprising week all the way around, don't you think?" Shaking his head in agreement, "Yes sweetie, it certainly has. We had better go upstairs and get some rest ourselves, because I want to be fully alert and rested for the ride in that red Firebird of yours." Rising, "We'll take it out for a spin in the morning, while the guys are fishing." They had reached the top of the stairs and Matt took out his phone to arm the alarm and turn out the downstairs lights. He walked Ronnie to her door. She turned and kissed him on his cheek and gave him a quick hug. He looked at her, "You looked stunning tonight, well done." Smiling she blew him a kiss, entered her room, and closed the door. Ronnie got ready for bed and climbed in, humming a new melody which she was working on, before drifting off to sleep.

Matt got ready for bed also. The phone rang and it was Geena. They spoke briefly and said good night. It had been a long day, but Matt was extremely proud of himself, as he was able to surprise Ronnie without a hitch. The guys seemed to like her, and she certainly was a hit with Jason. She had done a wonderful job preparing the meal and she was the perfect hostess. She looked stunning in her outfit, reminding him so much of how Geena did things in the same manner. It did not take him long to fall asleep. Matt was out for the count.

Chapter 24

Summit for 'the Crew'

Geena's trip to Paris had been extremely successful, and having Lee Ann with her, turned out to be a plus. They worked well together, planning every detail so things would work out smoothly. They had a blast together, shopping, touring, and dining out.

Now back in New York, Geena was hoping Lee Anne would be able to clear her schedule for a couple of weeks, so she could surprise Matt and spend some quality time with him. Despite the time difference between Paris and the States, they had managed to stay in touch with each other daily.

Lee Anne was busy making sure Geena's schedule was cleared, and Geena decided to call C J, just to catch up on things. "Hi C J, how are you and the family doing? I was hoping we all could get together soon. It has been far too long since we have all been in one place. We are long overdue to meet up for just some relaxation and fun." Glad to hear her voice C J told her to hold on, because he had JET on the line also. He merged the calls with the three of them. "Hey G, it is great to hear your voice," JET chuckling. C J also chimed in, "It sure is, Geena. It has been a while. Funny you should call now with the idea of us all getting together. It is great timing. Matt, Rob, and Jason are at Summit Meadows culminating a project. How is your availability now Geena?"

While they were on the call, Lee Anne came in and gave her a thumbs up. Geena responding, "I am clear for the next two weeks." Excited, JET began, "Listen guys, I think this is a great idea. I am in Atlanta, and I will be done with my clients on Friday. I could fly up with the jet early Saturday morning, pick you guys up and we could head down to Summit Meadows and surprise the rest of 'the Crew.' What do you guys think?"

Geena exclaimed, "I think that sounds great. Are you in C J?" Excitedly responding, "I sure am." They started to laugh together excitedly. "I will see you all early Saturday morning then," said JET. C J told Geena he would pick her up in the limo, so they could go together. She informed them she would be bringing someone with her. They hung up and Geena told Lee Anne the good news and invited her to tag along. Lee Anne was excited and told Geena she would be delighted to go, thinking it would be an opportunity to see JET.

Everything had worked perfectly, and Geena was glad she had decided to call C J at that time. In this manner, she would not have to reveal she and Matt were together. Now she and Matt could tell their friends, live and in person. Of course, she and Matt had agreed to tell their parents first before announcing it to everyone. She wondered if there would be a proposal in her near future. She knew she needed to start planning because after it becomes official, she did not want to wait a long time before they could be by each other's side on a regular basis. Planning was key to her success in business, and she was sure it would apply here also.

The rest of the week passed by quickly and it was now time to head for the airport. C J had called informing he would be there soon. During the week, Geena suggested to Lee Ann she spend Friday night at her place, to be more expeditious for their departure and she had agreed. They grabbed their luggage and headed downstairs so there would be no delay on their part. They did not have to wait long before the limo arrived. C J and Chet got out, and they greeted each other warmly. They grabbed the luggage and loaded them into the trunk. Chet opened the door for Lee Ann and Geena, while C J entered from the other side.

Chet slid into the driver's seat, and they were off to the airport. C J said, "It is great to see you both. It has been a while." Geena agreeing, "Same here. You know, Lee Ann knows JET, and this is going to be a surprise for him too. We are going to have a wonderful time."

They talked some more and before long they arrived at the airport.

They bounded out of the car and mobbed JET, glad to see him. Lee Ann came up in front of JET smiling, "Lieutenant Leslie Howard reporting for duty Captain," giving him a smart salute. Coming to attention and returning her salute, "At ease Lieutenant." They all laughed. "Oh my God L A, it's so good to see you again, it's been a long time," picking her up off the ground and swinging her around. "We were not allowed to do this in the military. You look fantastic, how have you been?" Lee Ann smiling, "I am doing fine, thank you. You look great also."

Chet and C J made sure the luggage had been stowed away and Chet said his goodbyes and drove off. JET bellowing, "Let's get aboard and get airborne. Geena, you are with me. I let the other pilot go. I hope it's okay with you?" Replying, "It is fine with me JET, you know how I love to be in the cockpit flying."

Everyone on board safely, JET and Geena began the final check of the aircraft and soon they contacted the tower and were airborne for Summit Hill, NC. It was a short flight, and they soon landed. The limo C J had arranged to pick them up was there. After stowing the luggage, they headed to Summit Meadows for their surprise reunion.

Once she settled into her seat, Geena was thinking Matt was in for a wonderful surprise. She could not wait until she was with him again and would feel his arms around her once more. She was not forgetting those wonderful kisses of his either. Sigh, just a while longer and she would not have to imagine it.

Chapter 25

Hail, Hail, the Gang is All Here!

The limo arrived at the house in what seemed like no time at all. The group was excited as they headed up the steps to ring the doorbell.

Matt was just heading to the kitchen for another pitcher of lemonade, as they were in the studio listening to Ronnie's recording session. Hearing the bell, he put the empty pitcher down and went to the door, wondering who was stopping by.

Opening the door, Matt was surprised to see them standing there. What followed was a loud chorus of, "Hail, hail, the gang is all here," as they started laughing and hugging each other, glad to see one another again. Geena grabbed Matt, hugging him, and whispered in his ear, "Surprise baby," giving him a kiss on his cheek.

Having taken a break from the session and waiting for Matt to return with the pitcher of lemonade, Rob and the rest heard the commotion going on outside and they got up to see what was going on. Matt, Geena, and the rest were now coming inside. Brick and Rob arriving first out of the studio, could not believe their eyes. They started hugging and laughing again.

Jason and Ronnie, now joining them were taking in the now jubilant group hugging and laughing with one another. Smiling, Ronnie came over and put her arm around Matt's waist asking, "What's going on Matt? You guys sure seem happy." Geena noticed the familiarity between the two and wondered who this beautiful woman was. Ronnie was aware she was being scrutinized and wondered if this was Geena.

Matt exclaiming, "Ronnie, these are my friends, my family. Everyone, please meet Ronnie and introduce yourselves. We have got a lot of catching up to do." They came over and introduced themselves. Ronnie thought this was going to be one great big party and there was going to be a lot of fun. Coming over to Ronnie, "Hi I'm Geena, it is a pleasure to meet you." Ronnie smiling and reaching out to hug her, "I was speculating to myself you might be Geena. I am so pleased to finally meet you. Matt has told me so much about you."

"This is so great, and what a surprise to see you gathered here. I am ecstatic to see you, this is amazing! I sure hope you are here for at least a few days," Matt said smiling and feeling overjoyed.

Geena was thinking Ronnie must be someone special to Matt. Especially if he had been telling her things about me, and there seems to be an easy rapport between them.

Everything settling down, the guys went out to bring in the luggage and take it to the various rooms. Ronnie enlisted the aid of the ladies to help her prepare a snack for the new arrivals. She knew she had enough for this evening, but she would have to order some things to be delivered. Then she thought better of it, once again feeling Geena was scrutinizing her, maybe she could ask Geena to go with her to get some things, so she would have some alone time with her. She wanted to make it clear she and Matt were simply good friends, deciding to be honest with her about how they met. From Matt's description of Geena, she knew honesty would be the best policy here. She also had a feeling she and Geena were going to become good friends.

Not wanting to reveal anything about their relationship yet, Matt texted Geena, requesting her to meet him in his office. Geena excused herself and started for his office. Upon arriving, she saw he was already there, leaning against his desk. He quickly came over, gently pulling her inside, closing the door and taking her into his arms. First kissing her behind her ear, down her neck and then finally looking into her eyes, he kissed her lips. She parted them and their tongues met with urgency and great passion. He had missed her so much and was glad to have her body close to his once again.

Geena's head was spinning. Every time this man did this to her, she would lose it, legs and knees going weak, Matt having to steady her. How she had missed being in his arms and yes, those tender and sweet kisses of his.

Not wanting things to escalate matters any further, Matt released Geena and they sat down together on the settee. He began, "I missed you and I love you. I am so happy you are here. I have so much to tell you and we have a lot to talk about regarding our relationship. We are obviously not going to be able to keep this from that crazy bunch out there, so I guess it is time to come clean, and to let them know what is going on. Judging by the way Lee Anne was smiling and looking at us, I surmised you told her about us when you were in Paris, since she is your best friend. I have not said anything to C J yet, because we have been busy, and I have been traveling."

"You are right Matt, I was so happy and so excited about the trip, I could not help myself, so I told Lee Anne. I hope you don't mind?"

"No, I do not mind. However, I think we should conference call our parents and let them know what is happening first, then if it is okay with you, I would like to call C J in, and we can tell him together. We can let everyone else know at dinner later."

"Sounds great Matt," Geena thought to herself she could speak to him about Ronnie later. This was more important, and her curiosity could wait.

They were fortunate to be able to get their parents on at the same time. They told them the good news; with each set of parents exclaiming, it was about time. They spoke for a little while longer and then said their goodbyes. Having finished the call Matt arose, taking Geena in his arms again and kissing her briefly before going to get C J.

Everyone was talking and having a good time. Matt noticed Jason and Ronnie talking and they seemed to be enjoying themselves. "Excuse me C J, may I please see you in my office a moment?" Rising and excusing himself, "Sure Matt, what's up?"

Reaching the office, Matt opened the door and went over to stand by Geena. They put their arms around each other, and Matt started to speak, but before he could get a word out, C J said, "I knew it, I knew it! You don't have to say anything. Looking at how happy you two are, all I have got to say is, it's about bloody time," rushing over to hug them.

Geena stating, "We just finished conferencing our parents and I am sure you will be glad to know they concur with you C J. I told my best friend, Lee Anne and Matt and I agreed we wanted to tell you together."

C J saying, "I knew something was up by the way Lee Anne kept on smiling and looking at you both. Congratulations! You know I love you both and I wish you much happiness." They thanked him and Matt suggested they had better return to the group before they put out an APB on them.

Geena returned to the kitchen with Lee Anne and Ronnie. They were chatting away and had already set about fixing dinner. Ronnie came over to her, "I was wondering if you would care to go to the market with me tomorrow to get some more things. I don't think we will have enough if we do not go shopping, and since you know them best, your assistance would be quite valuable. I want everything to be perfect for Matt's family. He is so elated to have you all here. Brick, Rob, and Jason have been here since Friday, and we are quickly bonding with one another. They are helping me record my music. I hope the rest of you will come into the studio to listen when we start back to work. I would love for you to hear my music."

Geena said, "That sounds great Ronnie. Speaking for myself, I most certainly would love to hear your music, and I am certain the rest will feel the same way." They finished preparing dinner and setting up the dining room table. Then they asked the guys to get cleaned up, and to join them in the dining room, as dinner would be served soon.

The gentlemen gathered in the dining room, joining the ladies and dinner was served. They joined hands and Matt requested Jason say the blessing. Jason asked a blessing over the food for the nourishment of their bodies, the hands that prepared the food and gave thanks for being able to have it. For the fellowship and the meeting of friends and family and for the new friendships being formed, also praying for Ronnie's recordings to be a success. They said amen and began to devour the meal prepared for them.

Matt stood and asked for everyone's undivided attention, looking over at Geena, who rose from her seat and came to stand next to him.

Geena began, "We are all family here and some of us have grown up together. I think all of you know how much we love you, and we know how much you love us. So, now that we are all here, we want you to know we are officially together as a couple. We have not yet formulated any plans, other than telling our parents and you guys, but when we do, we promise to let you know." Everyone started cheering and applauding them, as they stood there hugging one another. Brick stood up and said in his own comical way, mimicking Gomer Pyle, "Well golly gee, it sure took y'all long enough. It's about time!" Everyone busted out laughing because they had the same feelings. This was a long time coming. Brick picking up his glass continuing, "I can do funny and serious, so on a more serious note, Geena and Matt, you have been an inspiration to everyone gathered here this evening. You both have stood by each other and by all of us, helping us to attain our goals. Always being a source of strength and a bright ray of light. We all go way back, and I know I am not only speaking for myself, but I am speaking for everyone here. We wish you all the best in your continuing endeavors and in your personal lives. Everyone, if you will grab your glasses and raise them up. Let us toast Geena and Matt, that they will remain extremely happy and blessed." Everyone toasted and drank, then they applauded and cheered for them. C J came over to Brick's side saying, "Well done."

 Matt and Geena thanked them. Matt saying, "We have not done this in a long time. Why don't we plan to bring our families down for Thanksgiving, so we can all be together? In fact, we should think about Christmas and New Year's too. After all, we are family. Maybe we can make this a tradition. What do you think?" Everyone was excited and eagerly agreed to Matt's proposal.

 Things were winding down now, and they began pairing off. Everyone pitched in to help put the food away, cleaning the dining area, and kitchen. It was still early enough for Ronnie, Brick, and Rob to knock out some more work in the studio. Matt came up with an idea that could be enjoyable for them. "Why don't we fix the studio up like the setting of a jazz club? We can make it look like a live recording!" Everyone agreed and the guys rounded up some small tables and set them up, clustering chairs about. Geena said, "Bring your glasses to give it more authenticity." It did not take long for them to set the atmosphere in the studio. Brick would do the audio recording; Jason would do the live video recording and Rob would take some still photos. It was all done seamlessly, reminding them how they did things together back in the day. The girls found some material to cover the tables. Ronnie had never been a part of anything like this before and was super excited. She was going to have a live audience for her recording!

It was the perfect way to culminate the evening festivities. Ronnie performed with that special unique way of hers, smiling and looking into the eyes of her audience, engaging their attention to her performance, all the while making it seem she was singing to them individually. Geena leaned over and softly whispered in Matt's ear, "She is really good. I am loving this."

Ronnie finished the song she was playing, now just playing soft chords, she addressed her audience. My engineer has signaled to me he has everything he needs, so I am going to play and perform my final song. I think you will recognize it. She looked over, smiled at Matt and Geena, and began playing Roberta Flack's, "The First Time Ever I Saw Your Face." Matt stood with outstretched hand to Geena, who took it and rose, coming into his arms where they began to dance to their song. JET looked over at Lee Anne and did the same, smiling and looking into her light brown eyes as they danced.

Everyone had enjoyed the evening and gathered around Ronnie, complimenting her on her music and the performance, wishing her the best on her project. Brick made an announcement to everyone that she had agreed to become a part of Brickhouse Productions, telling them to expect releases from her soon. Further, he had signed Jason as well, letting everyone know he and Ronnie were collaborating on some music together, which they could also expect soon. They congratulated Jason as well.

They retired to the living room and then everyone started to go their separate way. Jason and Ronnie had stayed in the studio, Matt thinking they wanted to work on their music collaboration. He nudged Geena, "Let's go for a walk sweetie, now that we are no longer a secret." Geena smiling, "You don't have to ask me twice big boy, let's go!" They went outside onto the patio. They chose to sit in a dimly lit portion of the patio, so they could kiss. That was still personal for them, and they did not want to share the experience with anyone else.

Matt began to speak, but Geena put her hand across his lips and said, "Enough talk and speeches, just hold me and kiss me. I don't want to waste another minute talking." Matt complied. They were sitting quietly cuddling with one another when Matt whispered to Geena, "Look over there." Apparently, they were not the only ones who wanted to be alone. It was JET and Lee Anne. Geena softly saying, "I was hoping there would be a spark between them, that's why I brought her along. She had gotten this look in her eyes when she talked about how he had recommended her to be my personal assistant. I hope something happens good for them. JET sure was pleased to see her when we showed up at the airport this morning and he has not taken his eyes off her all evening."

They started kissing again. Soon after, Geena said, "Look over there." It was Ronnie and Jason. They were holding hands and were walking towards the gardens and fountain. They sat on the ledge of the fountain, Jason taking off his jacket for her to sit on, so she would not soil the beautiful dress she had worn in the studio. Matt saying, "Looks like Cupid has been working overtime. It's becoming crowded, let's head back inside, tomorrow is another day. This one has been grand."

Matt walked Geena to her room and kissed her good night and turned to go to his room. Geena reached and pulled him back, "Umm, more please." They did not notice Brick, who had gone to get a snack. He mumbled, "Why don't you two get a room?" Startled they looked around to see him laughing at them as he went by. Matt saying, "Go to bed young man, this is grown folk's business." Brick reached his door and entering muttered, "Yeah right, old folk's need to be in the bed too," laughing and shutting the door behind him. Geena trying to sound indignant, "The nerve... now, where were we?" Matt pulled her close again, "I think about right here," as he began kissing her again.

Hearing Lee Anne and JET coming back in, they broke it up as they approached them. Geena saying, "Seems as if we just cannot be alone." JET said, "I heard that. Maybe L A and I should join you." Lee Anne leaned in, pulling him close, giving him a kiss of her own. "Now, now boys, it is time for you to go home. Come on G, let's go inside and let these rascals go," both laughing and saying goodnight. JET and Matt said goodnight to each other and followed suit.

Ronnie and Jason had stayed outside talking, getting better acquainted with one another. They had a long full day, so Jason suggested they head back. He was becoming more and more infatuated with her at each passing minute, but did not want to tire her out, thinking he would have time to pursue her some more tomorrow.

Ronnie liked that Jason was considerate, and he was a gentleman. He was sweet she thought, and he had a gentle spirit about him, and she liked the time they were spending together. He was really a great saxophone player and had contributed a lot, on the music. He walked Ronnie back to her room and said goodnight. He was shy and quiet. She liked that about him as well. She gently reached out and pulling him close to her, kissed him good night. Umm, I like the way he kisses me, soft and gentle. Note to self, make sure he knows you like it, so he will initiate it himself. She let him go, smiling at him and saying good night, before she slowly shut the door, continuing to smile at him. He was still looking at her when the door finally closed. Good, I think he got the message. She got ready for bed and went over in her head all that had taken place today and then tired, she closed her eyes thinking, Matt had set all of this in motion. She was trying to think of ways she could do something for him in return. He has been so good to me. She finally fell asleep.

Jason could not stop thinking of Ronnie. She was so beautiful and lady like. He was really into her, hoping she liked him too. The way she just kissed him good night, he thought next time I am going take the initiative. I loved the way she kissed me and smiled. He fell asleep thinking of Ronnie.

Geena and Lee Anne had decided to share a room together so they could talk. Lee Anne saying, "Girl, you set me up. You knew JET was coming when you asked me to come with you." Geena saying, "I sure did. The way you talked about him, I took the chance and played matchmaker. Judging by the walk you ttok with him, the two of you holding hands and the way you kissed him just now, I don't think you are too upset with me."

"Alright, you got me good. I loved being with him every minute since he picked us up this morning at the airport." Geena laughing, "I know. Now let's go to sleep and rest. I have a feeling tomorrow is going to be a repeat performance," Geena thinking of Matt, and Lee Anne thinking of JET.

Chapter 26

Ronnie and Geena

Geena got up early. Showered and dressed, she quietly slipped out of the room, so she would not disturb Lee Anne. She headed downstairs, thinking she would make herself a cup of tea and then start preparing breakfast for 'the Crew.' Apparently, Ronnie had the same idea, as she was already sipping something hot. They looked at each and laughed, Ronnie smiling, "Help yourself."

Geena grabbed a cup and poured hot water into it. "May I join you?" Ronnie sipping her drink, nodded yes. Geena grabbed a tea bag and dropped it in her cup, mixing in two teaspoons of brown sugar. Settling down next to Ronnie she was thinking her first assessment was correct, they were going to become good friends.

"Looks as if we had the same idea. If it is alright with you, maybe we can do this together." Smiling, Ronnie sat her cup down, "I would love to Geena and while we are preparing, we can also make a list of the things we will need, making sure we have enough for everyone." Geena took a sip of her tea and said, "Sure thing. This crazy bunch knows how to pack it away. They have always been like that, especially when we are all together. If you are not careful, they will drive you nuts." They both laughed. Ronnie was thinking we are off to a fantastic start.

Ronnie and Geena had just finished cooking breakfast and setting the table when they heard everyone come downstairs, talking, and laughing with one another. Geena went into the living room saying, "Good morning everyone. Come on into the dining room, Ronnie and I have fixed breakfast for everyone." They said good morning and filed into the dining room, sitting where they did last evening for dinner. The only difference was, they left a space next to Matt, so Geena could sit next to him. C J starting the conversation, "I hope everyone rested comfortably last night, I know I did." Everyone nodding their heads and saying they did. Matt asked everyone to join hands and said the blessing.

Everyone dug in and filled their plates, exclaiming the food was delicious. Brick hamming it up as per usual, "Ronnie, if you are not successful with your record deal, and if Geena wants to stop globetrotting, you guys could have a successful business catering, or you could open a restaurant, I know I would be a regular." Matt thinking, oh, oh… here we go off to the races and the day is only beginning. Laughing, Lee Anne added in, "No, no Brick, then I will be out of a job, because I can't burn like these gals!" Everyone was cracking up and having a great time. Geena put in her two cents, "Don't worry girl, we will teach you, because judging from the way things were moving last evening, you had better learn to burn." Everyone was cracking up with laughter now.

Breakfast was winding down, and Ronnie said, "Geena and I are heading out to the market to pick up some things. Lee Anne, we are going to start you out on your first lesson. Get these crazy men in here to help you clean up the dining area and kitchen," laughing and grabbing Geena by the hand, they headed out, looking over their shoulder and saying together, "Bye, bye," as they headed out the door.

Matt was glad to see the two of them hitting it off and bonding. They were a pair of great women, and he felt blessed to know them.

Ronnie saying, "I will take my car. I hope you like convertibles. It is a beautiful day, and we can put the top down." Geena saying excitedly, "I sure do! I have a red Mustang, which I never get the chance to drive anymore. This will be fun." Thinking to herself, another thing we have in common, and girlfriend even has an extra pair of sunglasses I can use. I keep an extra pair in my car also.

They were enjoying the drive, when Ronnie saw an open field and she pulled the Firebird over, next to a tree which offered some shade. Turning to Geena, she started saying, "I am glad we are hanging together this morning. We are not in a rush, and I thought this would be a good time for us to talk." Geena thinking, I wonder what is on her mind.

"Undoubtedly, you must have been wondering who is this woman, that has just appeared out of the blue? A woman who seems to share a bond with Matt. I know you were trying to figure out some things, so I thought it best that I would help you out." Continuing, "Better to get it straight from the horse's mouth, as they say." Geena now intrigued said, "Please, go on," angling her posture in a comfortable position to face Ronnie, to listen to what she had to say.

Ronnie began from the beginning, how she and Matt met each other at the Starfire and all the crazy things that were happening to her. How he came to her rescue and of how untrusting her feelings were towards him initially. She explained how they started to bond on the trip to North Carolina, with Matt showing her understanding and having great patience with her. She even told Geena how she had started to develop feelings for him, thinking she was lucky to have found this fantastic man. She even decided to tell Geena what had transpired a few days ago, in regards to the horrific storm.

"Geena, please believe me, I had no idea of the extent of your relationship with him at the time. I was really frightened, and invaded his room, just like I used to do with my father. Matt was asleep and I startled him. Still being half asleep, he realized I was shaking and put his arms around me to calm me, saying "G it will be alright." Of course, I did not understand the reference at the time, and he went back to sleep, still comforting me. I snuggled up closer to him, feeling protected and safe. Feeling secure and letting my emotions take over, I started to gently caress him and kiss him. He stirred, and I thought it was okay, so I kissed him, and he started to kiss me back. I guess it was something in the kiss that startled him again and he woke up, looking at me with a crazy look on his face." Geena said nothing and continued to watch Ronnie.

"Somehow, looking at his face, I knew I had messed up big time and began to cry, apologizing profusely. Telling him I used to run to my dad when I was afraid of a storm. He looked angry and asked me if I kissed my father like that. I started to explain what was going on with me, and his look began to soften. I begged him to please forgive me and told him if he would just give me a few days, I would leave and not cause him any further problems." Geena thinking, that's my guy, always to the rescue.

Ronnie continued, "He put his arms around me, and he told me to calm down and go back to sleep. That it was alright, and he understood, further telling me we would talk in the morning. He kissed me on the forehead, and relieved, I went to sleep, again feeling safe and protected. In the morning, still holding me close in his arms, he began telling me how he loved me. But he made it clear to me he was in love with you, saying your name. I noticed the look on his face when he mentioned you and the soft way, he called your name. I knew at that minute what he was explaining to me. He told me to get the idea of leaving out of my head, because he did not want me to, and he would miss what we had developed. He said I was family, and this was my home too. Losing it, I gave him a final kiss and ran off back to my room." Geena was still looking at her, making no comment.

"G, I was so happy by the way he treated me, it had me humming all day long. I even thought I would love to meet the lady who made him look that way when he mentioned her name. I am sorry," tears starting to well up in her eyes. "I know I don't know you that well, but it just seemed cool to call you G. I don't want you to think I am being too forward."

Ronnie continued, "Please believe me, I would never hurt Matt, or you for that matter. I just developed feelings for a fantastic man and human being. You are blessed to have him love you the way he does. I hope one day, I can find such a love."

Geena was moved by her honesty and the way she shared her feelings with her. It must have been difficult for her to reiterate all those emotions she felt. Reaching over, Geena pulled her into her arms, "Ronnie, it is okay. All my friends and family call me G, and you are family too. I appreciate you telling me this, as I know it must have been difficult for you to do.

Just so you know, I never thought anything transpired between you and Matt, because that is how he treats me. I would expect nothing but that from him because it's just who he is."

Continuing, "I appreciate you telling me this and I appreciate you. Something in my spirit told me you and I are going to be the best of friends. Now pull yourself together and let's get going before I start crying too. We have been gone for a while now, and knowing those guys, they will put a posse together and come looking for us." Laughing, they set about completing their task and getting back to the house. Having picked up everything they thought they might need, they headed back to the house. The guys coming out to help with the packages. C J saying, "We were just talking about rounding up a posse to come find you gals." Ronnie and Geena looked at each other and busted out laughing.

Chapter 27

Girls, Time to Go Shopping!

Now that the guys had brought in all the packages, Geena, Ronnie, and Lee Anne set about organizing everything, keeping out what they were going to use for this evening's meal. Lee Anne asked what kept them so long. Geena said, "We were just chatting and getting to know each other better, and we lost track of time." Ronnie nodding her head, "Yes, and we found out we have some things in common."

Lee Anne smiling, "I really enjoyed your musical performance last night. It was like being at a live performance in a club. You are incredibly talented, and I cannot wait until your music drops." Matt entered the room, hearing the conversation. "I agree with your assessment, and she has multiple gifts. Ronnie, you should share what you did in the studio with them. I think you will like what she did there also."

Surprised, Geena asked, "What studio are you talking about?" Matt said to Ronnie, "Go ahead, show them, I know they will like what you have done."

Geena now intrigued, "Yes Ronnie, please show us. Have you been holding out from your girls?"

Ronnie answering, "No, I'm not trying to hold anything back. Matt has been the only person I have shared it with. I'm just kind of laid back about it, because I am not certain how it will be received, and I am somewhat nervous about showing it." Matt interjecting, "There is nothing for you to be hesitant about Ronnie, the work you put into it speaks for itself. I am positive they are going to love what you have done."

Excited, Geena urged Ronnie to show them. "Come on Ronnie! You are our girl, so show us already. We are already fans of yours, and if Matt says it's good, it must really be great. So come on, show us already! We are going to find out anyway."

Ronnie started to take them to the studio, "Okay then, come on I'll show you. Matt, you stay here please, because you are biased. I want to get their input, without you coercing them any further. The way you go on about it, I should engage you as my business manager," giving him a wink and a smile.

Geena said, "Pay no mind to Matt girl. If it is all of that, trust me, I'll be your business manager."

Turning on the light, "Well, this is it. Look around and tell me what you honestly think about it."

Geena and Lee Anne quietly walked around the room, taking in all the displays Ronnie had set up. They looked at the paintings and the photography. Then they went through all the fashion design sketches, occasionally stopping to look at each other, look at Ronnie, and then back to the sketches.

Geena exclaiming, "You did all of this yourself? This is fantastic!" Agreeing, Lee Anne said, "The paintings and the photography are simply amazing. You have quite the eye."

Continuing, Geena remarked and asked, "The fashion sketches are beautiful. Do you design gowns as well?"

Ronnie, nodding her head, "Yes, I designed those dresses because I needed some clothing. I am glad I did too. When Brick and Jason started to record me, they thought it would be best that I was dressed, just as if I were at a club. Then Matt came up with the idea for the club scene in the studio and the live audience. Well, as you know, it all came together."

Geena said, "Lee Anne and I were recently talking with one another and bouncing the idea around of preparing for a wedding. Now, seeing all your work, I was wondering if you would be interested in designing my wedding gown and the wedding party dresses, as well as the accessories for the men, so they would all match?"

Embracing Geena, "I would be honored G. Just tell me what you would like and consider it done." Lee

Anne saying, "This is going to be so much fun," now the three of them hugging one another.

"Now let's get down to business." Geena continuing, "I was serious about representing you if your work was good. From what I have seen here today, I am sure I can be of great assistance to you if you would like. We could start by hosting an event which would showcase your paintings and photography. I am certain there would be persons interested in purchasing your work, and maybe even consigning you to do work for them. As for your fashion designs, we could get our team to set you up with a website of your very own custom designs. Your designs will certainly make a big splash. If things go well, which trust me it will when we are finished with it, perhaps you could open your own shop." Lee Anne saying, "This coupled with the success of your music, is going to make you very busy and very much in demand."

Geena asking, "So Ronnie, do you think you would be interested in my firm representing you? We can do a lot for you, especially since we know and love you. We can also speak with Brick, because we often work together, and I am sure this would not be a conflict with your recording deal with him. After all, we are all family."

Excited, Ronnie responded. "This is all happening so fast, and I am so excited about the wonderful things you say you can do. My dreams are about to come true. Yes, yes! I would love for you to represent me. I cannot wait for us to get started. I'm up for it! Let's go tell everyone."

They were jumping excitedly now, hugging each other, crying tears of joy, and laughing, all at the same time.

They went back outside to tell everyone the good news. Everyone was excited and they were hugging her, genuinely happy for her. It was almost like a football game, 'the Crew' huddled around. Coming back to the line of scrimmage, ready to execute a magnificent play, which would surely lead to a game winning touchdown.

JET started things. "Ronnie, you are now with Brick and Geena. With that comes some other benefits and amenities. You never have to worry about ground or air transportation, because you will have at your personal disposal, JET Ground & Air Transports." C J continuing, "Also, you will be protected by C2C Security. Shortly, you will be given a watch, which will be paired to your smart phone. It has a state-of-the-art tracking system. In this manner, we will always know your location. By the way Jason, you will be receiving one also, as you are just as much part of this family as anyone else. All our team has one, right JET?"

Jason said, "Thank you!" JET saying, "That is correct. Lee Anne developed this watch and each person on the team has one. When activated, using GPS, we will be able to locate and track the wearer. It is solar powered and self-sustaining, needing no batteries, just needing sunlight to stay charged. Once fully charged, it can also be kept charged under normal lighting conditions."

Ronnie was overwhelmed. "Meeting Matt and all of you has been a blessing to me. You have no idea what this means to me. I lost my parents a few years ago and I have no other family. Now, I have been blessed with this utterly amazing family and I could not be happier. Thank you all. Thank you all so much for accepting me. Thank you, Matt, for being there for me, you are such a blessing."

Matt said, "You know Ronnie, we have been richly blessed also. We are here to help others and we continue to prosper and grow because of what we fondly dubbed, pathways to love. The sharing of gifts and talents towards others. That's the best way I can describe it to you. You have these amazing abilities, and you share them with others. Not only will you be successful, you will help others to be successful also. So, we thank you for being a part of us."

Geena wiping away a tear, "This is so emotional. If we go on like this, there is not going to be a dry eye in the room." Geena exclaimed, "Girls, time to go shopping." All the ladies giggling and laughing. Brick now weighing in, "Here we go. Any excuse to go shopping." The guys started to laugh, and Brick continued, "But can I just ask a favor before you go fill up the shopping bags? Can we get something to eat around here please? This has all been so emotional and I am famished. Pretty please!" Geena remarking, "See, I told

Girls, Time to Go Shopping!

you Ronnie, this bunch loves to eat. Come on girls, let's go fix something to eat for them. Come to think of it, I could stand eating a little something myself." They all busted out laughing.

The ladies headed for the kitchen, but Jason intercepted Ronnie. "I am so happy for you. After dinner, I was wondering if you would like to go for a walk with me again? I would like to speak with you please." She smiled at him and kissed him on the cheek saying, "Sure Jason, I would love to go." She turned and went to the kitchen with the other ladies.

The ladies quickly put together dinner and yelled out to the guys to get ready. They went up and came back down, just as the ladies were putting the food on the table. C J gave the blessing, and they enjoyed the meal prepared, talking, and joking with one another.

Dinner completed, everyone pitched in to help the ladies clear the dining room table. Food put away, dishes and utensils cleaned and put away, they headed for the living room, where they continued to chat with one another.

JET asked Lee Anne if she would like to go for a walk with him. She told him she would. They excused themselves and started out. Brick also excused himself, stating he had some ideas regarding Ronnie's audio and video recordings, and he was going to go work on them in the recording studio. He asked Jason to come and assist him. Jason looked at Ronnie. She whispered in his ear for him to go, because she had something to do in her studio.

She excused herself, leaving Matt, C J and Geena talking. Speaking for a while longer, C J now excused himself, stating he wanted to call home to speak to his wife Mel, and he wanted to find out what the baby had done today.

Geena and Matt went outside to their favorite spot on the patio. They held hands and just enjoyed each other's company, listening to the crickets, looking at the stars, and of course their favorite pastime, kissing one another.

Ronnie went to her studio. Earlier, when C J was congratulating and hugging her, he had whispered in her ear he wanted to speak with her. She asked him to meet in her studio. He was waiting in the studio when she came in. "Hi C J, what did you want to speak with me about?" C J began to enlighten her with what Matt and 'the Crew were doing to surprise Geena. He also told her Lee Anne was in on it and she had been keeping Geena busy, helping to keep her at a distance. Expounding further, he told her Matt had thought maybe she might be able to contribute some input regarding the project. He brought her up to speed on what they had done thus far, and the problems they had encountered.

She told him she might be able to help, but she would have to make a phone call first. Promising to get back to him as soon as she could, they ended their brief meeting. C J headed upstairs to call Mel, and Ronnie headed for the recording studio to free Jason.

Ronnie was wondering what Jason wanted to speak to her about. She was really intrigued. Each day that passed, Jason was becoming an essential part of her day. She now was really understanding what Matt tried expressing to her in their conversation the other evening. She was falling in love with Jason, and hoped he was feeling the same way.

She was incredibly grateful and was feeling extremely blessed at the way doors were now opening for her. New family, friends, and the marvelous things happening for her career. She couldn't even begin to dream about what has happened. God has given even more than she could imagine.

Only He knows what is in her future. It's such a blessing!

Chapter 28

The Gazebo

Ronnie entered the studio, "Hi guys. Jason, are you ready for that walk you promised me?" Jason looked over at Brick who said, "Go ahead Jason, I've got this. You two go enjoy yourselves." Jason smiling, "Thanks Brick."

Jason started towards her, "Hi Ronnie. Yes, I'm ready." Ronnie smiling at him, as they started out. Taking Jason by his hand, Ronnie said, "I've got an idea if you're game. Let's go for a ride in my car. I know a nice spot where it is quiet, and we can sit and talk." Jason agreed and they headed for the car.

He opened the door for Ronnie and then walked around to get in the passenger seat. They fastened their seatbelts and Ronnie fired up the engine of the Firebird. Since it was a warm evening, she pressed the controls and let the top down. They started out, the night air blowing gently by them. Ronnie drove to one of her favorite spots on the other side of town. It was quiet and there was a beautiful gazebo with a swing. There were flowers all around it. There was a pole lamp not too far away, providing some light.

Jason put his arms around her and gently picked her up, swinging her around. She put her arms around him while he was swinging her around. Placing her gently back onto the ground, he leaned down and kissed her. Head spinning, she kissed him back, finding it hard to believe all the wonderful things that were now happening for her. To think, just a short while ago, she felt she was at the end of the line, and she had no idea of what she was going to do next.

Taking her by the hand, they went up the steps to the gazebo and sat in the swing. Jason whispered in her ear, "Ronnie, I'm crazy about you. If you give me the chance, maybe, just maybe we can have what Matt and Geena have. I know you have only known me for a short while, but I am hoping that you feel the same way towards me."

Ronnie looked deeply into Jason's eyes. "A few days ago, I would have said you must be crazy. But now, unbelievably, I feel it too. It is crazy. I was listening to Matt earlier, when he was talking about the many pathways in our lives we travel and then one day we traverse down the pathway to love." Pausing and moving closer to Jason she continued. "To be honest with you, I've had my share of ups and downs, but there seems to be something special about you. We have this amazing connection and chemistry I have felt since we first met. If you are willing to try to have a relationship with me, I would have to say that I am willing also."

Jason kissed her, "All I can think about is being with you, ever since I first met you. You are so beautiful, not only on the outside, but on the inside where it counts. Your smile is amazing, and I especially love it when you smile at me." Continuing, "All my life I have been focused on my music, never dating, but just practicing and learning my craft. The only other thing I do, besides breathing, eating, and sleeping is fishing. I love to fish. It is quiet and I get to be alone with my thoughts. I find it to be calming and peaceful. Sort of the way you like to be at this gazebo. I am able to think about and expound on my music."

Ronnie kissed Jason and then said to him, "Meeting you has been a wonderful experience for me. You are so sweet to me, and I like the way you look at me. You've been kind and considerate towards me and most definitely you have been a gentleman. I am so glad I met you and I hope we do have the type of relationship Geena and Matt have."

Jason put his arms around Ronnie, pulling her gently close as possible to him, and he started kissing her along her nape, and he began to run his fingers through her hair softly. He moved to her sweet lips, kissing them tenderly, and slowly. Her lips parted to accept his warm kisses and their tongues met, gently playing with each other, then tasting each other, hearts beginning to beat harder and faster.

Ronnie surrendered, giving herself to him and enjoying being in his arms, loving the way he was pleasing her. Jason was enjoying the softness of her body against his and the way she held him, pressing her body into his. It was like electricity flowing between them. He gently pushed her away, caressing her shoulders and back. "I have never felt this way before and I am in unchartered waters. What I am feeling right now is nothing like I have ever encountered before and I don't want this feeling to go away, but something tells me I had better stop and stop now. Even though I have never been there, I know where this is heading and what it could lead to. Believe me, I want to go there with you, but only when we can do it the right way. I want you to know I will always honor and respect you as the lady you are."

Ronnie looked deeply into Jason eyes. "Somehow I knew I could bring you here and feel safe with you. So far, you have been showing me everything I have been looking for in a relationship. I have been mixed up and confused before, but I know I am not mixed up, or confused now. I feel so happy right now and I have a feeling this is something between us which is going to grow and last for a long time to come." They held hands and sat there swinging, back and forth. They stayed at the gazebo a little longer, then deciding to drive back home.

Matt and Geena were still in their favorite place on the patio, doing their favorite thing, when Ronnie and Jason drove up. Ronnie backed into the garage, and they came walking out, Jason holding her around her waist with his arm, and Ronnie holding her arm around his waist. Geena said to Matt, "Looks like they had a good evening." Matt smiled and started kissing her again.

Jason walked Ronnie to her room, where they kissed and said good night, Ronnie telling him she had a wonderful evening, closing the door slowly and smiling at him. Jason standing there loving it.

Shortly thereafter, Lee Anne and JET came back from their rendezvous. "Well G, it looks as if all of our children are safely home. I guess we should head inside too." Geena pulled him close to her again, "Not yet baby, I am not through with you yet," as she began kissing him again.

Finally, they headed inside, Matt arming the alarm system and turning off the lights. He wished Geena happy dreams and they kissed. Geena told him she would meet him in her dreams.

Lee Anne was already under the covers. "Getting in late again. You are making a habit out of this," giggling. Geena laughing, "We had to make certain all of our children were home. It seems you had a good time too." Lee Anne said, "I sure did. We did not do a lot of talking. We just held hands. JET had this beautiful music downloaded on his phone and we danced to it, swaying, looking at each other, and kissing under the stars in the garden. It was so romantic."

Matt heard Brick come up and go down the hall to his room. Thinking, I hope all is well with him. C J is right, he is acting somewhat different.

Brick went to his room and called Lena, telling her how much he missed her and wishing she were here with him. She told him how much she missed him and loved him. Brick told her the same. Tired, they said good night and went to sleep.

Chapter 29

A Time of Reflection

The next morning, Geena, Ronnie and Lee Anne were up early preparing breakfast for the group. Chatting endlessly and giving updates on the last evenings events. Each lady having their own unique romantic story to share.

"You know ladies, I never thought this time was going to be anything other than Matt and I spending quality time with one another. But I must say this whole 'summit' has taken on a life of its own. Our family has grown and been enriched. I personally can say I have been blessed with friends I am proud to say are like my sisters. Matt and the guys share this kind of bond and I'm only beginning to realize why it is so important to them." Geena continuing, "I am so grateful to have you ladies in my life and I hope I can be a blessing to you as well."

Lee Anne responding, "You are so right Geena, and I have a feeling there is more to come. This time we have shared has been nothing short of amazing. When you break it down and sum it all up, we have enhanced our businesses, and grown our personal relationships to an even higher level. Soon it will be time to return to New York and to start down different pathways once more. Speaking for myself, I am going to miss all of this, but I also look forward to what is going to happen in the future."

"Alright ladies," Ronnie wiping her eyes, "you are getting me all misty eyed again. Up until a couple of months ago, I never could have imagined what has transpired since my new connection to all of you. This has turned out to be far better than any dream I ever had for myself. I have gone from no family to nothing but family all around me. I too am feeling grateful and highly favored. When it seemed like there was no positive future in the mix for me, now suddenly there is. My future is now bright with many positive prospects and on top of that, I get to share it all with you, my new sisters."

Now they all were feeling misty eyed, they hugged each other. Geena adding, "I love you all."

They heard the banter and laughter of the men coming to join them. "Here we go ladies, showtime," Ronnie laughing, "I wonder what is in store for us today?"

"Ladies, ladies, good morning to you all," said Matt grinning happily and the rest of 'the Crew' followed suit with their own personal salutations. Brick said, "It sure smells good in here and I know it's going to smell even better on my plate." JET exclaiming, "The aroma is divine Brick, but I bet the taste will be as exquisite as ever." C J adding to the mix, "Well you guys duke it out on whether it smells or tastes better, Matt and I will simply just eat it." Everyone laughing good naturedly.

"That's right C J. Now let us take our places and give thanks for the blessings for this food and fellowship." Matt said the blessing and they began to eat and fellowship with one another once more.

Finishing breakfast, the men told the ladies to relax, and began to clean the dining area, washing the dishes and putting them away. Brick started to converse with the men. "Matt, I am glad you suggested we get together for Thanksgiving and the ensuing holidays. We should never allow business to overshadow our family. We have been apart too long. It has been a blast being together once again."

Matt asked, "How are we looking regarding that little problem C J?" Responding, "I did as you suggested Matt and I spoke to Ronnie. She advised she had to make a call and she would get back to me asap." Continuing, "The look on her face when she said it, was one of pure determination. I think your instincts were spot on about getting her involved." All the guys shook their heads in agreement, with Matt saying, "She is amazing, and I have no doubt she will get the job done. Jason, looks as if you have picked a winner." Jason smiling happily responded, "Thanks Matt, I agree. She is a keeper."

Rob shaking his head, "Young man, you just said a mouthful. I do not think she has even scratched the surface of what yet is going to come from her. By the way Brick, those stills of her at the recording session came out great."

"Fantastic Rob! It seems we are all taking an active part in her future. She sure is a welcome addition to our family," Brick said to the others.

Matt said, "I don't know what you guys have planned for the next few days, but Geena and I are going to enjoy each other and take advantage of the down time."

Acknowledging what Matt had said, it seemed everyone had their individual plans set for the rest of the stay at Summit Meadows.

Ronnie excused herself from Geena and Lee Anne, advising she had to make a call and went to her studio. When she awoke this morning, she began formulating a plan to help 'the Crew.' She thought of it yesterday while C J was speaking to her.

She made her call. "Hello Mr. Meyers, it's Ronnie. How are you and your family doing? I hope everything went well for you." Elated to hear from her, "Hi there Ronnie. We are all well thank you, and everything has turned out fine." Ronnie got down to business, telling him of everything C J had related to her and asking if he thought he could be of any assistance to them regarding their project.

"I am glad you contacted me Ronnie, enlightening me of this venture. Matt came through for everyone when I had to give up the Starfire. Everyone was appreciative of what he did for them. I promised myself that one day, if given the chance, I would repay him. This seems like it. I can have my team clear up those loose ends holding them up on their project. In fact, have C J and Matt contact me, as I have some enhancements they may like to employ, and tell them not to worry about a thing. My team and I have them covered."

Responding happily, Ronnie said, "Thanks Mr. Meyers. I will let them know right away. I made a promise to myself to be there for Matt and his team also, if ever the need should arise. I am so grateful to Matt, as he has supported and opened doors for me to forge ahead. I hope to speak with and see you again soon." Ronnie disconnected the call and went to find C J to let him know what had transpired. Ronnie returning said, "Thanks for understanding ladies. I will join you in a minute. Let me just go see how the guys are doing." Geena responded, "Okay."

Ronnie entered the dining room. The guys had finished everything and were just sitting there talking with one another. "Hi guys, I have some great news to share with you. Matt, you know doubt remember my former boss, Jacob Meyers? Well, I just got off a call with him. I explained everything C J related to me last evening. He asked me to have you and C J contact him. He also stated he had some enhancements you might like to employ. He has not forgotten how you helped him Matt and he also sounded extremely excited. Here is his number. Give him a call as soon as possible. Now let me get back to the ladies before Geena suspects something. When I get the chance, I will bring Lee Anne up to speed regarding the latest events." C J and Matt told her great work, and she was off to rejoin the ladies.

Matt speaking to the guys said, "I told you I had a good feeling about getting her involved. Looks like our girl has come through. We had better follow suit and get going with our individualized plans before G suspects something. C J and I can make the call to Jacob Meyers and get the ball rolling. Have a great day gentleman, be safe and enjoy yourselves. It is almost time to go home."

Matt and C J went into the office to contact Jacob Meyers, to work out the details of the project, which now looked like they were going to be able to complete on schedule. Time to add the finishing touches.

Matt and C J finished their call with Jacob Meyers and things were now progressing extremely well. Jacob had advised his team had an opportunity to work with basketball player and entrepreneur, Leland Jackson on a project, suggesting he might be interested in a partnership regarding this project. Also, his team had connections with Theo Porter, the self-made playwright and movie mogul and thought he might be interested in the project as well. Jacob said he could set up a meeting with them, so Matt and C J could run the project by them first-hand. Matt and C J were grateful for the opportunity and thanked Jacob. If all went well, this would help them to attain a more solidified position internationally.

Everyone had gone their way when Matt and C J came out of the office. C J told Matt he was going to make some calls regarding the project. All that remained was for Lee Anne to coordinate the time to go over the main event with television personality, Olive Winfield, and the funny man himself, Seth Howard. She would take care of that upon returning to New York. Matt found Geena and they left to enjoy the rest of their time together at Summit Meadows, before heading back to New York.

Chapter 30

Back to New York

The next few days everyone basically rested and did their own thing. Lee Anne, now having an ally in Ronnie, kept Geena occupied when she was not with Matt, allowing the rest of the team to finish the project unimpeded by her. Lee Anne was thinking there was only a little more time left before the project would be complete. It is not easy trying to keep things from Geena, but thus far she had managed.

She was glad Geena had asked her to accompany her to North Carolina. She had not been here before, but now understood why the group loved this place so much.

Lee Anne was enjoying herself at Summit Meadows. Coupled with the fact she and JET had been reunited, made it all the better. Thinking back to when they served together in the military, she remembered having a crush on him. Unfortunately, being in the location they were at and given the responsibilities they each had, there was not time to pursue any kind of relationship.

She and JET got comfortable with one another from the very onset. They were taking their time, reacquainting themselves with one another. She had a good feeling about him, and how everything was progressing thus far. Laughing to herself, Lee Anne thought, besides the location being conducive for relaxation and creativity, Cupid must hang out here, because love sure was in the air.

Everyone was coming back from their various outings. She had been enjoying her alone time. Knowing it would soon be time to depart, she had started packing her things, so she would be ready to leave. She now was anxious to return to New York and to set her part of the project in motion, and she needed to make sure Geena was kept busy and out of the way.

The girls got together and set about fixing dinner. Matt, JET and C J went to the office, working on the presentation for Leland Jackson and Theo Porter, which Jacob Meyers was setting up. Brick and Jason went into the sound room to do some editing on Ronnie's music and video. Rob joined Brick and Jason, going over the still photos.

Geena and Ronnie shared details on their romantic outings with Matt and Jason. Ronnie had taken Jason back to the gazebo on the other side of town, so he could enjoy the view in the light of day. Geena and Matt took a ride in the countryside and laid out a blanket under a tree to enjoy the day. Lee Anne was incredibly happy for them and hoped to be soon telling them of her romantic adventures with JET. She told them she had enjoyed her down time and she had started to pack her things for the trip home. Geena said she had also started to pack last evening and asked if Ronnie had started to pack yet.

"No Geena, I have not. I was thinking I was going to be alone again, and I would start working on some music which I've been going over in my head."

Geena shaking her finger no, "Nope, that is not the plan. What part of it is time to go shopping did you not get? Honey, you can do your music at the studio in New York, so you might as well get packing and get ready to go with us. By the way, you will be staying with me. Don't worry there is plenty of space. In fact, Lee Anne, if you do not have anything urgent to do at home, you should plan to stay with us too. It would be loads of fun."

Lee Anne acknowledging, "Sounds like a plan Geena, and Ronnie you do not have to pack a lot of things, because this shopping spree is for you." Ronnie, now laughing with excitement, "This is great! I am going to be hanging out with my best friends, my sisters. I guess I had better get used to the fact I have this amazing family now."

Geena saying, "That's right, get used to it. Besides, this way Lee Anne and I can keep an eye on you. You seem to be getting awfully close to Jason." Ronnie replying, "I am so happy we found each other, and he is sweet and kind towards me. There must be something in the air or water at Summit Meadows, because Cupid is working overtime."

Lee Anne saying, "Funny you should say that. Earlier today I was thinking the same thing about Mr. Cupid." They all laughed, Geena saying, "Yes, he seems to have been kind to us all."

Dinner was now ready, and the ladies went to summon the men to get ready to eat. The guys went to prepare themselves and the ladies finished setting the table. They gathered for one last dinner at Summit Meadows, before heading back home. It was a phenomenal trip for them. Matt asked Brick to say the blessing over the food and for traveling mercies tomorrow.

As per the norm, they ate and chatted away. JET said the plane was all ready for whatever departure time they decided for tomorrow. C J informed them the limousine would be there to pick them up. All he had to do was call and it would not take long for it to arrive here to pick them up. The ladies said they had enough food for one last breakfast, and it would probably be best they eat it, so it would not go to waste. Everyone agreed. Dinner was finished and everyone pitched in to clean up the dining area, wash and put the dishes away.

They gathered in the living room one last time, before deciding to pair off with one another. Ronnie began saying, "This has been one of the greatest experiences of my life. Meeting all of you has enriched my life beyond measure and I just want to let you know I appreciate and love each of you."

Responding, Geena said, "Likewise Ronnie. You have won over and warmed our hearts as well, and we are proud you are now a part of our little family." Everyone shaking their heads and nodding in agreement to what had just been said.

They talked a while longer and then split up to do their packing and for the lovebirds, one last time to be alone together at Summit Meadows.

The ladies were up early, as per usual fixing breakfast. Ronnie was humming away with a new tune which was on her mind. Lee Anne and Geena were lost in their own thoughts.

"Good morning ladies." It was Matt. "I just wanted to come and greet you before the others come down. I want to thank each one of you for pitching in to make this an extraordinarily pleasurable experience. The love you have shown us has not gone unnoticed and I want to make sure you know I appreciate it from the bottom of my heart. I love you all."

"Matt, thank you for acknowledging us, but it was not labor, but a labor of love. We are family and like family should, we have all pitched in to do our part to make this a pleasant stay," Geena said responding. "The ladies and I have been planning for Thanksgiving. We are going to contact Mel, Priscilla, and Peaches, so we can get their input. All you guys have to do is get us here safely."

"That's great G! We will have a marvelous time together. I am hoping our parents will be able to join us also. I am sure they would love it," said Matt finishing.

Geena saying, "As soon as we return to New York, I will contact them and make the arrangements." Matt smiling, "Thanks G."

As if on cue, the others descended, everyone saying good morning and chatting away as they usually did. They gathered in the dining area, where C J asked for the blessing over the food and for their safe return home. They enjoyed their last breakfast together on this trip, everyone excited about the Thanksgiving plans, when they would be together again.

JET advised the plane was fueled and ready for take-off and C J had called for the limo to pick them up, which would arrive shortly. Matt was taking his SUV, so they would have room for themselves and the luggage. Also, to return the trailer he used to bring Ronnie's car to the house, and he arranged for the vehicle to be returned to Summit Meadows by one of the garage staff.

"Geena and I are going to fly us to New York, so you can relax a while longer JET with Lee Anne, before you have to continue on to your destination." JET responded, "Sure Matt, thank you both, I appreciate it." C J advised, Chet and a second driver would be waiting with two vehicles to transport everyone to their destinations upon arrival in NYC.

All the luggage had been placed in front of their doors early this morning and the men set about getting them downstairs and packed into the SUV. They also helped Matt hitch up the trailer he was going to return. Once inside the limo, Geena said, "I know Rob and C J are anxious to get back home to see their loved ones, but I was thinking maybe we could gather at my place tonight and have a romantic dinner." Rob and C J declined the invitation, as they wanted to spend time with their families. JET said he loved the idea, and he would leave tomorrow, so he could have one final romantic evening with Lee Anne. Brick said he was going to pass, something about some unfinished business. Jason was excited to be able to spend a little more time with Ronnie, and of course Matt wanted to be with Geena.

Their plans formulated and settled, they arrived at the airport, got the luggage properly stowed onboard and they strapped in for the brief flight to New York, Matt, and Geena at the controls.

Geena couldn't resist, "Ladies and Gentlemen, the captain and I welcome you aboard. Please make sure you are buckled in, and your seats are in the upright position. Also, please be certain all loose objects are properly stowed in the overhead compartments, or under the seat in front of you. We are just about ready for take-off, just as soon as we receive the go ahead from the control tower. So, sit back, relax, and enjoy your flight to New York. We are on schedule and should be there shortly." Everyone was laughing, Matt smiling and thinking to himself, that's my girl.

Geena asked Matt to let her pilot the plane to New York, explaining to him she did not know when she was going to get a chance to fly again, because it was time to go back to the everyday grind of business. He agreed, as it afforded him the opportunity to marvel and look at this fascinating woman he was so in love with.

Geena noticing him looking at her and asked, "Why are you looking at me like that?" Matt replied, "Nothing sweetie. I was just admiring the view of the beautiful woman I love and adore." Smiling, "Aww, you say the sweetest things to me. I love you as well. I am glad we had this time to spend with one another." Matt replying, "Yep, it's back to the grindstone after tonight."

The flight had gone just the way they expected, and they were now approaching New York. Matt decided to pick up where Geena left off. "Ladies and gentlemen, this is your captain. We are on final approach and should be landing shortly. Please make sure all seat belts are fastened, and your seat is in the upright position. Please stow away any loose objects and prepare for landing. We thank you all for flying with JET Ground & Air Transports and have a very pleasant rest of the day." Brick exclaiming, "Those two are having a blast up there, and notice they put in a plug for your business JET," everyone once again laughing at Geena and Matt's comedic routine.

Having landed safely and taxied to the hangar, they disembarked from the plane. Chet and the other limo driver were there and waiting to help unload the luggage, placing them in the correct vehicles for transport. All the luggage being properly designated to the limos, Brick, C J, and Rob said their goodbyes to everyone and started off to their destinations.

Chet got everyone safely to Geena's place in no time. He was going to help with the luggage, but Matt said they were okay and could handle it themselves. Lee Anne came over to Chet, to tell him of the plans for Thanksgiving, and that he and his wife were invited. He thanked them and said he needed to check with his wife, but he was sure she would be excited at the invitation too, as he was unaware of any other obligation they might have. Waving goodbye, he told Lee Anne he would be in touch soon to let her know what their plans would be.

Chapter 31

Evening in New York

After settling in at Geena's place, they sat in the living room to talk for a while. Geena asked everyone what they would like to have for their romantic dinner. They decided to leave it up to the ladies, as they were happy with the selections, they made at Summit Meadows during their stay. The guys said they would oversee the evening's entertainment. The ladies said they were excited and looked forward to what they were going to contribute to this romantic evening.

The ladies informed the men they were going out to pick up some things for the evening's festivities, leaving them alone to plan and execute their contribution for the evening. They decided to keep it casual and intimate, wearing jackets, but no ties. Just enough to please their ladies. Jason advised he would play his sax for the live music, and, he had a smooth jazz playlist they could listen to on the stereo.

They prepared a list of items they would need for the evening. Matt asked them what kind of flowers they wanted to give their ladies. Finding that out, he called the florists to place the order and to set a time for the delivery. JET said he would go to the liquor store and get the wine for the evening. Not knowing what the ladies were preparing, he said he would make certain to bring a selection that would go along with anything the girls prepared. Jason said he would pick up an array of romantic cards they could choose from to give the girls, adding they should also pick up the girls some fancy chocolates. "Sweets for the sweet," he said. Matt laughing said, "You're catching on, and don't forget to get some fancy candles."

The ladies returned chatting away and laughing, bringing with them the things they needed to prepare for tonight's meal. The guys kissed them and left to set about completing their errands. Ronnie said, "Ooo, they looked kind of serious. I cannot wait to see what they have come up with for this evening." Geena adding, "You are right. Knowing Matt, I am confident it is going to be romantic, so we better put on something that will blow their minds. Not anything to fancy, just enough to please our guys," winking.

Lee Anne had asked the ladies to stop at her place on the way back, so she could pick up the watches to give Ronnie and Jason. She gave Ronnie hers before they returned to Geena's place, and she gave Jason his just before the men left.

They went about their tasks to prepare for the evening, each thinking of what outfit they were going to wear. They wanted to have everything ready when the guys returned, so they would have time to go to their rooms to change. Upon their return, they would ask the guys to do the same, which would keep everyone separated until they were ready to dine together.

Having completed their mission, the men returned. Geena hearing them, came out and laid out the format for the evening. Having done that, she gave the men their space.

Jason went and got his sax, tucking it out of sight in the living room and he and Matt paired his iPhone up to Geena's Bluetooth system. JET took the candles and wine into the dining area, placing them on the table, and making sure the wine glasses were in place. Finishing that, the doorbell rang. Matt told Geena not to worry, he would answer it. It was the flower delivery. Each man had gotten his lady a dozen roses, along with an extra rose, to place in her hair.

Satisfied everything was in place, they went to their room, cleaned up and got dressed, ready to pick up their date for the evening.

Geena and the ladies were ready and waiting for them, Geena saying, "I know those guys have something up their sleeves, because Matt made certain I did not come out to answer the door. I am excited to see what they planned." Lee Anne and Ronnie nodded their heads in agreement.

Matt knocked on the door and Geena went to open it. "Good evening Ms. Michaels. You and the other ladies kindly follow me into the living room please." Geena waved for the others to follow her. When they reached the living room, each man had flowers, a box of chocolate, and a card for each of them, giving them a kiss and presenting them with their gifts. Each man took the extra rose and placed it in their girl's hair, then took them into their arms and kissed them.

The ladies exclaimed how beautiful the flowers were. Matt had gotten Geena red roses, JET got Lee Anne pink roses, and Jason had gotten Ronnie white roses. Geena had put on the blue dress she wore for Matt when they were in Salt Lake City for their dinner. Lee Anne wore a pretty dress that was wine colored, and Ronnie wore the white dress she had on when she met Jason.

Upon seeing the ladies when they entered the living room, the guys were all grinning from ear to ear. Geena got some vases to place the flowers in. The ladies had prepared a small table for the appetizers. There was shrimp cocktail, an assortment of dips, a veggie platter, and cheese and crackers.

The main course was garden salad, baked potatoes with sour cream, and a choice between broiled steak and baked chicken, along with dinner rolls. For dessert there was, cheesecake and cherry pie.

They had their choice of coffee, or tea, and of course the wine the men bought for them.

The men lit the candles and dimmed the lights. They dined and talked with one another, reminiscing about the time spent and the things they had done at Summit Meadows. Finishing dinner, and dessert, they pitched in to clean the dining area, put the food away, clean and put the dishes away. The men then escorted the ladies into the living room, where they paired off as couples.

Matt stood saying, "Thus far the evening has been beautiful. The meal was scrumptious ladies and we enjoyed what you prepared and dining with you. We hope you like the flowers and candy and that you are enjoying yourselves as well. However, there is more in store for you. Tonight, you are going to be treated to a private one-night performance given by Jason Taylor. Jason, the floor is yours." Jason had slipped over and gotten his sax while Matt was speaking. "Good evening ladies and gentlemen. It is my esteemed pleasure to be playing for you this evening. I hope you enjoy and recognize some old favorites, as well as some of my own compositions. Sit back and cuddle up. Ronnie, the first tune I will be playing is an original and I am dedicating it to you… it's called, "Gazebo"… everyone, enjoy." Jason began playing smooth, melodic tones on his sax. When he finished playing the song, they began to applaud. Ronnie was so moved, she jumped up and kissed him saying, "Thank you honey." Jason began playing again, tunes they were familiar with, along with his own compositions.

Matt got up again saying, "I hope you all enjoyed the music rendered. Let's give it up again for Jason Taylor." They applauded and cheered. Matt continued, "Now we have reached a point in the evening, where we can all participate. Jason, please hit it." Soft music began to play throughout the room. Matt said no more, going over to Geena and wrapping his arms around her, they began to sway to the soft playing music. No more needed to be said, as the other gentlemen pulled their ladies into their arms and followed suit.

They danced to the music for a while, then sat down to talk with one another. It was now getting late and time for the men to go their ways. The ladies kissed their men good night and told them they had enjoyed themselves immensely, making the men promise to call when they had safely reached their destination.

Lee Anne excitedly remarked, "Oh my gracious. Those men are so romantic, and Ronnie, the song Jason dedicated to you was simply beautiful." Ronnie responding, "Oh my God, it was certainly all that and more. When we were in Summit Hill, I took him to one of my favorite places, with beautiful flowers in a field, and there was a gazebo set amidst it all. He must have remembered and composed the song while we were at Summit Meadows. He is so sweet, and I have fallen in love with him." Geena remarking, "I knew my guy was a romanticist, but your guys are not too bad themselves in that department."

Each man called his lady, letting her know he made it home safely. They talked for a while and then hung up, everyone happy how the evening turned out.

Chapter 32

Crooked Pathways

Rick is a career felon and three-time loser. If he is caught again, he knows he will be returned to prison, where he will never see the light of day again. He found the old, abandoned farmhouse and summoned the men, who have gathered. The place was not in an overly congested area, nor was there any high volume of traffic in the area. It would serve as an ideal location from which they could operate.

"Gentlemen, from this moment on, you are only to use your assigned names. I'm Rick and the rest of you have your assigned names and assignments. We must be in position to execute the plan with the utmost precision. Not adhering to these instructions will surely mean failure. Also, from this point on, there is no turning back. We need to be a close-knit team, so it is imperative everyone carries out their assignments exactly as laid out in the scenarios we have rehearsed. Are there any questions gentlemen? If not, let's go over each section of the plan one last time and make sure everyone knows what role they play."

Rick continued, "First, let's go over the equipment checklist and who is responsible for the various items on the checklist. Each man will have a fully loaded automatic handgun, which will all be identical. They were purchased off the street and the serial numbers have been filed off, so they are not traceable. The sacks we need are already in the van. Inside one of those sacks will be some money to pay off some local hoods, that I, have arranged to make it seem like they are driving a getaway car. They owe Eddie a favor and he will pay them off with the sack filled with money, just before they do their part. Then Eddie will join Bobby and myself in the bank. Those guys know what to do with that sack, by making some of their own arrangements, just in case they are caught by the police. By that time, we will be safely on our way in the opposite direction."

Eddie took over saying, "Jimmy is to stay here and watch out for this area until we return. He will be watching over the vehicles brought here separately by each man, fully fueled for use when we depart from this location. Each man is responsible for returning their vehicle to the car rental agency, once they have safely departed this location."

Pausing to look at each man, Eddie continued, "Chuck is responsible for changing the logos on the van once the heist is completed. Once Chuck drives the escape van back to this location, he will place his bike in the back of the van and switch to the second pair of stolen plates and logos. He will then drive the van to a junkyard. Once there, he will remove the logos from the truck, remove and destroy both sets of stolen plates and identification stickers from the windshield. The screwdriver will be wiped clean and left inside of the vehicle. Also, in the van will be all the attire used for the heist placed in a sack, which will be burned and placed back into the van, then the van will be demolished in a compactor as already prearranged. He will then depart, dispose of the bike at a biker's bar, where he will meet Rick, who will also ditch his bike there. From there, they will walk a few blocks to a hotel, where they can catch a taxi to the airport.

Each man will have a suitcase, fitted with a hidden compartment for the money stolen. The luggage will be transported to the airport in the three cars, where we will all meet. Upon each of you returning, you will change from your heist attire to your own personal attire, placing your share of the money in the false compartment. Of course, you will have other items to fill up the bag. All bags will be checked in at the curb side check-in at the airport. Make sure you have your tickets and boarding passes available. We all will meet in Mexico City at the pre-arranged location in three days."

Eddie is an ex-cop, who was relieved from duty because of sexual harassment at the stationhouse with the female officers and for excessive force used in the field. His wife divorced him because of mental and physical abuse. He loved to prey on and abuse women whenever he could. He lost his pension and needs the money from the heist to create a new life for himself, and he is willing to go to any lengths to achieve his goal. He helped Rick plan the heist, as he had inside information on the bank they were robbing. Information he was privileged to know because he once upon a time made deposits at the branch, for an account the precinct maintained there for community affairs.

Rick began again, "Jimmy will be responsible to disassemble the weapons used for the heist and the empty shells once we have returned to this location. Upon return, the weapons will be fired, and the empty shells collected. All weapons and shells will be wiped thoroughly of prints, then placed in separate sacks for disposal in different locations by each man. No bag will have any parts that will be able to complete an assembly of a weapon. Eddie and Bobby will assist Jimmy with the weapons and assist loading the luggage into the cars. They will then return the cars to the car rental locations."

Jimmy and Bobby were both young and inexperienced, Jimmy being a bit more toughened than Bobby. Neither of them had any kind of police record. Being on the streets with no jobs, both were susceptible to Rick's plan for doing this heist, which he was easily able to talk them into. He had assured them no one was going to be hurt and the job would be easy to pull off.

Rick continued. "Concerning the pre-paid cell phones in your possession. They were purchased weeks ago, each at out of the area locations. Each man will be responsible for deleting the calls, messages, and telephone numbers from their phones. Take out the SIM card and then destroy and dispose of both. We don't want the police getting any information from them. Does everyone understand what their purpose is? If not, now is the time to ask." He looked around, and there was none. "Good, there being no questions, let's get some rest because we have a busy day ahead tomorrow."

The plan gone over for the last time and everyone knowing what they had to do, they were now ready for some rest. Earlier they had found some old cots at the farmhouse, and they spread some sacks out over them to get some rest. They just needed to remember to pick up the sacks and put them back into the van in the morning. One man would stand guard and watch, while the others rested and then he would be relieved so he could get some rest as well. They would be on crooked pathways tomorrow.

Chapter 33

Wrong Time, Wrong Place

The ladies were up bright and early, ready to do some damage shopping. They prepared breakfast and sat down to enjoy their food. While they sat eating, they talked about their romantic evening with the guys and how much they had enjoyed themselves, each of them specifying which part of the evening they enjoyed the most.

Ronnie suddenly remembered the watch Lee Anne had given to her and went to get it, so she could show her how it worked. She opened the box and removed the watch. There were also two interchangeable leather watch bands of different colors, a necklace and matching bracelet. Lee Anne explained there were tracking devices in both the necklace and bracelet, which could be paired and activated from her phone.

The watch was charged by solar energy and artificial lighting. The bracelet and necklace were designed to keep a charge for seven days and could be recharged in the special box they came in. Ronnie decided to wear the watch and Lee Anne showed her how to pair it to her phone. It was not necessary to do anything else, as the phone was now operational and ready for tracking.

C J and Rob called to advise they would be in the city for a meeting and if the ladies wanted, they could meet up for lunch. The ladies jumped at the idea, because it meant they did not have to lug the packages around with them. They told the men they would call them to let them know where to pick them up. The men said it would be fine and they would probably be finished with the meeting at one o'clock.

Geena, Lee Anne, and Ronnie finished cleaning up the dishes and were ready for their shopping spree.

Rick and the rest of his crew had gotten up early, making sure they had everything needed. Once that was accomplished, they got in the van and headed for New York.

With a lot of shopping already done, the girls decided to call C J and Rob to set up the rendezvous point. Geena said she had some banking to do and texted the guys to meet them at the midtown branch at 1:30 pm. Rob replied to the text saying it would be fine and they would see them then. It was 12:55 pm and the girls decided to walk to the bank from where they were. They were on the east side and needed to walk a few blocks to the bank's branch which was located on the west side.

They arrived just as Chet pulled up with the limo, which was perfect timing. The men jumped out and grabbed their shopping bags. Chet opened the trunk, and they put the bags in. C J and Rob decided to walk inside the bank with Geena, Ronnie, and Lee Anne. Not being able to park there, Chet said he would circle around and park near the corner across the street. They headed inside the bank with the ladies.

Just as Chet parked near where he indicated, Rick and his gang pulled their van past him across the street and parked about four cars from the corner. Chet noticed three men get out of the van. Two were walking towards the bank and the other man walked across the street to a man standing next to a car, along with two other men. He handed the man a bag and then turned around heading back across the street towards the bank.

Geena went to handle her business, while the rest of her party stood to the side out of the way of the bank's customers, talking with one another.

Rick and Bobby entered the branch and tried to look like they were filling out banking slips, Rick looking around thinking everything was alright to proceed with their plan. Shortly thereafter Eddie came inside. There was no turning back now. They pulled down their ski-masks and pulled their weapons out, shouting for everyone to stay where they were, that this was a robbery, and no one would be hurt if they followed their instructions. They then told everyone to toss their cell phones into the bag being passed around and to lay down on the floor and don't move, threatening if anyone did, they risked being shot. One man stood at the door to quickly take control of anyone coming into the branch. They ordered the teller door be unlocked immediately, or they would shoot someone. The orders were obeyed, and Rick went back and ordered them to fill up the bags with the money from the safe and from the teller drawers. Eddie had been correct about the layout and that the safe door would be open because of the volume of transactions being made earlier. They picked this time because the vault would be open to put away the money taken in, so there would not be a lot on the bank floor. They were almost done. Just another minute and they would be gone.

Eddie was alert and watching everything, along with Bobby. He noticed Geena and thought to himself, she was one fine babe, wishing he could spend some time with her. He also noticed Lee Anne and Ronnie over to the side.

Chet was still waiting for everyone to return to the car. Chuck was in the van across the avenue from Chet, when suddenly there was a loud crash, followed by screaming. Both men heard and looked to see what happened. A car apparently lost control and crashed into a restaurant midway down the block from where the men were standing by the car. Chet noticed the three men jump into the car they were standing next to, and they sped away. Chuck noticed too and called Rick to let him know the plan was going south and for them to hightail it out of the bank right now, because the area would soon be inundated with emergency vehicles. Rick acknowledged. Eddie and Bobby heard the crash also and now were edgy because they had not planned for this. Eddie yelling and keeping the people inside the bank contained. Rick came over advising the other vehicle had already driven off. Eddie said they were going to have to wing it if they were going to get out of there safely.

"We need an edge just in case," he said. "If we take a hostage, they will not be as eager to try and apprehend us if the scenario should arise." With no time to think and having no other plan, Rick agreed. Eddie said, "I am going to take that one," nodding towards Geena. "In fact, take those other two over there. They are all petite and won't give us too much trouble," again nodding his head, this time in the direction of Ronnie and Lee Anne.

They rounded up the three women and told them if they did not cooperate, they would be forced to shoot them. This time Rick yelled out, "Nobody move or try to follow us, or else we will shoot the ladies." Eddie advised the women they each had a gun pointed at her back and they would not hesitate to shoot them. He said, "Walk outside calmly with us and do exactly as we say." They started walking for the van parked around the corner. They reached the van and pushed the women inside, where Rick said to cover their heads with the empty sacks left on the floor. Chuck put the van in drive and slowly pulled away from the curb.

Chet saw the men come out of the bank and immediately recognized Geena, Ronnie, and Lee Anne. C J used his watch to call Chet and alert him to what happened. Chet advised he had the van in sight and had turned on the tracking device inside the limo. Rob called JET who was still at the airport, to let him know what happened. JET advised him he would get airborne with the helicopter, call and pick-up Matt, who was driving, but still near New York. All 'the Crew' that could do anything was nearby and had been alerted to the events. JET was also tracking the girls movements from the chopper. C J and Rob came running over to the limo, "Let's get moving Chet," he ordered, just as the light turned green.

Chuck and the gang were driving towards the tunnel, going to New Jersey. Bobby upset, "I don't like what we're doing here. Let's drop these girls now. I'm telling you when you bring dames into the picture, things get complicated." Eddie snapped, "Shut up! We needed an edge, and this is it." Sensing she might be able to create some division and conflict among the group, Lee Anne said, "Maybe you better listen to him. You could just drop us off and we would be out of your hair." Rick saying, "Not on your life sweet thing. I bet you would like that. You're kind of feisty and fiery. I like that in a woman. For now, just pipe down until I decide what I want to do with you." Realizing what Lee Anne was doing, Geena said, "Please let us go, we can't do any harm to you. Please, please... let us go." Eddie put his arm around her, pulling Geena towards him, "Now you just shut your pretty little mouth up, until I tell you to open it. I've got plans for you too," whispering in her ear. Ronnie shrieking, "Leave her alone, leave her alone." Bobby telling her to be quiet and Eddie saying, "Don't be jealous baby, when I'm finished with her, I will save a little bit of me for you too," laughing.

Bobby complaining, "I did not sign up for this kind of drama. I've got a feeling this ain't gonna turn out good for us." Eddie again telling him, "Shut up kid. If you don't want any, I'll take care of your share," again laughing. Chuck saying, "I didn't sign up for this either." Rick yelling, "Keep your mind on driving this van and all of you shut up!"

Lee Anne was listening and thinking, every chance she got, she would try to cause division and conflict between them, hoping that would keep their minds off them, until C J and the others could come for them. She knew they would be tracking them by now and they would have alerted the others.

JET alerted and picked up Matt from his car. They were airborne again immediately. Matt called the others to advise they had the van under surveillance from the air and they were staying well back and out of view, so they would not alarm the robbers. C J acknowledged and advised he had contacted his old team from the Bureau, who were coming from the other direction towards them. Once the destination of the van was determined, they would help to set up a perimeter and a base of operations. He also informed them they were bringing the necessary equipment needed for this operation. Chet followed along the route the van had taken, staying well behind.

Chuck said, "We are almost there, and I have not noticed any other vehicles following." Rick saying, "Good. Even though we had to wing it, the rest of our plan can still be executed, and we have a bonus we can all enjoy tonight." Eddie grinning and running his hand up Geena's leg, "It won't be long now toots. Then you and I are going to have some fun." Geena screamed, "Get your hands off of me you pervert!" Rick saying, "Down boy, we are going to have all night to do what we want to them." Eddie responding, "Yeah, and I'm going to really enjoy myself with this one. You can have the other two, unless these other two guys want some. They can fight over them, but this one is mine, and I am going to enjoy every minute with her. She is so fine." Bobby saying, "We should let them go. This is going to be trouble." Lee Anne saying, "You had better listen to him." Rick shaking her, "Shut up you feisty sweet thing. You think your friend is the only one getting it. I am telling you; I am going to take care of you too baby."

Ronnie was listening to all of this and thinking to herself maybe she could do something to take advantage of her captor, enabling her to help Geena and Lee Anne. If she could trick him into wanting her, maybe she could get his gun away and use it. Her dad had taught her how to use weapons, and if she got one in her hands, she sure would use it.

Finally, they arrived at their hideout. Jimmy was shocked to see the women and wanted to know where they came from. Rick taking command again, "Don't worry about it. You and Chuck stick to the assignment that was given to you, and we will tie up the loose ends. Bobby you will stay here with us to contain your little friend and keep watch, while Eddie and I handle our business. Now everyone get about your work and do it quickly. Eddie and I want to have as much time as we can with these ladies. Remember Bobby, if you want that other one, she is yours. If not, when we are finished with these two, we will come for her too."

JET landed the chopper about a mile away, so the perps would not hear. Chet and the others picked them up. C J's old team had already set up a perimeter around the location. Nothing in and nothing out. One of the team circumvented the area and brought C J and the rest, the weapons that were needed. They quickly devised a plan of action, knowing Lee Anne was trained for this kind of situation and would handle herself well. If she could, C J knew she would send them a signal if she got the opportunity. The team also brought a drone with the capability of being able to read body heat signatures through solid objects. It was ascertained the ladies were still together and there were still three other men inside with them. Some of the team approached the farmhouse on all sides, getting as close as possible, without alerting the occupants inside. It looked like two were preparing to leave, but they would be apprehended at the edge of the perimeter and detained. For now, they just waited, not wanting to spook the gang, who might bring harm to the ladies being held hostage inside.

Ronnie heard what the one they called Rick say to her captor, "If you want that other one, she's yours. If not, when we are finished with these two, we will come for her too." Now was her chance. She leaned close and whispered, "Bobby, I know you do not agree with what Rick and Eddie are going to do to those ladies. Please, help me. I know they will really hurt me. I would rather surrender myself to you, than have those two animals touch me. If you will, I promise I won't fight you and I will do anything you say you want me to do to you. I promise. They are probably going to kill us anyway. Maybe you can talk them into letting me stay with you. I will be good to you. In fact, maybe you can trick them into tying up the other two until you are finished with me, and you would finish us off when they are safely away."

Bobby saying, "I don't know. If they think I am tricking them, they will not hesitate to kill me either. I don't know why I allowed myself to become involved with them in the first place. This was supposed to be an easy job they said."

Ronnie saying, "Don't worry about that right now. Put your arms around me and hug and kiss me on my neck. When they see you, they will think you have changed your mind and are into this now. I'll put on a good show and struggle somewhat, begging you to stop, but you keep on and make it seem you have overpowered me. I promise, I will make it worth your while. You can even have the other two when you are done with me. Then you can pretend to kill us and be on your way. We are in the middle of nowhere and we won't be able to do you any harm. Besides, you're kind of cute. If you are not going to be with those animals, I will stay with you. We can go somewhere nice together and you and we can continue to be with each other. Think about it. I think I hear them coming back. Start doing to me what I said, then they will take their woman and do what they want with them, but you will come out ahead, because you will have money and me too."

Bobby did not have much time to think. The door was opening, and Rick and Eddie were bringing their girls back in. He took the chance and started caressing Ronnie and kissing her like she told him to do. She pretended to put up a fight and resisted, whimpering, and pleading with him not to do this to her. He tried not to hurt her. She seemed nice and he thought maybe they could go away together if he did this right. She sure felt good underneath him, and he started to think maybe this was a good idea.

When Eddie and Rick came in and saw what Bobby was doing, they cheered him on, and Ronnie really started putting on a good show.

"Eddie saying, "Get you some boy," with Rick agreeing, "Yeah, go for it kid. Now come on with me little feisty one, it's time for you and me to get busy too." Lee Anne pretending to now be frightened, pleading, "Please don't hurt me." Responding, Rick said, "Don't change your tune now sweet cakes. Don't worry baby, me and you is gonna roll all night long." Geena followed suit and began pleading with Eddie, "Please be gentle with me, I won't struggle." Eddie began laughing and saying to Geena, "Yeah pretty missy, all your pleading and begging ain't gonna matter to me. I'm going to make you scream and holler all night long. Get inside and lay down, your time has come sweet thing."

C J and the team had just been informed the two men had been stopped and taken into custody at the outer perimeter south of them. The drone was showing the men were now each with a woman, who seemed to be struggling, when suddenly C J and his team heard two shots ring out. He gave the order, "Move in team on the double, flank both sides of the building. This may be the chance we were waiting for."

Ronnie's plan had worked. She told Bobby to continue caressing her and to put his hand up her skirt. When he did, he was so into her, he placed the automatic on the floor next to him. She wiggled and squirmed until she could reach the weapon. When she did, she flipped the safety off and fired two shots in the air. Startled, Bobby jumped up, while Ronnie held the gun on him and told him not to move. Rick and Eddie heard the shots, and when they started to jump up, Lee Anne kicked Rick in the groin and he dropped his weapon in front of her, which she immediately grabbed and cold cocked him beside his head with it. Geena also went into action, punching Eddie in his windpipe and when he went to grab it with his hands, he dropped his automatic, and she grabbed it, taking the safety off and pushing him down on the floor, pinning her knee against his chest, saying, "Move, and I will blow your brains out," placing the barrel of the gun in his gasping mouth.

Bobby hearing the commotion, looked as if he wanted to go in and help Rick and Eddie. He quickly changed his mind when Ronnie said, "Got an itch? Go ahead, scratch it," looking dead at him and clicking the hammer into position. "Trust me, I will help you. Now lay down on the floor, spread your legs, and place your hands interlaced behind your head."

The ladies had duped Bobby, Eddie, and Rick, lulling them into a false sense of security. By keeping cool heads, they were able to surprise and overwhelm their aggressors.

The men came barreling in the door, C J and Matt first. Matt went to the other room and yelled back everything was contained in there. "Geena," he said gently, "It's over baby, put the safety on and take the weapon out of his mouth." Geena with a fierce look in her eyes, one Matt had never seen before, said, "I should pull the trigger on this maggot. The world will be a much better place without him in it."

Matt said, "Please don't G. What will happen to us then? It's all over. Let the system handle him. He's never going to see the light of day again. We will make sure of it. None of them will." Slowly taking the gun out of his mouth, Geena said, "You almost got a real big bang Mr. Eddie Big Man. Go ahead and laugh now," letting Matt have the automatic.

The rest of the team came in and handcuffed the gang. A vehicle drove up with the other two members of the gang. Bobby looking at Ronnie said, "I told them this was going to be trouble. I knew it, I knew it." Ronnie responding, "I almost feel sorry for you, but you are old enough to know better. I know you were against this, which is how I tricked you into believing I would go with you. You were being gentle with me, going along with what I asked, so I will put a good word in for you when your trial comes up. That goes for the other two also, who left and did not want to take part in what those other two had devised. As for your other crimes, you are going to have to pay for them." Looking at the agent standing there, Ronnie said, "Take him, he's yours. I'm done."

Matt collected Geena in his arms and gave her a big hug and kiss, then turning to Ronnie, grabbing, and doing the same to her. Saying to Geena, "Please forgive me, but these are extenuating circumstances. I could have lost the two of you." Continuing, "G, please don't ever look at me with that crazy look you were giving that guy. I really thought you were going to blow him away." Geena said, "He had it coming to him. Perhaps he was lucky you were there. I was really thinking about it. By the way, if you ever grab Ronnie and kiss her like that again, you'll see those eyes again," winking at Matt and walking away to hug Ronnie and Lee Anne.

JET ran and grabbed Lee Anne and held her tight saying, "Sweetheart, I love you. I'm so glad you and the girls are alright." Lee Anne replying, "At ease captain, I love you too." JET asking, "What did you do to that guy? He was muttering that you were a feisty and fiery ball of fire." Lee Anne grinning, "Well, I guess he bit off more than he could chew." JET exclaiming, "I'm scared of you." Laughing Lee Anne said, "And don't you forget it either buster," grabbing and hugging him.

C J said, "Alright, let's get out of here. Chet is bringing up the limousine now." JET said to Matt, "I took the liberty of having your car picked up by the rental agency. You are probably going to want to stay over through tomorrow, or the next day. When you are ready, I will get you where you must go."

Lee Anne asked Ronnie, "How in the world did you get the weapon away from your guy?" She said, "It was simple. I told him he was cute, and I would cooperate with him if he would not let those other two animals near me, and that I would stay with. I also threw you two into the mix, telling him he could have the both of you. All he would have to do is trick the other two guys into thinking he would dispose of us all when he was done. He was scared and believed me. He got excited, and I grabbed his weapon when he laid it down when he was trying to get busy with me. I fired the two shots and dared him to move, telling him if he's got an itch, go ahead and scratch it."

Rob said, "Phew, those guys never realized with whom they were dealing. Messing with these fierce women, wrong time, wrong place."

Ronnie saying, "Hmm, I like it. Sounds like the title to a song I should write. "Wrong Time, Wrong Place." The all laughed. They settled back for the ride back to New York. Chet dropped JET off to get the chopper.

Chapter 34

Time to Finish Shopping

After Chet dropped JET off to pick up the chopper, Geena and the girls headed back to New York in the limo, with Matt, C J, and Rob. For the better part of the ride back, they were all quiet. The ladies had been through a trying ordeal, being able to keep level heads, ultimately helped them get through an extremely dangerous and volatile situation. JET promised Lee Anne he would catch up with her once he got the helicopter back to the airport. Brick and Jason called to say they would meet them at Geena's place. Everyone knew it was important for them to be together, now more than ever.

   JET, Brick and Jason had already arrived, and were waiting for them when Chet pulled the limo up. Ronnie jumped out first, running into the outstretched arms of Jason. Jason said, "I was so worried for you after we were alerted to your situation. I love you so much, and my world would be empty without you in it." Ronnie kissed and hugged him saying, "Jason, I am in love with you too. I'm so glad you are here with me."

Lee Anne ran to and jumped into JET's arms. "Lieutenant, you guys were awesome out there, like I knew you would be." Lee Anne smiling, "Why thank you captain, I knew you guys had our backs. If I was holding back before, I am not now, because out there proved to me, tomorrow is not promised. I'm in love with you and I want to forge ahead with our relationship." JET agreeing, "Yes L A, I am in love with you too, and I totally agree with you. I don't want to waste another day not being with you, so we need to sit down and come up with a workable plan for our future."

Geena said, "We are happy to be alright, but let's take this little party inside. Chet is parking the limo and will meet us upstairs." They went inside up to Geena's condo, Chet arriving a few minutes later.

Matt addressed the group. "Here we are again. This time we were brought together, because of a very grave situation. Thankfully, this is a happy occasion, as these ladies remained calm and worked their way through a dangerous and horrendous ordeal. We have always been extremely blessed to always be there for one another, and this time was no different. You ladies have proven yourselves time after time, and your individual personal ethics played an important role in this being a happy outcome. I know one thing guys. I don't ever want to have these girls come after me. Trust me when I say, what I saw out there with them was scary. You do not want them to be your enemy."

Everybody started to laugh. Matt ending up saying that, eased the tension in the room. Indeed, everything had turned out okay and they were grateful because they could have been gathered for a more solemn occasion.

Geena said, "Thank you guys for being there for us. There was never a doubt in my mind you wouldn't hesitate to come for us. I think we all individually knew we had to remain calm and to watch for an opportunity to come out on top. Ronnie, I must say I was a bit concerned for you, but Jason, I want to tell you and the rest of you too, do not take this lady for granted. She continues to unveil hidden talents we are not aware of yet. You should have seen her in action. She duped and overcame her captor, took his weapon, shot two rounds off as a warning and basically told him, got an itch, scratch it and I'll help you, pointing the automatic straight at him, daring him to move."

Everyone threw their heads back with laughter, relieved this ordeal came to a good ending, and the ladies were alright.

Lee Anne jumped in, "Don't let Geena fool you with her little dainty self. She overpowered her captor too. She hit him in his windpipe and when he grabbed for his throat gasping for air, she got his weapon, pushed him down on the floor, placed her knee on his chest and shoved the automatic into his mouth, with a look in her eyes I hope she never looks at me with." Everyone crying with laughter now. "Listen, listen... Matt had to talk her down, pleading with her to give him the weapon. I think he was afraid she might shoot him too," Lee Anne bending over with laughter.

Matt saying, "You are so right Lee Anne. I don't ever want to see that look again. Baby, we're good, right?" For the first time, Brick had nothing funny to say, as he was howling with laughter. One would have thought they were at a comedy club, given all the laughter that was going on.

Jason saying, "I guess I will have to say it for him, Brick unable to speak right now, so here goes. Golly, I'm hungry, when and what are we all going to eat?" Brick getting it together, "That's cold Jason, that's cold."

Ronnie jumped up saying, "After what we have just been through, you boys better pick up the phone and order, because just in case you don't know, we girls are not fixing anything." Everyone still laughing, Rob said, "That's a first, you ladies always want to be the 'hostess with the mostess.' I guess we've been told gentlemen, let's get these orders in so we can eat." They ordered from a nearby restaurant that delivers and continued to talk and laugh with each other.

After some time passed, there was a call from the lobby letting Geena know their order had arrived. Geena advised them to let them come up. the guys had everything set up in the dining room. They came in, said the blessing, and began to eat their meals.

C J said, "The food we purchased turned out to be a satisfactory tasting meal. Not like the way our girls prepare meals, but passable." Geena said, "It must have been more than passable, because you guys finished it up, there is no more left."

"Speaking of purchases," said Lee Anne, "What happened to all of our stuff from our shopping spree? Ladies, it's time to finish shopping." Matt saying, "Oh no, here we go again." Rob giving his input, "Yeah, that's what got us into this mess in the first place. What did happen to those bags?"

Chet said, They're still in the trunk of the limousine." C J said, "Come on guys let's go get them and bring them to the girls. They can do the rest of their shopping on-line. Personally, I do not want us to go through this ordeal ever again." The girls saying together, "Neither do we, so go get those bags boys." They were laughing as the guys went out the door to retrieve the bags. Brick chiming in, "That's right, that's right, no more shopping for you girls. On-line is the way to go."

The guys came back with the bags, and they settled down to spend some quality time with one another, giving thanks to be in each other's lives. The evening was winding down and C J, Chet, and Brick said their goodbyes to everyone. JET, Matt, and Jason remained with the girls. Finally getting late, they too got ready to leave, kissing their girl goodnight and promising to call when they got home safely. Matt and JET took Jason home and then they each got a room at a hotel near the airport, so they could get an early start in the morning.

    As promised, they called their girls, letting them know they arrived safely. They talked briefly and then went to sleep.

Chapter 35

Back to Business

Time seemed to pass by quickly since the hostage situation. Soon it would be Thanksgiving and time for 'the Crew' and their families to gather.

Geena and Lee Anne had managed to contact the parents and assisted them in making the travel arrangements for them to spend time at Summit Meadows. So they could get a jump start on the Christmas holidays, they got the parents scheduled for that as well, wanting to make certain all reservations were made well in advance of the holiday season.

The guys were equally as busy. They were coordinating with Jacob Meyers and his group in Texas, and everything seemed to be on track. In fact, having Jacob and his crew come on board when they did, was a much needed and timely addition. His family having done business there for many years in the area, enabled Jacob to get around some of the barriers blocking the project. They had found an abandoned airfield, which had a lot of acreage around it which could be purchased. This would give them an airfield, along with buildings for their specific needs.

The project called for a sports and convention center, studios for audio and video production, and a center for a basketball clinic. They also wanted to erect an amusement park on the end of the sprawling acreage, and they had plans to renovate and expand an abandoned hotel which was nearby. There would also be cabins built for a summer camp kids could attend, offering them wide open space for their activities. An ambitious project, but one which will create employment for the locals in the surrounding area, during construction, and when the project was completed. Plus, there was room for expansion.

In addition, Jacob's contacts, Leland Jackson and Theo Porter were interested in the project and what it would offer. After presenting a proposal to them, they allocated additional funding to be used for the project. Now the team had additional support and funding from them, along with Seth Howard's and Olive Winfield's funding.

Brick, Rob, and Jason were helping Ronnie complete her project. Brick was doing the final editing on her music recording, while Rob was working on selecting the prints to be used from the stills, for promotion and the CD covers. Jason and Ronnie were completing their music collaborations and personally becoming closer to each other.

Ronnie had finished some preliminary designs for Geena's wedding gown and bridal party. She also designed some accessories for the men. Now she needed to meet with Geena, to get her approval.

Matt flew out to Texas, JET dropping him off, before he went on to his destination. Matt had been back and forth to New York. He contacted the new owners of the building where the Starfire Café & Lounge had been. He gave them an offer they could not refuse, so they sold the building and the adjacent vacant lot to Matt. The vacant lot offered ample room for patrons to park.

He then contacted Jacob, suggesting he would be part owner of the building, along with Ronnie, Brick and Jason. He accepted, excited for the opportunity. Although he was good at his family's business, his interest was always in the entertainment field. After the project in Texas was over, he told Matt, he planned to return to New York. Matt said, "Perfect," suggesting another idea. "You guys could call your place, the New Starfire Café & Lounge." He also told Jacob he planned to surprise the others on Thanksgiving. He invited Jacob, who had to decline, since he had already made plans to be with his family.

When Matt finished in Texas, he returned to New York, where he had to conduct some personal business… selecting an engagement ring for Geena. He decided to ask Brick to tag along, suggesting they could have dinner together. Matt thought during this time, Brick would then share with him what was the matter. Brick went with Matt to the jewelry shop and while Matt went to the rest room, he selected a ring he saw, thinking Lena would like it. He told the jeweler he would come back later and asked him to hold the ring for him, placing a deposit on it. Matt returned, looking around he saw the engagement ring he wanted, and purchased it.

He and Brick went to dinner, but Brick didn't relate any problems to him, so Matt left it alone, wanting to respect his privacy. It was still early when they left each other, so Matt called Geena to ask if he could come over to see her. She said she was free, and he headed over to Geena's place, and spent some time with her.

All in all, it was a productive time for all of them, but the fruits would be well worth the time and effort spent.

The past few weeks had been hectic, but much had been accomplished. Geena had developed a closer relationship with Lee Anne and Ronnie. She regarded them more as sisters, rather than friends. She could relate her thoughts to Lee Anne, who always seemed to know instinctively what to say to her. As for Ronnie, she was glad she came into her life, and she could make a positive difference in it. It was a blessing Ronnie felt comfortable with both her, and Lee Anne. The three of them forged a bond which could not be broken.

Geena was musing how Ronnie handled herself with her captor. Her solid thinking enabled her to take advantage of him, providing the distraction they needed to overcome their situation. She will never forget the look of surprise he had on his face when

Ronnie was pointing the automatic at his face, and the way she told him, "Got an itch? Go ahead, and scratch it, I'll help you," was something like a scene from a movie, chuckling to herself.

The lady knew how to handle herself and she kept on surprising everyone with her many abilities. Not the sort of person one should take for granted.

It was a just a few more days until Thanksgiving. Geena, Ronnie, and Lee Anne had contacted the other ladies regarding what was to be done for the occasion. They knew what their individual roles were, thus enabling everyone to have a good time, without overtaxing any one individual. Geena thought they were going to have a marvelous time.

The last few days, Geena had been tossing around an idea. An idea she had been giving great thought to. Lee Anne told her that her lease had to be renewed soon. Geena was toying with the idea of having Lee Anne come and stay with her in the condominium she owned.

Ronnie had gone back to Summit Meadows, but she would have to be back and forth between there and New York, working on her music. Geena missed her and could not wait for her to return. She was also excited, because Ronnie had told her she was finished with her designs, and she wanted Geena to see if she liked them.

Geena thought she could also invite Ronnie to stay with her and Lee Anne when she was in town. Thinking, first things first, she would ask Lee Anne what she thought about the idea of the three of them living together. After all, they were always around one another, and being together had its advantages. There was plenty of room she thought. She would broach the subject with Lee Anne later today.

Ronnie could not wait to get back to New York. She missed Geena and Lee Anne immensely, and it felt strange to be apart from them. She and Jason talked every evening with one another. The absence of being with him was becoming more impactful, as they missed each other.

Matt and Geena had asked Jason to invite his parents for the Thanksgiving holiday. Jason advised Ronnie they were looking forward to being with them. He said to Ronnie, "My mother is a high school teacher, and my father is head of the high school athletic department." She said, "That's wonderful sweetie. I hope they will like me." Responding to her, Jason said, "Don't be nervous. They will love you, just wait and see." Ronnie replied, "I sure hope so."

She needed to be back at the studio to work out some things with Brick regarding her music project. JET told her he would pick her up with the chopper, so she would not have to drive up. She would finish her business with Brick and then she, Geena and Lee Anne could tie up any loose ends regarding Thanksgiving.

Chapter 36

Thanksgiving

Matt and JET had arrived back in New York on Monday and met with the girl's as prearranged, so they could go over the travel itinerary for Tuesday. Before they arrived at Geena's, she spoke to Lee Anne about her idea of sharing the penthouse with her and Ronnie. Lee Anne thought the idea was great, and they agreed Ronnie should be with them whenever she was in town. When Ronnie came, they told her about it and she was excited to say yes, remarking on how it would be great for them to be together.

When Matt & JET came, they of course shared the good news. Matt and JET were glad they would be together. Matt asked Lee Anne what she was going to do with her apartment. Lee Anne told him she was not going to renew her lease. Matt and JET looked at each other, both having the same idea simultaneously. Matt said, "JET and I have been talking about getting a place here in New York, but we just never got around to it. If you can, why don't you arrange for us to take over your lease, or renew and sublet to us? It certainly would alleviate us from having to find a place and your apartment would be just what the doctor ordered. It would be a plus to be close to you guys and be near the airport. The ladies thought it was a terrific idea.

Lee Anne advised she would contact management to make the necessary arrangements. She called them and was informed it would not present a problem. They would draw up a new lease, which could be finalized and signed right after Thanksgiving. Lee Anne thanked them and went back into the room to share the good news. Having taken care of that, they got down to finalizing the travel arrangements.

Matt and Geena's parents were flying in on Tuesday, and they arranged for a car to pick them up and bring them to the hangar. Rob, C J and Chet, would meet them at the hangar with their wives and the baby. Geena and Matt would pilot the plane. JET would pick up his parents on Wednesday morning and he and his dad would pilot the chopper. Brick, Jason, and his parents would fly in with them.

Matt had arranged for another SUV to be at the hangar in Summit Hill. He and Chet would drive everyone to Summit Meadows when they arrived. On Wednesday, he and Chet would drive to Summit Hill to pick up JET and his passengers. The ladies had already given everyone their living assignments when they arrived at Summit Meadows. Geena and Matt's parents being close for years, had decided they wanted to stay together utilizing the facilities over the garage. There would be plenty of space for everyone else in the main house to stay.

Geena, Ronnie, and Lee Anne were up early on Tuesday. Geena was extremely excited about seeing her parents. It had been a long time since they last saw each other. Although they often talked, or video chatted, it was not the same as being there in person. She was also excited to see Matt's parents. Back in the day, she and Matt would often have dinner at each other's home. She was always welcome at Matt's home, and he was always welcome at her home. Their parents had become the best of friends and have kept a close relationship through the years. This was going to be quite the reunion for them. Even more so now that she and Matt were together as a couple.

Matt was showered and dressed and already on his way to pick up Geena and the girls. C J had arranged for a limo to pick him up, before swinging by to pick up the ladies. The girls were already packed and ready to leave. They had prepared a light breakfast for themselves and for Matt when he arrived. Matt had called Geena from the limo, telling her he was on his way up. She was already standing with the door open when Matt got off the elevator. She grabbed him eagerly into her arms and gave him a good morning kiss. "Good morning baby, I love you. Today is the big day, and I am really excited about seeing our parents." Matt replied,

"Good morning sweetie. Yes, it is a big day. I get to hold you in my arms once more, and I get to see our parents," kissing her back.

Lee Anne and Ronnie were standing there observing. Lee Anne said, "Yuk, I think it is so unfair the way you two carry on all the time, without regard to who is around you," laughing. Geena responded, "Don't be so jealous. You will be with your man soon enough, and I bet you cannot wait until you are in his arms once more girlfriend," everyone laughing.

Matt and the girls ate their breakfast quickly and headed for the lobby with their luggage. The driver opened the door for the ladies to enter the limo, and then assisted Matt putting in the luggage in the trunk. They were on their way to the airport and arrived soon afterwards. C J and the others were already there when they arrived. Everyone greeted one another, glad to see each other again. The men unloaded the luggage from the car and stowed them on the plane. Matt and Geena got back into the limo and went to pick up their parents.

Their parents found each other after their flights had landed and were waiting when the limousine with Matt and Geena arrived. It was an emotional scene when they greeted one another, hugging, crying, and laughing at the same time, glad to be together after such a long period. Both mothers were extremely elated to see Geena, saying how happy they were for her. The fathers were just as happy for Matt, hugging him and saying how proud they were of him. They jumped into the limo and headed for the rest of 'the Crew'. Everyone was elated at seeing Matt and Geena's parents. Matt introduced them to Ronnie. They hugged and welcomed her to the family. If she did not understand what made Geena and Matt the way they were before, it was abundantly clear now. Their parents were extremely outgoing and welcoming towards her and they exhibited a love for one another, much the same way Geena and Matt did each other.

Everyone safely aboard and the luggage stowed, they were now ready for departure. Matt and Geena at the controls, got clearance from the tower and lifted off, headed for Summit Hill.

They arrived safely and headed for Summit Meadows. Once there, the guys unloaded the luggage and brought them to the appropriate rooms. Everyone settled into their quarters, agreeing to meet in the dining area for brunch. Summit Meadows was alive again, filled with chatting and laughter once more.

After brunch, everyone went to their rooms to get some rest. Geena, Ronnie, and Lee Anne had arranged for everything that was needed to be delivered. They set about their tasks of getting dinner prepared. Soon after they started, the other ladies joined them and organized what things were to be done for Thanksgiving dinner.

Everyone enjoyed dinner and went to get some rest. Tomorrow was going to be another busy and emotionally filled day.

Thanksgiving

JET had his reunion with his parents and having already picked up everyone else, he and his dad were airborne and headed for Summit Hill. JET had already contacted Matt to let him know when they would arrive. Matt advised him he and Chet would be there to greet them when they landed.

When the men gathered, the women had already started preparing breakfast for everyone. Matt received the call from JET, advising he was almost there. He and Chet got the SUV's and headed for the airport. They did not have to wait for long, as JET and his father landed the chopper a few minutes after he and Chet arrived. They greeted one another and set about getting the luggage put into the SUV's. Then they headed for Summit Meadows.

When they pulled up, the rest of the guys came out to help with the luggage. The new arrivals went inside, where greetings and introductions were given. On the flight, Jason's parents had asked Rob who was this girl their son seemed be so enamored with. They were surprised and eager to learn about this woman. Up until recently, all Jason seemed to be interested in dealing with, was his music, and of course, fishing with his father, or Rob.

Jason was oblivious to the conversation, as he and Brick were up front joking around with each other. Rob told them they should not be alarmed and assured them Ronnie was a lovely young woman. He said, "Just wait, you are going to love her like we do." Jason's mom said, "We will just have to wait and see."

Jason went over to Ronnie and brought her over to meet his parents. He sensed Ronnie was nervous and whispered to her, "Don't be nervous, just be yourself. It will be okay, you'll see." Jason continued, "Mom and dad, this is Ronnie. Ronnie, these are my parents, Jeff and Tina Taylor." Ronnie stepped over to extend her hand to Jason's dad, saying, "Mr. and Mrs. Taylor, I am pleased to finally meet you. Jason has told me so much about both of you. He is an incredible person, who I am certain you are both proud of," moving over to hug Jason's mom. Jason was smiling and said to himself, they already like her, I can feel it. Jeff was thinking, my son has found a real keeper. So far, I like everything about this young lady. Tina acknowledged, "It is our pleasure to meet you as well and we looked forward to this gathering for Thanksgiving." Ronnie answering, "Why thank you Mrs. Taylor. Once you are settled, please feel free to join the rest of the ladies and myself in the kitchen. We are finalizing the menu for today and of course for Thanksgiving Day. We would be delighted if you would join us." Responding to Ronnie, "Thank you dear. Once we have settled in, I would love to join the rest of you ladies."

Ronnie turned and gave Jason a kiss on the cheek, saying to Tina, "That is great Mrs. Taylor. See you soon," smiling she turned and left. Jason was now grinning from ear to ear. "See, I told you. She's wonderful."

Tina replying, "She seems like a lovely girl son, we'll see." Jeff whispered to him, "I like her son. That was no act. She is an extremely lovely young lady. Don't worry, your mother likes her too, I sense it."

Jason left them not in the least worried, because he knew Ronnie was special, and they could not do anything except to accept her. She would be a fine daughter, one whom his mom would be proud of. He went to seek out Rob and Brick. They and some of the other men had gathered to set things up for tomorrow's entertainment. Of course, he and Ronnie were going to perform some of their music. Rob was preparing a slide show of the photos he had taken the night of the live recording, along with the excerpts of video Jason had taken of Ronnie and the attendees. Matt's father, John, was giving them a hand. The rest of the men were chatting in the living room. They had pitched in to set up the tables and chairs for the performance in the studio tomorrow. Brick was even taking a part in the night's festivities. He was going to render a stand-up comedy routine. Tomorrow was going to be great. Jason was happy being a part of 'the Crew' and their families. Together, they were all one big happy family!

They settled down and ate dinner. Afterwards, everyone helped in cleaning up and came together in the living room, where they talked, laughed, and enjoyed each other's company. Jason's mother noted everyone seemed to have a high regard for Ronnie. She had to admit to herself, this young lady was someone incredibly special. She leaned into Jeff, saying in a low voice, "Honey, the more I see of this young lady, the more I like her, and I understand why our Jason is so smitten with her." Jeff saying, "Yes, she is a class act."

The evening was now winding down, and everyone went to their quarters to get some rest. Tomorrow was going to be a fantastic day!

Thanksgiving Day! Everyone was up early, no one wanting to eat breakfast, not even Brick. Some had decided to have tea, juice, or coffee. The ladies had planned everything well and there was almost nothing left to do. They watched the programming of the Thanksgiving festivities on television, until it was time to serve the bird and all the trimmings. The men stayed in the living room to watch the game, rooting for their favorite team to win.

Matt decided to tape the game, figuring they would not be able to finish watching it. They would not look at the scores on their phones and if per chance someone found out who won the game, they swore they would not reveal the outcome of the game. They could watch it together tomorrow at some point. Some of the ladies wanted to see the game also.

Everyone had agreed to dress for dinner. The ladies wearing dresses and the men jackets. They went and changed, as dinner was almost ready to be served. The men were dressed first and waiting for the ladies. As the ladies came down the stairs, each man went to help her and escort her into the dining room. They remained standing behind their chairs and Matt requested they join hands. Matt asked for the blessing of the food, gave thanks for their safe arrival, for the fellowship of being together once again, and for the uniting of those who were gathered for the first time. He asked for a special blessing for the youngest addition, C J and Mel's first child, that he would be richly blessed in his life. Amen. The gentlemen pulled out the chairs for the ladies to sit. Brick exclaimed, "Eat up and enjoy everyone, I know I am going to."

    The ladies had gone above and beyond preparing the dinner. There was an array of food prepared. Turkey & stuffing, roasted chicken, baked salmon, yams, macaroni & cheese, collard greens, string beans, rice & gravy, cornbread, rolls, cranberry sauce, apple sauce, pineapple, fruit salad, fresh garden salad, celery, and carrots. For dessert there was, peach cobbler, blueberry pie, sweet potato pie, apple pie, chocolate layer cake, strawberry shortcake, and coconut cake. There was wine, apple cider, lemonade, coffee, tea, and hot chocolate.

    There was plenty of food to enjoy and enjoy they did. They enjoyed the fellowship with one another and were grateful for the good outcome and safety of the girls from their harrowing ordeal, a few weeks ago. They ate, laughed, and talked with one another, having a grand time. Even the baby was gurgling, wiggling, and laughing happily.

The evening was progressing wonderfully when Brick stood up and excused himself from the table. He had a faraway look upon his face. Matt, Geena, and C J all noticed and looked at one another. Matt said, "Something is wrong. I'm going to check on him." Geena said, "No, let me go speak with him. Something is up with him and maybe I can find out what it is." Matt and C J nodded to her in agreement.

Geena found Brick just walking around the grounds, seemingly brooding about something. She approached Brick and said, "Are you alright? You left so suddenly, the guys and I were worried about you. You had a faraway look on your face, and now being here with you, it seems you are in deep thought about something. I'm here for you if you want to talk about anything. You know we all stick together."

Brick smiled at Geena and replied, "Nah, I'm okay. I was just looking at how happy everyone was around the table and," hesitating he stopped. After a few more seconds, he said he was okay and would be back inside in a few minutes and not for her to worry.

Geena said, "Okay," and headed back to the house. Thinking of the way he started to speak about how happy everyone was at the table was strange. Then it hit her. Of course, he was referring to 'the Crew.' He was talking about how everyone was happy with their significant other. Now she knew what was going on, having had those very same emotions not too long ago. Brick was missing someone... he must be in love.

Sitting down, she said to Matt, "I think I know what the problem is. C J asked, "Well are you going to share it with the rest of us?" Geena smiled and looked at Matt and then at Lee Anne. "Our friend just may be in love." Matt asked, "How do you know? Did he mention something to you?" Geena replied, "Not in so many words. Just the way he said something to me just now, coupled with the look he had on his face. Trust me, I know that look." Lee Anne jumped in, "You know G, I think you may be correct. That would explain why he has been acting so strangely."

They started to laugh. C J said, "We'll get some answers when he comes back in." Matt laughing and nodding his head in agreement. Geena said, "The poor guy has no idea what is going to go down when he comes back in here. Please, don't tease him too much." C J exclaimed, "The way he always clowns with us? Well now it's our turn to rib him."

Brick came back in and sat down at the table. Sensing everyone was watching him, he asked, "What's going on, did I miss something?"

Matt said, "No, no. It seems we are the ones missing out about what's going on with you."

Replying, Brick asked, "What?" C J said, "Not what, but who…who is she Brick?" Matt laughing, "Yeah, who are you hiding from us and not telling us about?"

"Okay, okay," Brick now laughing, "You got me, there is someone I met. You guys happy now?" C J asked, "Just how long did you think you were going to keep this from us?" Brick laughing said, "Well certainly not as long as Matt thought how he was keeping his feelings about Geena from us. I'm going to get my girl as soon as I can, and trust me Matt, she knows how I feel about her. No secret there." Everyone fell out laughing.

C J still laughing said, "Guess he's got you there Matt," everyone continuing to laugh. Brick continued, "Yep, one look at her when I met her, I took her hand and would not let it go until I told her how I felt. Nope, no dragging the feet over here Mr. Matt." Brick now picking up his fork to eat his dessert. Everyone was hysterical with laughter. C J said, "Way to go Brick, when are we going to meet her?" Brick said, "Soon enough. I have invited her to come here for the Christmas holidays. You'll just have to wait until then to find out who she is."

Matt still laughing, arose and said, "May I please have everyone's attention? Thank you. This has been a wonderful fellowship and it's not done yet. You ladies have outdone yourselves preparing this fine meal, which has simply been scrumptious." Brick adding, "Yes indeedy, pass me some more of that d'er peach cobbler please." John exploding with laughter, saying, "That boy has always been able to pack it away." Everyone joined in laughing.

Matt continued saying, "As you know, we are always finding and making new acquaintances. Earlier this year, I was privileged in making a few new acquaintances, which has resulted in a new partnership. I have a surprise tonight; with which I hope you will be happy. This person sends his regards tonight, along with his apologies for not being here since he is with his family. We have forged a partnership and are presently working on some projects we expect to be quite beneficial. I won't get into them right now because they are still in the developmental stages."

Continuing, "Ronnie, I believe you know this person. His name is Jacob Meyers, and he sends you, his love. We were able to negotiate a deal for a building in Queens, I think you will remember. We recently purchased the building and property. We call it and hope you like the name, 'The New Starfire Café & Lounge.' I'm proud to say that Ronnie, Jason, and Brick, you, and Jacob, are now the brand-new owners of this establishment. All that remains is for you to sign the papers."

Ronnie excited, jumped up and pulled Jason up hugging him. Brick dropped his fork, with his mouth agape. He was speechless. Matt laughing, "What's the matter now Mr. Brick, cat got your tongue?"

Continuing, Matt said, "The three of you have been working very diligently on projects and you have worked well together. C J, Rob and I thought you were the perfect persons to build this establishment. It will house your business Brick... Brickhouse Productions and will also be able to showcase your talents Jason and Ronnie. You will be able to do a lot of good for the surrounding community. There are more details, but I don't want to bore everyone, as there are more surprises in store for everyone gathered here this evening." The trio were elated and extremely surprised and began thanking the guys. Brick came over and gave Matt a big bear hug. Everyone offered their congratulations.

Geena rose, and asked everyone to toast to the success of, "The New Starfire Café & Lounge."

C J picking up where Matt left off, "We have planned something we hope you will enjoy." Rob said, "So let us pitch in and get this place cleared up and clean, so we can enjoy the rest of the events to take place this evening."

Everyone pitched in as requested. They were finished in what seemed like record time. They gathered in the makeshift lounge in the studio, most of them wondering what was going to take place next.

Brick served as the evenings host, opening with a comedy routine which had everyone crying with laughter. He introduced Rob, who explained with the help of Matt's dad, they had put together a pictorial collage of Ronnie's recording. Jason videotaped the remarks of those who were in attendance, which was also presented. Brick did some more stand-up and then he called on Ronnie and Jason to perform.

Ronnie and Jason performed songs from Ronnie's soon to be released project, as well as the collaborated material between them. Jason also performed some of his new compositions. Tina said to Jeff, "Oh my goodness, our son has gone to another level with his music, and it is fantastic. Ronnie is masterful at the keyboard and her vocals are amazing. They sound great together. I'm so happy for them. Honey, the more I see of Ronnie, the more I like her, and she seems to make our son extremely happy," crying tears of joy on Jeff's shoulder.

Ronnie and Jason ended things with Geena and Matt's song, "The First Time Ever I Saw Your Face." At the end of the vocals, Jason joined in playing the sax, while Ronnie played the keyboard. Matt and Geena stood to dance. Everyone else joined them. The song ended and Brick played some pre-recorded music so they could continue dancing.

Soon, the evening was over, and everyone went to their rooms, having had a wonderful day. Tina went over and hugged Ronnie and Jason, putting their hands together, and smiling, said goodnight to them.

Geena and Matt put on some jackets and went to sit in their favorite corner outside on the patio. JET and Lee Anne went for a walk. Ronnie and Jason went for a ride to their favorite spot, the gazebo, sitting in the swing and holding one another. Jason saying, "I guess we have nothing to fear now. Mom gave us her blessing tonight." Ronnie kissed him, and he kissed her back. They were oblivious to the chilly air because they had created a warmth between them.

Getting late, Ronnie said, "We better go back now. I don't want to keep mama's baby out too late." Laughing, they got up and went to the car for the short ride back home, parking the car and going inside. Lee Anne and JET had already returned from their walk. Geena said to Matt, "It looks as if our children are safely home, we had better get inside too." Matt joking saying, "Aww gee Ma, do we have to go in now?" Geena laughing, "Come on Pa, we have to be good examples." Kissing one last time, they went inside, Matt turned the lights off and armed the security system.

John & Sarah and Ken & Elaine looked at one another smiling, "I guess we can all go to bed now, the kids are safely in."

…Thanksgiving Day had ended!

Friday morning, Summit Meadows was filled with excitement and anticipation of things to come. The surprise announcement, Matt, C J, and Rob gave had certainly created a buzz among everyone. Ronnie, Brick, and Jason were besides themselves, teeming with excitement, and extremely anxious to start planning for a grand opening of The New Starfire Café & Lounge.

After everyone had breakfast, they called Jacob Meyers to start making plans and setting things in motion. Of course, they had to take in account the time difference between the east coast and Texas. Jacob was equally excited and suggested they video conference one another to make plans for the club's re-opening. Preferably sometime in the beginning of the year, certainly after the Christmas and New Year holiday season.

The next few days were spent enjoying time with one another, and the ladies started planning for the next time they would meet. They had their work cut out, as Thanksgiving was a big hit. After conversing about what plans should be made, it was decided the holidays should be about family and friends. They came up with various ideas which would allow everyone to participate. There would be the normal exchange of presents, and they would incorporate a secret Santa exchange. There would be plenty of food and of course there would be entertainment. Ronnie and Jason agreed to play Christmas music and they suggested everyone could join in to sing Christmas carols.

Matt's mom, Sarah, was excited to take part in the planning. She gave ideas for decorating Summit Meadows. She suggested that in conjunction with the town of Summit Hill they have a tree lighting ceremony for the townsfolk, set by the gazebo just on the other side of town. They could have someone dress up as Santa and have plenty of gifts for the town's children, after all, what's Christmas without children receiving presents.

Everyone thought it was a great idea and maybe it could become a tradition. Geena and Ronnie said they would get in touch with the Mayor and the Town Council. There would be a lot of work to do, but they were certain if everyone pitched in, the event would be successful. They were also certain the towns people would be involved too.

They told the guys who said they would be elated in participating. Brick said, "If you can't find a Santa Clause, I'll do it, ho, ho, ho."

The next few days were spent planning for the Christmas holidays and the planning of the grand opening of The New Starfire Café & Lounge. Then it was time for everyone to say goodbye. Geena and Matt's parents decided to stay on at Summit Meadows. Geena's dad said, "I can manage my business from here and your mom has given more responsibility to her partner. We are strongly thinking of retiring and doing some traveling like Sarah and John. The fact is, we have been talking with them about doing it together. It would be a lot of fun for us."

Elaine said to Geena, "Your friend Ronnie is certainly a talented young lady. I was wondering if she would be interested in partnering with my firm. Her designs are simply fabulous, and it would be advantageous for her to collaborate with my partner. I wanted to run it by you first to see what you thought about the idea. By extending our time here, I could be of assistance to Sarah planning the Christmas extravaganza."

Geena smiling, "Mom, daddy, I think that's a fantastic idea. You should enjoy yourselves and I am sure you would have the time of your lives with Matt's parents. As for Ronnie, I am positive she will be extremely excited about the opportunity to work with your firm regarding her fashions. It's a passion and a dream of hers to be successful at fashion designing. I will set it up so you can speak with her before we leave."

Ronnie met with Elaine and as expected, she was extremely excited about the venture. She advised Elaine they could elaborate on the joint venture over the holidays when she returned. Ronnie was going to be an extremely busy person and she was wondering with everything happening, how she was going to manage her affairs.

Lee Anne told her not to worry, because they would help her until Ronnie could find an assistant.

Knowing Geena's business was going to expand, Lee Anne had already started vetting persons to assist her. She had to be extremely careful, not to alert Geena about what she was doing. Lee Anne had found a few persons who would be up to the task. Ronnie was going to have a hectic schedule and would need someone to handle her activities. Then she would not have to be concerned about her flow of creativity.

Lee Anne was thinking she could choose one of the many candidates she is vetting for Geena's new business upgrade. It would be an ideal assignment working for Ronnie, as they would have to set up and maintain a staff, much the same way she does for Geena. Not as large as Geena's at first, but one which would grow because of the variety of activities Ronnie brings to the table. Lee Anne was confident she could find someone with the credentials needed to assist Ronnie.

Geena asked her mom to accompany her to Ronnie's studio. Ronnie advised her the preliminary designs were complete, and she needed Geena's input on how to proceed. Geena was elated at what she saw. Smiling, "Ronnie, these are stunning. Look at this mom."

Elaine said, "You have created a beautiful design for my daughter's wedding gown, and the wedding party designs compliment her gown."

Geena said, "I love everything here. Understandably, I have not chosen colors yet, because I am not certain when the wedding would take place. I would want the colors to reflect the season, and you can use the guide I prepared for you. I don't even know if Matt is going to propose."

Ronnie laughed, saying, "There is no need for concern there. That man is so in love with you, I am positive it won't be too much longer."

Elaine came over to her daughter, "Ronnie is right dear. Matt loves you so much. I've seen the way you both interact with one another, and I know he will be approaching you to ask you for your hand in marriage soon." Geena replying, "From your lips to God's ears."

Elaine said to Ronnie, "We just have to measure Geena, Lee Anne and yourself, then send the specifications to my company to have the gowns made. Any alterations needed can be made by a reputable seamstress when the time comes. You already have the list of colors Geena prefers for the various seasons, so once the date is decided, it will not take long for the gowns to be completed."

Ronnie smiling said, "Of course." Matt had already spoken to Lee Anne and her, regarding his proposal to Geena. The other thing Geena and Matt did not know, was Olive Winfield had the idea of having the wedding aired live. She and 'the Crew,' were still working out how to maneuver Matt into proposing on stage, when they presented Geena with their big surprise.

Since C J was Matt's best friend, he had assured them he would know the correct time to push Matt into action. Olive said her team would make the arrangements for their pastor to be flown out for the event and take care of the legalities. Little did Matt know; he was going to be surprised too.

The ladies planned a farewell dinner for everyone before leaving Summit Meadows. Everyone expressed the marvelous time shared with one another, and how much they looked forward to the Christmas holidays.

They enjoyed each other's company for one last evening.

Chapter 37

The New Starfire Café & Lounge

Brick, Ronnie, and Jason were glad to get back to New York, so they could start implementing the ideas they had come up with regarding the Starfire. They needed to choose the décor, choose a date for the opening, and select the entertainment. They were in constant contact with Jacob Meyers, who had advised them he would be in New York, a few days after the New Year.

There were areas in the edifice needing to be soundproofed. Work for building and lot had already begun. All the necessary improvements and renovations were to be completed no later than mid-March.

For the entertainment, Matt had suggested they contact the group Pacific Sunset to participate at the gala affair. They liked the idea and asked if Matt knew how to contact the group. Already anticipating what their response would be, he advised them the group would love to come and would work it into their schedule when Brick and the rest were ready. They just had to come up with a grand opening date to let them know.

Some friends from Jason's school recently put a female smooth jazz vocal group together called Hudson Flow. Jason and a few of his buddies agreed to play for them. They had the looks, moves, and the vocals. He was certain they would love the opportunity to play at the Starfire, being on the venue with a successful group such as Pacific Sunset.

Ronnie suggested they have a talent show, showcasing the talents of those in the local community. In this manner, they could begin to mentor upcoming talent, by offering vocal and instrumental training. Brick could also help to train those interested in becoming audio and video engineers. They agreed it would be a positive move for their business, helping to secure a positive image in the community. It would be beneficial for Brickhouse Productions, by placing the company in position to capitalize on any new undiscovered talent. He told the group he knew someone who could do stand-up, and he would ask if they would be interested in performing for them.

The photography and video duties will be handled by Rob and John. Jacob agreed to be the host and Brick would be the sound engineer.

Jacob Meyers advised them he had reached out to some of his former employees offering them positions.

Some were excited about the new venture and others declined. He was also able to retain the service of the chef he had employed at the original club, along with his staff. They agreed Jacob and Brick will manage the club due to the busy schedules of Ronnie and Jason having other projects.

Tryouts for the talent show will be at the club, the weekend prior to the clubs opening. Those moving forward will participate in the talent show the weekend of the grand opening.

The grand opening will be held the second weekend in April, with the rest of 'the Crew' being present. The talent show will commence Friday evening, 7 p.m. to 11 p.m. and Saturday, from 10 a.m. to 3 p.m.

The winner will be announced on Sunday evening and would also perform that evening, accompanied by Ronnie and Jason. Saturday and Sunday evenings will feature the showcased talent.

The basement would be utilized for Brickhouse Productions recording studios. There would also be room for two restrooms. The main floor would be the club and the kitchen to the rear. The second floor would be the Starfire's offices, including space for a restroom. The third floor would be a virtual set-up using this radical new headphone design. A friend of Brick's designed them. Patrons could see the live event on the main floor, but also utilize the headphones. The sets would allow them to not only hear the music but feel it as well. The design also allows the wearer to still hear sounds around them, while listening to the music. There would be plenty of space to dance and the sets are wireless, so the wearer would not have to worry about being entangled in wires. There would also be space for two restrooms. The fourth floor would have space for two apartments, front and rear. Those facilities could be utilized for out-of-town guests, who did not want to stay at a hotel. The rooftop would be enclosed, offering a rooftop café for entertainment during the warm weather months.

The parking area could offer monthly paid parking, for community residents during the club's closed hours, with off-hour security. This would create jobs for valet parking attendants during club hours and security personnel. C J advised he would hire extra manpower for the club, trying to utilize persons from the community, along with someone who was experienced from his staff. There would be enough space for employee parking, and there would be a side entrance for deliveries. Along the side of the building, would be an outside enclosed area for the parking attendants and security personnel.

Ronnie was thinking it soon would-be time for her to meet with Lee Anne, regarding her new personal assistant. I will also have to coordinate matters with Geena's mom, regarding Powder Puff Designs & Fashions. Geena also wants to meet with me to plan the showing of my art and photography at the Starfire.

Chapter 38

Just to Be Close to You

Everything was looking up. Since Matt's big announcement at the Thanksgiving dinner, Brick has been quite the busy individual. He now felt he once again had purpose. He was enjoying himself working with Ronnie and Jason. They have proven to be quite talented, and both have exciting careers in their future.

His friends are the greatest, still remembering how Geena came outside the house to speak with him. It's wonderful to know your friends care about you when you're going through it. They were genuinely concerned about his wellbeing and made it clear they would be there for him, because they were family. The exchange at the dinner table was hilarious he thought. Relieved he was alright; the exchange of banter had uplifted everyone's spirits.

When he returned to his room later in the evening, he called Lena. He was extremely excited to share with her the news regarding The New Starfire Café &

Lounge. She was ecstatic when he told her about what the group planned for the club.

"Sweetheart, this is fantastic news! I'm so happy for you and your friends." Brick was imagining that beautiful smile of hers as she responded to his news. "This is an exciting time, and I am elated to share the news with you Lena. I have been missing you so much, I guess I was brooding around. Well, everyone noticed, and they were worried about me. Geena figured out it must be a woman and related the observation to the rest of the group. They jumped into my case and demanded to know who it was and when were they going to meet you. The exchange was hilarious. Did they ever tease me; but I gave them as good as I got. You would have thought we were in a comedy club. We laughed and we laughed."

Lena responded, "Wow Brick, it sounds as if you have an amazing bunch of friends. You must all be close. I hope I will meet them one day."

Brick responded, chuckling, "It's funny you brought that up because I was thinking the same thing. I came up with this idea I would like to run by you."

Lena giggling, "What have you got up your sleeve now Brick?"

"I was thinking it would be great if we got together over the holidays. It has been a while since we saw each other. We are planning a Christmas holiday get-together and I would like it if you would come. Do you think you could take time off from your schedule and come to visit over the holidays? You know how much I've been missing you, and it would be wonderful to see you. It would be a perfect opportunity to meet my friends. I already sort of told them they would meet you then, no pressure though."

Responding, Lena said, "I feel the same way too. I miss you so much. I have been running around for the past year, dealing with an extremely heavy schedule. I have been thinking for some time now about taking some time off for the holidays. Yes, this would be perfect, being with you and meeting your friends."

Brick was elated. Lena had jumped at the idea and excitedly accepted his invitation to spend time together over the Christmas holidays.

"Okay then. It seems like I am on a roll, so here goes part two of my idea. I hope you will like it."

"Oh, oh," Lena giggling again. "What other plans do you have?"

Brick responding, "I would like you to come back and perform at the club when we open it. What do you think?"

"Sounds great," Lena said replying. "Seems like you are trying to keep a girl close by your side," laughing. "Mind you now, I'm not complaining, because this lady misses her man something fierce and I love every minute I get to spend with you."

Brick responded, "Yes, I know what you mean Lena. Perhaps when you come over the holidays, we can sit down and plan a course of action for ourselves. I knew this was going to be difficult, as our schedules have become increasingly more hectic. I am certain we will be able to resolve this problem when we see each other."

"You're right Brick. I'm sure when we talk, we will be able to work something out. I love you so much and I don't want to lose what we have."

Brick responding, "Don't worry sweetie, I know it has been tough on you as well, but I'm certain we can make this work. When I first saw you, I knew you were someone special. I meant what I said, I'm not letting you go. We have a relationship which is special, and I believe it is going to flourish. Planning is key in making this relationship a success."

"You're right honey. I'm excited to see you over the holidays and I know it is going to be wonderful. Santa Claus doesn't have to bring me anything. I just want to be close to you."

Brick thinking, that's just how I feel. Now all I must do is pick up the ring in New York and find the right time to propose to this wonderful woman.

Brick started singing, "Just to be close to you, girl," both laughing.

Chapter 39

Coordinating the Surprise

Now that they were back in New York, Lee Anne thought things were progressing well. With Ronnie working in close concert with her, they were able to keep Geena busy. This allowed the rest of the team to work unhindered on her surprise, with her being none the wiser. It won't be long now.

Not only was she looking for someone to handle Geena's affairs in New York, but she was also looking for someone to be Ronnie's personal assistant. She was certain she would be able to pick someone from the candidates for Geena. She was trying to kill two birds with one stone.

She had been speaking with JET at great length regarding their relationship. They both knew a coast-to-coast relationship would not work out well. She decided it would be an advantageous move if she were to handle Geena's affairs from Texas. JET agreed this was a good idea. He could relocate from California and

Coordinating the Surprise

open offices in the Texas complex, as he was planning to expand his business. This would allow them to be near each other on a regular basis.

Not only was Lee Anne trying to select someone to run the New York office, but she was also trying to put together a team for the Texas office and studio. Olive Winfield and Theo Porter have been extremely helpful regarding the selection of staff, which helped her immensely.

They also discussed the live show Geena thinks she will be hosting. She is in for the surprise of her life to find out she will really be opening for the Olive Winfield Show. But there was a twist. Olive will be taking over the hosting duties, along with America's funny man, Seth Howard.

This is going to be Geena's wedding day. In addition, it will be the first broadcast of "The Geena Matthew's Show." This will take place in her brand-new studio.

With CJ's help, Geena and Matt are going to be pleasantly surprised. He is sure he can get Matt to propose on the show. I have taken care of all the other arrangements with the assistance of Ronnie, and Olive's staff. It's going to be quite romantic for them. I have also made plans for anyone from Matt and Geena's staff, to be present at the event if they so desire. They are well loved and respected. Their family and many of their friends are planning to be present.

Lee Anne was proud to be a part of this undertaking. Geena and Matt have worked with and done so much over the years for numerous people. It was fitting those they helped be present to celebrate with them on their day. This has been an ambitious plan with the guys. Keeping it off Geena's radar and planning the surprise of surprises, right under Matt's nose, has not been an easy task.

Ronnie and Geena's mom had planned everything with Olive Winfield regarding Geena's wedding dress and the wedding party's attire. Olive made certain all the legalities were taken care of and along with Lee Anne, she has been in close contact with Geena and Matt's minister, who will be performing the ceremony.

Lee Anne went over all the arrangements again, making sure nothing had been left out. She wanted things to work without a hitch.

She also had a final interview with the person she believed was going to be the NY office manager for Geena. Her name is Felicia Gail Roberts. Felicia must quickly get up to speed, because once she starts, a lot must be done to make it a smooth transition. While Lee Anne was serving in the military, she met Lisha in Paris, and they became friends.

Lee Anne also has an interview with one of the staff, who looks promising in becoming Ronnie's new assistant. Her name is Cynthia Elise Richards. Cindy had proven herself countless times while working on projects with Lee Anne, and she thought Cindy would be perfect. She has a very pleasant personality, and she is thorough regarding her work. If she accepts, all that remains is for Ronnie to meet her.

Ronnie's new assistant will have to jump right in, as Ronnie's schedule has become extremely busy. Lee Anne would help her get started, as she was familiar with Ronnie's schedule. Cindy will also have to work close with Geena, concerning Ronnie's art and photography show, and Brickhouse Productions. I believe she will work well with Ronnie and will be able to see to her needs.

As for Lisha, she was glad to be reunited with her friend. They were close when she was in Paris. Thinking back, she remembered Lisha was struggling with some personal issues and decided to return home to the States. Upon her return, Lee Anne started working for Geena. While they were out shopping, they ran into Lisha and her sister at a mall in New Jersey. Lisha was looking for work, and Lee Anne told Geena she recommended her highly to fill a position on Geena's staff. With her recommendation, Geena hired her immediately.

Now it looks as if Lisha will be running the NY office. Lee Anne just had to play her cards right to make it happen.

Chapter 40

Ronnie's Affairs

So many wonderful things were happening, and doors were opening for Ronnie. It was an exciting time for her. She could not help but worry about how she was going to handle everything, as her schedule was becoming way busier than she anticipated. She was trying to remain calm, remembering Lee Anne and Geena had told her they would help her. Lee Anne had promised she would find her an assistant. Ronnie knew she could really use the help, as things were increasingly becoming overwhelming.

Her phone was ringing. "Hello." It was Lee Anne. "Hi Ronnie. I know you must think I have forgotten about you, but I haven't. I have some good news for you. I believe I've have found just the person you need to be your personal assistant. We've worked on many projects together and she is quite adept at what she does. She's honest, hardworking and has a great personality. I believe she is someone who will be beneficial and valuable to you."

Continuing, "Her name is Cynthia Richards. Cindy presently works on staff for Geena's organization, which is why I have not mentioned this at home, because I don't want Geena questioning what is going on. This is going to be an amazing opportunity for her, one of which I believe she can handle. I will be having a final interview with her this week. She seems to be intrigued and excited. Of course, this is all contingent upon your approval. I would love for you to meet her. How does your schedule look for the end of the week?"

Ronnie responded, "Lee Anne I look forward to meeting her. If you say she's good, then I am willing to go along with your recommendation.

I really could use the help, so I can get back to work, without having to worry about scheduling. I'm free this Friday. The work has been completed for our office at the Starfire. Perhaps we could meet there."

Lee Anne saying, "That would be great Ronnie. I will call her and set up the meeting for this Friday. I will get back to you confirming the appointment. Thanks for understanding about Geena. As you know, it is not easy keeping things hidden from our sister." Acknowledging, "Not a problem Lee Anne. She certainly does not miss much. Geena and I must meet soon regarding the art and photography show. I will remember to handle that myself, so she does not have to interact with Cindy."

"That's a good observation Ronnie. Upon your approval of her, I suppose we should bring her up to speed of what we are planning, so she doesn't spill the beans to Geena. I'll be glad when this project is completed girl. It has not been easy keeping Geena busy and out of the way. At some point she is bound to run into Cindy, but with us all being aware, I'm sure we will be able to cover and explain why she is around."

"You're right Lee Anne, but I am sure everything will be alright. See you later tonight at home." They said their goodbyes and hung up the phone.

After her call to Ronnie, Lee Anne called JET. "Hi honey, I miss you." JET responding, "I miss you too sweetie. I'm glad to hear your voice."

Lee Anne continued. "I don't think we are going to have this problem much longer. I believe I have found the person to run the New York office for Geena. Her name is Felicia Roberts." JET replied, "Sounds great L A." Lee Anne continued. "I have also found someone to be the personal assistant for Ronnie. Her name is Cindy Richards and Ronnie is going to meet with her later this week." Surprised, JET exclaimed, "Oh my gosh, Cynthia… Cynthia Richards? That's Chet's little sister. C J recommended her for the job on Geena's staff. This is great! Cindy is a really nice young lady, and I am certain she will get along with Ronnie."

"That's a great piece of information you imparted to me. We were wondering how we could keep her off Geena's radar, and this could be it." JET replied, "I have a suggestion that may help you. I'll be in town this weekend, and so will Matt. Why don't you ladies invite us over for dinner? We'll bring Chet and Peaches, who will just happen to have his sister and her husband at the house. We'll invite them to come along, and sometime during the evening, one of us will say to you in passing conversation, why not consider Cindy for the position. Of course, you will jump at the opportunity and Cindy will accept, with Geena being none the wiser. What do you think?"

"Wow," Lee Anne responding. "I thought I was good. That's real sneaky honey. I have to watch out for you," laughing. I'll let Ronnie and Cindy know, so they can play along. Thanks sweetie." JET responded by saying, "Anytime. I am glad to be able to contribute."

No sooner than Ronnie had gotten off the phone with Lee Anne, it began ringing again. Ronnie answered and it was Geena. "Hi Ronnie, it's G. Do you have a few minutes? I would like to talk to you about a couple of things."

Ronnie replying, "Sure Geena, what's on your mind?" Geena said, "I just got off the phone with mom, and she told me her partner is excited about working with you regarding your fashion designs. Mom said she could set up a conference call next week, and the three of you could go over the details. She also said if you agree to everything, you could finalize the deal when she sees you over the holidays."

"That sounds great Geena. Oh, you said you wanted to talk about something else."

Geena continued, "Yes, I wanted to let you know I have been in contact with some dealers who are interested in your artwork and photography. You and I need to sit down and figure out a time when you can display your work in a show. I think the perfect venue would be at the Starfire."

Ronnie was elated and excited at the prospect of having her own show. Her dreams were becoming a reality. They decided they would talk when they got together over the holidays. Geena and Ronnie spoke a little longer and said their goodbyes. Ronnie thinking, I hope I like the person Lee Anne picked to work with me. Just today alone, I see I can really use some assistance. If that phone rings one more time, I am going to be undone. No sooner than she thought it, the phone rang.

Relieved, because this time it was Jason. She told him everything which had transpired, and she invited him for dinner at the end of the week, with the rest of 'the Crew.' Jason gladly accepted because they had not seen each other in a couple of weeks. Their schedules had been busy, and it was hard to coordinate time for one another, other than their nightly calls. He told Ronnie he loved her and would see her later in the week.

Ronnie was thinking how much she missed Jason when the phone rang again. This time it was Jacob

Meyers. She quickly brought him up to speed on the progress at the Starfire. He thanked her and told her about what was transpiring in Texas. Things were progressing expeditiously, and they were on schedule for the spring event. Ronnie thanked him for his update and promised to relay the message to Lee Anne. After further small talk, they said goodbye. Ronnie thought, if this phone rings one more time, I'm going to scream.

Lee Anne and Ronnie met with Cindy as planned on Friday. After a brief discussion, Ronnie knew she would be a great fit. Upon meeting Cindy, Ronnie realized she liked her demeanor. She was easy to speak with and Cindy was showing what she could bring to the table to assist Ronnie. Lee Anne had briefed her regarding Ronnie's schedule and what would be needed to help her. Cindy did her due diligence and came to the meeting prepared to win Ronnie over with what skills she could offer her.

Ronnie had a good feeling about her and offered her the position. Cindy gladly accepted and advised her she would start getting Ronnie's affairs in order immediately.

Lee Anne expounded on the conversation she had with JET about the dinner on Saturday evening. Knowing what was going to take place, they just had to follow the lead given and play along. Geena would never know it was all planned.

JET and Matt arrived in town early Saturday morning. They had contacted C J and Brick earlier in the week, letting them know what was planned for Saturday at dinner. Brick said he would tag along with Jason, because he was going to enjoy every minute of the charade. Cindy called Lee Anne to inform her that her husband William, had to leave town unexpectedly on business. Lee Anne acknowledged, but that news was not going to interfere with their plans.

Matt and JET arrived early, asking the ladies if they needed any assistance. They told them to relax as everything had been taken care of. Everyone else showed up and they chatted until dinner was ready to be served. They ate, chatted, and laughed, having a good time.

C J asked, "Lee Anne, how is the search going for Ronnie's personal assistant? I know her schedule has become hectic." Interjecting, Ronnie said, "It sure has. I've been on pins and needles, trying to get everything done."

"Welcome to our world," Brick said, everyone laughing. Lee Anne answered, "I'm working on it. I'm sure I will find someone soon." Brick could not resist. "There is a lot of activity coming up and Ronnie is going to need all the help she can get."

Chet spoke up. "What about my sister Cindy?" She has worked in Geena's organization for some time now and I heard she is efficient at her job."

Geena exclaimed, "Lee Anne, that's it! Why didn't we think of this before? She has worked well on many of our projects, and she would be an ideal fit for the position. It would be an amazing opportunity for her. I will lose an important person from my staff, but think of it this way, she will still be in the family. What do you think Cindy… think you're up to the task?"

This was turning out better than they expected. Geena was giving the pitch for Ronnie's personal assistant. Brick thought this was hilarious and was sorry he could not comment without letting the cat out of the bag.

Lee Anne quickly responded before Cindy could say anything. "Yes, Cindy, this would certainly help me out. Geena is correct in what she said. This would be an amazing opportunity for you. You will be doing what you so adeptly have proven in Geena's organization and I'm sure Ronnie would love to have you build her staff."

Cindy suppressing laughing out loud responded, "Yes, I would love to. Of course, if it is alright with Geena and Ronnie."

Geena responding, "It's alright with me. I would never stand in your way of this opportunity. What do you think Ronnie? She has proven herself and I recommend her highly."

Ronnie smiling, "I think this is a fantastic idea and I certainly would welcome you with open arms Cindy."

"Great," Lee Anne said, "I can help you get started, as I am familiar with Ronnie's schedule already. We can get started on Monday morning."

Everyone was smiling and chuckling around the table, congratulating Cindy on her new position. Geena had unknowingly helped this charade be successful, none the wiser of what was being planned for her. Things could not have gone better. Going forward, Cindy would be handling Ronnie's affairs.

Lee Anne said, "Cindy, I'm sorry your husband could not be here tonight. I was looking forward to meeting him. You said he had to go out of town on a business trip when we spoke earlier. What type of work does he do if you don't mind me asking?"

Replying, Cindy answered, "No, I don't mind Lee Anne. He is a musician. He got a last-minute call to do some studio work in Philadelphia. When a gig pops up, he tries to pick up the work. We're trying to purchase a house, so every penny counts."

Brick asked, "What instrument does he play and what type of music does he enjoy playing?" Cindy replied, "Will is a bassist. He likes to play gospel, jazz, blues and R & B."

Brick exclaimed, "Wait a minute! Your last name is Richards, correct?" Cindy answered, "That's right." Brick continued, "Holy cow! Do they refer to your husband as, 'Tom-Thump the Bass Man'?"

Answering, "Why yes they do. It was a nick name given by his younger brother, Benjamin."

Brick was extremely excited. "Good gracious! You're talking about 'Baby Boom' Richards. Guys, these guys are a couple of bad musicians. I had the privilege of seeing them perform at a gospel music workshop a few years ago. 'Tom-Thump' is one of the best bass players I ever heard and his brother, 'Baby Boom' has one of the funkiest beats on drums you will ever experience. Wow, you're married to 'Tom-Thump'!"

Laughing, "Yep, that would be my man," replied Cindy.

Ronnie and Jason were now excited as well. "I played with him once on a gig of mine. My bassist was sick, and he filled in for him. Brick is right, he is an incredible bassist. Ronnie looked over at Jason, "Are you thinking what I'm thinking?"

Jason responded, "If you're thinking about asking him to play for Hudson Flow, then yes. I've heard him play, and he is terrific. Just what we have been looking for. It would be really cool if we could get his brother to be our percussionist too."

Cindy replied, "This is so amazing you know them. What a small world. I can't wait until I can tell him."

Cindy's cellphone was ringing. "Speak of the devil, it's Will. Excuse me while I take this call."

She got up and answered, "Hi honey. Did you make it safely to Philly?" Will responded, "No sweetie. I was on the way, but got a call advising the gig was cancelled due to an emergency. That's why I'm calling you to let you know I am on my way back. Is it too late to meet up with you and your friends? I'm crossing the bridge now and could be there in a little while. Even if it is too late, I still could come to pick you up and take you home." Cindy answered, "Wait baby, let me check. Hold on."

Cindy returned to the group. "Excuse me, my husband is on the line. He told me the gig was cancelled, and he returned. He says he is nearby, and he was wondering if it was too late to come. If so, he'll just stop by to pick me up and take me home."

Geena responding, "No, tell him it's not too late. Give him the address and tell him to come."

Brick chiming in, "Yeah, and tell him to bring his bass up when he gets here."

Smiling, Cindy said thank you. "Sweetie, it's not too late, come on over. I will text you the address. Bring your bass up with you, I've got a surprise for you." Will asking, "What kind of surprise sweetie?" Cindy replying, "You'll just have to wait until you get here. Hurry and please be careful." Will replied, "I will. See you soon."

Cindy returned saying, "He is on his way guys. Thank you so much."

"This is going to be fun guys." Ronnie, bring your keyboard out and set it up out here. Jason, you go down to the car and grab your sax. This is going to be amazing everyone. Just wait. You're in for a treat."

Everyone pitched in to clean up the dinner dishes. Geena said, "We can wait to serve desert. We can serve it when Will gets here, so we can keep him company while he eats." Cindy thanked everyone. Geena continued, "Not a problem Cindy, we do a lot of things impromptu."

Jason went to get his sax and Brick asked him to bring his portable recorder he keeps in the car. Brick helped Ronnie set up her keyboard, amp, and microphone.

Matt said to JET, "It's a good thing we were able to get Lee Anne's apartment. When we finish here, we won't have far to go." JET shaking his head in agreement.

Lee Anne had been in contact with her building's management team and Matt and JET were able to take over her apartment sooner than expected. She let them have the furniture that was there, and the guys gladly accepted, not having to furnish it themselves.

Shortly after Jason returned, Will arrived with bass guitar in tow. Cindy ran over to greet him, giving him a big hug and kiss. "Hi baby." Geena came over to greet him with one of her fantastic hugs, "Welcome Will. Please make yourself at home. Put your case down and follow me. We are all in the dining room and we have a meal prepared for you."

Will replied, "Thank you. I hope you didn't go to a lot of extra trouble on my account."

"Don't worry yourself. We get together like this all the time." Entering the dining area, Geena continued, "Everyone, this is Will. Please introduce yourselves."

Introductions completed, Will sat down to enjoy the meal prepared for him. Cindy explained what happened earlier and he said, "I've learned you never know what is going to pop up out of the clear blue. This time it's something pleasant. I remember playing with you, looking over at Ronnie. If I recall, there was a problem with your bassist, and I filled in for him. It was a pleasant experience and I really enjoyed myself playing with you. What a small world." Ronnie acknowledging and everyone laughing and agreeing.

Brick told Will what they planned after he ate dinner. He gladly agreed, saying, "It will be fun."

Ronnie and Jason played some of their music and the music for Hudson Flow. Will had no problem adapting to the different styles they were playing. He fit right in. Will said, "I wish my brother could have been here. He would have loved this jam session."

Brick interjected. "May we discuss some business with you Will? Ronnie, Jason, and I were discussing the possibility of you playing for Hudson Flow, and some other projects we are working on. The fact is, we would like to have your brother as well." Will was excited and anxious to hear what they had to say. They excused themselves and talked business.

They discussed Hudson Flow, the Starfire, and the upcoming plans, asking if he and his brother would be interested in playing. Brick explained it was a good opportunity and there would be plenty of work. If they were interested, Brick said he would set up a meeting with everyone next week at the Starfire.

Will was excited and accepted. He called his brother, who agreed to come to the Starfire for the meeting. Brick arranged for Hudson Flow to be present. Ronnie and Jason advised him they would also be there.

Disappointed about the gig in Philadelphia being cancelled, this had turned out to be a far better opportunity. From what he had learned thus far, the work would be steady, which would help him have a steady income. Now he and Cindy could pool their resources and think seriously about purchasing a home and having a family. This was great and he could not wait to share this exciting news with her. Things have a way of working out. When one door is shut, another door opens.

They joined the others, Brick asking Will if he would mind if he shared the news with them. Will said it was okay. Brick explained to everyone, and they were glad for Will and Cindy. Cindy ran over to Will, tears in her eyes, hugging him. This day has been a blessing for them.

Brick saying to Lee Anne, "Looks like you better get a few more watches ready. Looks like our family is growing again."

Jason put on one of his playlists and everyone danced. Soon it was time to leave, everyone saying good night.

Cindy was thinking, next week was going to be an extremely busy and productive week. She was looking forward to spending some alone time with Will on Sunday, because Monday, it was hit the ground running.

Ronnie and Jason were extremely pleased of the unexpected events which developed. Ronnie was also glad Cindy was on board. Her schedule was really picking up and she remembered she had the call this week with Geena, Elaine, and her partner. She was glad to have her, and she was happy for Cindy and Will's new opportunities.

Jason was also pleased. What a coincidence. They had recently lost their percussionist and bassist, who were given other opportunities and wanted to move on. The timing for this was fantastic.

Geena was thinking she and Lee Anne should contact Matt's mom regarding the Summit Hill Christmas event. Plans needed to be confirmed. Time was flying by and the event would be upon them soon.

Brick arranged to pick up Lena's ring next week. He called her to tell her he loved her and said good night, wondering when he should propose to her and how he was going to do it.

Matt and JET would be flying out to Texas soon, to meet with Jacob and the rest of the investors. Soon the project would be culminating.

Not needing to say anything, Ronnie and Lee Anne looked at each other and smiled. Yep, everything was working out perfectly. Geena putting in her two cents was hilarious. Now this turn of events with Cindy's husband, also turned out to be fantastic.

This could not have been planned better.

Chapter 41

The Best Made Plans

Lee Anne was thinking about last week and the developments which transpired. Some good ideas were formulated, now they needed to be implemented. Surprises also took place, which were positive for the projects in progress.

This week she was going to be working closely with Cindy on Ronnie's affairs. They would also be coordinating with 'the Crew' pertaining to Geena's surprise affair in Texas.

Lee Anne and Geena would be in contact with Matt's mom, Sarah. They were working on the Christmas Extravaganza for Summit Hill. Sarah was already receiving assistance from the town's residence. We contacted the Mayor of Summit Hill and the Town Council, who gave approval to have the affair at the Gazebo, located on the edge of town. They planned a call tomorrow to work out the details for the event.

Geena advised Sarah we would come to Summit Hill next week to give her assistance and help decorate Summit Meadows, for their Christmas party.

Today, Lee Anne was at the Starfire, to help Cindy get started. She had just driven into the newly completed parking area when Cindy pulled her car alongside of hers. Another plus about Cindy, she was punctual. "Good morning Lee Anne. How are you doing on this beautiful day?"

Responding, "Good morning Cindy. I'm doing fine thank you. How are you doing… ready to get started?"

Cindy smiling, "Yes, I am excited to see how much we accomplish today. I thought we would start by getting Ronnie's schedule in order.

Then make plans to set up some interviews for a small staff here at the Starfire. I already took the liberty of making some fliers for the community. Since Ronnie expressed the desire to utilize the people in the local community, I thought it would be advantageous for us to distribute them throughout the local businesses and churches. From there, we could set up interview dates, and see what we come up with before we reached outside of the community. All the details of how to contact us are on the flyer. This will be a great start to become a part of this area. Soon we will have to make fliers up concerning the talent show, so the contestants will have time to prepare."

Impressed, Lee Anne said, "That's great thinking on your part Cindy, which will help us to get off to a fantastic start. Ronnie told me she will be here later today to go over the schedule with us." They worked diligently preparing Ronnie's schedule and taking time to pass out the fliers around the community. Jason had arrived after his morning classes. He was off the rest of the day, and he assisted in distributing the fliers around the community.

Ronnie would be sitting in on the meeting with Will and Ben, to discuss plans for the Starfire later this afternoon. Hudson Flow would also be present. If things worked out well, Cindy made plans with a local restaurant for food to be delivered just in case they were hungry. All they needed to do was call.

Ronnie's schedule included calls related to the Starfire, with Jacob Meyers. She also had an important call with Geena and her mother, Elaine. They were going to conference call each other concerning the business partnership with A-Line Apparel. Elaine was retiring and was turning the business over to her partner Belinda Connors, and Ronnie. If all worked out, they would seal the deal over the holidays.

At home later this evening, Geena would be discussing her plans for an art & photography exhibit for Ronnie at the Starfire.

Ronnie had an idea to have a fashion show, to showcase her fashions, and utilize some of the young people in the community. This of course would take place after the grand opening of the club.

The grand opening would be a weekend affair, starting with the talent show and the winner being announced and performing on Sunday evening. Cindy made a call to the group Pacific Sunset, so they could place the date on their calendar. Cindy asked about them utilizing the quarters at the Starfire and they opted to stay at a hotel. Hudson Flow would also be advised later today, and rehearsal schedules coordinated with the musicians.
    Plans were made in conjunction with Brickhouse Productions, regarding Ronnie and Jason's recording release. Brick would assist in that area.
    All personnel involved in the grand opening of the Starfire had been contacted, with dates and times confirmed. The kitchen and dining area were almost complete. The chef and his staff would be in the week prior to the grand opening, to make certain everything met with his standards. The building would be inspected three weeks prior to the opening just in case any infractions needed to be cleared up. The completion of the building structure was ahead of schedule, and they made tentative plans for the interior to be decorated. All materials needed, chairs, tables, etc. were ordered and would be delivered in March, to get everything set up in a timely fashion. The plumbing and electrical work were nearly completed. Presently there is a working restroom on the main floor. Brick had arranged for the audio and visual equipment for the various areas. The studio should be completed by the end of the week.

Rob and John will be handling the photography and video recording of the event.

Ronnie arrived and met with Hudson Flow, Will and Ben. Brick, Jason, and Ronnie were elated the meeting was successful. Scheduling for rehearsals were made, which would commence on Friday of this week.

Later, at home, they went over Ronnie's calendar. Ronnie was relieved everything was organized. She now knew when and where she had to be. From now on, all scheduling for Ronnie would be coordinated through Cindy. They decided to order dinner, which came just before Geena arrived at home. They ate their meal, laughing and joking. Afterwards they planned the details for Ronnie's exhibit and fashion show, which would be after the grand opening of the Starfire. Geena was elated to inform them everything was in order and would be in place for the show. She loved the idea of Ronnie displaying her fashions and utilizing the young people from the community.

It was a long day and they had accomplished much. Ronnie advised Geena and Lee Anne she planned on returning to Summit Meadows with them. Everyone would be off for the holidays. Any work she needed to do, could be completed in the studio there. Geena asked if Cindy would like to spend the holidays with them. She graciously declined, stating plans were already made with her family.

Everything completed, Cindy headed for home. She was gratified with a rewarding first day of work.

Everyone had her number stored in their phone. Tomorrow, Lee Anne was going to meet with her and Ronnie, to coordinate the Texas event for Geena. Ronnie stated she would meet her again tomorrow, so they could contact Jacob Meyers. She would also be working with him, regarding the events of the Starfire. She would make certain those events were posted to Ronnie's schedule as well. She would have all appointments and plans on her calendar. There was never going to be a dull moment, and Cindy was loving every minute of it.

Chapter 42

Grand Rapid Falls, Texas

Matt and JET were in Grand Rapid Falls, TX. They had been with Jacob Meyers all day, working on the surprise for Geena. Having finished for the day, they decided to have dinner together.

The plans were being implemented and thanks to Jacob, the project was ahead of schedule. The only piece of the project that would not be ready for the grand opening in the spring, was the Grand Rapid Falls Amusement Park. Completion of the park would be around mid-June, so the park could be inspected before it opened. The opening of the park would not be until the beginning of July.

They decided to have dinner at a restaurant located in Pine Bluffs, which was a town about thirty miles from the project site. It did not take long for them to get there. The hostess led them to their table, and they let themselves unwind and get comfortable from the long day's work. They did not have to wait long for the waitress to come over and take their orders.

They were happy the project was nearing culmination. Matt said, "Thank you for coming on board Jacob. You and your staff have done a marvelous job on this project. I don't know how we would have been able to pull this off on time without your assistance."

Remarking, "It's been a pleasure Matt and JET. I look forward to other projects in the future, as it has been wonderful working with you. It's great when friends can come together and implement a project of this magnitude. It has created employment opportunities for the surrounding communities and will continue when construction is done."

JET agreeing, "This project is doing better than we projected. The response has been phenomenal. It was a great idea of yours to purchase the real estate for those buildings which were abandoned. In addition, the construction of more dwellings, will create homes for those persons who are working on this project. They will be able to purchase a home for themselves and their families."

Jacob responding, "That's the beautiful part. It has helped my family's real estate business, so you see, everyone is coming out a winner here. We've started looking into building a local school and medical center. This is going to be a large community, so we have enlisted some local politicians in the surrounding area, to assist forming a governing body for Grand Rapid

Falls. They will of course need a mayor, town council, and emergency personnel. There will be a necessity for teachers and medical staff, which will be essential."

Matt said, "JET, I think it's a great idea of yours to open an office here. Your expansion name, JET Stream International is great."

JET replying, "Thanks Matt. Knowing Geena's studio and offices will be here helped influence the decision. Lee Anne would have to relocate with Geena, and we thought this would be the answer we have been looking for to be together. Lee Anne has been grooming someone for Geena's New York office, so her decision to relocate here with me would not present a problem for Geena."

Matt jumping back in, "Speaking of Lee Anne, we are going to need her assistance out here with us. She needs to be here to coordinate the meeting with our investors and to work with Olive Winfield's staff. It has not been easy to keep Geena from discovering what is happening. I think I have an idea on how to get Lee Anne here without her suspecting anything. We simply tell her you are opening offices here and we need Lee Anne's assistance in recruiting a staff for you."

JET shaking his head, "That's a great idea Matt. We should do it in person for effect. Geena can't resist helping when one of us needs her assistance. We can have wheels up tomorrow morning and be in the Apple by midday. You know she will be glad to see you, and if we stay a couple of days, she'll be ecstatic."

Matt saying, "Sounds like a good plan JET. We can alert Lee Anne and she can prepare to introduce her replacement to Geena. We can tell G that we only need L A for two weeks, maybe less."

Jacob laughing, "You gentlemen sure know how to concoct and execute a plan. You don't waste any time getting it done."

Matt continuing, "Geena is always involved in whatever projects we are involved in, so it's difficult keeping things from her. She's usually tuned into us, so we have gone to great lengths to keep her out of this. I'm sure glad it's almost completed."

JET said, "Matt, we should get C J to come out here also. We'll include him in the plan, stating we need his assistance to set up the security for my new offices. That will really keep Geena off our trail."

Matt replying, "I will give him a call tonight regarding our plan. Then I'll call Geena, to tell her I will see her tomorrow. Gentlemen, I believe we have covered everything. Let's enjoy our meal."

Lee Anne was glad to hear from JET, and she was doing her part to make the plan work. I've alerted Felicia and advised her she will be taking over my duties temporarily for approximately two weeks. I will introduce her to Geena tomorrow. If there are any problems, she knows how to reach me. Lee Anne thought this was a great plan the guys put together. All she had to do was follow their lead tomorrow. She also gave a call to Cindy and Ronnie, advising them of the plan.

Matt gave C J a call, letting him know what the plans were. C J said not to worry, and he would be ready to leave.

Matt then gave Geena a call. "Hi sweetie, I miss you. I must be in town on business tomorrow, so JET and I are flying in. I thought I would stay a couple of days and we could have dinner together tomorrow evening."

Geena responding, "Oh Matt, that would be wonderful. I miss you too baby." They spoke for a while and then said good night.

Geena thinking, I love him so much and Matt thinking, I can't wait to marry this girl.

JET and Matt were airborne early the next morning, arriving in New York around three o'clock in the afternoon. C J arranged for Chet to pick them up. They called when they landed to let the ladies know they would be there shortly. They went straight to Geena's office. Geena already told Lee Anne they were on their way, and she was waiting in Geena's office when they arrived. Geena hugged and kissed Matt. JET enveloped Lee Anne in his arms, giving her a warm kiss.

They sat down, Geena saying, "Welcome home guys, it's so good to see you," Lee Anne smiling and shaking her head in acknowledgement. JET and Matt agreeing it was good seeing them too.

Matt wasted no time getting down to business. "We need your assistance Geena." Geena thought to herself. Finally. It's been a while since they have asked for my help. "What can I do to help you?"

Matt continued, "JET is expanding his business to Texas. We have already let C J know, as we need his expertise to set up the security. If she doesn't mind and you can spare her, we need Lee Anne's help too."

Lee Anne responding on cue, "What do you need me to do?" JET answered, "I need you to set up my office and get a working staff for the new location. It will not take too long. I know you ladies are headed for Summit Meadows next week, to help with the holiday plans."

Geena responded, "That should not be a problem. Lee Anne introduced me to someone this morning, who can fill in for her while she is away. She has been grooming her for this type of situation. This is perfect timing, right Lee Anne?"

Replying, "It sure is Geena. This will be a perfect test for her. I'll get her situated in the morning before I leave. It should not take me long to set JET's office up and get it staffed. JET, I assume you've already put out a request for people who might be interested in the positions?"

JET responding, "That would be correct Lee Anne. I need your expertise vetting the applicants, as you are familiar with my operation."

Lee Anne laughing, "What will I get in return for my services big boy?" JET laughing as well responded, "I will take you out and treat you to all the hamburgers you can eat, tonight and tomorrow night."

Lee Anne winking at Geena, "What do you think G, should I help him?"

Geena smiling, "I want a piece of this action too. You guys are going to have to do a lot better than hamburgers though. You will have to give us a romantic evening tonight, and JET you will have to give a repeat performance tomorrow evening with Lee Anne. If you want her, those are my terms. Take it or leave it."

Matt chiming in, "Well JET, I told you this wasn't going to be easy. The lady drives a hard bargain, and I suppose we'll have to comply."

JET answering, "Alright Geena, you've got me over a barrel. Shall we shake on it?"

Lee Anne saying, "Nope. You must seal it with a kiss. Matt, you have to give Geena a kiss too." JET looked at Matt smiling, and they went to their ladies kissing them, saying, "Agreed."

Business conducted and now concluded, they left for Geena and Lee Anne's place, to get ready for dinner. Matt and JET left their luggage there, and after changing they went to dinner.

After dinner, Matt and Geena decided to go back to her place. JET and Lee Anne wanted to stay at the restaurant longer, dancing to the soft music.

When they got back to the apartment, Geena put some music on and snuggled into Matt's arms, to enjoy their favorite thing to do… kissing.

JET and Lee Anne returned later and sat chatting with Geena and Matt. Matt said, "It's been a long day

JET. We better leave, so we can be fresh for tomorrow's departure." JET agreed and they collected their belongings, kissed the ladies, and headed for their apartment. They knew the drill. Upon arrival, they would call Geena and Lee Anne.

Geena looked at Lee Anne and said, "I'm glad we were able to help JET. It's been so long since they asked me for my help." Lee Anne replied, "I'm sure it's because they know you have been extremely busy."

"Yes, but I'm glad we were able to come through for them. I miss the projects we work on together. It's usually hard work, but I enjoy being with them." Lee Anne laughing, "You mean you enjoy being close to Matt." Geena laughing, "Okay, okay. So, you found me out. Good night Lee Anne." Still laughing, Lee Anne replied, "Good night Geena."

Matt said to JET, "That went a lot easier than I expected." JET agreeing and laughing. Matt called Geena and JET called Lee Anne, letting her know C J was picking her up in the morning. The couples spoke briefly and went to bed.

C J picked up JET and Matt first, and then swung by to pick up Lee Anne. They began telling C J what transpired last evening. Lee Anne laughing, "We got her again and it was so easy. Matt your girl is so helpful."

"Yes, she sure is. I told JET last night, it went easier than expected. We thought we would have to beg and plead, knowing the way she relies on you." Lee Anne saying, "Geena told me she missed working on projects with you guys, poor thing. I wasn't buying it. I told her she just liked being close to you Matt." They were in tears laughing, Matt saying, "Alright, leave my baby alone now." C J cracking up, "Matt to the rescue again."

They arrived at the airport, boarded the plane and they were airborne. They arrived in Texas around noon. Jacob Meyers met them, and they went to eat. He advised them the meeting was arranged for Friday morning. That would not be a problem. Lee Anne had her notes, and the meeting would not take long to complete. There was nothing else for her to do, as JETS California staff had already arranged to fill the positions for Texas. The theatrics were only in place for Geena's sake. So far, so good. Geena still did not know what they were planning. C J and Lee Anne had a plan in place for Matt, regarding the proposal and wedding. Olive Winfield said Geena's first show would get rave reviews. They will be surprised because it was going to be a live telecast.

Lee Anne and JET enjoyed the few days they had together immensely. Matt and JET were going to fly them back to New York when the meeting was through. C J worked with Jacob's staff, overseeing the security measures. He would be ready to leave after the meeting too. They would depart Texas on Monday morning. Upon arrival, they would spend the night. JET and Matt would fly the ladies to Summit

Meadows Tuesday morning, before they returned to Grand Rapid Falls.

The meeting went well on Monday, and everyone was pleased. Lee Anne went over everything on her checklist with Olive's staff. Everything was set and ready to be implemented when the time came. Lee Anne made sure everything was in place for Leland Jackson's basketball clinic. It would be called, The Leland Jackson Sports Complex.

The main center would be named, The Grand Rapid Falls Media Arts & Convention Center. There would be plenty of space for different venues and for private vendors. Any conceivable event could be held there.

Theo Porter agreed to sponsor plays and movies in the theater complex. He planned on opening multiple theaters across the nation. They would be called Porter Cinema Franchises.

Olive agreed to present two live specials a year, for the next five years. She would utilize Geena's studio, which was named GEM Studios. Theo helped the team, making sure the studio had everything that would be needed for live broadcasts and film production. Geena's headquarter offices are called Gem-Star Productions. JET would also utilize the building for his offices, JET Stream International. Galaxy Quest Headquarters would utilize office space in the building as well.

Grand Rapid Falls Airport (GRF) has three runways, hangars, a terminal complex, and control tower. There would also be a mall and a terminal restaurant.

JET would supply the shuttle buses and limos needed. The shuttles would provide free transportation to the Grand Hotel, which was approximately fifteen minutes away.

Grand Rapid Falls Amusement Park will be completed in mid-June, and the targeted opening date would be the first week in July.

About ten minutes away, there will be the GRF Veteran's Housing Complex, for veterans and their families.

Uncle Seth's Summer Camp is sponsored by America's Funny Man, Seth Howard. It will be utilized by inner-city youth for camp. The kids will be able to play all kinds of sports. They will be able to go swimming, canoeing, cycling, hiking, and camping. They also will be able to utilize the amusement park. Cabins have been provided for living quarters. During the off season, the cabins could be utilized by families for holiday vacations, such as Memorial Day, etc. The fees collected would be used for the kid's summer camp.

Jacob Meyers completed the meeting by giving his report on the homes being built for Grand Rapid Falls. His team was working with local politicians in the surrounding area to provide a local governing system.

Everyone was excited the project was near culmination and overjoyed with the amazing employment opportunities. The growth for employment would be ongoing, thereby allowing the town to grow.

The meeting was adjourned. The next time they meet will be at the opening of the complexes in May. They were already booking for future events. If things kept moving like this, they would need another hotel. Jacob Meyers said plans were already being drawn up for another hotel should it become necessary.

Reservations had been made at a restaurant for dinner. Tomorrow they would depart. The project was being implemented successfully.

The next morning, the team said goodbye to Jacob Meyers. He wished everyone a happy and safe holiday, reminding them he would be back in New York sometime after the holidays. They boarded the aircraft and JET and Matt lifted off for home.

Chapter 43

Preparation for the Holidays

Ronnie and Jason had been extremely busy working on the promotion and release of their recordings. When she came home, she was exhausted, going to bed. Geena understood, as this was a critical time for them, and everything needed to be in place.

Geena missed Lee Anne being home, and in the office. She realized what a great asset she was, not only as her personal assistant, but as her close friend and confident. They were like sisters. She had a fantastic bond with her and Ronnie. She felt blessed having them in her life.

Lee Anne's choice to work with Geena while she was away, was on point. Felicia had proven herself to Geena, and they worked well together. She kept on top of Geena's scheduling and affairs. Earlier in the week, she reminded Geena of a conference call, between herself, Ronnie, and A-Line Apparel. She was grateful she did, as it had slipped her mind. The call was a good one. Her mother's partner, Belinda and Ronnie had liked working together, and they agreed to continue to work with one another. Mom would help Ronnie seal the deal over the holidays.

Geena would have no problem having Felicia fill in for Lee Anne again, should there be a necessity. She was a good leader, working well with the rest of the staff. They seemed to like her as well. It was almost like having Lee Anne there. She was spot in recommending I hire her when I was upgrading my staff. Ready to call it a day, Geena gathered her things together, said good night to everyone, and headed for home.

Arriving home, she received a wonderful surprise. There, sitting in her living room, were Lee Anne, JET, C J, and Matt. She dropped her things, running to Matt and jumping into his arms, hugging, and kissing him.

Letting go of Matt, she turned around, and gave JET a kiss on the cheek. Giving C J a kiss also. Then grabbing Lee Anne, she gave her a big hug.

Matt said, "It looks as if someone missed us," everyone laughing. Geena responded, "I sure have. Ronnie has been so busy; I didn't have anyone to tease." Lee Anne responding, "It's good to be home. I missed you too. We should go out for dinner to celebrate."

The door opened, and it was Ronnie and Jason. Ronnie said, "That sounds like a great idea. Can we tag along?" Geena exclaimed, "You bet you can." Her sisters had returned home.

They had an enjoyable dinner, letting Geena know the trip to Texas was successful. Explaining JET's California staff had come through on their end. Jacob's staff helped in Texas, making Lee Anne's job easier. Jacob's team worked well with C J implementing the security system.

C J said, "I would love to stay longer, but I'm anxious to get home to see Mel and the baby." Geena said, "Get home safely and give Mel our love. Don't forget to give the baby a kiss from auntie."

Saying goodbye, "I'll be sure to do just that. Matt, I'll call you when I arrive home." Matt replied, "Okay C J. I'll see you over the holidays." He replied, "Mel and I are looking forward to it."

The guys stayed a while longer. They stayed with the ladies, until it started getting late. Saying goodbye, they left for home. Of course, they knew the drill… call the ladies.

Geena, Lee Anne, and Ronnie sat in the living room catching up, until the guys called to say they arrived home safely. Then the ladies retired. JET informed them at dinner, to be ready to depart for Summit Meadows tomorrow morning. He and Matt would stay overnight, before heading back to Texas.

C J arranged for Chet to pick everyone up in the morning, to take them to the airport. Jason met them at the airport. He wanted to be with Ronnie, knowing they could work in the studio at Summit Meadows.

They boarded the aircraft and soon were airborne. Geena wanted to be in the cockpit. JET agreed, knowing how much she enjoyed flying, especially with Matt.

They arrived mid-afternoon in Summit Hill. John met them with the Suburban. The men put the luggage in the rear, and they headed for Summit Meadows.

Sarah and Elaine were excited to see everyone. Matt and the rest of the men unloaded the luggage, taking them to everyone's room. Sarah said, "Elaine and I have already started dinner." Geena asked, "Is there anything we can do to help?" Elaine responded, "No honey, we have it under control. We will be able to eat whenever you like."

Elaine continued, "Ronnie, we can go over the final details and sign the paperwork tomorrow. For now, everyone can relax, and enjoy being together again. We will go over the Christmas plans for Summit Hill tomorrow and we can finish decorating here this week."

Matt had given Sarah and Elaine the number to call a service from town, to come assist them in cleaning the house, from top to bottom. They were efficient and completed everything in a timely fashion. They were equally excited about the event at the gazebo for Christmas and offered to help them if they needed their assistance.

John and Ken got the tree and set it up in the living room. They did not start decorating it, because they thought it would be great for everyone to have a hand in trimming the tree. With the rest of the guys helping, and young Jason, they will be able to hang the lights outside in no time.

John and the rest of the men came back down, joining the ladies in the living room. Everyone sat and talked about what they had been doing individually. Soon it was time for dinner, and they went into the dining room. John gave the blessing for the food and gave thanks for the safe return of everyone.

They finished dinner, put the food away, and cleaned the kitchen. Returning to the living room, they talked some more. Ronnie and Jason decided to go do some work in the studio. Jason was becoming quite adept at the controls. Brick had been teaching and guiding him.

JET and Lee Anne went for a walk, holding hands. They walked to their favorite spot in the garden. JET played his playlist on his phone, and they danced.

Geena and Matt headed for their favorite spot, cuddling up to do their favorite pastime, kissing. It was a clear and mild night out. They needed only to put on a light jacket. Geena and Matt's parents went back to their quarters, to play a friendly game of poker.

Time passed and JET and Lee Anne returned, going inside, and saying good night. Matt and Geena stayed out a while longer kissing, then came inside. Geena said to Matt, "Baby, I love being in your arms, with you kissing me." Matt replied, "I love holding you in my arms, and I adore kissing you. Your lips are so sweet." They kissed again and said good night.

Ken said, "The kids are home. I suppose we should turn in. Tomorrow is going to be a busy day." They said good night and went to their rooms.

Ronnie, Geena, and Lee Anne started breakfast. When everyone came in, they sat down and ate. The guys cleared everything up.

Geena, Ronnie, and Sarah went into the office, and conferenced called Cindy, and Belinda. They went over the paperwork once again.

They made sure everything was in order. Ronnie signed the documents and once the paperwork was filed, she became an official partner with A-Line Apparel. Powder Puff Design & Fashions would be a subsidiary of the parent company. Geena thought, it was great to have an attorney in the family, her dad, Ken. It made the legalities much easier.

Sarah left and Lee Anne entered, joining Ronnie and Geena. They went over the plans for Ronnie's exhibit and fashion show at the Starfire. With Lee Anne's assistance, they were able to arrange for news coverage. Geena invited curators, and dealers, who might be interested in purchasing, or showcasing Ronnie's work. She also invited people to attend, hoping they would offer Ronnie a consignment to do work for them. Lee Anne advised Cindy made fliers and passed them to the various businesses throughout the community last week, with Jason assisting them.

If anyone were interested in fashion designing, they could enter their designs in the contest being sponsored by Ronnie. The winner would receive a scholarship for a fashion design school. Their work would be featured on the Powder Puff website. Any sales generated from their design, would be given to them, or added onto their scholarship. Having completed their work, they said goodbye to Cindy and Belinda. Geena, Ronnie, and Lee Anne returned to be with the others.

They started to discuss the plans for Summit Hill, going over what was needed. John started. "When we picked up our tree, Ken and I spoke with the owner, who said he would donate a large tree for the event at the gazebo. Before we headed for home, we stopped by the hardware to buy some lights for here. We talked to the owner, who advised he would donate the lights for the tree. He also said he and his staff would hang lights and decorate the gazebo. He took us across the street to the gift shop, which was owned by his sister. She promised to donate the decorations needed at the gazebo. She had an idea on how to get others involved." Geena said, "Sounds good."

John continued, "She said she was going to contact the rest of the merchants on the main street in town, asking if they would decorate their windows. If they did not have enough to decorate, she and her brother would help them out with the lights and decorations."

Geena said, "This is great. It seems like the people in town are really getting involved." Sarah said, "I'm going to contact the crew that was here last week, to see if they still want to assist. They have those tall ladders, and they would be instrumental in decorating the tree." Matt interjected, "I'm sure they will do it. I know the owner and he is a great guy. I'm going to give him a call, to see if he can loan us one of his ladders, so we can string the lights here. Of course, we'll pay him." Sarah replied, "Son, I know you will be leaving, so I will handle it." Matt said, "Thanks mom." She replied, "You're welcome son."

Elaine said, "I contacted the schoolteachers and local daycare center, requesting they ask the children to write down one gift they want Santa Claus to bring them. They have collected the lists and given them to the owner of the toy store. Most of what the children asked for he has in stock, or he can order."

Geena said, "Let him know we plan to pay for the toys and will donate them to the children. Have we got a Santa Claus yet?" Elaine responded, "No dear, no volunteers yet." Geena said, "Not a problem. Brick said he would do it. We'll let him know, so he can get a Santa Claus outfit. Maybe his new girlfriend won't mind being Mrs. Claus." Everyone laughing, "I'm sure he'll love that," Matt said. Continuing, "Make sure he knows, so he can ask her. We can't assume anything." Ronnie said, "I have to call him, so I'll bring this up to him."

JET said, "Have them put a throne for Santa Claus to sit on at the gazebo. If it doesn't snow, he can make a grand entrance by helicopter." Geena said, "Great idea. The kids will love it."

Sarah said, "The hardware store owner also donated the candles which are battery-operated for all of the participants. He thought it would be a nice touch when we sing Christmas carols at the lighting of the tree. He has enough for the entire town and said he would store them for use next year."

Elaine said, "The local club owner said he would set up the sound system and have the necessary connections for any equipment that would be utilized. He also stated his DJ was available to spin music. He requested we let him know what our wishes are, so they can plan and be prepared."

Ronnie said, "Let him know I just need an amp and connections for my keyboard. So far, Jason and I are the only musicians playing. If he knows of any local musicians who want to play with us, tell him to let us know, so we can rehearse with them." Elaine replied, "Will do."

Sarah advised, "The women of the town volunteered to wrap the presents for the children. The gift store is supplying the gift paper and the church is allowing them to work in the basement. The pastor said the toys could stay there until they were placed around the tree on Christmas eve. The men of the church said they will pick the gifts up and transport them to the tree, the afternoon of Christmas eve. I figured a few of us could help Brick, by dressing up and being Santa's helpers."

John said, "We've got all the necessary decorations for here. All we must do is put them up. I'm certain with everyone pitching in, we can be finished by the end of the week." Sarah said, "The last thing we should do is trim the tree, when everyone else arrives next week. Is there anything else we have not thought of?" Thinking of nothing, they ended the discussion, starting to decorate the house.

Accomplishing a great deal, they decided to end the decorating for the day. Matt suggested they go out for dinner, at the town's local restaurant. They agreed, and Geena called ahead to let them know how many were coming.

Matt drove his SUV, and JET drove the second SUV. They arrived in town at the restaurant a few minutes later. The staff had everything ready for them when they entered, showing them to their table. They placed their orders, chatting and laughing. The other patrons knowing who they were, came over to thank them for having the Christmas festival at the gazebo. They told them it was a wonderful idea and they were happy it was going to be an annual affair.

Geena responded. "We are happy to do it. The holidays are about family and close friends. We thought this would be a great time for us to be together."

Their dinner was served. They ate and continued to chat, until it was time to leave. When they finished, they thanked the owner, and staff for their service and hospitality.

Ronnie asked if they could drive by the gazebo before they headed back home. Agreeing, they went to the edge of town to the site. The tree was already in place by the gazebo. Geena could see why Ronnie and Jason liked coming here. It was peaceful and beautiful. They stayed a few minutes, then started back to Summit Meadows.

Arriving, they sat in the living room talking and laughing. It was getting late, so everyone retired early, knowing tomorrow was going to be another hectic day.

As per usual, the ladies were up and about fixing breakfast. Geena said, "We sure accomplished a great deal yesterday. We should be able to finish the decorating for the house today."

Ronnie said, "I am amazed at the amount of work we have completed. I've never been a part of team like this before. When there is a task, everyone gets involved, until everything has been completed, leaving no stone unturned. I'm glad to be a part of this, as it's simply wonderful." Geena replied, "Yes, it is amazing. From the early days, we would work closely together, until whatever project we were working on was culminated. We are always there for one another."

Sarah said, "Here we go. I hear the happy banter and laughing of the guys. Sounds as if they are eager and ready to go."

The men were laughing and joking when they joined the ladies. Matt said, "Good morning ladies," the rest of the guys joining in. "Looks like it is going to be another beautiful day," kissing his mom on her cheek, and then going over to Geena to give her a big hug and a kiss. "My two favorite girls." Sarah responding, "Good morning son," and Geena saying, "Good morning baby. What time are you and JET leaving?"

Matt answering, "Somewhere around midday. We want to help the rest of the guy's finish stringing the lights on the outside. We're almost finished. We plan on getting back to the city by early evening and to get a good night's rest before we head back to Texas tomorrow morning."

Geena remarked, "Good. I don't want you to overdo it. It's a good decision to get some rest before heading back to Texas. We want both of you to be safe." JET replied, "We will be well rested before we leave. We will probably be back by Tuesday of next week, no later than Wednesday." Matt chiming in, "Yeah, next week is going to be a blast. With all the festivities planned, I'm excited, and looking forward to the holiday celebration." Sarah saying, "You sound like you used to when you were a little boy. This time of year, has always been your favorite."

Matt laughing, "I suppose so. It's exciting we are going to be together again. It's been a long time, and our family has been extended. This is going to be a wonderful time for everyone."

Ronnie said, "I know I'm looking forward to it. This has taken on a life of its own. Our family, friends, and the town coming together to celebrate for the holidays is truly magnificent, and I don't want to miss a minute of it." Everyone excitedly laughing and agreeing.

They sat down to eat breakfast, continuing to laugh and talk with each other. They expressed the sentiments they felt individually, regarding the upcoming holiday celebration.

Ronnie said, "I spoke to Brick, regarding him playing the role of Santa Claus. He called me back to let me know, he would be happy to be Santa, and Brenda said she would love to be Mrs. Claus. He also said, rehearsal had gone well with Hudson Flow. Jason and I will begin rehearsing with them after the holidays. Cindy has already worked out the scheduling."

Lee Anne stating, "Cindy seems to have your scheduling under control Ronnie. You should be able to enjoy your holiday without any worries."

"Yes," Ronnie replying, "I'm grateful to you for recommending her to be my personal assistant. She is doing a fantastic job."

Geena said, "It sounds as if she is going to be just fine, and it looks as if Brenda is going to meld right in with the rest of the family." Matt agreeing, "Sounds like Brick has been blessed with a winner. Everyone has truly been blessed and it will be wonderful to celebrate together."

Finishing breakfast, and cleaning up, everyone set about the task of completing the decorating of Summit Meadows for the holiday.

The men finished stringing the lights and decorations for the outside and came back inside to assist the ladies. Matt and JET said goodbye and headed to the airport, for the short trip back to New York. Geena and Lee Anne drove them to airport, kissing their guy's goodbye. Matt and JET promised to call when they landed in New York.

Geena and Lee Anne decided to stop in Summit Hill, to make sure everything was progressing smoothly. They spoke with the nightclub owner, who advised a few of the musicians were interested in playing with Ronnie and Jason. Lee Anne told him she would advise them, so a rehearsal could be coordinated. Everything else was going along simply fine and they headed back for Summit Meadows.

When they returned, the decorating was almost completed, just needing a few finishing touches. There were just a few minor things remaining to be done. The ladies were in the kitchen preparing to fix dinner. Lee Anne and Geena joined the rest of the ladies, giving them a report on the progress being made in Summit Hill.

Lee Anne said to Ronnie, "We spoke with the nightclub owner, who advised there were some musicians who wanted to play with you and Jason at the celebration. He said call to schedule a rehearsal with them." Ronnie said, "That sounds great. I will give him a call now to set things in motion. Do you have his number?" Lee Anne gave Ronnie the number, who excused herself to call the club owner.

Geena said, "We should take a ride into town tonight, to see how everything looks. I am excited to see what has been completed, and to find out if there is anything else, we can do to help." Elaine said, "I think that is a good idea sweetie, and since we are having an early dinner, it won't be too late to check everything out. I'm especially curious to see what they have done to the gazebo." Ronnie saying excitedly, "Me too! That's one of my favorite spots. I hope the guys aren't too tired."

The men came in to join the ladies. Jason laughing asked, "Too tired for what? What have you ladies been cooking up in here, besides the dinner?" Ronnie replying, "Since we are having an early dinner, we thought it would be a good idea to drive into Summit Hill, to see what they have done with the lights and decorations along the main thoroughfare and at the gazebo. We were hoping you guys wouldn't be too tired to take us."

John saying, "It should be fun." Ken agreed and Jason said, "Since we are having an early dinner, we can stop to get some ice cream, and then go to the gazebo to eat it."

They sat down eating dinner quickly, anxious to get to town. Finishing, they cleared the table, put the food away, and cleaned up. They jumped in the two SUV's and started off for Summit Hill. Upon arrival, they were not disappointed. The businesses along the main street were lit with holiday lighting. The houses on the side streets were also decorated. They drove around, looking at the winter wonderland. The town was simply beautiful. They stopped in the restaurant, ordering ice cream. They headed for the gazebo. It was simply beautiful. Ronnie jumped out of the SUV first, shrieking with delight at the sight before her. "Look at this! It's so beautiful," running ahead to the gazebo, Jason following behind her.

The path leading to the gazebo had poinsettias aligned on both sides, with mini-candy cane lights between each poinsettia, leading to the stairs. On each side of the stairway, were two giant candy canes, wrapped with strands of lights. The gazebo was decorated with holly along the railings, with colorful blinking lights spiraling the holly on the rails and around the top outer edge of the gazebo's roof. There was a bright red throne in the center of the gazebo for Santa to sit.

The arms, legs, and back were decorated with white lights. To one side of the gazebo was the Christmas tree, which was decorated with a host of different colored ornaments, of all shapes and sizes. The lights were strung around the tree, but they were not lit. The town decided to have a tree lighting ceremony. There were lights along the outer edges of the paths around the gazebo.

Although the tree was not lit, the ornaments were capturing the reflections of the surrounding lights. This made the tree beautiful, even though it was not lit. On the other side, was a stage built for the performers and the DJ. It had a roof, which was covered with tinsel, ornaments, and lighting.

It was picture perfect, stunning. The town really did a great job decorating the area. Everyone in attendance, will be in awe of its beauty. Christmas caroling around the gazebo is going to be a wonderful event. The children were going to be incredibly happy.

Finishing their ice cream, they headed back for Summit Meadows. The men had installed a timer for the lights around the outside of the house. When they returned, the tree and the lights were aglow. The ladies were impressed with what the men had done. Lights were aligned along both sides of the driveway. The structures all had strands of holly and lights hung from them. They had even decorated JET and Lee Anne's gazebo with lighting. The garden was filled with beautiful colored lighting. The men had done a marvelous job decorating the grounds.

Geena remarked, "Daddy, you guys have done a marvelous job. The grounds look so beautiful. Everyone is simply going to have a fantastic time." Ken replied, "We had a great time doing it. The crew that came here from town last week, brought us the ladders we needed, and decided to stay and help us. They said it was their way of paying back what we had done for the town. It was very neighborly and nice of them."

John said, "It always pays to be nice to people and be a blessing. When you do this, blessings always come back to you. Matt wanted to pay them, but they would not hear of it, saying they felt blessed by the caring and generosity which was being shown to the town."

Elaine said, "Geena, we are so immensely proud of you all. The way you have been there for each other, and how you have developed your friendships is a blessing for you. You always look out for each other and those you encounter. Your honesty, ethics, and talents have served you well. You have worked hard, and you have shared your gifts with others. I love you all." Sarah, John, and Ken agreed.

Jason said, "I am not one to say a lot, but I feel I have to say something now. My mother and father have tried to raise me by example, and I absolutely love them. Whenever I am around here with you, I feel as if my mom and dad are here. You are so much like them, and I feel comfortable around you because those same lessons my parents try to teach me, I find in you. It's easy to understand how Geena and Matt developed into the persons they are, because they have been molded and shaped by you. Not only that, everyone in this entire group is also similar in their ways. My parents always remind me, you are who you surround yourself with, so be careful who you associate yourself with. Now I know what they mean." Ronnie came over to Jason, giving him a hug and kiss on his cheek, whispering to him, "I am so proud of you, and I love you very much."

Geena said, "Wow guys, stop it. We're all going to be in tears in a moment." Ronnie's phone started ringing. It's Brick guys. Excuse me while I take the call."

They were laughing and joking when Ronnie came back. "I have some good news," she said. "Brick told me Brenda has a gig in D.C. on Saturday."

Ronnie continued, "He is going to meet her there and has made a reservation to stay the night. They plan on renting a car and on Sunday morning, leaving D.C. to come here. He says they should arrive sometime around midday Sunday."

Geena said, "That's wonderful. I am anxious to meet this young lady who has stolen my little brother's heart. Brick has said little about her, but from what he has said, it seems she is genuinely nice."

Jason chiming in, "That's great, but I know she better have a great sense of humor, because Brick is going to have her laughing all the time." John said, "She better know how to cook too, because Brick loves to pack it away." The room filled with laughter.

Most of the gifts were purchased online. However, everyone agreed to finish shopping in town tomorrow, as there were some remaining items to be purchased. This would give them time to wrap the remaining gifts, place them under the tree, and write their holiday cards.

Chapter 44

Spill the Beans!

Brick rented a car and left New York, heading for his rendezvous with Brenda in D.C. He was eager to see her and looking forward to her performance in the evening. He and Brenda agreed to spend time together, deciding to go out for dinner after the show. Brenda knew it would be late when her performance ended. She told Brick it would be best for him to stay at a hotel. He agreed and made a reservation in the same hotel she was staying at. They would get a good night's rest and leave early Sunday morning for Summit Meadows. This would be the start of their holiday, and they were eagerly anticipating the time they would be spending together.

Brick made reservations for dinner at a nearby restaurant. After the show, he and Brenda made their way to the restaurant. It was already late when they arrived, but they did not have to wait long before placing their order for dinner. They were elated to be united once again.

"I've missed you, and I am so happy to be with you," Brenda said. "I was counting the days before I would see you again." Brick responded, "I've missed you too. I am so happy we are spending this time together over the holidays. I can't wait for you to meet everyone, and I think we are going to have a fantastic time." They continued to chat, enjoying the delicious seafood dinner they had ordered.

Knowing they had an early departure for tomorrow, they agreed to head back to the hotel. Brick walked Brenda to her room and kissed her good night before heading to his room. He couldn't wait until they got to Summit Meadows. He was not sure when, but he was planning a special surprise for Lena over the holidays.

The next morning, they were up bright and early. Brick packed Brenda's belongings in the car. Besides her luggage, she had a few shopping bags with gifts in them. He already knew she was kind and thoughtful.

He also knew she was going to leave a lasting impression on everyone and would be warmly accepted and welcomed. Once on their way, Brick called Geena to give an approximate time when they would arrive. Geena told him to be careful and to call when they were nearby.

She and the rest of the ladies had prepared breakfast and were settling down with the men to eat. Geena told the group, "Brick called to advise he and Brenda were on their way. He will call again when they are nearby. He sounded extremely excited. I'm elated he has found someone who makes him happy. I can't wait to meet Brenda."

"I am happy for him too," Ronnie acknowledged. "It seems we all have something to be happy for. The blessings keep on coming. This is going to be the best holiday I've had in a long time. Having lost my parents, the last couple of years has been lonely. This is so special to me, because I've found a whole new family, who have embraced me."

"You're right Ronnie," Lee Anne agreed. "I am appreciative of the blessings we share. This has been an amazing year, and I have a feeling there is more to come."

Jason jumped in, "Okay, okay. If we keep going on like this, we're going to be teary eyed. So, I guess I'd better mimic Brick. Let's sit down at the table and get to eating. Get ready y'all, the real deal will be here soon enough." Everyone was laughing. Jason had done it again, in true Brick fashion.

They finished eating and cleaning up, everyone doing their own thing. Basically, relaxing until Brick and Brenda arrived. Matt called Geena to advise he and JET would be there with everyone on Tuesday.

Geena and Ronnie decided to take the convertible for a ride to town. It was a beautiful bright and sunny day. They invited Lee Anne to tag along. They had a few more things to pick up in town. They decided to hang out at the gazebo a few minutes after shopping. The town really did a marvelous job decorating the grounds around the gazebo, and the kids were going to love the beautifully decorated Christmas tree and Santa's throne.

While they walked around, they talked about Ronnie's show at the Starfire, after the grand opening. Ronnie said, "I'm extremely excited, and somewhat nervous about the event. My paintings, sketches, and photographs are going to be displayed for the first time to the public. Not only that there's the fashion show. I wonder if I've taken on more than I can handle. Geena responded, "Ronnie, you have nothing to worry about, because your work is beautiful, and people are going to love it."

"I can't help but worry," Ronnie said, "I've never done anything like this before." Lee Anne saying, "Geena is right, Ronnie. You've nothing to fear. We've got this, and now with Cindy being onboard, all you have to do is concentrate on getting your material together."

Ronnie sighing, "I suppose you ladies are right, I'm just nervous." Geena saying, "You're going to look back at this and have a good laugh about it. You are incredibly talented, and you are going to be quite successful in your endeavors. Besides, you've got your sisters beside you." Ronnie hugging them, exclaiming, "Sisters!" They had a wonderful time on their outing, laughing and talking with one another.

Geena stated "We had better start back. If my calculations are on point, Brick should be calling soon to let us know they are almost here." They went to the car and headed back for Summit Meadows. When they arrived, everyone had gathered in the living room, relaxing and talking.

Jason asked, "Did you ladies have a good time?" Ronnie answered, "When we are together, my sisters and I always have a great time." The ladies looking at each other laughing and saying, "Sisters!" They took the shopping bags upstairs to their rooms and returned downstairs to be with the others.

Brick said to Lena, "We are about an hour away from arriving at Summit Meadows." The ride had been pleasant, and they had made good time, not having any traffic to contend with. "I promised Geena I would let her know when we get close."

Lena responding, "I've enjoyed the ride, as it has been quite relaxing, especially being able to be with you. The time we had to spend apart from each other has been difficult, but it has proven we have something special. I'm eager to work out the details, so we can be together on a more consistent basis."

Brick saying, "We will have plenty of time to plan and work the details out during the next couple of weeks. I'm extremely optimistic about our future and everything working out for the best. I love you so much."

Brick excused himself from their conversation, and made the call to Geena, letting her know they were almost there.

Geena answered her phone when she was coming back downstairs to join the others. Upon reaching the living room, she told everyone Brick had called to advise he and Brenda were almost here. "I was so glad to hear from him, I forgot to ask if they had stopped to get anything to eat. It's okay though, as it will take no time at all to heat something up if they are hungry. I'm anxious to meet Brenda. Brick sounded excited on the phone." Elaine saying, "We all are dear. I'm sure she is someone special and I know if his parents were alive, they would be happy for him, just as we are. From what you say, and from what we have observed, Brick seems to be happy."

Jason said, "Judging from the bags you brought back, I know you had a good time shopping. What else did you do?"

Geena laughing, "You're getting like the rest of the guys. We do more than shop. For your information, we talked about the Starfire, and Ronnie's show after the grand opening, in the spring."

Jason laughing, "Now I truly feel like one of the family, since you said I sound like the rest of the guys," everyone laughing. Continuing, "I am looking forward to the events at the Starfire. The grand opening and of course Ronnie's exhibition, as her work is extraordinary."

John saying, "That's the way young man, put in a good word for your lady. She'll love you even more for acknowledging it, and don't let Geena fool you, those girls love to shop. They come by it honestly, right Ken?" Responding, Ken said, "Our girls are the same way. They love to shop and hang out together."

Sarah said, "Alright you two, don't you start." Elaine saying, "That's right." Just as she finished, they heard the sound of a car horn. John said, "Saved by the bell, it must be Brick. Come on everybody." Sarah said, "That's okay gentlemen, we'll get you back later on," everyone laughing and going to greet Brick and Brenda.

Brick and Lena were already out of the car when everyone approached. With open arms, Geena reached them first. "Welcome Brick and Brenda," hugging him, and then turning to Brenda. Everyone surrounded them and started hugging them as well. Geena noticed somewhat of a hesitation between Lee Anne and Brenda but thought nothing of it when Lee Anne wrapped her arms around hugging her.

Lee Anne was smiling at Brenda, and while hugging her she whispered in her ear, "You and I have some talking to do specialist." She turned to give Brick a welcome hug. Brick said, "Everyone, this is Brenda Helena Davis. Lena, this is my family. As you see, they are already making themselves known to you. Get used to it, because nothing will be the same for you after today," everyone laughing, gathering around to welcome her.

Geena pulled Lee Anne away from the group, asking, "What was that all about?" Smiling, Lee Anne asked, "What are you referring to Geena?" Geena responding quickly, "Don't play games with me Lee Anne. I saw the exchange between you and Lena. It seemed like there was some recognition between you two." Lee Anne said to Geena, "You don't miss anything. Nothing pressing that won't keep until later. I'll fill you in then." Geena said, "Make sure you do Lee Anne. This concerns my little brother Brick. If there is something I need to know, I expect you tell me, because you seem to know something I don't. I don't want Brick hurt." Lee Anne said, "I'll speak to you later G, I promise. Later, while they are getting settled, make up an excuse for yourself and me. We'll go to the office, and I will fill you in then." Geena said, "Okay, I've got a feeling this is going to be mind boggling."

Lena was keeping her composure, all the while questioning herself, why in the world is L A here? This is the second time she has crossed her path. Now, and once just before Thanksgiving. What is going on?

The men started helping Brick unload the car and bring their things to their rooms. Brick said, "Be careful of those two bags, they have Santa and Mrs. Claus' outfits in them, ho, ho, ho."

Geena said, "Are you guys hungry? We can warm something for you." Brick said, "That would be great G, we drove straight through." Geena said, "Go up, get settled and cleaned up, and we'll fix some food."

They started up the stairs. Geena asked Ronnie to warm something up for them, excusing herself. "Something has come up which requires Lee Anne's and my attention. It will only take a few minutes for us to address, and we will rejoin you shortly." Ronnie said, "No problem Geena. You and Lee Anne take care of what you have to do, and I will get things started." Lee Anne saying, "Thanks Ronnie."

Geena and Lee Anne went to Matt's office and shut the door. Sitting down on the sofa, Geena said, "Okay Lee Anne, spill the beans. What's going on here that I should know about? You seem to know that girl."

Starting, "Your observation and assessment is on point as per usual. We served in the military together. She was a specialist and an elite covert operative assigned to my team. She worked on many missions with JET and me. This is the second time I've seen her in the last month and a half. In my former capacity, I learned in my line of work, when it seems like coincidence, it usually isn't." Geena was listening to Lee Anne very patiently.

Continuing, Lee Anne said, "I know after our overseas assignment, she was recruited by the firm, and I haven't seen her since. That is, until the fiasco with those bank robbers last month. I recognized her as one of the team members. We looked at each other, and she winked at me. I know JET was not in position to see her. She stayed in the background. I thought she might be undercover, not wanting us to blow her cover, thinking she may have been investigating someone on the scene. So, I smiled and winked back at her. I didn't even tell JET about seeing her." Geena said, "So you think something more is happening here than meets the eye?"

Lee Anne said, "I'm not sure. That's why I told her outside, the two of us need to speak with each other." Geena said, "I want in on the meeting between you. If it's about a covert operation, I'll leave, but if it concerns Brick, I'm going to have a lot of questions." Lee Anne said, "Agreed."

Finishing their talk, they joined the others. Ronnie said, "We're you able to take of matters ladies?" Geena responding, "Yes Ronnie, thank you for holding down the fort." Ronnie acknowledging, "No problem." Brick and Lena joined them, settling down to eat the meal prepared for them. Brick said, "You guys sure have this place looking festive for the holidays." Ronnie said, "Isn't it great? You should see Summit Hill. It looks fabulous." Lena said, "I still have a few last-minute items to pick up. If you ladies don't mind, maybe you can take me to town later, so I can do some shopping."

The guys started laughing, Jason saying, "Here we go. Brick, we were just talking about the ladies shopping before you drove up." Brick saying, "Hmm, sounds like we'd better take two vehicles to Summit Hill. When these ladies get together, there is no telling how long they will take to shop."

Lee Anne said, "Brick, that is a marvelous idea. Geena, we could call and make a reservation at the restaurant in town. You guys hang out and we ladies will have time to shop and chit-chat. Afterwards, we can show you the town when all the lights come on. It's a beautiful sight to see. You're both going to love it. Don't you think that's a good idea Geena?" Geena said, "I think that's a perfect plan Lee Anne, what do you think Lena?" Lena smiling and shaking her head in agreement.

Ken said to John, "Something tells me there is more than meets the eye here." John agreeing, "Yes, I've seen that look in the eyes of those two before. Whatever it is, I don't want to know about it." Ken shaking his head, "Yep, I think it's best we stay out of it. I know that look in Geena's eyes all too well."

Brick and Lena finished eating. Geena said, "Daddy, you and John can drive the SUVs, and make sure everything is okay at the restaurant. We'll follow soon in Ronnie's car. We want to show Lena her studio."

Ken said, "Okay honey, see you soon. Come on everyone, let's get started." Lena asked where the rest room was. Ronnie showed her. Lena was thinking to herself, what in the world is going on here?

Coming back, Ronnie said, "Okay give, something is up with you two. Obviously, you wanted us to be alone. Come on, fill me in." Geena said, "Lee Anne knows Lena, and we are on a mission to get to the bottom of what is going on. Just follow our lead." Ronnie shaking her head, "Okay, I will." Lena returned and they went into Matt's office.

Lee Anne started, "Alright Lena, it's time to spill the beans. What's going on here? This is the second time I've seen you in a month, and you know how I feel about coincidence. I need an explanation please, and knowing you the way I do, I'm certain you're looking for answers, just like we are."

"Please Lee Anne, I am just as surprised to see you here, as you are surprised at seeing me. I'll tell you what I know, then maybe we can clear this up. First, let me make this perfectly clear. There is no covert operation going on here, and I'm not on any assignment. If I were, I would not discuss anything further with these two ladies being present. Brick has told me how close all of you are, so I can imagine your concern."

Lee Anne said, "Okay Lena, you must see why I am concerned here, knowing I know who you are, and what you do."

"You're absolutely correct Lee Anne. Let me start at the beginning, and I believe we can clear this up. You know me well Lee Anne, so this should not take too long. When I saw you last month, that was no chance meeting. I was in town visiting my old group when word of your abduction reached my former commander. I heard it was you. I told him I knew you, and because of the nature of my skills, I wanted in on the operation. Since I worked with him before, he agreed."

Continuing, "What you don't know is, I left the firm some time ago, to pursue my dreams. I'm not saying what my dreams are, because I know Brick is planning a surprise for you, and I don't want to spoil it. I might add, I'm glad I did because Brick's path crossed mine, and I'm so happy it did."

Lee Anne started putting it together in her head. "So, it was you in charge of the drone on the rescue operation?"

"That's right Lieutenant. I was not about to let someone else fly that drone when I was there. If you recall, I smiled and winked at you. I saw JET and C J there too, and I was not certain if something else was going on there, so I stayed in the shadows. When I drove up with Brick earlier, I was as shocked to see you as you were to see me. So, you see this time it truly is a matter of coincidence. Brick always refers to you all as his family, never saying your names. I haven't told him of my previous employment yet, but I planned on telling him over the holidays. Please Lee Anne, I need you to believe me. I love him so much, and I would never put him in harm's way. Meeting him has been incredibly special, and all I want is to make him feel the same way he makes me feel."

"Well Specialist Davis, that's quite a story you want us to believe," Lee Anne said. "What do you think ladies, should we believe her? Let's step outside, and you tell me what you think."

Lena saying, "Please do. My happiness, our happiness, depends on it."

Geena, Ronnie, and Lee Anne busted out laughing, Lee Anne saying, "Girl, we're pulling your leg. We believe you. Wait until we fill you in on this incredible year, which has been filled with many coincidences."

Lena saying, "Wow, you got me good. You had me scared there for a minute. Now I see firsthand why Brick loves you and why he always talks about you. You're really special."

Hugging her again, Geena said, "It's clear why Brick has been so happy since he's met you. Welcome to the family. Looks like we have another sister." Gathering around her and embracing her, "Sisters!" They were excited laughing gleefully. Ronnie said, "Phew, what a year we've had."

Geena said, "We'd better get going. We don't want a posse coming after us." Lena exclaiming, "What posse?" Lee Anne said, "We'll explain in the car." They headed out, Lena happy she had found new sisters, and was now a part of Brick's family.

On the way into town, Geena received a phone call. It was from Chet. "Hi Geena. I kind of messed things up, and I was hoping you could help me out." Geena said, "Tell me what's wrong Chet, maybe I can help you fix it." He continued, "Well, every holiday, my family is usually together. I forgot to tell my sister we were invited to Summit Meadows. When I finally did call her, she told me she turned down your invitation so we would all be together. Usually it's her, Will, along with his brother, me, and Peach's parents, who live in North Carolina. I feel so bad because we always spend the holidays together. I was wondering if the offer was still good, because if not, Peach's and I don't want them to be alone for the holidays and we will stay here to be with them."

Geena said, "No problem Chet, I understand. Tell them they are all welcome. We have plenty of space. We have a great big tree, with plenty of space for extra gifts under it. Come on, the more the merrier." Chet sighing with relief, "Thanks Geena, you're really helping me out here. I would never leave my sister and family out. We were so excited, I thought Peach's told her, and Peach's thought I told her. I'll let Cindy know and make the necessary arrangements for them to get there on my end. Thanks again." Geena said, "Ask Will to bring his bass with him, and let his brother know we have a set of drums here. All he must do is bring his accessories. See you all Tuesday." Chet saying, "Okay Geena."

Geena exclaimed; I've got great news! Cindy, Will, and his brother will be celebrating the holidays with us. Peach's parents will also be coming. I know you musicians are going to have a fantastic time." Ronnie elatedly saying, "That is great news. Jason and Brick will also be glad. We are going to have a blast. Lena, what are you and Brick cooking up?" Lena said, "Nice try girl. I'm not spilling the beans. You'll just have to wait and see. Don't worry, you won't have to wait much longer. Besides, if I tell you, Brick will be upset, and we all know we don't want that to happen."

Laughing, Lee Anne said, "I can tell you from personal experience, this lady is not going to divulge anything to you. She can keep a secret, trust me, I know firsthand. By the way Lena, we still must show you Ronnie's studio. You're going to love it, and you might get some use out of it." Lena responded, "I look forward to seeing it."

Arriving at the restaurant, Brick said, "We were just talking about rounding up a posse to look for you girls." Geena said, "Told you." They looked at each other and started laughing.

Geena told everyone Cindy, Will, and his brother were coming. Brick and Jason were excited to hear the news. They finished eating, went to the gazebo, and then headed back to Summit Meadows.

Chapter 45

Holiday Affair

Ronnie was up extra early, filled with inspiration to use the camera for some photographs of the sunrise. She walked around the grounds, taking various shots. Feeling further inspired, she drove into Summit Hills to the gazebo. She was able to take some great shots there as well, before heading back to Summit Meadows.

The ladies were up early Monday morning, bustling around in the kitchen preparing breakfast. Most of the food needed for the Christmas dinner already had been picked up or delivered. They would start preparing most of the food throughout the week, a little each day.

When Ronnie returned, the other ladies were downstairs. Geena said, "You certainly are up bright and early." Ronnie answering, "I woke up feeling inspired, so I grabbed the camera, and took some photos of the sunrise around the grounds. Then I jumped into the car and drove to the gazebo in Summit Hills. I got some great shots there also." Lee Anne said, "Sounds as if you had a very productive morning." Ronnie said, "Yes, I did. It has been some time since I did this. It felt great."

The guys were also up early, maintaining the grounds. They raked and bagged up the leaves. There had been a surge of gusty winds late last night, so they made sure the decorations were still in place. They had just finished putting everything away, when Ronnie and Lena asked them to come in and clean up for breakfast.

Gathering, they said the blessing and ate their food. Geena reminded them the others would be arriving tomorrow. They all could start trimming the Christmas tree, so everyone could place their gifts under the tree. The ladies also placed fresh fruits in baskets around the house. The house not only would look nice but smell nice too.

Brick, Ronnie, and Jason went to the studio, setting up and preparing the equipment for the in-house holiday show. John joined them, getting the camera and video equipment ready. Geena and Sarah walked around the house to see if any further decorations were needed to enhance the look. Everyone had done a marvelous job decorating and it did not seem as if anything else was needed.

Suddenly Geena turned to face Sarah exclaiming, "How could we have missed this?" Sarah looking surprised said, "Look at all of this. What could we have possibly missed?" waiving her hands in the air. Then a look of realization formed on her face. Looking at each other, they both said, "Mistletoe," both laughing.

Elaine came in and asked, "What are you two laughing about?" Lena and Lee Anne came in joining them, asking what was going on. Geena said, "We forgot to get mistletoe." Elaine started laughing with them. "I almost forgot myself, but don't worry, I have that area covered. I had completely forgotten I purchased some in town. They're in a shopping bag in the greenhouse."

Geena laughing, "Fantastic mom. I'll go get them and I'll ask dad to help us hang them around the house. We don't want Cupid to be upset with us." Lee Anne said, "As much as you and Matt love to smooch, I'm surprised this wasn't the first thing on your list." Geena saying, "Look who is talking. You and JET don't do too badly yourselves." Lena threw her two cents in, "I'm down for this. Brick and I love the fun and the recreation also."

Everyone laughing, Elaine said, "Well, I guess it's unanimous. Come on G, let's get the shopping bag and get busy. You grab the bag and I'll go grab your father." Laughing, Geena said, "That's right mom, go grab your man," everyone laughing.

They set about hanging the mistletoe throughout various parts of the house. There was plenty left over, so Ken hung some around the outside areas. There was mistletoe everywhere. Ken came back in and grabbed Elaine, pulling her under some mistletoe, saying, "Testing, testing, one, two, three," kissing Elaine. Geena said, "Aww, daddy." Ken said, "Don't be jealous, with your track records, I'm certain you will all catch up. I just decided to get a little head start," everyone laughing.

Sarah went and grabbed a camera. "I think we should take loads of pictures, start a scrapbook, and we will add to them every year." Elaine said, "That's a great idea Sarah. Don't forget to let John and Rob know, so we have plenty of shots."

Sarah said, "I bought some decorative battery-operated candles. We can place them around the house and on the tables for a special touch in the recording studio." Geena said, "I think that just about covers everything. Anything else we think of can be added on later."

Brick and the others had finished setting up everything in the studio and came out to join the ladies. Jason prepared a playlist of holiday music, which he turned on. The music was playing softly throughout the house. Not only did Summit Meadows look great inside and out, but there was also a pleasant aroma which filled the house, and the ambience of holiday music filled the air, along with the holiday spirit.

Another day was ending, and much had been accomplished. John said, "You ladies have been working unceasingly for the last week. Let's all go to town and eat at the restaurant tonight. Ronnie, you and I can get some photos of the town and gazebo all aglow.

In fact, I'll remind Rob when he gets here, we need to photograph the festivities at the town Christmas celebration." Sarah said, "That's a good idea honey, we were talking about doing the same around here, so we have a record of it." Geena said, "I'll call ahead and make reservations for us."

They got cleaned up and went to town. They had a wonderful dinner and when done, John and Sarah set about going around the town taking pictures. When they arrived at the gazebo, they found other people had the same idea about spending some time there. People were strolling about, holding hands, laughing and talking. It seemed their idea of hanging out there had caught on with everyone else.

Ronnie and Jason ran into the nightclub owner, who informed them there were three musicians who wanted to play with them at the event. Jason asked, "What instruments do they play?" He told them, trumpet, trombone, and guitar." Ronnie said, "That's fantastic!" He said, "There may also be two others. They play clarinet and flute. Do you think you guys can come into the club on Thursday to rehearse?"

Ronnie said, "I believe we can. We'll be bringing a bassist and percussionist with us. What about around four o'clock?" Answering, he said, "That sounds great. I'll arrange it so you can eat at the restaurant and enjoy each other's company after your rehearsal." Jason said, "Sounds like fun. See you Thursday." They continued to their favorite spot, the gazebo, staying there until it was time to leave.

Geena received a call from Chet, who advised her, "Peach's parents will arrive late Wednesday morning. They live in North Carolina, a couple of hours away, and will be driving in. Geena told Chet, "Everything will be ready for them when they arrive." Chet said, "Thanks Geena." Brick got Geena's attention, asking if he could speak to Chet. Geena said, "No problem Chet, see you tomorrow. Hold on, Brick wants to speak to you." Brick asked, "Chet, did you, Rob, and C J remember to give the 'Koach's Kids" their holiday gifts?" Answering, "Yes, already done." Brick said, "Fantastic! See you guys tomorrow." Chet said, "Okay." Satisfied, Brick handed Geena her phone saying, "Thanks G." She replied, "Sure Brick."

Everyone gathered back at the vehicles early because tomorrow and the next few days were going to be hectic. Arriving at Summit Meadows, Sarah said to John, "I'm not ready to go in yet honey. Let's go for a walk." John said, "Okay sweetie. Maybe we can find some more of that mistletoe. If not, we can kiss anyway." Ken and Elaine had similar ideas, and went to Geena and Matt's favorite spot, where they snuggled and kissed. Elaine said, "Mmm, I see why Geena loves it here. Kiss me again sweetie," Ken obliging her.

Ronnie and Jason headed for the studio, deciding to work on music for a little while.

Lena said to Brick, "Honey, I need to speak with you." Brick said, "This sounds important. Come on, we can use Matt's office." Lena brought him up to speed regarding her previous career. Brick was paying close attention to her story. When she finished Brick came over to her, and gently pulled her into his arms. He said, "You're a woman who is special and I am proud you're in my life. Thank you for your service and thank you for wanting to share this with me. It changes nothing. You are fierce and most of all, I know you love me. I want you to know I love you very much," looking deeply into her eyes and then kissing her.

It was getting late. Everyone was returning to their quarters. Brick walked Lena to her room, kissing her and saying goodnight. Jason took Ronnie to her room, kissing her goodnight. Ronnie slowly closed the door, smiling at Jason, with him loving every passing second. John and Sarah returned from their stroll, running into Ken and Elaine. John said, "Did you enjoy your smooching?" Ken winking, "Probably just as much as you and Sarah." They laughed, going to their quarters.

Geena said, "Sounds like everyone is in, turning the alarm system on. Goodnight Lee Anne." Lee Anne responding, "Goodnight Geena." Both delighted their guys had landed safely in New York.

Matt and JET arrived safely back in New York from Texas. They let C J and Rob know they were back, then went out for some dinner. They let Geena and Lee Anne know also, calling them again when they returned from dinner. C J advised them arrangements were made for everyone to be picked up, to be taken to the airport. He also arranged to have JET's parents picked up when they landed from Canada. Matt told C J they would drive to the airport themselves, so they could make sure the aircrafts were serviced and ready for take-off.

Arriving early, JET and Matt made sure their aircraft was ready. They were doing the final check of the plane when the vehicles arrived with everyone. They were glad to see one another and excited about the holiday. Matt and the guys made sure the luggage was stowed away properly and assisted the ladies on-board. JET and Paul checked out the second aircraft.

Everyone safely seated on-board, they taxied to the runway and after receiving the go ahead from the tower, they lifted off for Summit Hill. Matt called Geena, giving her the approximate ETA. She advised him the guys would be there waiting for them when they landed. She said, "Everyone is excitedly anticipating your arrival. I can't wait to see you baby. You guys be safe." Matt saying, "We will. See you soon sweetie." Geena and Lee Anne were anxious to see their guys.

Ronnie and the rest of the ladies were up early preparing brunch. They were making sure everything would be ready for the new arrivals. John and Brick were going to drive the Suburban's. Ken and Jason would drive the SUV's. They departed for the airport, so they would be waiting when the aircraft landed.

They did not have to wait long. John pointing said, "There they are." Landing their aircraft, they taxied to the hangar and the waiting vehicles.

Glad to see each other, they assisted the ladies and baby to the vehicles, then transferred the luggage from the planes to the vehicles. Working together, they were swift with their chore and were now ready to head for Summit Meadows.

They talked excitedly about being together once again, and how they were eagerly looking forward to the various events. It did not take them long to reach Summit Meadows, blowing the horns when they drove up. Geena and Lee Anne were ahead of the others, running straight into Matt and JET's arms.

The others were close behind, gathering around, and welcoming them to Summit Meadows. No sooner than they gathered around the new arrivals, there was the sound of another car horn. Geena looked at Peach's and said, "Surprise." It was Peach's parents. They had called Geena, advising they would be coming in a day earlier, so they could arrive and surprise Peach's.

Matt took control saying, "Welcome everyone. Let's take this into the house and get everyone settled, otherwise we will be out here all day. Guys, please lend a hand with the luggage and take them to the proper quarters."

Geena adding, "You can get yourselves settled, and then come back down. We have prepared a fantastic brunch for everyone. How does that sound to you?"

Everyone was excited, moving into the house. The ladies showing them to their quarters, and the men set about the task of getting their luggage to their rooms. With all the manpower, it did not take long to get everything and everyone to their proper quarters.

Coming back downstairs, they gathered in the dining area, giving thanks and enjoying their meal.

Geena said, "If anyone has anything still needed to be purchased, we will be more than happy to take you to town. We have been preparing food all week, but for the last few days we have been dining at the restaurant in town. If you would like, we could do the same this evening. We would love to show you around, as the town has gone all out decorating and it looks beautiful." Ronnie said, "There is going to be a Christmas tree lighting ceremony on Christmas eve. There will be loads of entertainment, which I'm sure you will enjoy." Lee Anne adding, "When we return here, we will have our own celebration."

Sarah said, "We decorated all of Summit Meadows, but we thought everyone would like to take part in trimming the tree, and then placing your gifts under them." Brick said, "You're going to like the show we have put together for your entertainment." Tina said, "Trust me. You're going to love it. We were here for Thanksgiving, and it was simply wonderful."

Everyone was excited, saying they could not wait for all the gala events planned. Cindy said, "I'm so excited, I could burst wide open. It sounds like we are in for a grand time. I'm grateful all our families are here, making us one great big happy family."

Matt said, "That's the general idea. We're hoping everyone enjoys themselves enough to make it an annual event." Everyone applauded and agreed they liked the concept.

Geena said, "I'll call the restaurant to make the reservations for this evening. I'm so happy and I'm looking forward to our time being together. If anyone has any suggestions, or wants to do something else, please feel free to tell us. If there is anything you need, please don't hesitate to let us know. We would like for everyone to enjoy your stay." Peach's exclaimed, "Let's start trimming the Christmas tree," everyone agreeing.

John said, "Come on guys, let's get the camera and video equipment. We will probably be able to take a lot of great shots." Jason turned on the music, and everyone began singing as they decorated the tree. They were finished in no time, and had a great time doing it.

John said, "Gather around the tree so we can take some photographs of everyone together. We'll also take shots of the individual families, and any other shots you may want." Rob said, "I was able to capture a lot of footage on video. Before you leave, I will compile the footage I took and put it on a DVD. I'll make copies for you before you leave."

Matt said, "Of course, if any of you brought a camera, feel free to take your own shots. There are areas around the grounds you might like to capture, so feel free to explore."

Ronnie said, "We better get going to the restaurant. If we leave now, we will be able to eat and still be able to view the sunset. Soon after, the lights in town will start coming on and at the gazebo. You're going to love it. If you have a camera, you might want to bring it, because you're going to be able to take a lot of great shots."

They piled into the vehicles and headed for Summit Hills. Arriving at the restaurant, they enjoyed their meals and each other, talking, laughing, and having a fantastic time. Ronnie was right, the sunset was beautiful, and the lights started to come on shortly afterwards.

Jason's parents and Peach's parents were walking together. Tina said to Delores, "This is simply beautiful." Delores nodding, "It sure is. I bet the tree lighting is going to be beautiful. I'm looking forward to it."

Everyone walked around town and the gazebo, snapping pictures and having a marvelous time. Soon, they headed back for Summit Meadows. When they arrived, the grounds were aglow with twinkling lights.

They went into the house, enjoying each other's company. Some decided to take walks around the grounds, while others stayed in the house talking to each other. There was a group who wanted to go into town tomorrow. Ronnie and Jason said they would take them.

Matt and Geena went outside to their favorite spot. "You've all done a marvelous job decorating the house, and the town is simply beautiful. Everyone seems to be enjoying themselves, don't you think?" Geena shaking her head in agreement, "Yes, everyone seems happy. This was a wonderful idea, and it's turning out better than I expected. I'm glad we decided to make this an annual event. We seem to be getting closer and more comfortable with one another." Matt agreed with Geena.

"I've missed you G. It's great holding you in my arms again." Geena pulled Matt closer to her, kissing him warmly and tenderly, only stopping briefly to say, "I've missed you too baby." Matt gently pulling her back, kissing her softly. First on her nape, then behind her ear, before letting his lips travel to hers. Geena thinking, this man always drives me crazy when he does this, enjoying every minute, their kisses growing more urgent.

Matt was thinking, this woman fills me with delight, and she drives me nuts. I love the way she melts into my arms, pressing her body close into mine. I don't know how much longer I can hold out. I want her to be with me all the time. The surprise I'm planning for her will be well worth the waiting. I can hardly wait to propose to her. Matt said to Geena, "Here comes JET and Lee Anne." She said, "Jason and Ronnie are coming too. Let's head inside, tomorrow is another long day and I know you must be tired. You've had a couple of busy days." Matt said, "No argument from me sweetie, but before we go, give me one last kiss please," taking her again into his arms, Geena not resisting and willing to comply. She loved being in Matt's arms.

Jeff, Tina, Paul, and Marie were in the kitchen eating a snack when JET and Lee Anne returned. Shortly after, Ronnie and Jason came in, then Brick and Lena. They went up just before Matt and Geena came in.

Brick and Lena returned from their walk, going into the house. Matt said, "Looks like the kids are all back. Let's go in sweetie." They went in, Matt setting the alarm. Geena said, "It looks like everyone has turned in," as they walked up the stairs.

John said, "The kids are all back." Nodding, Ken said, "Great. You guys want to play another hand before we turn in?" Sarah said, "Sure, sounds like a plan." Delores said, "Your turn to deal honey," Jacob dealing out the cards.

In the morning, Ronnie again awoke feeling inspired, but this time she wanted to visit the gazebo in Summit Hill first. She did not want to go alone, so she called Jason to go with her. Jason thought it was a fantastic idea and said he would be ready to go in a few minutes. They met downstairs, Ronnie coming over to Jason and giving him a good morning kiss. Jason was thinking this was a great way to start the day, holding Ronnie in his arms and kissing her back.

Jason said, "Good morning honey, I'm glad you called. This is a great way to start the day." Ronnie smiling, "Good morning. I thought it would be nice for us to catch the first rays of sunlight. Come on, let's go. It will be a shame not to be at the gazebo on time and miss it."

They got the car and drove off to Summit Hill. They parked the car on the edge of town and walked to the gazebo. Ronnie and Jason weren't disappointed, catching the first rays beaming through the trees. Then a fiery ball, ablaze above the gazebo, which casted a shadow along the ground. Sunlight was sparkling off the lei around the top and sides of the gazebo. It looked like a spaceship in the middle of the field.

Ronnie took a lot of great shots. They stayed a few minutes more before driving back to Summit Meadows. It was going to be another beautiful day. Jason told Ronnie he was going to the studio to do some work, kissing her before he went in. Ronnie went into the kitchen and joined the ladies. She said, "Good morning," everyone responding.

Geena said, "I see you felt inspired again." Smiling, Ronnie said, "Yes I did, but this time I took Jason with me. I was able to take some good pictures." Lee Anne laughing, "Are you sure that's all you took?" Ronnie smiling and winking at her, "I may have gotten some other things too." Lena said, "It sounds like you got more than pictures girl," everyone laughing. Tina said, "I like how you two are starting your days out together. It's sweet dear." Ronnie said, "Thank you Mrs. Taylor," going over and giving her a big hug.

When Jason entered the studio, he found Brick and Rob working. He said, "Good morning gentlemen." Looking up, they said good morning back to Jason. Brick said, "We were just going over the details for the events coming up." The door opened, Will and Ben entering. They all said good morning. Will said, "We thought we would practice for the rehearsal tomorrow." Jason answering, "It looks like we all had the same idea. The only one who is missing is Ronnie. Maybe I should get her so we can do this together." Ben said, "Sounds good. When we meet with the others tomorrow, we will already sound tight, which will make everything easier. We should be able to develop a good flow."

Jason went to get Ronnie, explaining what was going on in the studio. She looked around to say something, but Geena was already ahead of her. "Go ahead Ronnie and do your thing. We've got things covered." Ronnie said thanks, "We'll be finished soon, and then we can take those of you who want to shop into town." Geena said, "Don't worry about it, Lee Anne and I will take them." Ronnie said, "Thanks again G."

No one was hungry, so no breakfast had been prepared. It seemed everyone was content with getting something to drink and grabbing some sweet buns. Matt, C J, and JET were busy on the phone with Jacob Meyers, working on details for the Grand Rapid Falls event. Jacob reminded them he would be returning to New York after the holidays. He had been in constant contact with Ronnie's assistant, Cindy. Everything seemed to be on schedule in Texas and New York.

Geena and Lee Anne took the group who wanted to shop, to Summit Hills. Those who were not working on any projects, just relaxed and had a free day for themselves. Before Geena left, it was agreed they go into town tonight to eat. Most of the food was already prepared for dinner Christmas eve. Only the desserts remained, which would be made in the morning.

Matt and the rest of the guys finished their call with Jacob and joined the ladies, sitting around and talking in the dining area. Brick excused himself, going up to his room to make a call to Seth Howard.

"Hi Uncle Seth, how are you doing?" Seth answering, "Hey young man, I'm fine. Thanks for asking. To what do I owe the pleasure of this call?" Brick responding, "I wanted to ask you for a favor," explaining what he was planning.

Seth said, "I sure can. This is fantastic news. I was just speaking with them last evening about you. They wanted to know who this guy was Lena chose to be with over the holidays, rather than coming home. I hope you don't mind, but I told them you were a nice young man. I also told them what I felt your intentions were, and of how well you were handling the situation. So, you see, this call is perfect timing." Brick said, "Great Uncle Seth. Thank you very much." Seth said, "Let me set up a video chat, and you can handle your business."

Lena's parents responded to Seth's video invitation within a few minutes. He introduced Brick to Isaiah and Karen Davis. Brick said it was a pleasure meeting them and thanked them for this unorthodox meeting. He apologized about not being able to meet them in person, and alluded to his plans for their daughter, asking for their blessings.

Seth said he introduced them, and he already gave Brick his blessing. Isaiah and Karen were impressed with Brick's thoughtfulness, and they believed the young man when he related his feelings about their daughter.

Isaiah said to Brick, "I don't want to be rude, but is that your real first name?" Responding, "No sir. That's my nickname. My actual name is Samuel David sir." Seth laughing, "I saw the look on your face when I told you his name was Brick big guy," continuing to laugh.

Brick said, "Thanks a lot Uncle Seth," laughing. They all were laughing now, Seth saying, "I knew you would handle your business. I just wanted to see his face." Brick thanked them again. They spoke a few more minutes before the video chat was terminated.

Brick was both relieved and elated. His plans were coming together, thinking Lena is going to be surprised Christmas eve. Now, on to the last thing to do on his list before tomorrow. He went to get C J and Matt, telling them he would like to speak to them. They excused themselves, going to the office to talk. Brick said, "You're my big brothers, and I want you to be among the first to know what I'm planning," explaining what he had done.

Elated, they jumped up hugging him, shaking his hand. They offered their congratulations. "Matt said, "I'm proud of you. Lena seems like a wonderful young lady, and I'm certain both of you will be happy."

C J jumped in, "Now we just have to get him married to Geena."

Laughing, Matt said, "Don't start with me C J." Brick joining in said, "I'm not in this, I knew what to do. I've got mine," laughing as they went out the door. "Remember, mum is the word." Upon their return, Geena asked, "Is everything okay?" Taking her in his arms and kissing her on the cheek, Matt said, "Things are just fine sweetie."

Almost dinner time, they departed for the restaurant in Summit Hill. They finished eating and walked around town, ending up at the gazebo. The area was alive and electric, filled with excitement in the air, others also walking around the grounds enjoying the evening.

Not wanting to be out late, they went back to the vehicles and headed back to Summit Meadows. It was decided everyone could open one gift on Christmas eve. Brick thought it was a good idea, and it would be a perfect time to surprise Lena with his proposal.

They further enjoyed each other's company before splitting up to do their own thing. Having the same idea, everyone returned to the house early, retiring to their rooms. Thursday was going to be a big day, making sure everything was in place and ready for the Christmas celebration, here and in Summit Hill.

The excitement continuing to build, everyone was up early, pitching in to make a buffet breakfast. Gathering in the dining area, they ate and joked with one another.

Rob said he had taken some great pictures of the Koach's Kids holiday celebration and thought it would be a great idea to incorporate them in with the festivities here. Ronnie agreed, suggesting they create a gallery at the gym, with photos of the various events and activities. C J and Brick thought it was a great idea and thanked her.

Brick suggested they could hang photos around the Starfire, utilizing photos from the guest performers, and the various events. Ronnie agreeing and saying it would be easy to include it into the décor.

The musicians were excited about the rehearsal at the club later, and the dinner afterwards, everyone agreeing to meet them there to make it a big celebration. Geena got right up to make a reservation. She said, "We sure have been keeping them busy." Laughing, Lee Anne said, "I'm sure they don't mind G."

Matt and JET decided to drive out to the airport, to make certain the helicopter they were utilizing for Santa was ready. They also wanted to speak with the owner. He was adamant about not wanting to take any compensation for the rental of the helicopter, citing he wanted to do his part for the town's celebration.

Elaine said, "We should be finished baking, and we will be ready when it is time to leave." Sarah asking, "Can anyone think of anything we may have overlooked?" No one had anything to add. Brick chuckling said, "At this point, if we did, I suppose it will have to wait until next year," everyone laughing. Jason said, "Here we go, the Brick Comedy Hour," everyone laughing. Brick responding, "Stick to your horn kid, Santa tells the jokes."

Lena couldn't resist, "Oh, is that right Santa baby? I think Mrs. Claus may have a couple up her sleeve." Everybody was cracking up, C J saying, "Oh, oh. Looks like Santa has got some competition." Ronnie adding, "Look out Santa baby!" Everyone was in tears from the laughter. The way this week was going, they were going to need next week to rest up before New Year's.

The musicians left for their rehearsal. Matt said to Geena, "We won't be long G, kissing her goodbye." JET kissed Lee Anne, and they left.

The rest of the group stayed with the ladies in the dining area, waiting for the desserts to finish baking. Matt and JET were satisfied with the helicopter and returned to Summit Meadows.

Meanwhile, the musicians had gathered at the club and the rehearsal was moving along at a fast pace. They were in the pocket, playing well, grooving and enjoying themselves. The club owner remarking they sounded great together. They were almost finished.

Everyone enjoying themselves, Geena said, "I suppose we'd better leave for the restaurant. Ronnie and the other musicians should almost be done. It probably will be best if we eat and return here early to relax. We have an exciting and busy day planned for tomorrow." Everyone agreed. They left to meet the musicians at the restaurant.

Finishing the rehearsal, the musicians packed up and prepared to take the short walk to the restaurant. The club owner said they could leave their instruments there and pick them up when they returned for their cars, which were parked in the club's parking lot.

Jason and Ronnie were trailing behind the group, holding hands. Jason said, "That was a great rehearsal. It sounded like we have been playing together for a long time." Ronnie agreeing, "Yes, I'm glad we got our groove on yesterday. Today seemed to be a continuation of what we did."

They got to the restaurant just as Matt and the others arrived. Matt asked how the rehearsal went. They told him it went well. They had the restaurant just about to themselves, as they were shown to their tables. The owner asked for everyone's attention, the room becoming silent. He said, "We're a small family town. In case you didn't know it, the night club owner is my brother and so is the mayor," beckoning his brother to come stand beside him.

Continuing, "We have been extremely blessed and fortunate with your presence here in Summit Hill. My brother the mayor, could not be with us this evening, something about running the town," pausing for effect, everyone laughing. "I'm certain the windbag will have something to say tomorrow, you know politicians, they can't resist." Brick saying, "Oh this is just great, everybody is a comedian," everyone continuing to laugh.

The owner of the restaurant continued, "We just want to let you know how much we appreciate you. You have brought our town together and it is wonderful we will be celebrating this holiday with you. There are more announcements, but I'll leave something for the mayor to do. I don't want to upset his busy schedule," the laughter continuing. "We want to thank you by letting you know; tonight's dinner is on us." They cheered and applauded at the announcement.

Matt stood and approached the owner, shaking his hand, asking if he could say something. The owner told him to go right ahead. "Thank you all for showing us your hospitality. We have been greatly blessed this year and decided to come together as a family to celebrate this past Thanksgiving. Speaking further, we decided to celebrate this holiday together as well. Someone suggested incorporating Summit Hill into the mix. We contacted your brother the mayor, and the Town Council," pausing, everyone laughing. Continuing, "They were excited about the idea, and the rest is history. The town got busy, and here we are. Thank you again." Brick yelled out, "Thanks for keeping it short

Matt. Now let's eat!" Everyone laughed. Dinner was soon served.

Aware of the time, they finished, said thanks again and started back for Summit Meadows. Ronnie and the musicians got their belongings from the club and followed. Reaching home safely, they relaxed and retired early, as Friday was going to be an even busier day.

Matt and JET were going to meet the owner of the helicopter and find a safe place to land, away from the gazebo. They decided to leave early so they could return to Summit Meadows to pick up everyone.

When they spoke with the helicopter owner yesterday, they realized trying to land the craft close to the gazebo would not be safe. Not wanting to get the choppers blades entangled with any light strands, they came up with a contingency plan. Better safe, than sorry.

One of the men in town had a Dodge Ram which was red. They arranged for the sheriff to escort the truck to the gazebo, with Santa and Mrs. Claus on board. The sheriff knew of some other guys with similar trucks, who agreed to join the procession, bringing Santa's helpers. They agreed to pick up Santa's helpers and to meet where the chopper was going to land. There would be a procession from the LZ to the gazebo, with all the fanfare. Sirens blaring and lights flashing, the kids would love the excitement.

They found a safe area where the chopper could land, creating a safe perimeter with flares. Matt and Jet would light the flares when the chopper approached, guiding the pilot in for a safe landing. They all would jump into the vehicles, and process to the gazebo. Mission completed, Matt and JET returned to Summit Meadows.

They ate something light and relaxed with the others, until it was time to leave. Geena told everyone, the plan was to go to the event in Summit Hill, return to Summit Meadows, get cleaned up, and have dinner with one another. After dinner, they would gather around the tree, and everyone would be allowed to open one gift. Afterwards, they would gather in the studio for the performance planned for them.

They left early, so the men could help transport the gifts stored at the church, to the gazebo. Everything was going according to plan.

The towns people had gathered at the gazebo, and it was almost time for Santa to make his appearance. The mayor asked for everyone's attention. "This is a great event which has been planned for the people of Summit Hill. There has been an abundance of cooperation from you all, to make this a success, and I thank you. I am proud to announce, the Town Council has unanimously approved Summit Hill make this Christmas tree lighting ceremony, an annual event." Everyone was cheering and applauding. The children were jumping up and down with excitement and glee. The mayor continued, "Further, they also approved there be an annual New Year's Eve countdown, to be held right here at the Summit Hill Gazebo. What do you all think about that?" Again, cheering and applause. "Ms. Lee Anne Howard has designed an apparatus which will light up, after the countdown begins, bringing in the New Year. So, bring your horns and noise makers to help celebrate New Year's Eve. Hey, listen everybody, what's that I hear… could it be Santa?" The children began jumping up and down with excitement, yelling out, "Santa, Santa." The DJ began playing "Here Comes Santa Claus."

The chopper flew past them, not flying too close, moving towards the landing zone. Matt and JET lit the battery-operated flares around the perimeter and guided the pilot in for a safe landing. They jumped into the waiting vehicles, ready to begin the short ride to the gazebo. The lights were flashing, with sirens and horns blaring as they approached the gazebo and Santa's throne. The children were laughing and yelling, jumping up and down with excitement.

Santa helped Mrs. Claus out of the decorated truck saying, "Ho, ho, ho. Merry Christmas boys and girls, Merry Christmas one, and all," waving to everyone. Mrs. Claus and Santa's helpers following suit, as they headed for Santa's throne.

Santa said, "Ho, ho, ho! Have you all been good boys and girls?" The children excitedly answering, "Yes Santa, yes Santa!" Brick and Lena were enjoying themselves. "Very good, ho, ho, ho. Come on Mrs. Claus and Santa's helpers, let's give these gifts out to these wonderful children, ho, ho, ho!" Mrs. Claus started calling the names of all the children, and Santa's helpers passed out the gifts to the eagerly waiting children. She said, "Make sure you take them home and place them under the tree. Santa will be there later after you're asleep, to bring the rest of your presents. Don't forget to leave Santa some milk and cookies, and Merry Christmas!" The children were saying, "Thank you Santa, thank you Santa!"

Santa said, "Ho, ho, ho! I must go now to get my reindeer and sleigh. I have a lot of deliveries for all the other children everywhere. Bye boys and girls." Santa, Mrs. Claus, and Santa's helpers got into the vehicles, heading back to the chopper, lights flashing, siren and horns blaring. As the chopper flew past, everyone heard Santa on the exterior sound system, "Merry Christmas to one and all, and to all have a good night… ho, ho, ho!" The children were jumping and waving goodbye.

The mayor said, "Don't go anywhere, the fun is just beginning. We've a live show prepared for you before you return home for your individual family celebrations. Play some music Mr. DJ, everyone be merry and dance!" The DJ started playing music and everyone began dancing. Brick and everyone changed out of their costumes, returning to the celebration.

Ronnie and the musicians started the live show, performing and singing Christmas songs. Everyone joined in, having a good time. Cognizant of the time, they ended the show. All the lights were turned off, except for the Christmas tree, and the battery-operated candles everyone had. The musicians started to play, "Silent Night, Holy Night."

Ronnie said, "Come on, join in everybody," as everyone started singing, waving their candles high above them. They finished and the band yelled out Merry Christmas to the gathering. Everyone was hugging and saying Merry Christmas, departing for their homes. The night was a great success. The band packed their things, thanking each other, and headed for home.

Reaching Summit Meadows, the musicians set up their instruments and equipment in the studio, so they would be ready to perform. Everyone went to change and to prepare for dinner.

The ladies had everything organized and ready to serve. They had set the table earlier today before they left for Summit Hill. They gathered in the dining area, said the blessing, and began to eat. Still excited, they began talking about the celebration at the gazebo. Sarah said, "Those children were so excited and happy." Peach's mom Delores agreed and said, "They were absolutely in a frenzy when the helicopter flew over, and when Santa and his entourage pulled up. To be honest, I was just as excited."

Geena said, "Brick, you and Lena did a marvelous job, in fact, you did so well, you should play Santa again tonight when we gather around the tree." Brick jumping right in, "Ho, ho, ho! Have you all been good boys and girls?" everyone laughing. "Ready to help me again Mrs. Claus?" Lena laughing, "I sure am. After all, I can't let Santa have all the fun." Elaine said, "Yes, you all were extremely organized."

Cindy said, "Oh my goodness, you musicians were just fabulous. I was really enjoying myself. You sounded great together. The ending was wonderful. The singing of "Silent Night," everyone waving the candles, was a moving finish to the celebration. Rob and John said they were able to capture some great video footage and photos of the event.

Matt said, "You all worked extremely hard planning and executing this event. It was truly a labor of love, and it's fantastic the Town Council voted to make this an annual affair, along with a New Year's Celebration. Lee Anne, that was a great idea you had for the New Year's Eve celebration, reminiscent of Times Square." Lee Anne said, "Thank you Matt. Everyone had marvelous input for this holiday affair. When we start something, we sure get into it!"

Finishing their meal, as usual, everyone pitched in to help put the food away and clean up. Geena said, "Let's all gather around the tree and continue with the festivities." John and Rob went to get the cameras, and Jason put the music on softly in the background. Cindy and Lee Anne organized an area for the gifts which were going to be opened tonight. Santa started, "Ho, ho, ho!" Gather around boys and girls," calling out for "Mrs. Claus!" Answering, Mrs. Claus said, "Yes Santa baby." Santa saying, "Let's pass out the gifts, ho, ho, ho!" After all the gifts had been passed out, Mrs. Claus said, "Here's your gift Santa baby," saying she loved him.

Not to be outdone, Santa said, "I happen to know you were an extremely good girl this year, and this is for you my special girl." Brick gave her a beautifully wrapped box, asking her to open it. Inside the box was a white gold chain, with a diamond heart hanging from it. "That represents my heart I am willingly giving to you. I hope you will treasure it always." Lena saying, "It's beautiful Brick. Yes, I will always take care of your heart," turning so he could place it around her neck. Brick said, "Do you like the other item in the box?" She said, "There's nothing else in the box."

Brick responding, "Sure there is. Look again please." Showing him the empty box Lena said, "See, there's nothing else in it." Brick scratching his head, "I can't believe this."

Taking her hand and placing it in his, he began saying, "Lena, when I first saw you, I knew you were someone special and I knew I found someone I wanted to spend my life with. When I was introduced to you, I took your hand and placed in mine, just as I am doing now. I said to you I would never ever let it, or you go. I called and spoke to your parents, requesting their blessings, which they gave, along with Uncle Seth."

Getting down on his knee, opening the small box from his pocket, he said, "I love you so much. Brenda Helena Davis, will you grant me the pleasure of sharing my life with you, and gladden my heart, by becoming my wife? I love you so much."

Lena was trembling, tears of joy flowing from eyes, and smiling. She was nodding her head up and down. Finally finding her voice, she said, "Yes, yes Brick. I would love to become your wife, I'm so in love with you," pulling him up to her, and going into his arms kissing him.

Everyone was happy for them. Geena came over to Brick and Lena, hugging them both. Gathering around them, everyone offered their congratulations and best wishes. While they were gathered around them, Geena slipped outside. Ronnie saw Geena leave, going after her. Matt also noticed, having an idea with what might be wrong with her.

Ronnie said, "G, are you okay?" Geena said, "Sure Ronnie, I'm fine. I'll be back in a minute. I just needed some air." Ronnie responded, "No you're not alright. You are upset because you are wishing Matt asked you to marry him." Geena saying, "Don't get me wrong, I'm extremely happy for them both, but I'm just wondering when it is going to be my turn. I love Matt and I want to be with him. I'm not selfish, but I just want to be happy." Ronnie went over to Geena and began hugging her, asking her not to cry.

"Geena, I know you both well and I know Matt loves you. Matt is special, and you know it. What Brick did was extremely romantic. However, you know Matt likes to do special things for you. Geena, you told me so yourself. The way your first date was, he made sure everything was romantic and perfect for you. You must know he has to be planning something special for you. Just be patient. You know, as well as I, whatever he is planning, will top this and be special for you both. Now pull yourself together, before everyone thinks something is wrong, and let's go back inside."

Geena said, "I know you're right. It's just I'm becoming anxious. Thank you for coming to see about me. I love you and I am glad you are in my life, my little sister," hugging her.

They went back inside. Lee Anne came over, "Everything okay?" Ronnie said, "Everything is fine. We were just discussing some details." Lee Anne said, "It's great news about Brick and Lena." Geena saying, "Yes, I'm so happy for them both. Come on, let's go back over and join them."

Geena said to everyone, "This has been an amazing evening thus far, and there is more to come. Let's all grab our dates and gather in the studio to enjoy the performance which has been prepared for us."

Pairing off and taking their significant other's hand, they went into the studio. Brick said, "Hey everyone, use these headsets to listen to the performance, and let me know if you like them." Brick was the MC, opening with a few jokes, everyone laughing, Brick setting them up for the rest of the entertainment to follow.

Jason, and the rest of the musicians played, along with Ronnie, who also sang, everyone enjoying the performances. Brick asked Lena to come up front, telling everyone they were in for a treat. Lena had them all laughing uncontrollably. Lena finished, Brick said, "We are almost done with everything. Just a couple of more things to go."

Geena leaned in close to Matt, saying, "I've been trying to figure where I've seen Lena before. Now I know why she seems familiar to me. She was in Salt Lake City, and received an award for Best New Comedienne, remember?" Matt nodding his head said, "Yes, now I do remember. She is quite a funny lady."

Brick continued, "I told you there were going to be a lot of surprises. So far, have I kept my word, and are you enjoying yourselves?" Everyone applauded and agreed. He said, "This is so much of a surprise, the next participants don't even know about it. You could always count on them to do something special, and it always turned out to be beautiful. So, not to keep you in further suspense, Geena and Matt, please come to the front and gladden our hearts with one of your beautiful renditions."

Elaine leaned over to Sarah, "It's been so long since those two have performed together. Brick is right, some are going to be extremely surprised." Sarah, John, and Ken nodding their heads in agreement. Brick said, "Come on you two, you're not getting out of this. Let's go!"

Matt looked at Geena and said, "He set us up very smoothly. I suppose we have no choice. What do you say?" Geena said, "Yep, he got us good. We're going to have to think of something to pay him back." Matt saying, "We will. Why don't we do that arrangement of "O Holy Night," we used to do?" Geena said, "Okay, do you remember it?" Smiling, Matt said, "Do you?" They started towards the front, Matt for the piano, and Brick handed Geena a microphone.

Matt said to the musicians, "Feel free to play along. We'll be in the key of F major. Ronnie, please play strings on the other keyboard."

Matt began to play, the others joining in, recognizing "O Holy Night." Geena began singing, everyone surprised. Not wanting to miss this, Rob grabbed the video camera, and John grabbed the camera to take some photos. Geena sang beautifully with her soprano voice, Matt and the rest of the musicians accompanying her. When they finished everyone rose and applauded their beautiful performance.

Brick said, "Surprise! Did everyone enjoy that?" Everyone still clapping. "I know somewhere down the line, I'm going to have to pay for this, but it was worth it to hear them again. It's been a long time."

Brick continued, "Well, in for a penny, in for a pound. You guys stay right where you are and close us out. This is something we can all take part in." Brick looked at Ronnie and Matt, as they began playing "Silent Night," Ronnie and Geena singing a duet. Then Jason did a verse on the sax before everyone else joined in singing with them.

After finishing, Jason put on some soft music to dance by. Excited about the headsets, everyone asked Brick about them. John said, "These headphones are fantastic. I could hear the music, feel the beat to the music, and still hear what was being said around me." The rest of the group was also excited. Brick responding said, "A good friend of mine developed the headphones, which will be available to the general public in the next few months. I will be utilizing them on our virtual floor at the Starfire for the grand opening." Ken said, "That's a great idea Brick. People are going to love them. Your friend has a fantastic product." Brick said, "Thanks for trying them everyone. I wish I had a pair to give you, but I need these for the club. Don't worry, they will be available to you soon. My friend will be elated knowing you liked them." The men moved the tables and chairs to the side, making space in the middle of the floor for them to dance. Nat "King" Cole's, "The Christmas Song" was playing. It was a beautiful way to end the evening. Everyone said Merry Christmas and headed for their rooms.

Matt said to Geena, "Let's go for walk sweetie, kissing her on her cheek." Geena said, "Ok baby, let's go." They walked around the grounds for a few minutes, saying nothing, just holding hands. Of course, they ended up in their favorite spot on the patio. Matt began, "G, I have something important to say to you regarding this evening. I saw your reaction tonight and it seemed you were a little upset. I believe I know why, so I want to clear some things up. I know being apart from each other has become taxing on us. We have been extremely busy with our careers, making choices to forge ahead. I want you to know I love you very much. It's been hard on me too, because I don't wish to be separated from you any longer. It's been unbearable. You are in my thoughts every day, all day. Please, don't give up on us. They say, good things come to those who have the patience to wait it out. We're almost at the finish line, sweetie. My life would have less meaning if you're not there to fill it. I love you." Geena started to cry. "Sweetie, please don't cry. I don't want to make you sad. I want to fill you with happiness, the way you make me feel," wiping her tears away. Geena looked at Matt and said, "Baby, these aren't tears of sadness. They are tears of joy. You do make me feel happy and blessed. Loving you is wonderful."

Matt gently pulled Geena closer to him, wrapping his arms around her. She felt so safe and at peace when she was in his arms. He caressed the back of her arms, sending goosebumps up and down them. Matt began kissing the back of her nape and behind her ear, making her start to tremble. Then his kisses moved across her cheek, finally meeting her waiting lips. Always trusting him, Geena allowed herself to let go, enjoying being in his arms, enjoying the sensations he always evoked. She parted her lips to accept his kisses, responding to him, all her senses were being heightened.

Matt enjoyed being with Geena like this. The feeling of holding her in his arms, was exquisite and exhilarating. He loved the way she allowed her body to surrender in his arms, trusting he would not take advantage of her. It felt like she was absorbing his love, creating a warm sensuous aura which swept over them both. He always had this feeling of sensation for Geena, which heightened as time went by.

It does not matter when he is apart from her. This magic has always been a part of him, and he knew it always would be.

Elaine said, "Turn the lights off guys, and come join me. There's something beautiful I want you to see." Turning off the lights, they came to join her at the window. She said, "Look at our children. They are so in love and have always been. There has never been a doubt in any of our minds they would be together one day." Sarah said, "Yes, they have always looked out for one another, as well as their friends. I always knew Geena would be our daughter, and Matt would be your son." Ken said, "The depth and caring they both have, probably would have gotten in their way, not allowing them the success they have found. But I think they have figured out they can do it together now." John said, "I think your assessment is right Ken, and I have a feeling wedding bells are in the air, coming very soon."

Sarah said, "Look everyone, it's beginning to snow." Elaine said, "Yes, and it looks as if our lovebirds see it too."

Matt stopped kissing Geena, looking deeply into her eyes he said, "I love you G, always have, and always will." Geena responding said, "Ditto baby," briefly kissing him again. "Look Matt, it's beginning to snow." Grabbing her hand Matt said, "Come on G." They looked up at the snow, as the first snowflakes gently swirled and danced around them. Matt took Geena into his arms. Holding her close, they began to dance.

Elaine and Sarah both sighed, Elaine saying, "That's so beautiful," everyone shaking their heads in agreement. John and Ken took their girls into their arms and began to dance with them. The romance and love remained with each couple, just like in the beginning.

Matt and Geena danced together, looking at the snowflakes, and then into each other's eyes. Geena said, "We'd better go inside now. This is so romantic," kissing him gently on his lips. Matt smiling, "Aww shucks, do we have to?" Geena laughing at him, took him by the hand, leading him inside. Matt armed the alarm, scooped up Geena, and headed up the stairs. He gently placed her back onto the floor, kissing her good night. Geena pulled Matt back to her, wrapping her arms around him, kissing him, and wishing him a Merry Christmas.

Ronnie also had been watching from the window, thinking good for them. It looks like he has everything under control. That Matt sure has a way about himself. He is so romantic. Going to bed, she was glad it was rubbing off onto Jason. The phone rang. It was

Jason. He called to wish her a Merry Christmas and say he loved her. Ronnie wished him a Merry Christmas and told him she loved him. She loved the way he was romancing her, closing her eyes, drifting off to sleep, and dreaming of Jason.

Christmas Day! As everyone came downstairs, it seemed as if they all had a song in their heart. They were either humming, singing, or whistling a tune. Things were picking up from yesterday's festivities and love was in the air. They ate little for breakfast, leaving room for, and excited about Christmas Day dinner later. After finishing, they gathered around the Christmas tree, and unwrapped the rest of their presents. They were having fun, singing Christmas carols, laughing, and enjoying themselves.

Ronnie said, "I was so surprised last evening to find out you could sing Geena. You have a beautiful voice, and Matt, you've been holding out on me. I suspected you were hiding the truth from me. I enjoyed you both, immensely." Brick said, "Matt never fancied himself as a musician, but don't let that fool you. He plays the keyboards, sings, directs, and orchestrates. He's even written original compositions, and why he hasn't published them, only he knows. He was a choir director for many years. He loves all types of music, especially gospel, and smooth jazz." Matt said, "Okay, okay Mr. Blabbermouth," changing the subject. "It seems you were holding out on us too. Lena, you are an extremely funny lady. You had us all in tears last evening."

Lena said, "Thank you. That's how I met Brick. I was performing a show, mesmerizing him with my performance of course," everyone laughing. "Later in the evening we were introduced to each other, and he wouldn't let go of my hand."

Brick interrupting, "That's right. I put a leash on her quick and in a hurry. Beautiful and funny, I knew she was the girl for me. I was not taking any chances of letting her get away, no Sir, thank Ya!" Everyone cracking up. Continuing, Lena said, "As you see, he comes up with a few good lines. I might say, some of which he used on me quite effectively. He captured my heart."

Brick said, "I've engaged her as one of the acts for the New Starfire Café & Lounge when it opens next year." Matt said, "That is fantastic news. At least we know now someone will be there that is funny." Everyone was laughing uncontrollably. Geena said, "That's right, you tell him baby! Brick, it's time to pay for your transgressions."

Brick said, "Ouch, they're ganging up on me." Lena said, "I think it's payback time honey. You guys can come on the road with me anytime." Brick said, "Honey please, not you too!" They were all laughing and having a good time. Rob said, "You can take it big boy," laughing.

Peach's dad Jacob said, "This is a tough crowd, they just keep coming for you. I thought our family was rough, but this takes the cake. I'm going to remember this for a long time." Delores adding, "Yes, thank you so much for inviting us. We are having a marvelous time." C J said, "We're glad to have you. One great big happy family."

JET's parents told everyone how much they enjoyed Thanksgiving, and now this, the holiday affair. JET said, "We have had comedy, romance, and music." C J said, "Don't forget about our girls here. Just before Thanksgiving, we had some action and drama."

Mel saying, "Yes, and we are grateful everything turned out alright. You guys going to the rescue." Matt said, "Not that they needed our help," laughing. "Those guys never knew what hit them. These ladies are fierce." Lee Anne said, "They have a long time to think about what happened to them. Don't mess with us, right ladies?" Ronnie and Geena jubilantly saying, Lee Anne joining in, "Sisters!" Geena saying, "Now we have a new one." They began chanting, "Lena, Lena." Lena coming over to embrace them, as they all jumped up down, "Sisters, sisters!"

Jason said, "Glad they are on our side. I don't want to mess with them. They are a force to be reckoned with." Chet said, "You're right Jason."

They settled down for Christmas dinner. The parents saying how they were proud of everyone, citing the way they are involved with each other, supporting, and giving back to the community. Elaine said, "This has been a wonderful family experience. Cupid has been extremely busy with you this year. In the coming years,

I expect we will be hearing the pitter patter of little feet. Time for some grandchildren," everyone laughing.

Geena said, "Okay, okay mom. Everything in due time you know. First things first. Some of these guys still have to put a ring on it," everyone laughing. Matt laughing said, "Look what you've started Brick," JET and Jason chiming in, "Yeah," laughing. Ronnie said, "You boys better get your acts together," winking. "Matt already told you we're fierce, and you don't want to cross us," the girls chanting, "Sisters!"

Geena stood, "Getting back to the serious side. It has been absolutely wonderful having you all here this week." Matt standing beside her and agreeing. We want you to relax and enjoy this week together. Nothing formal is on the agenda until New Year's Eve, when we will celebrate the coming in of the New Year with Summit Hill. Feel free to roam around doing what you like. If you want to go into town, just let us know. We will be more than happy to accompany you. Enjoy!"

They resumed talking with one another, then proceeded to clean up the kitchen, dining area, and putting the food away. They gathered in the living room, continuing to enjoy one another. Jason put on some soft music. Dancing, talking, and laughing was the highlight of the evening. Eventually, the couples paired off, doing their own thing, some strolling around the grounds. The parents got together and were having fun playing cards. Geena, Matt, JET and Lee Anne were sitting together. JET said, "excuse me ladies, I need to speak with Matt about the planes, it won't take long." Geena saying, "No problem guys, we'll be here."

Leaving the room, JET began, "We do have to check on the planes this week, but that's not what I wanted to speak to you about." Matt said, "I kind of figured that out. What's up JET?" Answering, JET said, "I plan to ask Lee Anne to marry me on New Year's Eve. I saw a ring at the local jewelry store in town, but I don't want her to suspect anything. So, if you go with me, she'll be thinking we are dealing with the jets. Those ladies of ours are sharp. I plan to let my parents know this week."

Matt smiling, "That's wonderful JET and it's a good plan. It is difficult getting things past those two. I'll be glad when the next few months have passed, and we can end this sneaking around." JET said, "Great! Thanks Matt. Now we had better get back in there with them." Matt laughing, "I'm right behind you."

Lee Anne said, "Everything okay?" JET said, "Yes, we were just deciding when to go into Summit Hill next week. We will go some time Tuesday, or Wednesday. We don't want to wait until the last minute to service the planes. I'll probably ask my dad to go with us." They continued to talk a while longer, before pairing off, and going their separate ways.

Brick and Lena were hanging out in the studio. Ronnie and Jason took the car, driving to Summit Hill and going to the gazebo. C J and Mel played with the baby around the Christmas tree. Chet, Peaches, Rob, and Mel joined them. Lee Anne and JET went to the garden. Matt and Geena went to their favorite spot, doing their favorite pastime.

Everyone returned early. They stayed in the living room talking, before heading to their individual rooms. Brick and Lena went to the kitchen to get a snack, Ronnie and Jason joining them. They finished and went upstairs, saying good night.

Matt and Geena came in, arming the alarm. Matt walked Geena to her room and kissed her good night.

Sunday morning, some of the couples went to church in town for the Christmas service. The children put on a wonderful play. Returning home, everyone relaxed. For the next few days, they took time to relax and spend quality time with each other.

Monday, the ladies took Lena and her mother to Ronnie's studio. Lena was in love with her fashion designs, asking if Ronnie would design a gown for her wedding. Ronnie said she would be delighted.

JET brought his parent's up to speed regarding his New Year's Eve plan. He asked his dad to go into town with him. Paul said he would be delighted to go with them. They went to the airport to check on the servicing of the planes. Then they went to the jewelry store, where JET picked out the engagement ring he wanted for Lee Anne. The group headed back for Summit Meadows, JET happy and excited.

The musicians met at the club during the week and had a jam session. Rob, Jason, and Jeff went fishing.

Jason got the chance to speak with his dad, and Rob concerning Ronnie. He expressed how he felt about her, telling them he was going to propose to her. He said he knew they had careers that were just beginning to flourish, and they were young, but he had a good feeling about her.

His dad told him, "When you find your soulmate, sometimes there are exceptions to the rule. Your mom and I married young, but much like you, I knew she was the one. The difference being, both of our parents were gone, but you will have us to help you along, just in case you want to make us grandparents. So, know you have a support system, not only with us, but with Rob, and your family back at Summit Meadow. I'm sure they will be there for you as well. Jason hugged his dad and Rob saying thank you, knowing how much he was blessed having them, and his mom in his life. He knew they loved Ronnie just as much as he did. They caught no fish, but they bonded, growing closer.

Matt, JET, C J, and Brick went into the office to talk about Grand Rapid Falls, and the New Starfire Café & Lounge. Brick told them he and Lena were planning their wedding a week after the Starfire grand opening. He said it was going to be a small wedding, and he asked Matt to be his Best Man, and C J to stand with him. He would also be asking Rob.

Matt told him he would be honored, then began relating his plans. He said he planned on asking Geena to marry him the evening of the Texas event at the banquet. C J smiling, "It's about time," embracing Matt in a bear hug, winking at the other guys. Matt said, "C J, I would like you to be my Best Man, and you two to stand with me." They told him they would be delighted. He told them they would be away for a few months honeymooning and enjoying a much-needed vacation. C J asked, "Where are you planning on going?" Laughing, Matt said, "Like I plan on telling you," everyone laughing. "You'll find out when we return."

JET said, "Lee Anne and I are planning a September wedding, hopefully after you and Geena have returned from your extended honeymoon." Chuckling, Matt said, "Don't worry, we'll be there with bells on."

Matt thinking to himself, soon it would be New Year's Eve, and then it would be time to leave, getting back to business. The next few months were going to be extremely busy, but so what, they were always busy. At least he and Geena would finally be together.

New Year's Eve arrived, and they went to Summit Hill, gathering with the rest of the town at the gazebo. The mayor hit the switch beginning the countdown, the lights filling up each section before reaching the top. Reaching the top of the globe it started flashing, everyone exclaiming, "Happy New Year!" Horns were blowing, and there were plenty of noise makers. Everyone grabbing their significant other, kissing and wishing them a Happy New Year! JET grabbed Lee Anne and got down on his knee to propose, telling her how much he loved her. Lee Anne excitedly jumping up and down, accepted his proposal, pulling him up, kissing him, and telling him she loved him. Everyone was excited for them, surrounding, and congratulating them.

The group then headed back to Summit Meadows, planning to spend New Year's Day together.

Most of their packing done, they planned on leaving Summit Meadows Tuesday, everyone agreeing to stay so they could help take the holiday decorations down and put them away. Matt planned for the crew to come back out to help take down the lights. Geena wanted everything to be in order before they left. Finished taking down the decorations, they stored them away. They went to town to eat their last dinner together. Geena had called ahead making the reservation for them. They had dinner, and then walked to the gazebo one final time, before returning to Summit Meadows.

They spent their last evening walking around the grounds. Peach's parents would be leaving in the morning, driving back home. They would be home approximately when they reached New York. Paul and Marie were catching a flight out of JFK for Canada, arriving back home sometime around three o'clock in the afternoon. Geena and Matt's parents planned a trip, looking forward to traveling together.

They got up Tuesday morning and packed everything in the vehicles. Matt and Geena arranged for them to eat breakfast at the restaurant in Summit Hill. When they finished, they said their goodbyes, Peach's parents driving off, promising to be at the Starfire grand opening and the rest heading for the airport, lifting off and heading back to New York. JET and Matt planned to spend Tuesday evening with Geena and Lee Anne, before leaving late Wednesday morning for Grand Rapid Falls, Texas.

It was the end of the Holiday Affair!

Chapter 46

Preparations for the Starfire

Ronnie called the chef of the Starfire on Monday, to let him know she would be back tomorrow and planned on seeing him during the week. She also wanted to find out how everything was progressing. He said the kitchen and staff were ready to go, but wished they had a chance to work together before the grand opening.

Ronnie told him about the groups plan for Tuesday evening, suggesting the group could have dinner at the Starfire. She advised him the staff would be paid for the evening. Excited, he told Ronnie he would call her back to advise if the staff would be available. It wasn't long before he called back, letting her know it would be alright. Ronnie told everyone and they liked the idea, making plans to dine at the Starfire.

The flight back to New York did not take long, and they landed safely at JFK. Everyone said their goodbyes and headed for their individual homes and destinations. Matt and Geena's parents planned a trip together, promising they would be back in time for the New Starfire Café & Lounge grand opening. Promising the same, Paul and Marie headed home for Canada.

    C J and Mel decided to go home, wanting to spend some quality time with the baby. Chet, Peaches, Rob, and Priscilla went home to unpack, saying they would meet everyone later at the Starfire. Cindy and Will decided to do the same. Having an extra bedroom, Geena invited Lena to stay with her, Ronnie and Lee Anne. Saying thank you, Lena gladly accepted. She planned to return home to pack for her transition to New York. She and Brick found a lovely home, and she was excited about the move. JET and Matt offered to fly her home, before going to Texas.

    Matt and JET went home, promising the girls they would come over to spend time before they went out to dinner, Jason and Brick deciding to stay with them. Geena, Lee Anne and Ronnie went home and unpacked, showing Lena to the guest bedroom. While they were waiting for the guys to return, they spoke about the grand opening of the Starfire, Brick and Lena's wedding, and Ronnie's show.

    It wasn't long before the guys came over. They sat in the living room laughing and talking, until it was time to meet the others at the Starfire. When they arrived, they were greeted by a full staff. The valets parked the cars, and once inside, they were greeted by the hostess and taken to their tables. There was soft music playing when they arrived. Joining the others, they sat down, placing their order with the waitress.

Geena remarked how lovely the Starfire looked and was impressed with the hospitality and service thus far, the others agreeing. Cindy said everything was on target for the grand opening. The food was served, everyone enjoying their meal. Chef came out to find out if they were enjoying everything. Ronnie, Brick and Jason let him know they were pleased with the meal and with the quality of service provided.

They were having a good time. As a preview, Ronnie and Jason played some live music and Lena and Brick did a comedic routine. Finishing their brief performance, Ronnie and Jason played Matt and Geena's favorite song, "The First Time Ever I Saw Your Face," with everyone dancing. Jason put the soft music tracks on again, and everyone continued to dance. Soon they called it an evening, heading back home.

Matt, JET, Jason, and Brick went home with the girls. They stayed for a brief period because tomorrow it was back to business. Reaching home, the guys called the girls to let them know they arrived safely, speaking with them briefly before saying good night.

The following morning, Matt and JET decided to have breakfast at the girl's place, before heading to the airport. Brick and Jason also came over, Brick wanting to say goodbye to Lena. Afterwards, they were meeting Cindy at the Starfire, along with Geena,

Ronnie, and Lee Anne. They wanted to make sure everything was on point for the grand opening and to go over the upcoming events.

The girls told Lena not to worry about planning the wedding. They knew she had to get ready for the move and said they would help her. For the next few months, Lena made certain to change her scheduling of events to be in line with her new location. In this manner, the transition she was making would be more amenable for her. She would be in New York from time to time, helping Brick get the house situated. When they finished, she planned to stay there, until they were married.

Saying their goodbyes, Lena promised Brick she would contact him when she arrived home. Matt and JET told Lee Anne and Geena they would call when they reached Grand Rapid Falls, and as always, telling the girls they would speak to them every evening.

After leaving JFK, Jason and Brick drove to the Starfire to meet with Cindy. Lee Anne followed them in her car with Ronnie and Geena. When they arrived, Cindy was already there waiting for them, going over the menus with chef. Geena said to Lee Anne, "It looks like you chose well picking Cindy to assist Ronnie with her operation." Lee Anne saying, "She is doing great, and she is always punctual." Ronnie said, "She fits in well with the rest of us, and she always seems to know what I want." Geena saying, "The mark of a great personal assistant."

Geena said to Lee Anne, "Felicia has been doing a marvelous job as well. She has been on top of everything while we were gone." Agreeing with Geena, Lee Anne said, "She has been doing a great job, and the staff likes her."

Ronnie said, "I'm almost finished with the designs for Lena's wedding. I will have them finished by the end of the week, and ready to send them by email for her approval. I want to finish them, so I can focus my attention on the grand opening and the show." They got down to business planning the details of the events coming up.

Cindy informed Ronnie she had spoken to Belinda Connors, who advised their new website would be ready for launch soon. Ronnie asked if it would include the main site for A-Line and the connecting site for Powder Puff. Cindy said yes, and the sites were presently being updated to include all of the new designs.

Next, they went over the rehearsal scheduling for the musicians and Hudson Flow. Cindy also contacted Pacific Sunset, going over their scheduling, making sure to reserve time in the club for their rehearsals. Cindy said, "Jacob Meyers called to inform me he will be back in New York the end of next week." Ronnie said, "Great! It will be great seeing him again." Continuing, "Please don't forget to let Will and Ben know what the rehearsal scheduling is for Hudson Flow." Cindy said, "I won't forget. Will and Ben are so excited to be working with them."

Meanwhile, Brick and Jason went in the studio to check the sound system, also checking how the system was working on the other floors. They made certain the connections for speakers and microphones were working and checked the video feed. C J would be coming in a couple of weeks, to make certain the security system met with his requirements.

When they finished, they went back to join the ladies. Brick told Ronnie, "Your CD's will be ready to be released in the next couple of weeks. I have you set up to do some local television performances, and guest interviews on some radio shows. I will coordinate the dates and times with Cindy." Brick continued, "I'm sure people will want to purchase them at the grand opening, so I've arranged for plenty be on hand."

Cindy said, "That's great. We should make sure there are enough here for Ronnie's show as well." Ronnie said, "It's hard to believe this is happening." Lee Anne said, "You guys have worked hard to get here. Now it's time to show everyone just who you are, and in the next few weeks everyone is going to hear how good you both are. I am sure your show is going to go well. Including the community in the grand opening of the Starfire, and Ronnie's show was a great idea."

Geena said, "The response has been overwhelming. Felicia will send over the list of applicants for the talent show, and she comprised a list of those who wanted to be a part of the fashion show." Brick said, "This is working out great. We have people from the community who are on our staff. We should be able to provide the young people with scholarships. This is a plus for everyone."

Cindy said, "I was speaking with Jason's parents while we were in Summit Meadows. They informed me they had connections with some people who might be able to assist us getting those scholarships. Not only for this community, but for the community where Koach's Kids is located, providing them with athletic scholarships."

Geena said, "This is so amazing and wonderful. Because of our efforts, and the crossing of the many pathways, we are achieving the goals we always dreamed of doing." Brick said, "You're right Geena, and I am certain there is more to come. We just need to keep forging ahead." Jason said, "It seems the more we bless others, we are blessed too." Geena said, "Yes, we have been truly blessed and I believe Brick is correct. There is more to come, so we have to keep on working."

Tired, they decided to call it a day. Everything was on schedule and in the next few weeks, their plans would be ready to be implemented. Chef was kind enough to prepare them dinner. They were grateful. They ate, talked a while, said good night, and went home.

Jason and Ronnie went to the city to see the tree at Rockefeller Center. Brick went home so he could talk with Lena, who had called earlier to let him know she arrived safely home. JET and Matt called earlier, letting

Geena and Lee Anne know they arrived safely in Grand Rapid Falls.

They were sitting in the living room talking when Jason brought Ronnie home. He didn't stay long, leaving and promising her he would call when he got home. Ronnie showed them some photos she took of the ice-skating rink and the Christmas tree. Before she went to her room, to finish the designs for Lena's wedding, she said to Geena she had another idea for the show.

Geena asked, "What do you have in mind Ronnie?" I wanted to ask your opinion about including Matt and Rob's work in the show. As I am sure you know, Matt has a terrific eye and has done some great work. I also got the chance to see some work of Rob's. I saw them when he was showing me the photos, he took at Summit Meadows last week. I haven't said anything to them, wanting to know what you thought of the idea first."

Geena said, "I think it's a great idea. I've seen work from both, and I have always tried to encourage Matt to show his work. Maybe now is the right time. I think you should ask them." Ronnie said, "Thanks G, I will ask them this week. They already have enough work to display. Well, good night ladies. I want to finish those designs for Lena." They said good night to Ronnie, and she went to her room.

The guys called their girls, speaking briefly about the day. Even though they were together for the last couple of weeks, already they missed each other, wishing they were together. They related their love to each other and said good night. Then it was time for lights out, as tomorrow was going to be another extremely hectic day.

The next day was much like the time spent yesterday. Going over the scheduling, preparing the club for the events, and planning Ronnie's show at the Starfire. They were also in touch with Lena, assisting her, and her mother with the wedding plans. Ronnie advised her she would have the designs by the end of the week.

Ronnie had also started on the designs for the fashion show. She just needed a few more to go along with the designs she already had. Belinda Connor sent her some designs she could include in the show. Ronnie also decided not to include any of her paintings. She felt more time was needed, and she did not want to rush the work. Geena agreed with her. There would be plenty to display with the photography, and the fashion show.

Cindy spoke briefly with Jacob Meyers, updating him on the progress. Brick and Jason also stopped by to do some work in the studio. C J and Rob were working at Koach's Kids. Ronnie called Rob and Matt to ask if they would participate in her show at the Starfire. Rob agreed and Geena was right about Matt, as he agreed to show his work also.

They set up the audition schedule for the talent show contestants, advising them of the dates and times. Hudson Flow was slated to start rehearsals with the musicians next week. Wanting to get a head start, the musicians decided to come together for rehearsal at the end of this week. They wanted the same type of flow they had over the holidays.

Brick and Jason only stayed briefly, heading over to help C J and Rob at Koach's Kids. The girls finished up early, so they could do some food shopping. They came home and prepared something to eat. After dinner, Ronnie went to her room to finish the designs for Lena and sent them to her. Lena told her she loved them. Ronnie already sent her measurements to Belinda, who would have them made.

Geena and Lee Anne spoke further about Ronnie's show. Lee Anne asked Rob to send the photos he wanted to display. Ronnie told Matt what pictures she wanted from him. He promised he would get them to her soon. They called it an early evening, each speaking to their guy briefly before going to sleep. Geena and Lee Anne decided to stop by Geena's office tomorrow, planning to work there for the rest of the week.

Before she fell asleep, Lee Anne was thinking things were progressing well. Olive Winfield had called earlier today, advising she would call the office this week, to follow up on the plan, inviting Geena to host her show. Lee Anne fell asleep, chuckling to herself. Geena was going to be shocked.

In the morning, Geena was already in the kitchen when Lee Anne entered. "Good morning G, how are you today?" Responding, "Good morning Lee Anne. I'm fine thank you. How are you?" Lee Anne said, "I slept like a baby." Geena said, "Join me. There's some hot water on the stove, and try some of this pastry, it's delicious. Ronnie fixed it for us and is already gone." Lee Anne saying, "Thanks, I will."

They spoke briefly before leaving for the office. Felicia was there to greet them. "Good morning ladies. It's great to see you both." Geena said, "Good morning Felicia." Lee Anne said, "Good morning. How was your holiday?" Felicia answered, "It was wonderful thank you. I hope you both had a pleasant holiday as well."

Getting down to business, Felicia said, "Geena, your schedule is light for the rest of the week." Answering, "That's great Felicia. You've done a terrific job. If you don't mind, I will be needing Lee Anne by my side for the next few weeks, and I would like you to continue your current role." Felicia said, "That won't be a problem Geena, I've been having a wonderful time working with everyone."

Geena said, "If you need us, we will be in here for most of the day. I'll let you know when we are leaving." Felicia said, "Great, see you later." Lee Anne said smiling, "I'd better be careful. I may have to find a new job." Geena laughing, "Not on your life. I don't know what I would do without you." They started working on Ronnie's event, paying attention to the changes Ronnie requested.

Later, Felicia came back to the Geena's office. "Sorry to bother you Geena, but I thought I should bring this to your attention myself. There is a lady on the line who would like to speak with you. She says her name is Olive Winfield." Geena and Lee Anne stopped what they were doing, looking at each other. Felicia continued, "I know this is surprising, but I have to admit it sounds like her. I told her you were in a meeting and asked her please to hold on. She is on line one." Geena said, "Thanks Felicia, I'll take it from here."

Geena said to Lee Anne, "That's strange. If it's her, I wonder why she is calling me?" Lee Anne said, "You're never going to know until you answer her call. It's not every day you get the chance to speak to your idol."

Geena answered the call, "Good morning Ms. Winfield. Sorry to keep you waiting." Olive said, "Good morning Geena. I know this is a bit irregular. I imagine your assistant was taken aback I called personally." Geena responding, "Yes, she was. She did say it really sounded like you. I have to say, I'm also surprised." Olive laughing said, "I know Geena. I figured you would be, but I wanted to speak with you personally. I have been watching you for some time and I am a fan of your work." Geena said, "Thank you Ms. Winfield. That means a lot to me coming from you." Olive answered, "First, please call me Olive. I know you are probably busy, so let me explain why I am calling you, because I need your help."

Geena said, "Sure Ms. Win...," catching herself, "sorry Olive. You need my help!? How may I be of assistance to you?" Olive said, "As I said, I am impressed with your work, and I have need for your services. I am planning a special in May, and I would like for you to co-host it. You will be working with 'America's Funny Man,' Seth Howard. Would you be interested in assisting me?" Geena was shocked and did not answer. Olive said, "Geena, are you still there?"

Geena pulled herself together, "Yes, yes Olive, I'm still here, sorry. You sure know how to surprise someone. I'm speechless." Laughing, Olive said, "So, I take it that's a yes, and not a no?" Quickly responding, Geena said, "It's a yes Olive. I can't believe this." Olive answering, "That's great Geena. I'll have my people contact your personal assistant. Is it still Lee Anne Howard?" Geena responding, "Yes, it is Olive."

Olive said, "Good. They will be in touch with her early next week. Thank you for accepting, and I look forward to meeting with you both soon." Geena said, "Thank you for the opportunity Olive, and I look forward to meeting you as well." They said goodbye, and Geena hung up the phone, asking Lee Anne to have Felicia come back in the office.

Lee Anne was laughing to herself. *Geena is in shock. I wish I had a video of her, while she was speaking with Olive.* While Lee Anne was getting Felicia, Geena used the time to compose herself. *I had a conversation with my idol, Olive Winfield. Wow, she's requested for me,*

Geena Michaels, to co-host a special in May, with Seth Howard. This is amazing and unbelievable!

Lee Anne and Felicia came back in. Geena said, "Sit down ladies, and let me tell you what just happened." She briefed them on what transpired during the conversation. Geena told Lee Anne, Olive advised her people would be in touch with her early next week. She said to Felicia, "It looks like you're going to be utilized longer. I hope you don't mind. Lee Anne will bring you up to speed with our other projects. We'll see you later."

Saying goodbye to Felicia, they left. Lee Anne wanted to know all the details, but Geena said, "I don't want you to wreck the car, so let's wait until we get home, plus we can share the news with Ronnie."

When they arrived, Ronnie was already at home with Jason, who was about to leave. Geena said, "I have some good news I would like to share with you. Are you able to stay a few more minutes Jason?" He said he could, and Geena elaborated about her call from Olive Winfield.

Ronnie and Jason said it was great news, congratulating Geena. Jason stayed a few more minutes, kissed Ronnie and left, telling Ronnie he would speak to her later. The girls pitched in, fixed a light meal for themselves, and continued to talk about Ronnie's show.

Ronnie said she had a few calls to make, excusing herself. Lee Anne spoke with Geena a while longer. "I am going to head to my room Geena. I'm expecting a call from JET. I really miss him. I suppose Matt will be calling you soon too." Geena said, "I know what you mean. I miss Matt also. He's going to be surprised to learn what happened today. I hope he will be coming home from Texas soon."

Matt called, and Geena gave him the news regarding Olive Winfield. He said, "That's wonderful Geena. I know you are excited. I'm sure she will want to meet with you and Lee Anne soon. Did she tell you where the show was going to be?" Geena said, "No, she didn't. She said her staff would be in contact early next week." Changing the subject, "Matt, I miss you. When will you be coming home?" Matt said, "I know Geena. I miss you too. I will be better able to tell you next week. Things are going well here." They spoke about the other events and said good night.

Lee Anne told JET what happened, JET saying, "Geena is going to be one surprised lady when this is all done." Laughing, they said good night.

The weekend passed quickly. True to her word, Olive Winfield's staff got in touch with Lee Anne. They told her Olive would like to meet with them Wednesday in Grand Rapid Falls, Texas. They said the talks should last no more than two days. Lee Anne made reservations for a Tuesday flight. They worked with Cindy and Ronnie, going over the details for the show. They spoke with Matt and JET, letting them know of their plans. Matt told them they would pick them up at the airport and made dinner reservations for them.

The guys picked them up at the airport and took them to their hotel. They picked the ladies up for dinner and spent a quiet evening with them. Not wanting to keep them out late, they took them back to the hotel early, knowing the next couple of days meetings were important.

Matt told Geena they were planning on coming to New York for the weekend. He said they could all return together, and Jacob Meyers could join them. Lee Anne told Geena she only made reservations for one way, just to be sure they had time to finish the meetings with Olive Winfield. Geena said that's perfect because she was itching for some flying time. Matt said they could stop in Summit Meadows, so he could pick up the photos Ronnie wanted for the show. They made plans to leave on Friday morning, which should put them back in New York by sundown.

They left Friday morning as planned, Geena and Matt flying them to Summit Hills. After they landed, Matt and Geena drove to Summit Meadows to pick up the pictures, while the others waited at the airport. Returning to the airport, they lifted off for New York, arriving just before sundown. They decided to have dinner together. They dropped Jacob at his new apartment at the club, saying they would see him next week. Matt and JET went back to Geena and Lee Anne's. Ronnie and Jason were at the house when they arrived. Matt told Geena he and JET planned to stay through the weekend. The girls were happy they were staying.

Geena said the meetings with Olive Winfield went well, and she was excited to do the show. Seth Howard was not able to be there but teleconferenced with them on Thursday. She told Matt everyone was supposed to dress formally for the show, as there would be a banquet after the show. Matt said, "It sounds real fancy. What's the format for the show?" Geena said, "Olive's special guests are Theo Porter, and Leland Jackson. She will be honoring them, depicting their success, and showing our viewers the work, they do. She wants to highlight the way they give back to various communities through charities and events." Matt said, "It sounds interesting. Those two guys are heavyweights." Geena said, "Yes, I'm proud to be a part of the project. I still can't believe Olive wanted me." JET asked, "Why Geena? You have worked hard, and you are respected for your work, and your ethics. She only confirms what we already know," everyone agreeing. Geena said, "Thanks guys. This is extremely exciting, working with my idol." Matt said, "I'm proud of you G." The group spent an enjoyable weekend together, Ronnie and Jason joining them.

    Matt and JET left early Monday after breakfast with the girls. Geena and Lee Anne dropped them off at the airport before heading to the Starfire. They were meeting Jacob and the rest of the team. The club's inspection was scheduled for later in the week. Jacob was satisfied everything was ready, and the building was totally completed. The inspectors came

Wednesday, finding everything in order. They filed the paperwork. The club would have the necessary permits by the end of the week. Next week the auditions for the talent show start, and the grand opening is slated for the weekend. Rehearsals were in full swing, and everything was progressing nicely.

Chapter 47

The New Starfire Café & Lounge Grand Opening

The rehearsals between the musicians and Hudson Flow went well and they were ready for the grand opening. Ronnie and Jason's rehearsals flowed between them, and they were excited about the club's opening this weekend. Brick was pleased the audio and visual equipment was in place throughout the club. He was able to transmit live audio and video streaming to all floors. His friend's headphones were a big hit with the musicians.

Between Jacob Meyers and chef, the staff was ready for opening night. C J had the security team in place, which was comprised of men from his security force, melding in some new personnel from the community.

The ladies did a fantastic job with the interior design, and incorporated photos of celebrities who were associated with the Starfire. They picked well known musicians throughout New York and the surrounding area, to be the judges for the talent show. The auditions had already started, and they would end this weekend. The winners would be announced Saturday evening, and perform Sunday, accompanied by Ronnie, Jason, and the band.

Pacific Sunset arrived on Wednesday, rehearsing at the club and they were ready to perform this weekend. Matt and JET returned earlier in the week, assisting in the final preparations. Lena had arrived and with the assistance of Brick, had most of her things settled in the house. The guys helped getting them settled, so their home would be ready when they returned from their honeymoon.

Geena and Matt's parents returned from their adventure, getting settled in the hotel. John assisted Brick with the audio-visual equipment at the club, and Sarah offered her expertise in interior design to Lena.

Brick let everyone know his friend was coming to the grand opening, and he would be bringing headphones for people to purchase. His friend is also donating headphones to the talent show winners.

Peach's parents and Lena's parents were checked into the same hotel Matt and Geena's parents were staying. JET's parents flew in from Canada. C J made transportation provisions for the parents, throughout the duration of their stay.

Elaine's old friend and business partner Belinda Connors arrived, saying to Elaine, "I wouldn't miss the next few weeks for anything. The kids have worked so hard, and I'm excited for them. I sent Lena's wedding gown to her. She said it fit perfectly, needing no alterations. I also sent Geena's ensemble to Olive Winfield in Texas. I'm pretty certain our girl will maintain that fantastic figure of hers."

Elaine said, "I have no doubt about that. Thanks for coming. I was glad you called to tell me you were coming. We are going to have a fantastic time for the next few weeks." Belinda answering, "Yes. I'm especially happy to be here for Ronnie's show. She is going to receive fantastic exposure, which will undoubtedly work in her favor." Elaine said, "She is a very talented young lady, with a promising career in her future."

Sarah came over, "Hi Belinda. It's great seeing you again." Belinda acknowledging, "Hi Sarah. It's wonderful to see you. The kids have done a great job preparing for the grand opening." Sarah said, "Yes, they have. It's amazing how they all work together so seamlessly. I came over to suggest the ladies gather and help Lena and Brick. They have been extremely busy preparing for the clubs opening.

I spoke with Lena, and she said she would really appreciate any help we can give her. Their wedding will be right after the grand opening. They have also been assisting Ronnie for her show in a couple of weeks. They will be jumping right back into the thick of things when they return from their honeymoon."

Elaine said, "Count me in. I'm sure the other ladies will be eager to assist too. By combining our efforts, it should not take long to put things together for her. I'll contact Geena to get the ball rolling, and I will also call Lena's mom."

Belinda said, "I'll help also. This is an exciting time. So many wonderful things are happening, and I'm glad I can be a part of it. I'm especially excited about the trip to Texas for Geena's big surprise. I know everyone has been working extremely hard. She is going to be so surprised. Elaine said, "Yes, she is. Matt and 'the Crew' have had their hands full keeping this from Geena. It's been difficult because she likes to be a part of everything." Sarah said, "It's all worth it and she is going to love it."

They had finished talking, and just in time. Geena came in with Ronnie, and Lee Anne. "Hi ladies. What are you up to?" Elaine filled her in on the plans to help Lena and Brick, asking her to set things in motion with the rest of the ladies. Geena replied, "Lee Anne and I will get things started. We stopped by to make sure you were settled in okay."

Ronnie said, "I'm still amazed with everything going on, we still are able to look out for one another. I feel so blessed to be with this amazing group. Our wonderful extended family always comes through. I'm looking forward to this weekend, and the wedding." Geena said, I'm excited too, and for your show coming up. You're going to be extremely busy." Ronnie said, "This is a dream come true, and I'm loving it."

The Starfire's grand opening was in full swing. The community was supportive, more so than anticipated.

The local businesses proved to be incredibly supportive, even the local churches. The families and friends were present to support the young people participating in the talent show.

Pacific Sunset and Hudson Flow gave fantastic performances. Lena had the crowd in an uproar. Her routine was hilarious. She made herself available to sign autographs at the end of the show. Ronnie and Jason were a big hit as well. Jason surprised everyone by calling Matt to the stage to play keyboard. He had collaborated with Matt on two songs which were written by Matt. The songs were included on Jason's CD, "Pathways to Love," and "Snowflakes."

Saturday, the final three contestants were selected by the judges. They gave terrific performances individually and combined their talents for a final song with all the contestants. The winner would be announced on Sunday, and will perform with Ronnie, Jason, and the band.

Cindy and Lee Anne made certain the event was well covered by the media. Ronnie and Jason's CDs were a hit. They each provided time to their new fans, signing autographs and posing for pictures. The groups Pacific Sunrise and Hudson Flow gave superb performances. Pacific Sunset signed autographs and posed for pictures with their fans. There was an overwhelming response for Hudson Flow's first official outing. They posed for selfies for their new fans. Brick announced

Hudson Flow would be working on a CD, to be released later in the year.

Sunday, the talent show contestants were announced. A pianist, Cheryl Elizabeth Sharpe placed third, winning a check for one thousand dollars. The second-place winner was James Thomas Murphy, who was a vocalist and guitarist. He won a check for two thousand dollars.

The grand prize winner was a singer, Sharon Darlene Wilson. She won a check for three thousand dollars, and a recording contract with Brickhouse Productions.

Brick was impressed with James Murphy, offering him a contract with Brickhouse Productions. Pacific Sunset was equally impressed with his guitar playing and vocals and asked if he would be available to go on the road with the group to perform as an opening act. James was working as a musician, having little success at being discovered. He was ready to give up his dream, until he heard about the talent show, and he decided to give it one last chance. He was glad he did.

Good fortune came along for pianist, vocalist Cheryl Elizabeth Sharpe. She was a delightful talent. Ronnie realized she was going to be extremely busy and spoke to Brick and Jason about an idea. She felt Cheryl could play and sing with Hudson Flow. There were a couple of times she played for them in rehearsals when Ronnie was busy. They connected and worked well together. She was in her last year of college and the opportunity would be perfect for her. Brick and Jason thought it was a great idea and they spoke to all parties concerned. Everyone agreed, Brick advising he would have the paperwork drawn up.

Jacob Meyers asked Brick if Hudson Flow and Cheryl could be regulars for the club on weekends, reminding everyone how Ronnie got her start there. Cheryl could perform at the club in the same capacity Ronnie had. Hudson Flow could come into the Starfire on weekends. Another wonderful idea for the club.

Brick's idea for the virtual performance floor was a big hit with the younger patrons. It could also be utilized for separate performances when there was a live show on the main floor at the same time. Brick's friend and his headphones were a hit with the young people. They could not stop talking about them. He sold out but got plenty of orders.

Things could not have been better this weekend. The grand opening of the New Starfire Café & Lounge was a resounding success. Civic groups, business, and personal bookings for the venue were being made for upcoming events, and the restaurant was doing extremely well. There was fantastic support from the community, and it seemed the Starfire had a bright future.

Monday was proving no different than any of the days from last week. Extremely busy. The focus of attention was now on Lena and Brick's wedding preparations. The ladies, along with Lena and her mother, were giving the new house a woman's personal touch.

They planned to be finished by Wednesday. The wedding was scheduled at the church Brick and 'the Crew' attend, this Friday at four o'clock. Brick's cousin was the Senior Pastor and would be officiating. The reception would be held at the Starfire.

The ladies completed everything at the house. Brick and Lena were grateful for everyone's help. Their home was decorated revolving around their personal tastes, every detail overseen by Lena.

Finally, the wedding day was here. Sarah planned the wedding and reception with Lena. She utilized her own personal touch and skills, which delighted Lena and her mother. The church was beautifully decorated. There was an ivory-colored aisle runner, and each pew was decorated with three gold bells, attached to an ivory bow, accented with buttercup, or peach roses hung alternately from each pew. The altar railings were tastefully decorated with buttercup and peach lei.

The wedding party consisted of Lena's Godchild, who was the flower girl. She wore an ivory-colored tea-length ballerina dress, with a buttercup tiara. She also wore ivory-colored patent-leather "baby doll" shoes. Her petal basket was peach, trimmed with small gold bells, filled with ivory, and peach rose petals.

Ronnie, the maid of honor, wore a form fitting tea-length peach dress, with three-quarter length sleeves. Her headpiece was ivory-colored, laced with peach and buttercup baby-breathes. Her shoes were ivory-colored four-inch heels, with a peach crisscross ribbon vamp overlay. The bouquet consisted of peach and buttercup roses, tied with a flowing ivory-colored ribbon.

The best man and the groom wore a two-piece tuxedo, by Emporio Armani, peach colored bow tie & matching pocket handkerchief, by Ronnie of Powder Puff Fashions & Designs, Ivory French cuff, slim-fit pleated bib formal shirt, by Eton, white gold initialed cufflinks, and Florsheim's men's tux cap-toe, lace-up black oxfords, w/hidden eyelets.

The bride wore a square neckline and plunging V-neck open back fitted ivory crepe full-length gown, with three-quarter length sheer puff sleeves, gathering into lace cuffs, thin peach waste sash; by Jenny Yoo Myla; drop pearl earrings & matching pearl necklace; three-inch open-toe ivory-linen pumps, with a peach crisscross ribbon vamp overlay, by Gucci; peach colored ribbon head piece, layered with baby breathes, by Ronnie of Powder Puff Fashions & Designs; Bouquet: peach roses.

The music for the wedding party to walk in was pre-recorded, prepared by Jason. After reaching the front, Ronnie went to the piano to play the song chosen by Lena and Brick to played. Jason joined her, playing his sax. The song was, "Just to Be Close to You." John and Rob handled the video and photography for the wedding. After the ceremony, the wedding party posed for pictures, then headed for the reception at the Starfire in the limousines C J provided.

Sarah's choices for decoration at the club were done with simplicity, but dignified and elegant. Ivory-colored fine-linen table clothes, with matching chair covers. The table centerpiece consisted of peach and buttercup lei, surrounding an ivory-colored battery-operated candle, housed in a crystal and gold trimmed candle holder. These items were given as a gift to the Starfire, by Matt and Geena. The recessed lighting in the club, added to the ambience.

The guests were all seated by the time Lena and Brick arrived. Matt and Geena served as Master & Mistress of Ceremony. As the wedding party entered, they announced their names. Then it was time for the happy couple to enter. Matt said, "Everyone please stand to your feet to receive our happy couple." Geena continuing, "Mr. & Mrs. Samuel David Johnson." Matt humorously adding, "The Bricks." Everyone was laughing and applauding as they entered.

Dinner was quietly being served as Matt and Geena continued. Geena asked for everyone's attention. "Ladies and gentlemen, we have a special treat for you. With us this evening is Lena's uncle. You may know him as, America's Funny Man, Seth Howard." The guests were applauding as Seth came forward to the microphone.

"How's everyone doing out there?" A thunderous response was given by all, "Everything is fine Uncle Seth," followed by laughter. For a few minutes, he gave a hilarious performance, everyone laughing hysterically. Seth ended by telling how Brick and Lena met. "One look at Lena stopped the 'Brick man' in his tracks.

I introduced them and told Brick to handle his business. Well, he did just that. He took her hand into his and would not let it go. Look, look over there. He still has it and won't let go." Brick yelled out, "Not in this lifetime." Laughter filled the room. Seth continued, "In all seriousness, I wish you the absolute best, and a lifetime of success and happiness. I love you."

Matt said, "We will now have remarks and a toast by the maid of honor, and best man. Ms. Ronnie Rodgers and Mr. Charles Jackson, better known as C J. Please come forward. Ronnie and C J gave their remarks, asking everyone to join them in a toast to the bride and groom.

Geena continued, "Now it's time for the bride and groom to have their first dance as husband and wife. They will be joined by the father and mother of the bride. Joining them will be the best man and the maid of honor." Lena's father came over to dance with her, while Brick danced with her mother. The guests joining them on the dance floor.

Everyone enjoyed themselves and further remarks were given by the guests. Lena and Brick thanked everyone for coming, then fed each other wedding cake, and the rest was served to the guests. Geena remarked, "Ladies, it's time for the tossing of the bouquet, so all single ladies please join me on the floor." Lena tossed the bouquet over her shoulder, landing into the outstretched hands of Geena."

Matt said, "Gentlemen, please join me on the floor for the traditional taking of the garter." Brick said, "Excuse me, just one minute. I love tradition, but tonight we are going to deviate. Y'all are not gettin' ready to look at those gams tonight." Everyone laughing. Continuing, "Now, I'm not insensitive, so I brought ya one. Git ready, here it comes." Brick shot the garter straight at Matt, who caught it. "Well, look at who caught it," everyone laughing. "Don't you guys think this is apropos?"

Everyone continued celebrating as the happy couple departed for their honeymoon.

Geena, Lee Anne, and Cindy were speaking with Ronnie, regarding her show next weekend at the Starfire. Geena saying to her, "Brick and Lena will return from their honeymoon in time for the show." Ronnie said, "The ceremony was beautiful. You and Matt did a fantastic job at the reception," the ladies agreeing. Cindy said, "It's back to business on Monday. We need to make certain we tie up any loose ends."

Everyone agreed and looked forward to enjoying the weekend.

Chapter 48

Culture for the Community

The ladies relaxed over the weekend, spending time with their families and beaus. Monday morning, Geena, Lee Anne, and Ronnie ate breakfast together, reflecting about the Starfire's successful grand opening. They also spoke about Brick and Lena's wedding, which was beautifully planned by Sarah.

After breakfast, they headed for the Starfire. They were going to meet Cindy to go over the details for Ronnie's show. When they arrived, Cindy drove up, and parked beside them. "Good morning ladies, we meet again," accompanied with a wink and smile. Ronnie responded, "I hope you had a pleasant weekend." Cindy replied, "Yes, I did thank you. I hope you ladies had a wonderful weekend as well. Acknowledging, they went inside to get down to business.

It was decided the exhibit would take place in the virtual room on the third floor, from four o'clock to six-thirty. Dinner would be served beginning at seven o'clock. Anyone could attend the exhibit, however, if they wanted dinner, a reservation would be required in advance. Most people made their reservations already. Of course, Ronnie would be there to greet and mingle with the guests, along with Matt and Rob.

Geena engaged guides, who would aid anyone who wanted to make a purchase. Hors-d'oeuvres were to be prepared by chef and served, allowing everyone to view the work displayed. The fashion show was going to take place on the main floor, where dinner would be served. For the entertainment, Ronnie and Jason are going to perform music from their newly released CD's. John and Rob were handling the video and photography, while Brick would handle the audio.

Jacob Meyers advised he would be utilizing a full staff, and C J had provided for extra security on the premise. He and the staff would make certain everything was in place for the event on Saturday. He also stated, Sarah aided with the décor. The preparation for the placement of the exhibits was done by Geena earlier in the day.

Satisfied with the arrangements for the event, they departed for home to change for dinner. Plans were made over the weekend for everyone to meet at the Starfire for dinner at seven o'clock. The last few weeks were extremely hectic. Everyone was planning to spend the rest of the week relaxing and enjoying themselves.

The week passed by quickly, and at long last, it was time for Ronnie's show. Geena, Ronnie, and the rest of the ladies went to the Starfire early Saturday morning, to make certain everything was in order. When they arrived, the club was already buzzing with excitement, the staff bustling about to put things in place. Jacob was overseeing the work, and chef and his crew were busy working in the kitchen.

Brick and Lena returned from their honeymoon late Friday night, and met the ladies at the club. Lena said, "Good morning everyone. It's so good to see you all." Geena replied, "Good morning. It's good to have you back. You both look fabulous, and you have this glow about you. By the looks of it, you had a wonderful honeymoon." Brick saying, "We sure did. We had a fantastic time. We'll fill you in later when we get together later this evening. But right now, I've got to check the audio equipment, to make certain everything is on point."

Jason arrived, walking up behind Brick and saying, "It's great to have you and Lena back. Everything should be in order Brick. I followed your instructions to the letter. There were some logistical changes regarding the setup, so I compensated. I hope you like what I did." Brick replied, "I'm sure I will. Excuse us ladies while we check the system out."

Lena said, "See you later sweetie. I love you." Taking her in his arms and kissing her, Brick responded, "I love you too honey, and I'll be counting the minutes until we're together again." Lee Anne said, "That is so sweet. Girl, it sounds like you two are still on your honeymoon." Lena replying, "We are, and I'm going to make certain it continues. I enjoyed myself immensely. We had an amazing time."

Sporadically during the morning, the others arrived, lending a helping hand where it was needed. It was almost noon, and the Starfire was ready for the festivities. Everyone went home to change, agreeing to be back at the club around two o'clock, for a final walk through.

They met back at the appointed hour, going over things step-by-step. Geena was the MC for the fashion show. She checked her cards to make certain they were in the proper sequence. Jacob had the honors for the entertainment portion of the show.

It was time. The guests were arriving for the exhibit. The guides and staff got busy, welcoming them to the Starfire, and ushering them to the exhibit. Ronnie, Matt, and Rob greeted the guests, answering questions, and socializing. In the virtual room, Jason and Brick utilized the video screens, showing the websites for the fashions, photography and music. It turned out Brick and Jason's idea for showing Ronnie's work was a good one.

Before the fashion show even got started, people were requesting if she could design wedding fashions for them. Cindy and Belinda were busy scheduling appointments. Geena introduced Ronnie to influential persons in the fashion industry, who showed interest in her designs. The photography displays also generated interest. Orders were being placed for prints of Ronnie's work, along with Matt and Rob's. People were also interested in the décor of the venue, which generated business for Geena. The exhibit was a fabulous success.

Guests were arriving, as it was almost time for the fashion show. The exhibit over, guests who had reservations went downstairs for the show. After the last person left, the area was closed and secured.

Soft pre-recorded music played as the guests arrived, and orders were being placed for dinner. An excitement filled the air, the guests anxiously awaiting the show to begin. There was positive feedback regarding the exhibit. Guests who were not able to attend the exhibit earlier, expressed a desire to see the exhibition.

There were so many requests, Geena made provisions for them to see it, while the musical performance was going on. An announcement was given by Jacob Meyers. He explained guests could see the exhibit and enjoy the performance on screen at the same time. Brick's idea of creating a virtual room was again working out positive for the Starfire.

The evening was shaping up quite nicely. Geena asked Lena if she would render a comedic performance. Lena was elated, telling her she would. Jacob came to the microphone, "Ladies and gentlemen, we have an added treat this evening. We have comedian Brenda Davis with us. Just back from her honeymoon, please put your hands together for Brenda Davis-Johnson."

The room filled with applause as Lena came to the mike. As per usual, she had everyone hilariously laughing.

When she finished, Geena went to the microphone, the fashion show beginning. As the models walked around, people were enjoying the show, impressed with Ronnie's fashions. The contestant who won the fashion talent show was announced by Belinda and awarded a scholarship. At the end of the show, Geena provided information regarding the fashions, and exhibits, advising information was included on the programs, and cards left at the table. Geena called Ronnie, Rob and Matt, to the stage, introducing them. "Please feel free to speak to them, or you may speak with any of the capable staff to assist you."

Jacob Meyers came back to the microphone taking over. "I've had an enjoyable time thus far. How about you? Are you having a good time?" The guests cheered, applauded, and said yes. Continuing, "That's great. Get ready to put your hands together once again, for Ronnie Rodgers and J.C. Taylor. Come on, come on, give it up."

Coming to the stage, they were warmly greeted with applause. Ronnie graciously thanked everyone for attending, playing soft chords on the keyboard, in that style of hers which was becoming signature. She and Jason acknowledged the musicians playing with them. Rick Harrison on guitar, Will 'Tom-Thump' Richards on bass, and on the drums, Benjamin 'Baby-Boom' Richards. The musical renditions coming from this group was magical, everyone enjoying their performance.

At the end they posed for pictures and signed autographs. People bought the CD's, which Brick had on hand. Finally, the last of the guests left, another successful event at the Starfire behind them.

Ronnie gathered the staff and expressed her gratitude for their hard work and input. "We have become family, working hard, but still enjoying each other. Over the past few weeks, we have been able to bond closely with the community. Without your support and hard work, the Starfire would not be the success it has become. We wanted to let you know how valuable you are, and we appreciate you. I had chef prepare us a light buffet, so we can celebrate and relax together. There will also be something extra in your paycheck. Now relax and enjoy yourselves."

They enjoyed themselves immensely, dining and joking with each other. Lena and Brick shared the highlights of their honeymoon, as only they could do it. They were funny individually, but together they were over the top, keeping everyone laughing. When done, everyone pitched in to clean up, so they could leave in a timely fashion.

Everyone had gone home, leaving Ronnie and this amazing close-knit family together. They stayed at the Starfire, listening to music and dancing. Brick said, "Y'all have fun. As for me, I'm collecting my girl and I'm heading home, bye." Lena said good night and they were gone, wanting to enjoy their new home. Her parents had an early flight for Monday morning. Uncle Seth left after their reception last weekend.

Geena said, "I guess it's time we head out too, so Jacob can lock up and get some rest." Fortunately, Jacob did not have to go far, as he resided in one of the apartments upstairs.

Before leaving they decided to have an early dinner tomorrow, before everyone departed for home on Monday. Geena and Matt's parents had planned another adventure together. C J and Rob were planning summer events for Koach's Kids. Will and the rest of the musicians were going to be busy with Hudson Flow and various other projects.

Belinda was returning home Sunday evening. She and Cindy were going to go over the scheduling for Ronnie. They would let Geena know about the orders for Matt and Rob. JET and Lee Anne were flying his parents' home to Canada, planning on staying with them for a week. Not having to worry about Geena for a week, Lee Anne could collaborate with Felicia, regarding the upcoming event in Grand Rapid Falls.

Matt and Geena flew Peach's mom and dad home to North Carolina. They were planning to stay at Summit Meadows a few days, Ronnie and Jason tagging along. While there, Matt wanted to have a discussion with the Mayor of Summit Hill.

Matt came up with an idea to build homes for veterans and their families. The mayor was open to the idea, saying he would pitch the idea to the Town Council. Matt discussed the idea with Jacob Meyers who agreed to oversee the project after the Grand Rapid Falls project.

After Matt met with the mayor, he and Geena had a marvelous week, along with Jason and Ronnie. While there, Geena received a call from Lee Anne with some wonderful news. Some friends of JET's mom and dad had been in New York visiting friends when Ronnie had her affair at the Starfire. They were impressed and inquired about doing something similar in Toronto. Paul and his friend were collaborating with them on the project.

Geena and Ronnie were excited and agreed to help them with their project, telling Matt about the new venture. JET asked Geena if Lee Anne could go and assist him in Texas. She agreed, knowing that Felicia would be on top of her affairs.

Matt thought the venture could not have come at a better time. It was time for JET, Jacob and himself, to be headed for Texas. The time for Geena's affair was just around the corner, and they needed to be there to oversee the project. JET advised Geena he and Lee Anne would meet them in New York at the end of the week. His dad and a friend of his dads were tagging along. They would fly the team back to Toronto. Ronnie contacted Cindy, needing her to contact Brick to make plans for Hudson Flow and their band to meet her, Jason, and Geena there.

At the end of the week, they met in New York and departed for Toronto. Brick arranged for Sharon Wilson to play at the Starfire, while Hudson Flow was away. JET's dad also invited Lena, who was doing a show in Detroit. She accepted, letting him know she would meet them there once her show finished in Detroit. The affair in Toronto was the next weekend. The plans in Toronto were already in place, needing only Geena and Cindy to add in the additions to the affair.

Matt, JET, Lee Anne and Jacob headed off for Texas to get ready for Geena's surprise. Everyone knew what needed to be done, in Texas and Felicia was taking care of things in New York.

Chapter 49

Affair for a GEM

The unexpected trip to Toronto was a success, generating further engagements for Hudson Flow, Ronnie, and Jason. Upon returning to New York, Geena only had a few days to finish getting ready for her assignment for the Olive Winfield show. She was overjoyed to be working with Olive and was eager to prove herself to her idol.

Ronnie and Jason were busy at the Starfire. Ronnie told Geena she would see her in Grand Rapid Falls. She and Jason were going to be there before her, so they could rehearse for the show. She knew Olive was going to be keeping Geena busy with Seth, Leland, and Theo. She would be going over their backgrounds and interview material.

All the plans in Grand Rapid Falls were finalized. Travel arrangements and hotel reservations were made for the guests by JET and C J. Olive Winfield arranged for a first-class ticket for Geena on a commercial airline, arriving two days before the event. Olive booked a reservation for Geena in a nearby town for the first night, planning for her belongings to be transferred to the wedding suite in the GRF Hotel. She would personally keep Geena busy and out of the way.

Everything was arranged. Felicia, and Matt's NY assistant Grace, closed Geena and Matt's New York offices. Both staffs were in Grand Rapid Falls conducting business from there. Everyone pitched in to help with the surprise for Geena. Keeping their fingers crossed and praying no one would let the cat out of the bag. So far, so good.

When Geena arrived, she had to hit the ground running. Olive informed her they would be filming and conducting interviews with Seth, Theo, and Leland for tomorrow's show.

Olive made reservations at a restaurant for an informal interview with them. She had a crew on hand and made sure there would not be any interruptions.

Geena had done her homework on the three legends. She knew about the accomplishments made regarding their professions. She was aware of the various ventures they were involved in, and their contributions given to charities and communities. Geena spoke to them about their latest joint venture in Grand Rapid Falls. Olive knew Geena was extremely talented, but even she was impressed by her thoroughness.

Everything was captured on video by the crew. Geena and Olive went over the material, making sure they had everything needed to make the show successful. Even though the day had been long conducting the interviews, Olive was not taking any chances. She called Lee Anne and Ronnie to meet them at the restaurant after the interviews. They would see to it Geena was kept busy for the remainder of the evening.

Olive winked at them as they approached Geena, saying goodbye. Lee Anne and Ronnie hugged Geena. Lee Anne said, "We saw the end of the interview. You did a terrific job and I think Ms. Winfield was impressed with your work." Geena answered, "I think it went well and I hope she liked the way I conducted the interviews." Ronnie said, "I don't think she would have left if she wasn't satisfied."

Geena said, "I'm nervous and excited about tomorrow." Lee Anne said, "Well don't be. You know how to do this with your eyes shut. Olive would not have asked you if she felt you couldn't handle the job. You are great at what you do, and tomorrow everyone is going to know."

They talked further until it started getting late. They said good night, telling Geena to get some rest. Matt called and spoke briefly with her before he said good night, telling her he missed and loved her.

The time has come, and the stage is set. Everyone and everything are in place. Matt and the rest of 'the Crew' are elated. The air is filled with electricity and excitement. Matt said to C J, "We have pulled what seemed like the impossible off, right under Geena's nose. Man, she is going to be surprised." Responding, C J said, "You can say that again. We still were able to manage our affairs and keep this all from her. I can't believe it. We did it! Brick chimed in, "Just think of it. She was involved in a couple of instances and wasn't aware of it. We are going to have fun with this."

Matt said, "Look at this! Family, friends, colleagues. This is a fantastic turn out. Everyone is here. I am so proud of her." C J said, "You are so right. Our girl has been a blessing to not only us, but to a lot of other people. She deserves this and more." Olive came over, to speak with them, "Congratulations, you guys have pulled it off. I'm so happy I can be a part of this." Matt responded, "Thank you Olive. With your help, we were able to make this a reality. I'm glad you liked the overall project. Assisting us to get Theo, Leland, and Seth together, really helped put this over the top." Olive said, "Thank you for allowing me to take part."

C J said, "Matt, please step over here with Brick and me." Moving away from everyone, Matt said, "What's up guys, everything is moving according to plan, right?"

C J responded, "Sure Matt, but Brick and I were thinking. We know you are planning to propose to G this evening at the banquet. But don't you think it would be romantic to propose on the live telecast? Geena will love it." Matt didn't notice, but Brick was signaling Olive to come over. Matt replied, "I don't know. I thought it would be romantic to propose at dinner, with family and friends nearby."

Perfectly timed and on cue, Olive came over. "A proposal to who, Geena?" C J said, "Yes. We're trying to tell Matt, Geena would love it."

Olive said, "I think it's a wonderful idea. The ratings for Geena's first show will be through the roof." Brick said, "See Matt, Ms. Winfield thinks it is a great idea too. You know you can't let our girl down." C J and Brick played their part well, with assistance from Olive. Matt said, "I suppose you are right. Okay, I'll do it, but when shall I propose to her?" Olive stepped in with a plan she felt could be executed.

Matt liked the idea, thinking it would be easy. Neither one of them were afraid of the limelight, therefore, it would not be difficult to pull off. Little did Matt realize the wool was now being pulled over his eyes. Brick could hardly contain himself. He was so excited. Laughing to himself, he thought this is going to be so much fun. Now, everything is in place.

Olive said, "Places everyone. I've sent the limousine to pick up Geena, who will be arriving shortly. C J said to Matt, "Have you got the ring?" Matt replied, "Yes, I've got it," laughing, "I hope she accepts." C J and Brick laughing, with him. C J said, "I don't think you have to worry yourself about that."

Geena just stepped into the lobby when the limousine arrived to pick her up. This was a big day for her, and she wished Matt could be here to share it with her. She knew he was extremely busy but thought maybe she should have invited him. Whatever he was doing, she knew it was important and did not want to distract him, knowing he would come if she asked.

The drive was only a few minutes away, and she was almost there, excited about the show. She was grateful Olive Winfield asked her to do the show. The driver pulled up to the rear of the studio.

Someone was there to greet her and took her to Ms. Winfield's office. Olive stood up, giving Geena a warm hug. "Hi Geena. Are you ready for this exciting show?" Geena said, "Some butterflies in my stomach, but I'm ready." Olive laughed and said, "Me too, but you've got this. Did you enjoy yourself with your friends?" Replying, "Yes, I did. They're really like my sisters. We watch out for one another. They didn't stay late, telling me to go to bed so I would be alert for today." Olive answered, "It looks like they were right. You seem refreshed and ready to go."

There was a knock at the door, and Leland, Seth, and Theo entered. Leland said, "Hi ladies. We just wanted to say thank you for the way you conducted the interviews yesterday. We felt comfortable." Theo added, "You made It feel like it was being at home." Laughing, Seth said, "You sure did. I was ready to tell you all my secrets," everyone laughing. Olive said, "All I had to do was stand there and watch. This lady is extremely proficient at her job." Laughing, "She reminds me of when I started out. Guys, she is the real deal."

There was another knock on the door, a voice calling out, "We're ready for you on set in five Ms. Winfield."

Olive said, "Thank you. Well, is everyone ready to get the show on the road?" They stood up and headed for the set to await the introduction of the show.

Olive was announced, and she went out to greet the waiting audience, warmly met with applause. "Well, hello there everyone. It's so nice to have you here today, and the viewers who are tuned in at home. We've a special show today, with plenty of guests and surprises. First, today I am happy to share the stage with an extremely talented co-host, who is going to get us started. Everyone, please give a warm welcome to Ms. Geena Michaels." Geena entered the set, greeted by warm applause. "Hi everyone, I'm happy to be here." Smiling. "Thank you, thank you."

Geena continued, "It is my pleasure to introduce our guests for today. With us are three fantastic gentlemen. They are well known to everyone. Each achieving goals and setting a high standard for others to follow. Achievers, who are trailblazers at what they do individually. Working untiringly, giving themselves to the community, giving funds to various charities, and spearheading various projects to assist others."

Smiling and continuing, "Which brings us why we are here today. Please help me greet these gentlemen. Award winning playwright and movie mogul, Theo Porter; nationally acclaimed basketball star, Leland Jackson, and America's funny man, Seth Howard." Cheering, the crowd gave them a standing ovation.

Geena continued, "Yesterday, I had the esteemed pleasure interviewing these gentlemen. I have some footage from the interviews which will explain why these men came together, combining their efforts. Let's look at the footage."

Everyone watched, learning about Seth Howard's summer camp for inner-city youth, and the seasonal cabins for families during the holiday seasons. The sports complex named after Leland Jackson, providing sports, educational programs, and scholarships for youths. The theater and performing arts center, developed by Theo Porter. The complex will be the first of many, in a chain of similar theaters across the country. Geena spoke with each man, allowing them to expound on their projects. She addressed the audience once again.

"Grand Rapid Falls now has its own airport, which houses a mall for shopping and a restaurant for dining. There is housing for veterans and their families to live. There are two major hotels and a medical center. An amusement park is scheduled to open just before summer. This mega project has created employment opportunities for the local and surrounding communities."

The air was buzzing with excitement, as the audience received the good news, and applauded. Olive Winfield came back. "I'd like to thank Geena Michaels, for a wonderful presentation, and these gentlemen for their visionary efforts for Grand Rapid Falls."

Continuing, Olive stated, "I promised you a show filled with surprises." Winking into the camera, "That's right, there's still more. For your musical entertainment we have Pacific Sunset, and Hudson Flow. To help us get our laugh on, comedienne Brenda Davis, followed by singing sensation and pianist Ronnie Rodgers, accompanied by jazz saxophonist J. C. Taylor."

The entertainers came out and performed. When the performances were over, Olive had her staff come out with gift bags for the audience. Inside the gift bags were the performers recordings, and autographed photos of the guests. Everyone was ecstatic. Olive said, "These gifts have been provided by our guests and performers. I hope you enjoy them."

Olive continued, "Geena, to my knowledge, you have been involved in many projects yourself. You're involved with a group, affectionally known as 'the Crew.' Can you tell me a little about this group?" Geena said, "Sure Olive. Most of us grew up together, and we've worked on many projects, trying to give back to the community whenever we can."

Olive said, "That's putting it mildly everyone. My staff and I have researched this group, and I want to tell you they have made some amazing accomplishments. Which brings me to the next segment of our show. We know the extent and involvement of our guests, but how did this project in Grand Rapid Falls get started? When was the overall vision conceived? Our next guests may be able to provide the answers to these questions. Ladies and gentlemen, let's receive Robert King, Samuel Johnson, Jonathan Troissant, and Charles Jackson, Sr."

The look on her face was one of astonishment. Geena was shocked.

As her longtime friends came on the set, Geena's thoughts were spinning wildly. They were greeted warmly by the other guests, as if they were extremely familiar with each other. They came over to embrace her. Brick laughing said, "Has the cat got your tongue?"

Before she could respond, Olive was speaking again. "These are her best friends, family. They have been through a lot together through the years." Olive showed clips of the interviews she had with them, which explained how involved they were in this project.

Olive addressed the viewers again. "This fantastic team has worked on this project since last year. Did you know anything about this Geena?" Answering, "No, I didn't. I'm overwhelmed because I usually work side by side with them on these types of projects. Now I am finding out they have been involved with this project for a year. I'm totally shocked."

Smiling, Olive said, "Would you like to explain C J?" Geena thought, how could she know his nickname is C J? He began, "This has been one of the hardest projects we have ever worked on," the rest of the guys nodding their heads. "G is usually in the trenches right beside us, but this time we endeavored to keep her away from the project. In order to do this, we enlisted your help, along with these other fine gentlemen."

Olive said, "You look stunned. We have more surprises in store for you Geena. We have a video connection for you to see, along with the rest of the viewers. Allow me to introduce you to the missing man from this group, George Matthews. Matt, can you hear us?" Geena could not believe her eyes and ears, it was Matt. Olive knew his nickname, just like she knew C J's. Matt's voice snapped her back. "Yes, Ms. Winfield, I hear you fine." Olive said, "Matt, can you bring some clarity to what's going on here?" Geena thinking, yes, please do! "Sure Olive. We wanted to surprise Geena, and in order to do this, we had to come up with ways to keep her out of the way. We got everyone involved."

Matt continued, "We got her staff, family, and friends to help us. Jacob Meyers also played a major role in the development of this project. In some instances, Geena helped us too, and she didn't even know it. I'll keep this short. If you can roll the footage, we shot previously, it will take the befuddled look of hers, off her face."

The clip revealed Geena's new headquarter offices, and GEM Studios. It also showed the newly expanded offices of JET Stream International. The new headquarter offices for Galaxy Quest was also introduced. The short clip was narrated by Olive and Matt, explaining the overall project.

Matt said to Geena, "I'm sorry I'm not presently on stage with you guys, but I've been watching remotely. Geena you are doing a fantastic job and..." Olive jumping in, "Looks like a connection issue. Geena, you look surprised and happy, but you seem to be a bit melancholy." Answering, "Yes, I am surprised and happy. This is so overwhelming, but somewhat bittersweet. Usually the whole team is present, and I'm sorry Matt is not here. I want to thank him, along with the rest..."

The audience was now applauding, cutting Geena off from finishing her statement. She wondered why they were applauding. She looked at the guys with a quizzical look upon her face, as if they had an inkling. Smiling, Brick was pointing behind her. She turned to see what he was pointing at. It was Matt, standing behind her!

He reached down, helping her up from her seat, giving her a warm hug. She couldn't believe her eyes, he was here, holding her in his arms. Matt said, "Surprise! I would not have missed this for anything. I'm so proud of you. We all are. This has been difficult for both of us. Missing, and wanting to be with each other. Keeping this hidden from you was not an easy task, but well worth the wait."

Matt got down on bended knee, the audience gasping an awe, and listening intently to every word being spoken. Tears were beginning to well up in Geena's eyes, knowing what was coming next.

Matt took out the engagement ring from the box, saying, "We've been waiting what seems like forever for this moment. I love you, and if you will have me, I want to share my life with you. So, Geena Elaine Michaels, I'm asking you to become my wife, and requesting you give me the honor of becoming your husband?"

Geena nodding her head, smiling, crying, said yes. Matt slipped the ring onto her finger. Geena pulled Matt up to her, hugging him. Brick started chanting, "Kiss him, kiss him," everyone joining in.

They kissed, while Ronnie and Jason softly played in the background, "The First Time Ever I Saw Your Face." Beginning to dance, Olive said to Seth, "Please break that up. They're going to have everyone sobbing." Seth complying, "Alright you two, this is not the club. We've got a show to finish."

Olive said, "This brings us to our final surprise. Everyone was asked to dress formally for the banquet after the show. Well, no banquet will be taking place, but there is a reception. Your wedding reception! How about that for a surprise?" Matt said, "I'm not certain Geena is going to go along with this." Geena said, "I don't even have a wedding dress." Olive stated, "All taken care of. With everyone's help, we've arranged everything for you. Marriage license, your minister is here to perform the ceremony, music, and your gown. Even your guests. Look in the audience. Recognize anyone?" The lights were brought up. Geena looked out and exclaimed, "Oh my goodness. Who's watching the office?" Someone yelled out, "Go get your man G." Everyone laughing. Olive said. "Go back, sign the paperwork, and get ready to enjoy the rest of your lives together. Lee Anne, please help your sister get ready."

She continued, "Meanwhile, let's enjoy America's funny man, Seth Howard, then let's hear more from Ronnie Rodgers, and J. C. Taylor, while we wait for Geena and Matt." Seth had everyone doubled up with laughter, and they enjoyed the music of Ronnie and Jason once again.

The paperwork was taken care of, and Lee Anne whisked Geena to a dressing room. Once there, with the help of Elaine and Sarah, they helped her prepare for the wedding. Geena said, "Lee Anne, I can't believe you hid this from me for so long." Lee Anne replied, "Believe me, it wasn't easy. We were doing things right under your nose, sometimes we had to be careful not to laugh out loud. Some of the situations were funny. What is amazing, we never had to lie to you about things. You came up with solutions which we laughed about when you were not around us."

Sarah said, "Dear, so many people love you, and were involved in this deception. I've never seen a secret of this magnitude stay hidden for so long. So many people knew what was going on, it's simply amazing."

Elaine said, "Oh honey, you look so beautiful. I'm extremely happy for you." There was a knock at the door. It was Ken. "Ahh, look at my girl. I am so proud of you." Geena said, "Okay mom and dad, stop it. You're going to have me crying in a minute." Lee Anne said, "Don't you dare. Everything is perfect, don't ruin it."

Lee Anne gave Geena blue diamond earrings with pearls, for the something blue. Sarah gave her a pearl necklace which belonged to her mother, for the something borrowed. Elaine and Ken gave her a new white-laced handkerchief. There was a knock at the door, "Are you ready Ms. Michaels?" Geena answered, "Yes, I am." Elaine and Sarah left to take their places. Ken said, "Come on sweetie. Let me walk my girl down the aisle." Geena said, "Okay daddy. Lead the way, Lee Anne. Thank you for standing with me."

Responding, "Wild horses couldn't have stopped me, and don't worry, I've got Matt's wedding band."

Matt and C J were preparing to leave for the altar. C J said, "Let's get the show on the road. I've got Geena's wedding band in my pocket." Matt said, "Thanks C J for helping me get through this project and for standing with me today." Brick gave C J gold and diamond cufflinks, which Matt had selected for him. C J thanked him and said, "No problem. We always stick together, now let's get you hitched."

Olive thought of everything. While everyone was waiting, she had her crew set up a chapel for the ceremony, with chairs for the family and close friends. The way it was set up, everyone in the audience would be able to see, and there was an overhead large video screen.

Olive said, "Everything is set, and we are ready to go. Before the ceremony begins, let me share what the bride will be wearing."

She described Geena's wedding ensemble. A shear ivory beaded lace overlay, with a V-neck bodice and shear long sleeves; an A-line fitted ivory full-length skirt, with deep rear pleat, and a short, beaded head piece. The outfit is designed by Ronnie of Powder Puff Fashions & Designs. Ivory satin three-inch sling back heels, by Ros Hommerson. Blue diamond and pearl earrings, and a matching bracelet. The bouquet consists of water lilies, baby breathes and peach roses.

Ronnie and Jason were playing soft music, as the groom and best man entered. The processional began with Lee Anne, followed by Ken proudly escorting his daughter to the altar. He shook hands with Matt and placed Geena's hand in Matt's hand. Their minister performed the ceremony, and they exchanged their wedding vows. After the vows, he said, "You may now salute your bride. Ladies and gentlemen, I present to you, Mr. & Mrs. George Edward Matthews."

The ceremony was over, and Olive closed the show. "I hope you have enjoyed todays special. I know we all wish Geena and Matt much happiness. See you at the roast," smiling and winking, "I mean the reception." Everyone crowded around Geena and Matt, offering them best wishes and congratulations. The studio began to empty, as people who were attending the reception left. The bridal party, family, and close friends posed for wedding pictures, before going to the reception.

Brick served as the Master of Ceremonies, announcing the family and guests. Then announcing, "Ladies and gentlemen, the Maid of Honor, Ms. Leslie Howard, escorted by the Best Man, Mr. Charles Jackson, Sr."

Continuing, "Please stand on your feet, put your hands together, and help me welcome, Mr. & Mrs. George Edward Matthews." Matt and Geena entered to rousing applause and cheers. They slowly made their way in, pausing for people to take pictures, and finally reached their seats.

Brick continued, "Now you all know I like to have fun, and let me tell you this, I'm going to have plenty this evening. I want you to have a great time. We have fantastic live entertainment for you. There is no sitting and relaxing allowed this evening. So, dance, sing, laugh, and be happy for our new couple."

There was the usual first dance by the bride and groom, followed by the maid of honor, and the best man. Then the parents danced with the bride and groom.

Brick said, "Geena and Matt, I hope you guys have your dancing shoes. It looks like a lot of people want to dance with you. Don't even try to leave early for the honeymoon. You've waited this long. Security, make sure you keep your eyes on these two, they're not going anywhere. We have plans for them." Everyone was laughing.

Dinner was served and the entertainment was just as Brick said it would be, fantastic. In between the performances, speeches were given, and toasts were made. Anecdotes were shared by those close to Geena, which explained how everyone was in on the game to fool her. "Yeah, that's right, Ms. On Top of My Game Geena." Brick never missing an opportunity to keep everyone laughing.

Just as Olive predicted, the reception turned into a roast. Geena could not believe all the things which took place right under her nose. She said, "You guys got me really good, and you, my darling Matt, you've got a lot to answer for," kissing him. Matt stood up, taking Geena by the hand, leading her to the dance floor.

Taking her into his arms and looking down at her he said, "Things really have heated up since Salt Lake City," laughing. Geena responded, "Yes, and that kiss on the forehead," looking up at him with a twinkle in her eyes. She sighed, and kissed Matt again, saying, "I love you, and I want you to know my insides are overjoyed with happiness, Mr. Matthews." Matt said, "I know exactly how you feel. I anxiously counted the days going by, with great anticipation for this day to arrive. I love your Mrs. Matthews," kissing her.

Watching them, Brick said, "Okay you two, break it up! I need some dessert, so let's cut this cake," Brick keeping everyone laughing. They cut the cake, and as it was being served, they thanked everyone for coming. Brick called on Lena to assist him. Lena said, "All you single ladies, take your shoes off, and come to the floor. It's time for a lucky lady to catch the bouquet." All the ladies gathered on the floor, excitingly waiting for Geena to toss the bouquet. Lena said, "Are you ready? One, two, three, let her go." Geena pretended to throw the bouquet, then stopped. Lena said, "Oh, oh. She got you. Just a little payback," everyone laughing. "Let's try this again Geena."

Lena continued, "One, two, three, let her go." Geena tossed the bouquet over her shoulder with precision, Lee Anne reaching out and catching it. Brick said, "Okay Matt, your turn." Matt interjected, "In the words of a good friend, y'all not lookin' at my woman's legs." He reached into his pocket, walked over to JET, and handed him the garter. "Here you go buddy, go grab your girl."

Everyone was laughing, Brick saying, "There he goes again, trying to be the funny man." Lena said, "I think he got you again baby," everyone continuing to laugh. The festivities continued, and everyone was having a wonderful time. Matt said, "Hey Brick, I sign the checks for security. Geena and I are out of here." Lena said, "Wow, he got you again. Baby I think you better leave him alone in the future."

Matt and Geena walked out holding hands, starting for the honeymoon suite. While on the elevator, Matt took Geena into his arms, kissing her softly and tenderly. They walked to the door. Matt looked down, kissed Geena on the forehead, and turned to walk away. Geena reached out grabbing him, "Not tonight big boy, you're not going anywhere," pulling him back. Matt scooped her up into his arms, carrying her across the threshold, and shut the door with his foot.

He placed her gently down onto the canopy covered bed. Geena pulled him into her arms, Matt responding. First, kissing her nape, and moving slowly to the back of her ear. Then he moved around to her cheek, gently kissing it, before continuing to her soft waiting lips. Matt loved the way Geena always held him close to her. Softly caressing him with her hands. First, down his neck, moving down his back. Geena was thinking, he's got me trembling again. This man sure knows how to make me feel good. When Matt reached her lips, she parted them, as she met his lips and tongue with great anticipation. Geena thought. Nope, he's not going anywhere tonight!

Chapter 50

Up, Up and Away!

Matt awoke early. He was laying on his side looking at Geena. The light of the new day gently cascading softly across the beauty who was beside him. Last night had been pure ecstasy. They gave themselves to one another softly, gently, unceasingly. Discovering, searching and charting new and unexplored territory. Matt always felt truly blessed knowing this wonderful woman, and now they truly belonged to each other.

Geena stirred, opening her eyes. As she focused in on Matt, she smiled, "Good morning Mr. Matthews." He gently ran his fingers through her hair, "Good morning Mrs. Matthews. You looked so peaceful and beautiful, I didn't want to disturb you." Still smiling, "You're so sweet honey," softly kissing him on his neck, cuddling up in his arms.

Geena loved the way Matt held her in his arms. She always felt safe and special. Last night was wonderful.

They were attentive and tender throughout the night. They made love, they talked, and they laughed. Sometimes they just held one another. She felt elated, knowing this was just the beginning of a new adventure they would be sharing.

Geena let go of Matt, starting to get up. He gently reached out, pulling her back to him. Hugging her, "Don't be long sweetie, I've got plans for you Mrs. Matthews." Smiling and winking back at him, "I've got plans for you too, Mr. Matthews. I'll be right back," Matt chuckling.

It wasn't too long before she returned, sliding under the covers and reaching for him. Matt moved quickly, before she could get her arms around him. "My turn. I'll be right back." Geena smiling, "Make sure you do, I've got something I want to try." Matt said, "Intriguing."

Matt came back and slipped under the covers. She said, "That didn't take long." Responding, "I'm anxious to find out what you're planning to try. Just what do you have in mi...." Before he could finish, Geena was in his arms.

First, kissing him on the side of his neck, then moving to his shoulders, and then back to his neck, repeating the same on the other side. She then kissed him behind his ear, softly letting her fingers caress his chest. Her lips moved to his cheek, and slowly around to his waiting lips. She kissed him on one corner, then moving to the other corner. She gently kissed his lips, slowly, softly.

Parting his lips, their tongues met. Her warm tender kisses were driving him crazy. Matt's heart was racing wildly as he kissed her in return. Gently he turned Geena on her back, responding to the pleasure she was giving him. Time elapsed with what seemed like an eternity.

"Umm, that was wonderful. Anytime you have the notion you have something you would like to try, please feel free to indulge yourself. Trust me, I'll be yours to do with as you please. I love you G." Smiling, "I love you too, Matt. We'd better get cracking, because the way I'm feeling, this could go on all day. We have to get packed, and then meet everyone for breakfast before we leave."

Matt smiled, "Not to worry sweetie. Just pack a few essential things. Travel light, travel right. Lee Anne and Ronnie will take care of our things. We're going to be gone for a while, and I figured we can get what we need, as we need it."

They got up, and quickly prepared themselves to meet everyone for breakfast. Geena said, "By the way Mr. Matthews, where are we going for our honeymoon?" Replying, "West my sweet lady, west. On an adventure, following the sun until it brings us back home."

Smiling, Geena said, "Sounds intriguing." Matt continued, "We are going to take the jet. I know how you love to fly, so you will be able to get plenty of flying time. We will be going to a lot of places, and we are going to have loads of fun. There are a lot of scenes waiting for us to photograph. The world is at our feet, and we are going to take time to enjoy it. Our teams have everything planned, so things run smoothly while we're away. If we want to be involved in something, we can do it on our terms. I have been planning this for a long time. If there's anything you want or need, just let me know, and our teams will get it implemented to your satisfaction."

Geena said, "Sounds as if you thought of everything. You have gone to great lengths to make me happy, and I appreciate all you've done. You guys really kept me in the dark." Replying, "Yes, we did. It was a team effort. Not an easy task hiding things from you and keeping you in the dark. I am certain everyone is going to tell you the lengths we took to keep this a secret from you." Shaking her head, "You sure did put one over on me, and from what I heard last night, right under my nose."

They went down to meet everyone, and as expected, things got busy very quickly. Holding hands, they entered the dining area. Brick stood up saying, "Ladies and gentlemen, the blushing bride and her groom." Everyone was laughing and commenting how radiant she looked. Not to leave Matt out of the commentary, C J said, "Matt looks as if he just won the Grammy for best movie." Matt said, "Better than that. I won the Geena for the rest of my life."

As per usual, they ate, talked, and laughed, having a marvelous time. They filled Geena in on what they did to surprise her, and how she inadvertently became involved in some of the plans. Geena said, "I can't believe how many were involved in this. How my family, friends and staff kept this secret is amazing. I love you all and I love you Matt."

C J said, "Olive Winfield was of great assistance, not only fooling you, but fooling Matt too. His plan was to propose to you at the dinner. She wasn't having any of it, saying the viewers would love it." Lee Anne said, "She was right. Geena, the ratings for your first show were through the roof. The response has been great, agents wanting to get their people showcased and spotlighted on your show."

Geena said, "I still can't believe I have my own show. This is so amazing and wonderful." Ronnie said, "That's what I said. It's unbelievable the way you and everyone helped me. I am grateful to have played my little role. It was fun pulling the wool over your eyes, sometimes right under your nose. Ms. Geena, who is always on top of everything. Sometimes Lee Anne and I had a hard time not to laugh, it was so funny." Everyone was laughing and laughing. They had a fantastic time.

Soon, it was time to go. Everyone went to the airport to see them off. Matt and Geena walked around the aircraft, inspecting it before liftoff. Smiling, Geena looked up at Matt and said, "Time to kick the tires, and light the fires." They started up the steps, and upon reaching the top, they turned, waving farewell to everyone. Ronnie and Lee Anne made certain JET and C J had all their belongings onboard.

Final checks were made once inside the cockpit, for the aircraft, and the tower was contacted for liftoff instructions. Matt said, "We're headed for San Francisco-Oakland and from there, Honolulu, Hawaii. We should be there before sunset. We'll probably get a lot of great shots. Your camera is in the box behind you. Do you want to take the controls sweetie?" Excited, Geena said, "You know I do," taking the controls. Geena expertly taxied to the runway assigned. As she turned onto the runway, she powered the engines and the jet surged forward.

Up, up and away!

Epilogue

Pathways to Love

Matt and Geena had a wonderful flight to the coast. Matt was at the controls, and Geena was busy snapping pictures of the Rockies. She also got some shots of the Golden Gate Bridge before they landed. They spent a few hours in San Francisco, before moving on to Hawaii.

They landed in Honolulu just before sunset, Matt getting some great shots before landing. Matt gave JET the itinerary and he arranged for the jet to be serviced, along every leg of their journey. They checked into the hotel. Settling in, they decided to take a walk along the beach. They found a place to have dinner, enjoying the cuisine and the show. They had a wonderful time, finally deciding to return to their room.

Geena looked at Matt and wondered why he was being quiet. "Honey is everything okay? Are you feeling alright? You've been so quiet."

Replying, "I'm sorry sweetie. Everything is wonderful and I couldn't be happier than I am at this moment." Geena said, "You could have fooled me. You looked so far away." Matt said, "Sorry about that. My mind went back in time to when we were young adults and we first met, also reflecting about the rest of our friends. We have been through so much together, always supporting and being there for one another. When I met you, even way back then, I knew you were the one for me. We always worked well together. Solving issues almost effortlessly. I told my dad how I felt about you from the very first time I met you. You have always been special to me and a great supporter."

Geena said, "I never knew you felt that way back then. It's funny though. When I met you, I had this desire to always be around you.

I always felt safe and special around you. I've loved working with you on all the various projects we were involved in through the years. I had such a crush on you. I realized I wanted to be with you. Everything I did, was in preparation for when we would be together. I didn't know when, but I knew someday we would be together. The hardest time for me, was when I went away to school. I missed you so much. I knew I had to concentrate if I was going to achieve my goals, and I needed that time away. If I didn't you would have been a distraction."

Matt replied, "I know what you mean. I felt that way when I was in the military. I turned down a promising career there because I knew I had my own goals to achieve. I worked hard because I was determined to carve out a life for us so you would be happy. I set the standard high for myself because I knew I wanted you in my life. Being my closest friend, C J would stay in my case about you. He knew how I felt about you and he stayed on my case, telling me I should tell you how I felt. Many times, I started to, but I stuck to my original goal."

Geena came over to Matt, cuddling in his arms. "Oh Matt, I have loved you forever. Somehow, holding on to the belief we would be together as a couple. I loved when we all worked on projects together, because it meant I would be around you constantly. The hardest part was when you took me home and said goodnight. Hugging me or kissing me on the cheek. I felt like I was your little sister. I always wanted to reach up and kiss you. When we were in Salt Lake City, I snapped, making up my mind it was now or never."

Matt laughed, "Yeah, you made it pretty clear kissing you on the forehead was not the way to go," now both laughing. "To tell you the truth, I wish you could have heard the conversation I was having with myself in my head. You would have died laughing."

Matt continued, "We're together now at last. We have all worked hard, trying to make a difference in our lives, and for those we've met. We've done some good work and we are not through yet."

Matt chuckled, "That's what I was thinking about when you asked what was wrong. What we have achieved is amazing, and we have traveled many routes to achieve these goals. Always determined and never giving up, we have helped many. Every one of our friends has this goal to make a difference for their family, friends, and community."

Geena kissed Matt on his forehead, "Payback," both laughing. You're right honey. Sometimes it's like we don't have time for anything else. It's like we have a game plan. It's amazing we are alike, but still, we are individuals. I believe this is why we work well together and have achieved our goals. It gave us a combined strength and love".

"I often wonder why we click the way we do, but you've hit the nail right on the head G. We have a love for each other and for what we do. Being able to help others is what makes us tick. The world is hard enough, but we have tried to make a difference in it, rather than talk about it. This is such a beautiful world. It would be wonderful if we could all come together, to just have respect for one another. To build up, instead of tear down. To lift one another up."

Geena said, "You're right honey. We all have our own life journeys, but sometimes we need to stop along the way and share our gifts with others. There are many ways we can traverse, but letting our love reach out for others could make the difference. As we journey down life's different paths, letting our love shine."

Geena and Matt looked at each other smiling. Then saying together.

"Pathways to love."

Pathways To Love – Poem

By James Gilliam

Pathways to Love:
Necessary tools needed to acquire for the journey that you aspire, and let not the journey begin until there's inner peace, a peace within.

Complaints/Compromise:
Because unknowing can breed confusion, anything can happen so just be pliable, able to adapt with a new idea.

Expectations/Exceptions:
Letting go to be used. Seeing the way, you need to choose, but being prepared letting good decisions cause opportunities heightened by love.

Judgments/Adjustments:
Creating harmony, judgments of no one, acceptance of adjustments because we're not judges. Freewill and choice enables insight and hindsight to directions, just as a beacon lights the pathway, so should it be on the pathway to love.

Pressures/Pleasures:
Aspiring ideas requires subtle pressures, nudges needed in order to enjoy the pleasures on the pathway to love.

About the Author

Born and raised in the Flatbush section of Brooklyn, New York. He was educated in the New York City public school system and in the United States Army. While serving, he achieved the rank of sergeant, and is a Viet Nam era veteran, serving until he was honorably discharged.

Raised in an area with diverse ethnic backgrounds, he developed close friendships in the community, school, and church. He and his friends enjoyed playing softball, stickball, and football. They also enjoyed riding their bicycles everywhere. When it rained, they enjoyed going to the movies, bowling, playing checkers, chess, or just getting something to eat.

Other activities included the after-school center, the Flatbush Boys Club, Cub Scouts and Boy Scouts, later becoming a Scout Master. He was also involved in countless church programs, later becoming an ordained Deacon. He was a music major in school, studying violin, vocal singing, orchestral and choral directing. Later using these gifts in the church choir. Over the years, he has organized, developed, and directed vocal groups and choirs, both in church and the military. He's traveled and performed, throughout the United States, Mexico, and South America.

He has worked as a driving instructor; in savings and commercial banking; the airline industry; the NYC MTA, and finally with a major telecommunications company, where he worked for twenty-seven years before retiring. He enjoys traveling, and his hobbies include, playing and listening to music, astronomy, photography, and writing.

This is Mr. Putney's fulfillment of a lifetime dream to write a novel, that is uplifting and inspiring. This is his first novel, and it reflects the nurturing he experienced growing up in his community.

Acknowledgements

First and foremost, I give thanks, all glory and honor to my Lord and Savior, from which all blessings flow.

I would like to thank all my family and friends for their support in helping to make this book become an actual reality. I'm extremely grateful for your kindness and patience. For your time, valuable input, consultations, and feedback, enabling me to complete this offering.

Thanks to Julie, Lex, Dave, and Lisa for listening and giving constructive criticism. To Donna and Scottie for your vital input, initial editing and assistance with the layout and structure. To all the incredibly talented musicians who shared their talents and gifts towards the music.

I'm thankful to my cousin, Mr. James Gilliam for his inspirational poetry. Please be sure to go to his site, (words4alloccasions.com), to check out his services.

To my nephew, Mr. Charles Brown, for getting my website constructed, (pathways2love.com). I encourage you to look at it, and I hope you will enjoy, and be inspired by its content.

Special thanks to Mr. Ben White (ben@domeaudioinc.com). Look for some exciting and special headphones from Dome Audio coming soon.

Lastly, I am excited and thankful for all of you who purchased this book. I hope you enjoyed it and will encourage others to purchase it. Please feel free to leave your comments on my website and be sure to look out for future offerings.

Enjoy your "Pathways to Love." Thank you – H. Thomas Putney

CPSIA information can be obtained
at www.ICGtesting.com
Printed in the USA
LVHW091225141221
706078LV00001B/5